Maximilian I Emperor of Mexico

Recollections of My Life

Maximilian I Emperor of Mexico

Recollections of My Life

ISBN/EAN: 9783337218775

Printed in Europe, USA, Canada, Australia, Japan

Cover: Foto ©Raphael Reischuk / pixelio.de

More available books at **www.hansebooks.com**

NEW EDITION, WITH A PREFACE

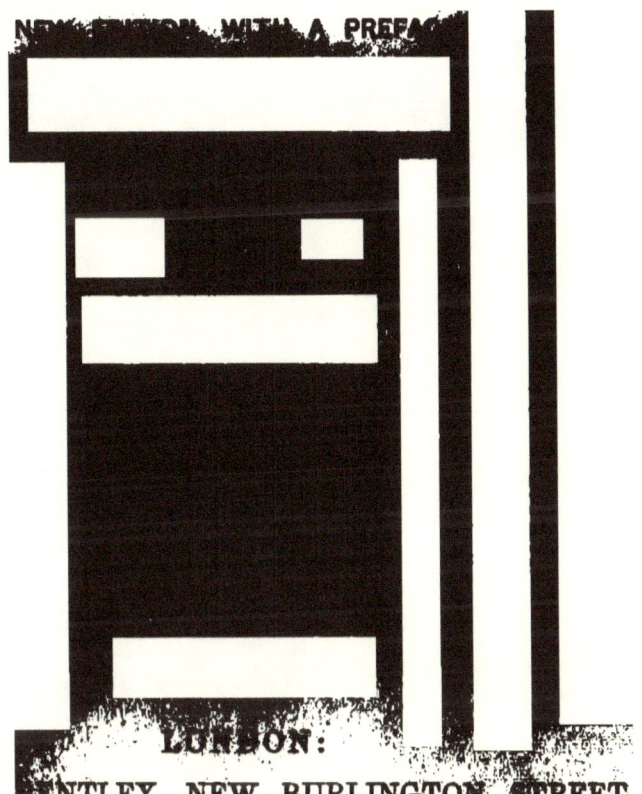

LONDON:

BENTLEY, NEW BURLINGTON STREET.

Publisher in Ordinary to Her Majesty.

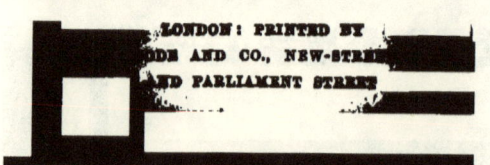
LONDON: PRINTED BY
[SPOTTISWO]ODE AND CO., NEW-STREET SQUARE
[A]ND PARLIAMENT STREET

ADVERTISEMENT

BY THE ENGLISH PUBLISHER.

———◆———

A YEAR has elapsed since the mournful tragedy of Queretaro closed the career of one of the most gifted, genial, and chivalrous of princes; of one who seemed destined, by his liberal and enlightened policy, to develop the wonderful resources of a great empire, and to advance the cause of civilisation over the world. This was not to be; betrayed by his trusted officer into the hands of his ruthless enemies, nothing but his blood would satisfy them, and Mexico will probably again fall into the same anarchy from which she might have been rescued by Maximilian.

The public will feel an additional interest from his sad fate in the following graphic account of the voyages and travels of this estimable prince.

The work was not originally intended for publication, and only fifty copies were struck off at the 'Geheime Staatsdruckerei' (privy state printing-office) in Vienna, for his family and most intimate friends. It was written shortly after he had reached his majority; for he was borr at Schönbrunn on the 6th of July 1832.* The narra tive extends from the 30th of July 1857, and concludes or the 19th of January 1860, while exploring the wonder: of the Mato Virgem, the primeval forests of Brazil.

The idea of publishing this work only occurred t(Maximilian a short time before he was called to ascend the throne of Mexico. To the care of Baron Müng-Bellinch-hausen, so well known in German literature under the pseudonyme of Frederic Halm, he confided the super-intendence of it through the press. The first Germar edition of the first four volumes was published by Messrs Duncker and Humblot, at Leipzig, in August 1867; the fifth, sixth, and seventh, on October 24, 1867.

Political considerations induced the German publisher: to postpone it towards the close of that year; but these impediments were removed in 1866. In Mexico the Emperor occupied himself in revising it, indicating cor-rections, additions, and, above all, suppressions, renderec necessary, in a great measure, by the altered state o political affairs which had unexpectedly arisen. These circumstances caused the postponement of the appearanc(of the book once more; and matters might have remainec in the same state even now, had not the news of the deatl of Maximilian induced the Emperor Francis Joseph, fron

* While staying at Madeira, he jots down the celebration of the anniver-

fraternal affection, to give orders to resume and complete the printing of the work.

The German publishers are in possession of a contract for the publication, signed, in the name of the Emperor Maximilian by the Mexican Consul-General, Staatsrath Herzfeld, and the Intendant-General and Prefect of the Court Library, Baron von Münch-Bellinghausen. This gives Messrs. Duncker and Humblot the right of publication; and in virtue of this contract, and acknowledging its validity, the Saxon Government gave the requisite 'Verlagschein,' permission to publish the book. Two editions of the German publication have been exhausted in eight months, and a third is in preparation. The right of translating it into English was purchased by Captain Otto Corvin, and by him transferred to the English publisher. The original German edition did not contain any preface nor introduction, and, therefore, the English translation had none. At a later period, on the appearance of a French translation, the German publishers furnished materials for a preface, from which a few particulars are here given. The French translator thus eulogises Maximilian :—

'The Prince possessed an enthusiastic and ardent soul, a warm and loving heart, a mind keenly alive to all that was noble and beautiful, a poetical imagination, dreamy, and essentially romantic. This last quality was especially notable in him; it was that upon which the

Prince most piqued himself. The lively and sensitive imagination, the chivalrous and romantic turn of mind, observable in him in childhood, and which remained until death, were characteristics of him, and may in themselves give some explanation of his strange and tragic fate. Severe judgments have been passed on Maximilian by his enemies. He has been pronounced to be an ambitious dreamer—one who was glad to escape the difficulties of his position, and who eagerly seized the first opportunity to place a crown upon his brow. All his apprehensions and scruples, the profound repugnance which caused him to hesitate so long before accepting the crown, are lost sight of by these persons, who forget how many times he refused to be proclaimed Emperor, and that he only ultimately consented on the advice of the European powers. After he had been elected, and after long negotiation, he accepted, with the assent of the Emperor, his brother, the Imperial Crown of Mexico, which had been offered him on the 3rd of October 1863, at Miramar, by the commissioners despatched to him by the Assembly of Notables, who met at Mexico, bringing him the result of the vote of the Mexican population.'

He sailed from Trieste in the Austrian frigate "Novara," and landed at Vera Cruz, May 24. The Emperor and Empress made their public entry into Mexico, June 12, 1864, amidst unanimous acclamations. During three years, Maximilian occupied himself in re-organising his empire; but the civil war, maintained against him by the insurgent chiefs, stopped all beneficial progress, and the withdrawal of the French army left him alone to contend with his enemies, and rapidly brought about their triumph. On the 5th February he left Mexico to place himself at the head of his army to encounter Juarez. He was defeated, and was eventually betrayed by his traitor officer, Lopez, for 3,000 ounces of gold! His execution quickly followed. On the 19th of June he was shot. This event is one of the most melancholy of modern times. His mental struggles and distress may be best described in his own words, written on the eve of the fatal decision which was to conduct him to Mexico :—

'Must I separate myself for ever from my beloved country, the beautiful land of my early years ? You wish me, then, to quit my gilded cradle, and sever the sacred tie which binds me to my country—the land in which the sunniest years of my childhood had been passed, where I had experienced the exquisite feelings of early love. Must I leave it for shadows and mere ambition ? You entice me with the allurements of a crown, and dazzle me with foolish chimeras. Ought I to lend an ear to the sweet song of syrens? Woe be to him who trusts to such flattering promises! You speak to me of a sceptre, of a palace, and of power; you place before mine eyes a boundless future. Must I follow you to distant shores beyond the vast ocean ? You wish that the woof of my life should

. . . . PAGE

. . . . I

ANDALUSIA AND GRANADA 155

I.

ITALY.

1851.

ITALY.

Road of Trieste, July 30, 1851.

I WAS GOING to realise my much longed-for desire—a voyage at sea. Accompanied by several acquaintances, I put off the dearly-loved shore of Austria. This moment was one of great excitement to me, for it was the first time I confided myself to the sea for a long trip. We dashed rapidly through the waves, and already, at about a quarter past 7, amidst the strains of the national hymn, we went on board the frigate 'Novara,' our future floating palace, of which the name itself was a good omen to every Austrian. The gentlemen who had accompanied us took their leave, the stairs were hauled up, and the last connection with the shore cut off; I was not able to send more than a few lines to my parents, written in the utmost hurry in the cabin of the commander. It began to get dark, and they were weighing the last anchor; this work was, however, of very long duration, and great exertions on the part of the crew were required, as a new-fangled French invention about the capstan impeded the movement and brought us frequently to a stop. Unfortunately, at this moment a man was hurt so severely in his chest, that he had to be carried to the hospital. The steam corvette 'Lucia' had taken us in tow, and at last, at 9 o'clock we began to move. I arranged my cabin as well as possible: it was spacious, airy, and agreeable, and might be called pretty, had it not been, that, according to the wretched arsenal-taste, the colours of the furniture and curtains were in a too glaring contrast with each other.

H. M. Frigate 'Novara,' July 31, 1851.

This morning, from 8 to 12 o'clock, I had my first watch; the sea was much agitated, the ship rocked considerably, and soon a heavy continuous rain poured down. The persons around me were suffering in the highest degree; indeed, the trial was rather hard for the first day. After some time the wind became so contrary, that we had to unfasten the tow of the steamer, and commenced tacking towards the land. We had the coast of Istria in sight, but it was too much wrapped in clouds, and the weather was too bad to notice any interesting details.

August 1, 1851.

In the morning we had the Monte Osero, and some islands of the Quarnero in view; the weather was tolerably fair, and the sea less agitated. Notwithstanding this, everybody was still sick. I had my watch from 8 until midnight, and was so sleepy as to fall down; my boots were too tight, and my feet tired, so that it cost me some efforts to persevere till the hour of the ghosts. The horizon became cloudy, and flashes of lightning shed now and again the brightness of day over the ship. As no object impeded the view to the horizon, and the water reflected the light, the eye was sometimes even painfully dazzled. Such sights, on a grand wide stage, can only be seen by a traveller at sea.

August 2, 1851.

The coast of the Neapolitan kingdom, with the commencement of Abruzzo, came in sight, and we approached within eight leagues of the Italian shore. The little town of Viesti could be discerned with the naked eye. The country seems to be very mountainous, rather well timbered, and streaked by yellow stripes of earth. The town is not an important one, and is situated on one of those yellow hills. There are, along the entire coast, and at no very great distance from each other, old towers, which were built as a protection against the former invasions of the Turks. Before Viesti we met many Neapolitan fishing-smacks, with peculiar sails. The intense heat of the sun reminded us that we had entered the southern regions.

August 3, 1851.

What Nature is able to do, what powers she can command and work with, how the waves dance, how air and clouds wrestle with each other, can only be seen on the Alps, with their awful lakes surrounded by rocks, or on the wide endless plain of the sea. There the over-awed soul feels the littleness and vanity of man, and yet his courage and pride swell at the thought, that it is his intellect which cleaves the mountain-waves, and understands how to direct the lightning of the heavens. Such a soul-stirring moment we enjoyed this night. There was a tremendous combat going on amongst the elements; the flashes of lightning were more glaring than daylight, the thunder crashing in short detonations louder than the report of the most powerful gun, violent gusts of wind shrilly shrieking, and the rain pouring down. I got up at about 4 o'clock, put on my clothes in haste, and went for a moment on deck to enjoy the unusual spectacle. Mass, ordered for 10 o'clock, could not take place, for the chaplain was not well, and the movement of the vessel was too violent. However there was a review and music between 10 and 11 o'clock, as usual. The Neapolitan coast came again in sight; we approached the land within two leagues, so that we were able to distinguish very well the town and Cape of Otranto, both offering nothing extraordinary.

Everywhere the towers before mentioned are to be seen; the land is desolate and monotonous; we hope that the

coast opposite, so much praised, will prove more attractive;
else the palm of beauty will remain to old and much-
cherished Hellas, and the generally praised shore of Naples
will scarcely equal the splendid gulfs of Patras and Lepanto.
Towards the decline of day, we passed the Capo di Leuca,
and its church, which is a place of pilgrimage. By the
light of evening this country appears a little more to
advantage. The sun disappeared, pure and bright, in the
sea, and its setting was a splendid spectacle. There was a
southern glow and southern colouring in the twilight, that
warmed my heart.

August 4, 1851.

I rose at 3 o'clock, as my watch to-day was from 4 to 8
o'clock. It was my good luck, on my first 'mattutina,' to
enjoy the most splendid sunrise.

Day brought us to the coast of Calabria; the south
coast offers rocky, bare, picturesque hills, leaving it to
the splendour of the sun to colour and transform them into
enchantingly poetical pictures. The frigate was unfortunately too far from the land to distinguish details. We
were sitting quite comfortably at luncheon, when, at about
half-past 11 we were suddenly startled by a splash in the
water. Apprehending an accident, we rushed on deck: and
then was heard the dreadful cry of 'Un uomo è caduto in
acqua!' All was in confusion. I rushed to the quarter-deck,
and saw the pitiable sight of the poor sailor, who had fallen
from the dizzy height of the 'Mars' yard, struggling with
the waves to reach the ship, from which he was, however,
separating more and more. The boat was lowered with
the utmost possible haste; the 'salva uomini' had missed,
but the lightning apparatus had gone off and smoked and
steamed at the stern of the ship. These were moments of
the most dreadful pain, moments of horror; the question
was asked, again and again, 'Will the poor man be able to
hold out; will he have the strength to combat with the

waves?' The boat pushed off at last; it came nearer
and nearer to the unfortunate man, who was seen at last
to take hold of its gunwale, and, the Lord be praised, he
was saved. He was carried to the hospital, but had not
lost consciousness, and got off without being hurt to any
extent.

To-day the spectacle of old Etna was expected, like
that of a Messiah, but all looking out and spying and
guessing was in vain; the venerable old fellow would not
make his appearance, or rather was altogether out of
sight.

August 5, 1851.

I had my watch from 4 to 8 o'clock; they were four
most interesting hours, during which pictures of past history
rushed by me. There old Etna rose from the morning
vapours; old Etna, the witness of so many past ages,
the witness of so many disappointed desires of so many
people, and of the degeneracy of powerful nations. There,
in blood-coloured twilight, were glowing the mountains
of Sicily, at the foot of which had been committed so
many national crimes. On a sudden the sun sparkled on
the hills of Calabria. Italy's hot sun, that poisoner of·
Sicilian blood, strikes with a thousand arrows proud
Messina, whose towers, palaces, and strongholds burst in
splendour from out the green, luxuriant gardens. It is
the same Messina which was founded by the cunning,
unruly heads of Greece; in which the poet makes the
sister-bride weep over two beloved corpses; in which a
thrust into a French heart was the signal for the Sicilian
vespers. But God also pronounced his judgment against
this city, and the palaces of Messina still afford evidence
of the verdict, as since that terrible earthquake only one
story remains to the most beautiful of them, and the roofs
now replace the vanished rooms of state.

The sun conquered night, and dispersed the dark vapours;

in bright splendour the Pharo stood before our delighted
eyes; now in the daylight the outlines of the land were to
be distinguished, and at the foot of the Calabrian mountains, washed by the blue sea, appeared the lovely town
of Reggio, floating in the green of a southern vegetation.
Palm-trees waved proudly, vines and lemons smiled in-
vitingly, and the light air brought us the refreshing balm
of southern plants. In the background, on both shores, the
volcanic mountains were seen in their sharp picturesque
lines. The tones of colour were as glowing as the southern
heart and eye required, and were such as to warm the
soul of northern men. We were sailing tranquilly through
the azure waves, and our glasses were kept in constant
activity, as, unfortunately, we were not allowed to set foot
on this classical ground. Messina was seen more and more
distinctly; the palaces, forts, and churches were distinguished so plainly by the glass, that I could even read, on
a long building on the shore, the inscription, 'Palazzo di
Città.' What we Germans, in our humility, call house,
is named a palace by the bombastic Italians. Amongst
the buildings we were most struck by a steeple, with
ascending spiral arcades, and windows. The city is large,
and rendered beautiful by its luxuriant gardens. The
country lay before us in a splendid panorama.

All was harmony in the still, holy, morning rest; even
Etna was breathing gently, the vapours from its crater
rising only like a mist.

The shores now became narrower, and we came to a
new theatre of historical events, the much-celebrated straits
of Scylla and Charybdis. The awe breathing through the
songs of Homer; the horrors revealed to us by Schiller's
'Diver,' vanished before reality. A bare neck of land,
with a rather considerable village, and a solid although
not high lighthouse, were seen from afar; at the end of this
prominence is Charybdis and its abyss peaceably closed

before us. At the other side, at the foot of the mountain, spring out of the sea the teeth of a black rock, with a castle on its top, which is connected with the land by a bridge; this is that most picturesque object, Scylla. Peaceably and without a pilot, we steered through the not very considerable water-strait, in which once Ulysses trembled, and which robbed the tender page of his life. On account of the roaring, hissing, or howling, unfortunately, I could hear nothing. The sweet daughter of the king seems no longer to bend over the height, to look for the traces of the bold swimmer. We were now again on the high sea, filled with enthusiasm by the view, unfortunately too short, of the beautiful coast, which we had enjoyed. I took my little book out of the cupboard, and read :—

Kennst du das Land, wo die Citronen blüh'n?

Splendid as is the view of Messina, that of the gulfs of Patras and Lepanto is still more so. On our left we now saw the islands of Vulcano, Lipari, and Panaria, and before us appeared Stromboli—all volcanic formations, as may be seen from their shape. These islands have no considerable circumference, but Stromboli reaches a height of two thousand feet, and has a great resemblance to a sugar-loaf flattened at the top; it slopes abruptly to the sea, and only a few fishermen find shelter at this point. The vital fire of Vulcano has been extinguished for some years, but Stromboli is still smoking and spitting, in such a way as is pleasing to behold.

August 6, 1851.

In the forenoon we saw the coast of Policastro. I had my watch from 6 to 8 in the evening; the sunset had been beautiful, the fiery ball, floating in a golden glow, sank gorgeously in the sea; the mountains of Salerno were delineated distinctly in grey masses, like the hills of Asia

Minor; and, partly shrouded by heavy clouds, appeared the mountains of Policastro. Poetical as this spectacle was, it was sad for the sailors, for a calm laid its leaden wings upon our ship, which lay on the smooth sea, transformed into an island. Scarcely had the gold on the waves towards the west faded, when they were dipped in silver by the moon.

August 7, 1851.

How little we had advanced during the night may be judged by the circumstance that, at about 10 o'clock, when the air cleared, Stromboli once again made its appearance; but this time we were at least rewarded by clouds of smoke rising from its crater. I therefore pardoned its proximity, and even tried to sketch it; it seemed to be strongly in a state of ferment, for clouds of smoke increased, and formed a dense canopy over its head; two peaks of smaller islands, beyond the Pharo of Messina, were visible. During the forenoon the wind freshened up a little, so that at half-past 3 I saw another of these unruly fellows—Vesuvius.

August 8, 1851.

Like the Greeks before Troy, we are lying before the entrance of Naples. Every day one expects to reach it, but there is never a favourable wind stirring. The sea is like a mirror this morning, and we find ourselves only off the height of Licosa. The shore is to be seen rather distinctly, and a small place on an eminence—probably the town of Licosa—can be detected. The mountains are very high, and slope ruggedly to the sea, but they appear bare, and their form is not particularly remarkable.

August 9, 1851.

At half-past 7 I was awakened to see the splendid, picturesque forms of the islands of Capri. This castle of rocks rose proudly, and its angular romantic lines were sharply delineated against the southern sky. Before the principal shore rise tower-like cliffs, like the outworks of a fortress, of which one is pierced, and forms a natural water-gate. Rocky as the island is, it seems to be tolerably well populated and very fertile, and is the birthplace of the far-famed Capri wine. From whatever side we had an opportunity of seeing it, favoured by the course of our ship, it always appeared picturesque, always noble in form. Here rose timbered slopes, there rugged rocks down to the sea; now castle-like forms appeared on the crest of the hills, and everywhere charming variety.

We had scarcely time to enjoy this prospect when the islands of Ischia and Procida made their appearance—all rocky islands, and yet romantically shrouded in green. Now we began to enter the gulf of world-famed Naples. The day was, unfortunately, not very clear, but the panorama was slowly unrolling before our eyes; hills were forming, masses of houses showing as we came nearer; single colours were detaching themselves from the general tone; the forms of single houses came out; questions were asked—explanations about the most prominent points given; glasses were in requisition; in a word, there arose that inward restlessness and bustle which always take place on approaching a remarkable locality, never seen before. But in my heart I felt a great disappointment. During my voyage in Greece I had been told that Naples was greatly to be preferred to what I then saw. One fellow-traveller had placed it so far above anything I had seen that I had made up my mind not to like it so very much. With such ideas, one is much inclined to judge by first appearances. I found the city too small, the hills behind it too low; would have preferred to see it rather at the foot of Vesuvius, densely wrapped up in clouds, and would altogether have liked to make improve-

ments here and there. The day, as I said before, was not
clear; the lines of the hills were not drawn in full distinct-
ness, the colours not enlivened by southern brightness;
sky and sea did not show that deep blue which is beautiful
above anything, and never to be forgotten by any one who
has once seen it.

We came nearer, and already the Castles of St. Elmo
and Uovo, the Villa Reale, and other distinguished places
could be made out, but still I did not yet find the city
to my taste. I preferred that side towards Vesuvius, and
farther on towards Castellamare and Sorrento, where were
high hills and green luxuriant land, and where the country
appeared to me picturesque. Now the frigate turned
round the Castle Uovo, which projects into the sea; the
royal palace, with its massive forms, its green terraces,
and majestic site, made its appearance; houses were
stringed to houses, palaces springing out, and I felt
that Naples was a great and a beautiful city. We cast
anchor, and waited longingly for the 'pratica' which was
to give us permission to land. But it was long before
we were satisfied. We had no certificate of health from
Trieste, and the most learned authorities of Naples would
not permit us to go on shore without it. Thus we had
to wait from 1 to 5 o'clock. The weather cleared up,
and soon the panorama commenced unfolding more and
more. To the right, on the sea-shore, was rising proud
Vesuvius, with its dark mysteries, and at its foot the little
town of Portici. To the right of Vesuvius stretched a
manifold-formed mountain range, till, opposite Capri, and
in its numerous recesses, shone out, amidst orange-groves,
Castellamare, with its royal palace, situated on a height,
' quì si sana;' Sorrento, with its name consecrated by the
poet; and the little town of Massa. To the left of the
volcano, which was still covered by a small cloud, stretches
a wide fertile plain towards the city, which reclines on

low hills enveloped in gardens. Yet, notwithstanding the length of this plain, the row of houses between Portici and Naples is scarcely interrupted.

There is life in the masses of houses in Naples; one does not see those regular tiresome rows as in modern cities. As the principal points came out, we saw the royal palace, with its picturesque bright brick colour, and its fine orange-bowers, which rise in lofty arches like the gardens of Semiramis; the Castle of St. Elmo, which crowns with a pyramid of houses an eminence in the centre of the city; the Castle of Uovo, which, to the left of the palace, rises as an outwork from the sea, and is only connected with the city by a bridge; the Castle Nuovo, with the grey stronghold of the Anjous, once the residentiary palace of the princes of Naples; and the massive Italian palace Capo di Monte, rising between villas and gardens on the heights overlooking the city, and built by Charles III. as a summer residence for the Neapolitan kings. Between the crowd of houses peep out the cupolas of the churches, which are roofed with glazed tiles, and sparkle in the sun.

At our anchoring place Castle Uovo concealed the long alleys of the Villa Reale, and the street and row of houses behind it, called Chiaja, which is used by the Neapolitans as a Corso. Immediately behind this castle stands, on a terrace built on the sea, a small royal palace, called ' Chiatamone,' in the gardens of which a fine cluster of trees refreshes the eye. To the left of the city the sea is also embraced by a wide crescent like that to the right, and from its terrace long rows of villas shine upon us. At the end of this is cut in the rock the far-famed ' Grotto of Posilippo,' from which can be seen the port of Puzzuoli, with its fort crowned by a castle, and the stronghold of Baiæ. Here follow the islands of Procida and Ischia, which close this remarkable panorama.

Whilst we gazed at all this with curiosity, we got a little
foretaste of the peculiar Neapolitan life. On several over-
crowded boats and sailing-vessels, which were darting past
us through the foaming sea, we saw lazzaroni and fishermen,
with their brown lively faces, red overhanging caps, and
that costume which approaches so nearly a state of nature.
One of them changed his shirt quite coolly in view of the
frigate, surrounded by his fellow-travellers.   After some
time a boat approached our ship; it was our minister,
Field-Marshal Lieutenant Martini, who from his boat held
a conversation with our commander, and then, on account
of the 'pratica' not being yet received, returned to the.
shore to wait for us there.   At last, at about 5 o'clock,
we jumped into the boat which was to bring us to shore.
While steering towards the quay of Santa Lucia, which is
situated between the Castle Uovo and the royal palace,
our frigate saluted with twenty-one guns; this thundering
greeting was answered by a land battery.

The nearer we came the more we could make out the
peculiarities of the city.   The houses are built close to each
other, and are very narrow and high; some have only one
window in front; the roofs are terrace-like, and almost every
window is provided with a small iron balcony ; and what
is there that is not hanging or standing on these balconies?
what things amusing and not amusing are there not waving
down?   The balconies are an important point in southern
life, as you may see at once from these in Naples. Here
flutter sheets and fans; there are blooming flowers and
monks, all in Italian 'sans gêne.' We jumped on shore
after nine days at sea, and found ourselves suddenly, as by
witchcraft, transplanted into another world—a world so
confused that we required a long time to find our way in
it.   At the first step in Naples we were besieged by representatives of popular life.   There, were standing two
Capuchins at the side of the street, with spectacles on

their serious noses, that they might examine the new
arrivals with a more acute eye; there, moved about a black
three-cornered Abbate hat through the noisy, screaming
crowd; there, thronged on the army of the lazzaroni to
surround the bashful traveller. There was a life, a whiz-
zing, a roaring, which the German ear is not used to.
Our brains began to spin, and how was this rush of
impressions further increased when we, with the minister,
got into a 'batard' to drive through the celebrated
Toledo, the artery of Naples! At home this hubbub
would have been taken for a riot, perhaps for a mas-
querade in the carnival; but here it was only the every-
day state. I was so surprised, so astonished, that only
a few figures out of this motley mass remained impressed
on my memory. The people here are full of life, not dull,
or shut indoors, as in so many other cities; all they do
is done before strange eyes, for they live in the street,
and that is a principal charm and chief amusement to the
newly arrived observer. All shops are free and open; the
eatables are piled up in the middle of the city; amongst
the finest southern fruit, pigs, sheep, dogs, and children
play; the latter, who are sometimes in a complete state
of nature, walk boldly, like genuine Murillos, in their
Adamitic costumes, between macaroni stalls, and cooking
shops, snatching their food from wherever they can get it,
even if they find it in the dirt. At almost every corner
are seen gaudily painted wooden chests, with an arch or
columns, ornamented with oranges and foliage, from which
shines the image of a Madonna. Behind these columns
move long kegs, horizontally or vertically, according to
their use; from these kegs fresh water is poured out, and
the men who work this simple machinery are the celebrated 'acquajuoli.'

The popular vehicles belong also to the most remarkable
things of Naples; they are two-wheeled cars drawn by

one, two, and sometimes three horses; the horses have at
one of their ears a pointed tuft of feathers, and their odd
harness is mounted with brass, and frequently provided
with bells.   Immediately behind the horse sits the driver;
between the wheels a seat is raised for two or three persons; yet the Neapolitans understand how to arrange it
in such a manner that twelve to fourteen persons standing, hanging, and sitting on such a narrow space, can be
drawn by a little horse in trot.

The celebrated Toledo is not at all pretty; the houses and
the street itself are in the grandest disorder, and covered
with a sort of artistic, poetical filth.   Half up this street,
which crosses the whole of the city, is a fine although not
large place, called ' Largo del Mercatello,' of which one
side is closed by a crescent-like building, belonging to
the Jesuits; the style shows its proprietors.   The road
rises towards the hill, and over a finely arched bridge we
came upon the region of gardens.   We had scarcely left
the interior of the city, when we found the road shaded
by trees, which are a chief ornament of Naples, and most
refreshing to the eye.   Through some serpentine windings we came to an iron railing provided with a guard,
and found ourselves before the splendid palace Capo di
Monte.   It is colossal, as are all the buildings in the Italian
style of the last century.   Columns and windows are cut
out of mighty blocks of grey stone; of the same material
are the lofty and wide doors of the halls.

The columns, also of grey stone, support in the interior the chief part of the building, and form yards and
spacious lofty corridors, through which one can drive con-
veniently in a carriage.   The walls are bare bricks, the
colour of which forms a good contrast to the grey.   The
palace is surrounded by a garden in the English style,
in which tolerably large grassplots, by their dryness, have
just now a rather disagreeable appearance.   As a compen-

sation there are some small palm-trees, and profusely blooming oleander shrubs.

I drove into one of the fine and airy arcades of the palace, and paid a visit to my aunt Clementine. She received me dressed in deep mourning for her husband, the Prince of Salerno, who died several months ago. I found her with her daughter Aumale. We spoke much of our Viennese relations and of the good old times! The rooms in which I found my aunt are of an extraordinary size, with gate-like doors and windows, lobster-red brick floor, and scanty furniture; a genuine Italian arrangement. I also paid Count Aquila a visit; he is living in a house at the side of a palace, but I found neither him nor his brother Trapani, who is residing in the palace. We then had a walk in the park, which extends far behind the palace; it is in the old Italian style, with wide straight avenues, which are not, as in the French gardens, stiff walls, but are arched in regular embowered walks. The garden is rich in trees, which, for the greatest part, are covered with bushy ivy. The pleasure grounds are partly irregularly wild and partly in artificial order, which gives them a peculiar charm, assimilating them to the character of the Italians, their creators. The eye follows with pleasure these long avenues, which so frequently cross each other, under the dark green of which one finds protection against the fierce sun.

This fine park, stocked with hares and pheasants, is only used for the sport of the King, and entrance is granted only to a few favoured persons. We returned to the city, by the celebrated 'Ponti Rossi.' The road running on the height of Capo di Monte leads towards the plain between Vesuvius and the city. One garden here joins another, all ornamented by pine-trees of a rare size, and numberless grape-vines ; and the views enjoyed from the driving alley are splendid. The sun was just descending, the

weather had become clear, and Naples and its surroundings showed what charm they may exert on the heart of
the stranger; over mine also the victory had been won.

In the background Vesuvius rose mightily, at its foot
spread the fertile plain far towards the mountains of
Caserta; to our right on the slope was the city, the wide
extent of which was only to be seen now. Before and
behind us was an exuberant southern vegetation; far off
the mountain chains of Sorrento and Massa appeared in
half-dark blueness, and before them was the wide gulf.
The road on which we were driving is called 'Strada dei
Ponti Rossi,' after two old Roman aqueducts, built of red
bricks, and under which the road passed. But it is not
by these antiquities that this road became celebrated, but
by the splendid and matchless views from it. I was
converted, and count myself now amongst the admirers of
the sense-ensnaring Parthenope. Beautiful as Hellas is,
splendid as the Gulf of Lepanto, yet these countries lack
the full charm of green vegetation.

Descending from the height, one again enters the
city by the 'Strada Foria.' The first immense building
that strikes the eye is the large poor-house with a massive gorgeous façade, built by the order of Charles III.,
and called 'Reale Albergo dei Poveri.' Everything
great that has been created in Naples and its environs
originates from this King, who commenced his work
when sovereign of Naples, and finished it for his son.
Scarcely arrived in the city, new pictures of life presented
themselves. We met elegant 'fourgons' driving along the
street, in trot towards the country; but their freight was
the dead, which, according to the Neapolitan custom, are
forsaken by their relations after their decease, and are
thus carried to the 'Campo Santo.' One of these vehicles
was surrounded by little boys, dressed as cherubims,
with burning torches in their hands, sitting on seats

arranged outside. We met also one of the celebrated Neapolitan brotherhoods; it was a long procession of snow-white forms, following, two by two, a crucifix and a priest. The whole body of these ghostlike brothers was wrapped up, and only their eyes glittered through white rags, hanging down over the face from their pointed hoods. Each class institute among themselves a similar brotherhood, to nurse their sick, and do the last honour to the deceased at the common expense. Curious also was it to observe in this street the sight of small bridges on dry land; they are built for the emergency of rain, which falls here frequently with such violence that it transforms the whole street into a torrent. The Neapolitan does not remedy such an evil at the root, he prefers the odd way of building, in case of need, these remarkable means of communication.

We now turned into the Toledo, at the corner of the 'Reale Museo Borbonico.' This latter is a truly majestic building, also built in the old Italian style of grey stone and bare brick walls, and is used for the preservation of the antique and modern treasures of art belonging to the kingdom. Evening had come, and with it the liveliness in the street doubled. If, before, the lower classes were to be seen, now there were crowds of rich, who, after the indispensable siesta, throng the streets, to breathe the fresher air. At that part of the Toledo which is outside the 'Largo del Mercatello,' the carriages jostled together. In Vienna, which is so full of life, this entanglement of carriages would have been taken for a stoppage produced by some accident; but here it is only an everyday amusement, and notwithstanding the murderous noise to be heard from all sides, and that the carriages drive into each other like wedges, no lasting confusion occurs, and no accident happens. After the most ear-piercing concert, the single equipage is detached, to rush into some other crowd. This

bustle reminds one of the Fresco in Venice, where, in the
Canal Grande, are crowds of vessels, only that there the
moving powers are oarsmen instead of horses. The noise
is considerably increased by the vendors and beggars,
as the first praise their goods in the most comical and
most shrieking manner, and accompany their resounding
speeches with the most curious mimicry; but the beggar
tribes of the whole kingdom hold their congress at Naples;
especially at the street 'dei Ponti Rossi,' we were perfectly surrounded by cripples, who unveiled their wounds
and ailings in every possible manner to the eyes of the
passers-by, and galloped alongside the carriage with the
most wonderful velocity, to extort money by all kinds of
vocal and gesticular modulations. From the Via Toledo,
we proceeded to the house of our minister, which is situated at the Chiaja behind the Villa Reale. We there got rid
of our uniforms, and enjoyed for a time from the balcony
the view on the enlivened corso, a long and wide street
between the avenues of the Villa Reale, situated immediately on the sea and separated from it by a railing and
a row of newly built houses of tolerably symmetrical appearance. There also carriage after carriage was driving
past; gentlemen and ladies on horseback moved to and
fro; and all was merriment and amusement. This seems
to be the Neapolitan Prater.

We then drove along the Chiaja in the direction of the
sea-road of Puzzuoli. Both equipages and toilets were fine
and expensive, but there was never in the *tout ensemble*
a truly elegant harmony; you see beautifully built carriages, with dirty drivers without gloves, and old women
with elegant pink bonnets. It is striking, that generally amongst the fair sex one scarcely ever sees noble
or fine faces, the features having a somewhat Moorish
character.

Driving along, observing and gazing, before we came to

the house of the minister, we met a high phaeton and a
reddish-haired stout fellow, driving his horses in the
English fashion, who very politely flourished his hat when
seeing our minister. I asked who it was, and was highly
delighted on hearing that my eyes had seen one of the
great and mighty, one of the rulers of the universe, one
of the chief weights of our century, one of the golden
planets of the European constellation, it was the youth-
fully vigorous—Rothschild. The Via Puzzuoli on which
we were driving now offered the most charming views.
There is, on one side along the street, the tufa stone
mountain, with its villas and gardens. The poor lazzaroni have worked into it cave-like dwellings, and there
are also high arches hewn in this soft stone, which may
serve as entrances to shops. On the other side of the
street, the ground falls steeply off to the foaming sea, but
nevertheless it is covered at many places with country
seats. As the Via Puzzuoli turns round the roadstead,
the city is to be seen in its full extent, with its picturesque
forts and its green heights, the luxuriant splendid plain,
the mighty Vesuvius, and the amphitheatrical mountain
of Sorrento.

The two most remarkable objects on the Via itself are
the hoary ruins of a large palace, built projectingly into
the sea, commenced by the Viceroys of Spain but never
finished, which building is wrongly called the palace of the
Queen Isan of Naples. A mighty palm-tree, with a splendid
luxuriant crown, in one of the gardens rises abruptly at
the road side. I have seen the palm-trees of Athens
and those of Nauplia; they are much higher, but I saw
none so beautiful, so luxuriant, and spreading its crown so
proudly as this, and no artist comes to Naples without
sketching it; its very numerous leaves are of considerable
length, they bend in gentle arches towards the ground.
The palm is a plant of the fancy; an enchanted fairy

child, snatched from the dream of a god; its shaft rises
straight and wonderful, whilst the pleasing and soft undulations of its leaves are an alluring dance of the Graces.
The sun had vanished long ago, thousands of lights appeared on all sides, and though the life of the day was
finished, there awoke a new and perhaps still more animated and interesting night-life in Naples. The glimmer
of the lights on the quays was reflected in the sea, and
drew golden furrows in the slightly rippling waves. But
it was the full clear moon, that enhanced the light to an
ideal, when she shed her silver beams dreamingly over land
and sea. Now my heart rejoiced; I humbly struck my
colours, and bent my defyingly elevated head before the
old bard who sings the ever-young song—

Kennst du das Land, wo die Citronen blüh'n?

I then shared the fate of all the German tribes wandering
to the south, who are struck with admiration, and are
captivated involuntarily by the mighty spell of Italy.

Having returned from our drive, we stopped at the entrance of the Villa Reale, and strolled through it in the soft
moonshine under the splendid walks of olives and evergreen
oaks, and other shady trees. But these are not the only
attractions offered by this place. Marble copies of celebrated antique masterpieces peep from among the green,
dark arbours; water basins with delicate fountains, statues,
and luxuriant water plants which whisper mysteriously.
The most celebrated of these basins is ornamented by the
Rape of Europa, beautifully carved in marble; unfortunately it was too dark to admire perfectly its particular
beauties. A second extensive basin was made of a large
piece of red granite, which had been excavated at Pæstum;
it is called the basin of Salerno, because it was set up in
that town immediately after its excavation. There is also
between the groups of trees a temple with the bust of

Tasso ; and a friend told me that a guard was placed here to compel the visitors to take off their hats before the poet. I stepped close to the bust, and the soldier did accost me, but only to warn me not to approach too near the great man. If poor Torquato, who was mortified so frequently in life, could know with what etiquette he is surrounded after his death, his stony, serious face would smile derisively. Or is the guard intended to remind one of the former captivity of the poor poet ? We stepped out of the avenues on a half-round terrace projecting into the sea, and saw dark figures lying on the balustrades. We believed them to be Egyptian statues of a mysterious form, but discovered, on approaching nearer, good-natured Neapolitans, enjoying on these stones the cooling breeze in ' dolce far niente.' The view from this projection was again splendid, charming, and new. From it were to be seen the Via Puzzuoli with its inhabited caves, which we had recently left.

The name of the Villa Reale leads one to imagine that it belongs to a summer residence, or a cottage of the King; but it designates only a railed park with walks, small flower-gardens, single palm-trees, and little guard-houses at its different entrances, as entrance is prohibited to the lazzaroni, and only decently dressed promenaders are seen here. We stopped for a moment at the iron gate fronting the city, to refresh ourselves at one of the ' acqua-juoli ' with water out of a wooden keg; then we went along the quay of Santa Lucia, the true region of the lazzaroni.

The streets are filled with boxes, in which the most curious eatable productions of the sea are piled up and protected against the sun by a somewhat inclined um-brella. Everywhere are to be seen cooking shops, heaps of fruit, and small tables on which some ring-shaped pastry is for sale. A number of small oil lamps light up these arrangements, which are surrounded by a mass of braying people. Women and children rush upon the promenaders, with the most varied offers and requests. Beggars from all sides surround and plague the passers-by. Besides all this confusion, one must take care not to step on one of the lazzaroni, who are lying about on the ground, sleeping. Stepping down a staircase to the lower quay immediately upon the sea, one sees a new feature of Neapolitan life; hundreds of chairs stand there on the wet slippery ground; elegant and dirty people, secular and ecclesiastical, are sitting comfortably about; and what do you think they are doing? Are they taking coffee, or more probably ice cream? No! they drink nothing else but an abstergent sulphuric water, carried round in large tumblers by lazzaroni women, and eat with it the above-mentioned ring-shaped pastry; and these are, as Field-Marshal Lieutenant Martini said to me, 'Le delizie di Napoli.' There is nothing to reply but, 'De gustibus non est disputandum.' The sulphur spring furnishing this horrid beverage is on the quay, in a vault below the highway. We entered it; the ground is wet, the grey building is supported by pillars, and at the end of it a flight of steps, where the lazzaroni world, with their tumblers, crowd to catch the nectar that is bubbling out there, for the mortals sitting on the quay. The spring belongs to the people, who use it freely.

Before the quay on the sea are erected—another peculiarity of Naples—filthy wooden booths, connected with the land by narrow bridges, and imposingly called ' bagni di mare.' But the water in these baths is so brown and dirty, the booths so disgusting, that, according to our ideas, there would be no great pleasure in visiting them, and yet at these balconies men and women sit crowded together, and seem to have their gossiping rendezvous. After having vastly enjoyed this evening, in which our senses had to take in so much in so few hours, we stepped into our boats, and quickly and quietly, in the pure light of the moon, we returned to our water palace. The city, with its myriad lights, its bright glittering quays, was amphitheatrically spread before us, and for a long time after we left, we heard the noise of the people.

Road of Naples, August 10, 1851.

At half-past 2 we had to leave our hammocks, for the battle-cry of this day was—Vesuvius! To the old sire of Naples, the greatest lion of the neighbourhood, the first visit must be paid. It was not half-past 3 when our boat left the ship, rowing towards Portici, where we were to find the aide-de-camp of our minister, and the horses which were to carry us up the mountain. But we had ventured to go away without a guide, and were now rowing near the coast along the little town of Portici, without knowing the appointed landing-place. For a long time we sought our port in the grey of the morning, asking fishermen and shippers; but the fishermen and shippers spoke Neapolitan, and Neapolitan is not Italian. Thus we might have squandered away in search the finest hours of the morning, if, on a sudden, the light of a torch had not appeared, giving us to understand, by sundry movements, that our boat should row towards it. We obeyed the signal, and were soon in a secure port. We mounted on horseback. What an agreeable feeling it is to be in the saddle again, after a week's living on board ship; and although the horses were small, and one could only balance oneself instead of sitting upon them, we proceeded quite briskly. We passed first through the streets of Portici and Resina, where, in preparation for one of the church festivals, so frequent in Italy, sundry flags were hanging on ropes across the streets. After having passed through several streets, our road led us between gardens full of the most luxuriant grape-vines, and particularly large cacti, all in the freshest and most brilliant green, notwithstanding the advanced summer. The ground began to ascend, and we came upon an excellent wide road, built by the present King, and leading to the hermitage. It runs mostly between chestnut-groves and vineyards, in serpentine windings up the mountain. At each turn the view of the sea, the city, and the plain, became more expansive. We were still in the shade of Vesuvius, when the sun commenced painting the country at our feet with golden tints. The wide plain was covered with spots of fog which looked like lakes, or parts of the sea, between which, the land, with its steeples and woods, came out like islands. I preferred this view to the one I had yesterday; for here, surrounded by exuberant green, one gets a conception of the boundless richness of nature, and the profuse gifts with which the Creator has endowed this favourite part of the earth. As a contrast, or rather as a complement to this luxuriant picture of nature, appears rich Naples, which, unlike other cities, is not separated by walls or ramparts from the country, but blends with the green of the landscape by its gardens and villas. To complete this splendour, this Paradise of a country and this city of life and animation are washed by the waves of a splendid large gulf; and thus land and water are lying at the feet of the admirer who wanders over that rich slope, and unite to form a picture one perhaps may never find again, of a terrestrial Eden.

I like to pass over the immediate space in quick time, the sooner to reach the desired place, and to stay there at leisure; we spurred, therefore, our lean little horses, and in wild chase—now trotting, now galloping—and put in the best of humours by this irregular riding, we were rapidly nearing the volcano. We soon saw, to the right and left, the places covered with lava, but they were also already covered with verdure; the living vegetation had conquered the dead mass, and the ground formed from the ashy rain had become serviceable to man. The ashes which, after a certain course of time, become fertile, are extremely fine, and of a greyish-yellow colour. In Pompeii, which had been buried under them, the excavations, newly undertaken, are easy; whilst Herculaneum, which had been overflowed by dense masses of lava, offers far greater difficulties.

We approached the hermitage; the richly overgrown promontory on which we were riding became narrower and narrower, and after a turn of the road we suddenly saw a large lava stream, the result of the last eruption, running between the promontories and Vesuvius. Like a petrified river, the brownish-grey lava extended, awful and lifeless, a charmless picture òf horror—a mass, stifling every germ of life, a spectacle not to be equalled by anything in this world. One can imagine, on looking at these cooled waves of lava, how they, following the law of nature in their course, irresistibly bore away with them everything, embracing it glowingly with their fiery arms, and pressing it to death in hot lust. The overflowing waters are also dreadful; they rush, devastating and destroying the fertile fields; but at last they cease, and the visited land, although laid waste, reappears. But the red-hot flood springing forth from the crater of Vesuvius buries everything; the lava cools, and forms a rocky crust over the once green grounds, and thousands of years must pass before sufficient fresh soil is collected to enable new plants to germinate. The banks of this awful Lethe were overgrown, and still we moved on green ground. We had reached the hermitage, a point well known to tourists. A small house and a little church stand there, unscathed, on the cone, shrouded in the most beautiful green; on its right and left frequently flowed blood-red cascades; the sea of fire swelled on to the little church, but the flood always divided at the house of God, and the house of the hermit

remained untouched in the middle of destruction. The
fine lime-trees testify to the age of this dwelling, which
is situated on a small terrace of earth, and overspread it
with their shadowy roof. The little church is to the right,
leaning against the house, and by the side of it is a fine
garden, from which there is a picturesque view. From
this height one looks far over the wide landscape, over that
country which is blessed by God, and over the blue flood.
Here one enjoys life to the full, in the golden haze of the
sunshine. I had never had my desire, and seen a hermit;
empty hermitages I have met with frequently, and many
neat little summer-houses to which that name had been
given; I had read of those pious men, in many awful
stories, and had been anxious, for a long time, to see one
of these solitary creatures. Although the tradition was
wide-spread, that the hermit of Vesuvius was a very
gay fellow, having somewhat of the fiery element of
his supporter, he was still a hermit, had the long garments and the long wavy beard, and that was sufficient.
But again I was disappointed, again my hopes vanished.
The world-famed hermit, dispenser of the blood-red
Lacryma Christi, was gone to his fathers, with all his
poetry, to be replaced by every-day prose. It soon fell to
our lot to see the new inhabitant of the cell: no brown
cowl fluttered about his lean shaky body, no beard
waved as a banner of hope to the tired pilgrim, no hair-
rope girded the feeble loins; no, a hackneyed, every-
day figure stood before us. The aspect was somewhat
startling, so out of harmony were the dress-coat and
the inexpressibles of the poor guardian of the Lacryma
Christi. He had hoped, it seems, for a whole flock of
strangers, and he had been waiting with the mass, and
offered to read it on our return. We were very glad at
this, and very thankful to the poor man, for otherwise we
should have had to attend service in Portici. Whilst

contemplating the view, we heard the finest, purest song
of a feathered songster, which is rare at this time of the
year; perhaps it sang of the old romantic time, when
hermits did not as yet drink Lacryma Christi, and men
still lived according to Nature, and were rewarded by her
for it.

After a short rest, we started for our goal. We were
still riding on the green cone, but the ground between
the lava channels continually got narrower, and vegetation
more scanty. The excellently planned road brought us to
the Royal Observatory, a fine solid building, much ornamented with lava, which had been commenced ten years
ago. A little garden spreads, terrace-like, before it, and
contains in lava excavations an interesting collection
of those plants which grow on Vesuvius. The building
has been erected by the present King, and is useful, as the
wide horizon seen from it offers an opportunity for obser-
vations which would be otherwise impossible; but it is not
now inhabited by any savan. To live in a house so
situated in this region of lava would be a sacrifice which
a Neapolitan would hesitate to make to science. After
leaving the Observatory, the projecting earth ends in a
sea of lava; the vegetation exhibits only herbs and single
scanty shrubs; the channels of the lava unite, the hoofs of
the horses strike volcanic blocks, and one comes to the
valley between Monte Somma and Vesuvius. The beautiful life of the earth is seen now more rarely, one is
surrounded by the colourless picture of a general nothing.
Dark fields, grey blocks, black masses, hills of moving
ashes, and cracking burnt-out lava, surround the little
troop of poor travellers who venture into this vast, endless,
awful realm of the dead, in this discord of nature, in this
valley of melancholy. Once the two summits of Monte
Somma and Vesuvius were united, but the interior of the
earth revolted, the mountain burst, and out of the wide

yawning jaws poured forth flood upon flood, which at last
cooled, and became that colourless, motionless, dead sea,
surrounded by ashy sand, which now separates the two
summits. The eye wanders wearily over these monotonous masses, which cover the mountain, and from which
life has flown. Very far off one sees the wide God-
blessed country, the city of joy, the smiling plain. The
gradation of the gradual decay is remarkable; the old
lava lying for thousands of years is covered with green ;
and on the lava of centuries dry shrubs vegetate in the
fine ashes as well as flowers which do not require a good
soil. In the lava thrown up in modern times, and on
small tracts over the whole mountain, single seeds germinate. Nature would dress the country in her green, but
the wild eruptions of the volcano do not permit it.

Our horses climbed with much adroitness the dismal
masses of lava, and we soon arrived at the foot of Vesuvius.
The valley between the two heights is not very wide, but,
considering that it is only a chasm in the once-united
summit, one wonders at the hidden and awful powers of
Nature. The great eruptions which imperilled the surrounding country, and of which the most recent and
devastating one took place in February 1849, are all to be
traced in this valley; the hot blood from the wounds of
the earth were poured out either on the mountain slopes
towards Resina and Portici, or on the other side towards
Pompeii. The smaller eruptions take place from Vesuvius
proper. Monte Somma has remained calm and quiet
since the time of the destruction of Herculaneum and
Pompeii, and Nature is already commencing to spread life
over the rough mountain.

We had now arrived at the point where one must con-
fide to one's own feet or the arm of the guides; the horses
were tied up, and the gendarmes who had accompanied us
from the hermitage, on account of some robberies, re-

mained at this place. Some men, provided with leather straps, insisted on dragging me up; but on such occasions, however troublesome, I prefer always trusting to my own legs. One sees here what man can do when he has to reach an important object; were it not for the flaming crater floating before our eyes, one would perhaps not climb up this painful and tedious way with such steady perseverance. First, we waded up a steep path of fine ashes, and this part of the undertaking may be compared to the tortures which Romans and Greeks assigned to the lower regions. One ascends with difficulty; one hopes to reach a higher point; then the ashes suddenly give way, and the foot again sinks into the grey mass, so that in this manner we take three steps onwards, and two downwards. But we looked at the expedition from its humorous side, and so it became much easier. By the side of this meadow of ashes is a field of bare pieces of lava, mostly from two to three feet in diameter, to which the guides led us after having brought us for some time through ashes. There was not much gained by the change, for, although the support gave way if it were too much trusted, yet you could jump over the ashes easily; but here the feet and the poor boots suffered greatly. Panting in the sweat of our brow, we climbed from one piece of lava to another; the heat got more and more perceptible, our exertions greater and greater; but we proceeded with good spirit, having the mysteries of the crater before our mind's eye. This lava path comes in a direct line from the top of the mountain to the valley. The pieces forming its contents are similar in colour, shape, and weight, to the slakes which fall off at our iron works. Before we reached the height we found crystals of selenite amongst the lava; they are small, of tetragonal shape, and have a greenish-yellow colour. Each step we took on these moveable stones seemed to us dangerous, for the higher we climbed the nearer appeared the

danger of rolling down the mountain, together with the
edged lava on which we were walking.   Sometimes it
happened that the support on which we were leaning gave
way from under our feet with a dull noise, but then
another stone would stop the one rolling, and give us time
to jump nimbly on to another.   After we had climbed
under great difficulties half our way, we were conscious
of a cooler air, and a slight sulphuric smell.   The clouds
surrounding the summit of Vesuvius came and disappeared; but we did not care much for that, as the view
was not the principal object in our ascent of the mountain.
The closer we came to the much-longed-for goal, the more
eager grew our exertions; one of the men who had accompanied us had already reached it; and only a few more
efforts, a little more panting, and we should arrive also.
We found ourselves in a dell between the two topmost
summits.   What a spectacle, what an inexpressible sight!
The slopes were covered with white sulphur, the lava
ground was black, the ashes grey; yellow and red pieces of
brimstone lying there singly; from under the great pieces
of lava vapours were gushing forth; the view around was
concealed from us by the caldron-shaped eminence; steam
and fog covered the firmament, and the air was now rough
and cold, now warm and sulphury.   Everything breathed
death and destruction.   One had a sensation of the working of mighty, unknown powers beneath; one saw colours
one had never seen before, and felt surrounded by an air
of another kind; we could not think we were living on the
rich earth, but in chaos, amongst the primitive elements
from which God had created the world; amongst the
poisonous vapours before water and air had been separated,
and before the sun had enlivened the world.   It was one
of those impressions which are indescribable; one must feel
and experience it, to have a perception how Nature works
here, to understand how little man is, and how little his

knowledge. We were not yet at the edge of the crater, and I was already more excited by the spectacle surrounding me than by anything I had seen before. Every traveller has certain stereotype movements, when first seeing certain noted localities of the world. If he comes for the first time to the shore of the sea, he collects shells with a childish eagerness. If he comes to the south, he lays hold in haste on the unknown fruit. If he comes to Vesuvius, he seizes upon the different many-coloured pieces of sulphur which at once strike his eye. Men have a strong inclination to collect, and to throw away what they collect. We did our best, and stooped down to cram our pockets. I made an examination also of one of the blocks under which, from fissures, the hot steam arose. The fine moist lava sand lying before one is so hot, that one is not able to keep the hand in it longer than a few moments. Everywhere these openings are to be found, which must have some connection with the interior of the mountain. Sometimes these vapours are without smell, like those arising from hot water, and spread only a moist heat; others, however, are so sulphuric, that one feels a pricking sensation in the chest, compelling one to cough.

We left the small but grand valley by a narrow path, which has been made out of the rolling ashes at the back of the chief cone. Whoever is giddy and has no secure step must shun this way. To the right is the exterior wall of the great crater, where are found lava rocks of the oddest form, out of which vermilion-red sulphur shines. To the left the ashy mountain falls off precipitately to the valley between Monte Somma and Vesuvius. The spectator walks on a narrow path in a soft mass of ashes; but this narrow path leads to the crater, and one does not mind the danger, and is highly gratified by the sight of the valley beneath. Here one can recognise the course of the great eruption of 1849. Great heaps of ashes and

lava are mixed in the direst confusion; hills and valleys
of grey and black colour appear like immense fire-holds;
but there is nowhere a chasm of any extent—the eruption
tore open the ground, threw up lava and stones, but the
opening which it made was filled up again by the material
falling back into it.   At that time the stream of lava
coming from the orifice in the valley opposite the hermitage took its course in the direction of the plain, towards Castellamare, in which Pompeii is situated.   The
villa of a Neapolitan prince and his vineyards were, on
that occasion, buried.   From where we stood we could
see distinctly, as I said before, the way taken by this fiery
stream.   A new crater on Vesuvius announces such a
phenomenon by emitting smoke and flames some long
time before.

Our path still ascended; we passed the dangerous place
with caution and steadiness, till at once was unfolded before us, in awful majesty, the aspect of the yawning abyss.
We stood on that edge, formed on one side by the mountain slope, on the other by the steaming crater.   Even in
the nursery, they tell us of the mighty fire-mountain with
its deathly abyss.   In travelling sketches the tourists take
pains to bring this grand picture before the mind of the
eager reader; and so Vesuvius ever floats before the eye
of our mind like an indistinct object; one gropes in the dark
towards it, and has an idea that no pen has yet succeeded
in describing conceivably what one sees and feels here.   It
is indeed impossible for any one to convey in words that
impression, and no imagination could construct an approxi-
mate picture.   It was the same with me!   I had so
frequently heard of this crater, so many of my acquaintances had visited it, yet I was quite differently affected
on seeing it than I had expected.   A wide abyss extended
before my eyes; the upper crest of which was, at several
places, considerably higher than that on which I was stand-

ing, therefore the edge was not equally high and was shaped like a mountain cauldron. The edge on the crest of the crater is exceedingly narrow, in proportion as the width of the pyramidal rising walls enclosing it more and more decreases. On the exterior side the sloping ground consists mostly of pure ashes and lava, but in the interior the regularly sloping ashy walls and the rugged lava rocks are covered by broad fields of sulphur, glowing in the most striking and glaring unmixed primitive colours; the edge and a few yards on the outside are also covered with these sulphur crystals. The principal tints are the brim-stone-yellow and glaring vermilion-red, which latter is generally seen in veins in the yellow fields: but one sees also, particularly at places where hot steam is pouring out, reddish-bluish-purple and verdigris-coloured tints. These latter are mostly insupportably hot, moist from the steam, and covered with a white substance similar to hoar frost. These varied tints give to the crater a very marvellous, unnatural appearance; the colours are so glaring and yet lack freshness. It is a cold lifeless spectacle, and the con-trast between this glaring colouring and the toneless grey of the ashes and lava is too striking to be beautiful. The interior shape of the crater is the exact counterpart of that of the exterior. Vesuvius is an upright-standing cone; the excavation of the crater has the shape of a reversed cone. The continuation of the funnel was hid before us by a lava rock projecting over the deep valley on our side. Large masses of steam gushed out of the interior, but, like as at a charcoal kiln, small columns of smoke come out of many different places of the walls of the funnel, so also on the outside of the edge of the mountain single little clouds of steam came up. These outlets generally occur under larger blocks of lava, which are covered with many-coloured flowers of sulphur. When the milk-white clouds of steam were very strong, the inside of the crater could not be seen distinctly; but from time to time the clouds were lifted up, and then we were allowed to see what was going on in the cauldron; then the abyss was at rest, as after a long, deep breath, and one could examine the awful depth; and indeed these holes have something jawlike, like those of the dragons of the fabulous age. The brimstone glitters like the smooth invulnerable scales, and has even the colours with which fancy paints these monsters. From the interior come the poisonous vapours which envelop the dragon-hunter with the vapours of death.

In the place where I stood, on the edge of the abyss, I felt lost; it seemed to me that I was no longer on this earth, but standing on the boundary of another world. I felt alone amongst all the terrors of nature, in this eternally stirring desert, in this soundless chaos. I felt surrounded by the horrors of the fabulous world, and, without the presence of my friends, terror would have driven me away. I did not feel steeled enough to resist such impressions; I was overpowered by the inconceivably mysterious spell of this subterranean working. And there is truth in these impressions: it is the language of nature that frightens the conscience of man, and which convinces him of his vanity; it is the deep unknown power of these elements which, when slumbering, are not noticed by thoughtless man, but which, awaking now and then, admonish irresistibly. How powerful must be, therefore, the first sight of Vesuvius and its mysterious laboratory, where the beholder is separated from the hot floods only by a thin crust, through which the stinging steam is oozing, and which conceals from him the spectacle of the destroying flames, a crust which may burst every moment, and yield before unfettered powers. But as soon as there are a few of us together one does not feel lonely; in the face of nature one becomes the merrier, and hurries on recklessly

over the 'road of horror.' To show the heat of the steam
coming from the openings the guide placed some eggs,
which an old man had brought, together with some bottles,
in the hot sulphur before one of the small orifices; in the
shortest time they were boiled, and we ate them with some
brown bread. I had not for many a day so enjoyed a
déjeuner à l'impromptu, and it appeared to me as if no
cook succeeded so well in boiling eggs as old Vesuvius.
Inwardly I toasted a few dear friends in sour Lacryma
Christi. According to an old custom, the bottle went
round, then it was sacrificed to the crater, into which
it rolled jingling down. Our cicerone and another guide
ventured rather a long way down the slope of the crater;
the first to give us the spectacle of rolling down pieces
of lava, the other to fetch for us some of the many-
coloured sulphur formations. Very peculiar is it, when
these pieces of lava, rolling down from point to point,
produce the noise of distant thunder, which resounds
slowly from the walls, till it dies away at last, leaving the
impression that the crater loses itself infinitely in the
bowels of the earth.

The cicerone proposed to take one of the two roads
round the craters; that crater near which we stood is
newly formed, the other is that of 1839. We proceeded
along the narrow edge, but our company had nearly lost
courage. The sulphuric vapour enveloping us acted on
our lungs, and we experienced the awful feeling of suffo-
cation, and indescribable pain seized us; and as a last expe-
dient, I thought of hurrying down the off side of the ashy
ridge, to get a little fresher air.

My companions voted for returning, but I found it so
interesting to walk round the crater, that I suggested
that we should try what our lungs could stand. I went
on and the rest followed, *bon gré mal gré*. I walked
close behind the guide, the others followed at my heels.

I defended myself as well as I could, and put the handkerchief before my nose and mouth, and thus steered
through the steam which the wind was driving strongly
towards us, and two or three times I thought my
courage would entirely forsake me. After much toil,
we conquered the evil powers, and reached our goal;
the pain subsided, and we could examine what was
before us.

The upper irregular circumference of the second crater
was, like the former, between twenty to thirty yards in diameter; the hollow narrows, funnel-like, and the walls were
also perhaps still more glaring, being covered with sulphur-
fields. The particularly remarkable feature of this crater
is, that you can see its bottom. The stones thrown down
produced a thunder, but one saw them arrive at the bottom,
to which, indeed, one might, I believe, descend without
great difficulty with the help of ropes, if it were not for
the sulphuric vapours; but these would suffocate the over
curious; the temperature of the ground also may be too
high, for even the place on which we were standing was
in many spots so glowingly hot, that it was impossible to
stand there for any length of time. This crater towards
the sea-side could be seen much better than the other, as
the vapours were not so frequent or so dense. It seems
to rest sometimes from its impetuosity, and we could
walk around it without being hindered by the stifling
sulphuric exhalations. When the clouds surrounding
the summit of Vesuvius parted in their rapid flight, por-
tions of that splendid panorama could be seen extended
beneath our feet, floating, as it were, in a veil-like white
haze, like a picture in a dream. Standing on this theatre of
destruction we were spell-bound, seeing, as in a fairy land,
the sea and its beautiful shore. As the mist shifted the
pictures disappeared, but only to display new ones. Before
leaving the edge of the crater the cicerone descended with

great boldness to a projection over the depth, and thrust
his stick in one of the many holes by which the ground is
perforated, assuring us that the wood would be lighted
here by the flames of the lower regions. I could not
forbear following him to the rather dangerous spot, and
placed myself by his side on the dizzy projection. Our
sticks were wedged into the hole, but, after some turning
and stirring, the guide abandoned his attempt. With incredible temerity, he ran down a part of the wall of the
crater, as if it were a smiling meadow on a soft slope, and
yet a single slip of the foot would have hurled him to
certain destruction; though he would not have been the
first sacrifice devoured by that abyss. A longer stay at
this place would not have been advisable, as the soles of
our boots became extremely hot. We took one more look
at the awful abyss, in which yellow and vermilion fields of
sulphur were shining. Once more we admired the power
and grandeur of nature, and then retired to a little
hollow, which smoked only in a few places, to refresh a
little our tired limbs; and here we took, between lava
blocks and ashes, a frugal luncheon. Living things seem
so little in harmony with Vesuvius, that one sees with a
sort of surprise, lying between the grey masses, many remains of refreshments and breakfasts. Kernels of fruit,
and peels of oranges and lemons lie about, forming an
odd contrast with the soulless desert around. But all life
does not shun poor Vesuvius: a few insects buzz about,
and the lizards glide over lava and sulphur. I found also
immediately beside the hot sulphur, several poor dead
scarabees; but whether it is true, as is currently said, that
Vesuvius in his last eruption threw out a great quantity of
small and unknown animals, I cannot guarantee, although
this mysterious mountain might very likely indulge in
such curious freaks.

After having dispatched our luncheon, we returned to

the point to which we had climbed three-quarters of an hour ago, steaming with perspiration like beasts of burden. Here a pleasure of the rarest kind awaited us; for the approach which had cost us so much trouble and toil, we could now fly down, and reach the valley between Monte Somma and Vesuvius as quick as lightning. The famous gliding through the ashes was to be gone through. I had often heard of such a thing at home, but could never form a distinct idea of it. With mad delight I threw myself forward, and jumped into the ashes, the whole company after me. You think you must irresistibly slide down the mountain, without having any will at all; but the feet sink softly in the yielding ashes, and one can stop, when at the greatest speed, by throwing back the body; a step which is sometimes required in this rapid journey.

The feeling is indescribably agreeable; one gets a notion of the splendid feelings of a bird of prey, when winging itself from the height of the air down to the deep valley. But indeed our company rather resembled, *sauve le respect,* a herd of young he-goats, which, after a long winter, are led for the first time to the green meadows. Capers are seen, bleatings are heard, and the herd does not know what to do with itself for pleasure and joy. Thus it was with us: half dead with laughing, we vied nevertheless with each other in jumping, with a feeling of mad rapture. I often jumped yards-wide into the sloping ashes. Sometimes I stopped for a moment, to prolong the pleasure and to recover breath for fresh laughing, and to observe my companions in the different phases of jumping. One was so glad to be once again allowed to be a child with all one's heart, and on a legitimate occasion, and to give unrestrained vent to merriment. We were flying, running, and jumping at the same time over the ashes. We were rushing madly down the ashy hill, like the furies of antiquity, only with this difference,

that our companion was good-humour, not curses.   In a
few minutes we had reached the foot of the cone.   The
number of quarter-hours required for the ascent would
have represented the number of minutes in descending, if
one had not stopped now and then.

Before remounting our horses, we scratched out of the
ashes and lava a few scanty plants to take with us, but
unfortunately they afterwards died.   We left the awful
valley.   I turned frequently round to look again at old
Vesuvius, the chemical laboratory of nature, where it is
permitted to man to approach the primitive powers.
Before the spectator is a naked bare picture, painted in
colours, of another world, with a grand and impressive
vigour.   He feels himself re-transplanted to a time, when
the foot of a race of sinners had not yet made an impression on the earth, filled with germs of life, when the
soft mass of clay was not yet animated by the breath of
the Most High.   Still the Spirit of God seems to float
over the land and the waters, musing over the rough
material before pronouncing the all-stirring words of life,
' LET IT BE.'   Vesuvius is a remnant of chaos.   Thus the
past speaks to us, through the spirit of fire; and also
gives us a warning of the future.   As God created, so He
will destroy.

As the fire purified, and as out of mist and smoke the
earth arose in its splendour, and God himself enjoyed his
work and said, ' *It is good*,' so once again will smoke and
mist arise, and withdraw this foul old ball from the blessed
eye of the Creator.   But let us fly before these awful thoughts
to the little church of the hermitage, to pray forgiveness
for our sins.   When the whole company was assembled in
the poor chapel, the priest read the holy mass, and then
we returned, in quick time, between splendid vineyards, to
Resina.   The day had become clear, the view still clearer,
and Naples, amidst the brightest green, washed by the

laughing sea, lay in full splendour at our feet, before our enraptured eyes.

In the best of humours, happy with what we had accomplished, we were speeding along an excellent road. In contrast with our merriment was a corpse carried on an open bier, covered only with a cloth, and going to the friendly cemetery of Resina. As everything in Naples is done freely and openly, so no coffin encloses the dead of the poorer classes. Somewhat tired, and in dreadfully disordered clothes, we reached our boat, which awaited us at Portici, and which brought us back to the frigate.

Having rested a little, I had to put on my uniform and jump again in a boat to go to Capo di Monte to a *dîner en famille* with my aunt and cousin. The afternoon was splendid and hot, the city glowing in rich magnificence. At the steps of the quay of Santa Lucia the carriage was waiting, into which we jumped, surrounded by the bustle of people in the most peculiar costumes. One must visit Naples to know the meaning of eternal noise, continuous activity, and restless life. I was so much occupied yesterday with the Via Toledo, with its manifold sights, that I quite forgot to mention the royal palace and the broad place extending before it; yet it is perhaps, in regard to architecture, the most brilliant thing in the city. The façade of the palace towards the Piazza, of rough brick walls ornamented with grey stones, is imposing and regal. Under the middle balcony, through a wide entrance, the main guard is kept, composed, as it seems, of the different military branches. Here, on all sides, we see the lilies, intimating that here rules still a dying branch of the Bourbons. Over the grandest, as over the pettiest work, from the Museo Borbonico to the last sentry-box—nay, to the neat form of the bad butter in the loyal coffee-house 'Europa'—the 'lily' waves, and seems to be promoted from the humble position of 'the lily of the fields' in the time of Solomon, to the highest places by the influence of the Bourbons. Though the use of this flower is here carried too far, still I love these symbolical crests, which remind one of an ancient power. Opposite the city façade of the palace is a large church, built of white stone, in the shape of a Greek rotunda, from which, to the right and left, branch off wide arcades, surrounding a great part of the place. It was built *ex voto* by Ferdinand I. after the recovery of his land, robbed from him by the French. As an enemy of Greek architecture for the use of Christians, I don't like it; but as heathenish work, it cannot be denied that it possesses an imposing harmony. On the right, seen from the royal palace, stands another smaller palace, which is used to lodge foreign princely visitors. A dwelling was allotted to me there, but I preferred my comfortable house. On the other side arises the unpretending palace of the Duke of Salerno, rendered so celebrated by its site and charming garden. From the sea one observes, peeping over the roofs, the tops of beautiful trees. As my uncle had no male heirs, this charming residence fell back to the Crown after his death. There are on the Piazza two fine equestrian statues of Charles III. and Ferdinand I., which have already acquired that greenish-blue hazy colour which no art, but time and weather only, can give to bronze. Once again through the Via Toledo, with its noisy life, to the hill, Capo di Monte, imbedded in green.

After dinner we strolled through the desolate wide state rooms of the stone palace. Taste and comfort, life and convenience, are banished from these wide halls. There are the stiff straight lines and ornaments of the time of the French empire, lacking the warm soul of past ages, and spoiling the fine proportions of the interior. There is a peculiar picture gallery in this palace, intended to support the feeble modern art of Naples. There are, however,

nothing but frightful subjects of past history and mythology; gaping wounds, dying heroes and heroines, and awful
corpses fill the rooms of the summer palace, to which they
are only so far fitted as the extremely natural costumes of
those represented are fit for the summer season: I never
saw so perfect a collection of naked bodies in horrid daubs
as I saw here. To judge from them, art must be indeed
in a very low and primitive state in this country.

My aunt invited me to take a drive with her and her
daughter. Through charming green avenues and laughing
gardens we rolled along the height of Capo di Monte, to the
Villa Regina Isabella, which had become noted on account
of its site. We soon arrived at the property of the Queen-
mother. By a long avenue running between oleander, rose-
bushes, and grape vines, we came to an open place richly
ornamented with flowers, on which, built in Grecian style,
the villa stands. We descended from the carriage and
entered the neat yard of the house. A slim being received
us in a green dressing-gown, whose tonsure and covering
for the feet discovered to us the house chaplain. We had
evidently disturbed his comfortable privacy by our visit.
He brought us through the pretty rooms of the ground
floor to a terrace, from which one enjoys perhaps one of
the finest views on God's wide earth; it is one of those
happily selected places, from which the view is not enjoyed
as a corollary to the splendour around, but where, by the
excellently selected spot on which one stands, one is
placed, as it were, outside the picture as an observer and
admirer; where the eye is not compelled to squander its
attention on details, but where all charms, all effects of
light, combine to one point, and the whole works powerfully on the soul in beautiful harmony. On a terrace
lying higher still, to which we were next led by the ecclesiastical custodian, the view around was still more comprehensive. As the last work of an artist dying at the pinnacle

of fame is generally the most saturated with his genius, so the sun never paints so vividly, never in such glowing tints, and with such magic lustre, as when he is parting and pressing his last kiss upon earth. He is possessed of the secret of creating a longing after his departure, he always leaves behind a hope, a desire, to see his golden image again; for the prospect of decay in this world awakens the anxious desire of resurrection in another. A still, magnificent evening was gilding Naples' splendid gulf.

The villa stands on a free airy height, and from it the green ground falls sharply off towards the city and the sea; and it is this point of vantage which heightens so much the impression of all seen from it. Vesuvius and the picturesque mountain chain of Sorrento were bathed in a blue haze; at the foot of the hills shone the different towns and villages; and the happy plain betwixt them and Naples was like a rich carpet spread between them; and the sinking sun gilded the cupolas and roofs of the capital, which was surrounded by a wreath of villas, and by the hills of Posilippo, with the southern green of their luxuriant gardens. Behind us rose the heights of Cămaldoli, with the celebrated monastery. Before us a palm waved its beautiful and regal head; beneath us lay the Chiaja, with the avenues of the Villa Reale, from which the calm mirror of the sea extended in untarnished brightness. Looking on this matchless picture, and this eternally young nature, in which the fresh flowers of Europe mingle with the luxuriant richness of the tropics; looking on this Southern glow, with its Oriental metallic light, one recalls the proud saying of the Neapolitans: ' Napoli è un pezzo del cielo caduto in terra!'

Although the interior rooms of the villa are of very little interest to the stranger, we yet looked over them. They have the stamp of a mixed household: two spheres of life are united in this house, which, though they ought to be able to be blended with success, here form a sad and discordant state of things. The father of the present king died, and his widow, Queen Isabella, married a nobleman of the country; and, after having taken such a step, instead of retiring with her new husband to some quiet nook of earth, she bought this charming villa, that she might stand here with one foot in the court and the other in private life. She wished to enjoy the leisure and the amusements of a private lady, and yet could not renounce the fading splendour of royalty. She died recently, and left her house at the disposal of her husband, who is serving as a colonel in the army of his step-son and living in a barrack. The Villa Regina is forsaken now, and its possessor comes only from time to time for a short visit.

It seemed strange to find in the house of a private man the family portraits of the Royal Family. The whole is furnished with a comfort which has not quite renounced its former magnificence. Amongst the occasional very costly furniture, I was struck by a kind of throne, of which the richly-embroidered stuff was surrounded by golden ornaments. Astonished to find such a piece of furniture in a drawing-room, I asked the house chaplain—who, like a genuine Italian, was leading us about *sans gêne*, in his mean-looking green dressing-gown, although he must have known very well who my aunt was—where this rich royal arm-chair came from? He answered that the Queen-mother had received it from a *Madame Roschilde*. It was only when he had repeated this name twice, which had in his Italian mouth a peculiar sound, that I perceived its Hebrew character. In the lower rooms of the house there is a kind of universal collection, a small museum, where there is something of everything, but nothing particular. We thanked the chaplain for the favour of having shown us about, and stepped into our light carriage.

I now became acquainted with one of the greatest

charms of Naples, the fine wide roads on the heights of the Capo di Monte. The present king caused them to be built, and ornamented with the most splendid and finely arched avenues. Driving through these gigantic leafy halls, one could fancy you were in an English park rather than in one of the ordinary roads of communication in the neighbourhood of a city. It is a beautiful and luxurious idea of the King of the Two Sicilies to surround his residence with green trees and shrubs, and so to arch over his admirable roads with a cool shade.

It was Sunday; everywhere was life, everywhere the people moved about happily, and on all sides we were greeted by the noise of the streets. The peculiar equipages common to Naples, the two-wheeled cars, with the poor little horses, which have to trot along with a company of twelve to fourteen persons, throng the centre. A Vetturino succeeds in bringing together inside them representatives of the most different classes of society. In this vehicle one sees the three-cornered hat of the servant of the Lord, the sword belt of a Swiss soldier, the fluttering coloured ribbons of a Calabrian girl; the cap of a lazzaroni waving by the side of the never-resting fan of an old citizen lady; and here we have the problem solved of which I spoke before, of how to find room for fourteen human beings in a car originally intended only for four. On the shaky seats of the car the people do not sit two and two, but three and four are closely packed, whilst the driver balances himself on the shaft, and alongside of him on the bars of the skeleton of the car the youthful world finds a place. Even steps do not remain empty, for they are as wide as a human foot. Behind the seats, and turning one's back upon the team, one has a very good view of the country left behind, although this pleasure has to be enjoyed on a very narrow seat. But there still remains a place between the two large wheels under the bottom of the car, which must be made available: a large basket, fastened by chains or ropes, hangs there, furnishing another place in which one of the passengers rocks most comfortably. With the population of such a two-wheeled car one could colonise an island very well. Such a vehicle would furnish priests, soldiers, peasants, and even beggars. Sounds of bells and of speaking, sometimes even instrumental music and singing, coming out of a cloud of dust, advise you from a distance of the approach of these equipages.

Hundreds of other comical figures are seen in the lively streets; and especially striking to the stranger are the avenues surrounding the city, the Abbati. My aunt and cousin were constantly laughing at my exclamations of astonishment at the number of priests we met. We met a young priest on a tall horse, with his three-cornered hat, his long flowing gown, and a hunting whip, and another who was driving comfortably a two-wheeled equipage.

On the turnpike road leading to Rome, we passed a large plain, on which the military festivities take place. Close to the road stands a small building for the Queen, from which she may look at these reviews. Along the Strada del Campo, passing the large poor-house, we crossed the railroad leading to Pompeii, and drove to the large quays outside the city. One enjoys this view of the plain and of Vesuvius, the outlines of which were marked on the delicately tinted evening sky. We arrived in the city at twilight. This is the moment, when a new and doubly animated life commences in Naples, where music and rejoicings compensate for the departure of the sun, and the absence of its glowing rays. Hundreds of lamps and lights are lighted up on the quays, and reflected in the sea; festoons and garlands indicate the different festivals of the many churches; volleys of guns shake the air;

rockets ascend; wheels of many-coloured fire whiz around the Madonnas; the theatres open their noisy halls; the squeaking of the marionets calls the lazzaroni to a popular meeting; hundreds of cooking shops display their treasures in the glowing light of crackling flames, or in the gloom of little dull lamps. For a few bajocchi the hungry people fish in the macaroni basins—some smart ones do it for nothing—and when the stomach is full, feel happy under the free blue sky in the delicious evening air.

Over all the rejoicings of the city, over all its busy life, sails calmly, through the blue sea of ether, the full, majestic moon, the ancient witness of night life, which looks with good-natured mockery on the merry restlessness of this hot-blooded people, who continue the brightness and the stir of the day to that part of it allotted to rest. The hundreds of lamps fade to little sparks before the over-powering light of the moon. She has lost the red glow with which she appeared behind the vapours of Vesuvius, and mirrors her pure and faultless countenance in the still surface of the gulf. She is calmly enthroned on the wide firmament, like a beautiful proud woman, conscious of her sublime and incontestable victory. The sun is the star of a fresh new life, of aspiring thoughts; he warms and makes young again; at his departure sad longings take possession of the heart; but the moon is the constellation of memory and of delightful melancholy! She brings back again the dreams of the past; in her pure mild mirror pass slowly and softly visions of happier times, and memories of blissful moments.

The evening was devoted to one of the greatest celebrities of Naples, the Teatro San Carlo. This grand theatre owes its origin to the genial pomp-loving Charles III., who had it built in 1738 in 270 days, after which rapid creation it was solemnly opened on the day of St. Charles, the birthday of the founder. It was afterwards rebuilt in 1816, having been destroyed by fire.

I know nothing of the question of feet and inches, but when I entered the large, beautifully illuminated hall, it produced on me at once the impression of being the most imposing theatre I had ever seen. Six tiers with thirty-two boxes in each, rise one upon the other, embellished abundantly by columns and rich golden ornaments on a red ground. The stage is of unusual width and height, reaching to the second tier and arching up to the ceiling of the theatre. The brightness of the golden ornaments has become somewhat subdued by time, which gives to the house a most dignified appearance. These ornaments are moulded in the pomp-loving taste of the last century. The house is just lighted to the right point, and has not the exaggerated eye-blinding tendency of our more modern theatres. Opposite the stage, over the main entrance, under a heavy canopy richly covered with golden lilies, is the large court box; it rests majestically on the crowns of two golden palm trees, the old Egyptian model of the column. To the left from the entrance, close to the stage, are four boxes thrown in one, for the general use of the royal family. There is a curious custom here, that on the appearance of a royal prince in the theatre, a soldier steps forward on the stage with his gun, turns, in face of the whole audience, towards the royal scion, presents arms, and looks at him continually till relieved, which is done every five minutes. 'So many countries, so many customs!' an old, never-to-be-forgotten saying. The theatre is filling more and more; in the pit fans rustle and wave; but it is not the fair sex, only, who handle them. No! they are the rough hands of men who, compelled by the heat, call to their aid the weapons of coquetry. The gentler portion of the children of earth is banished

from the Platea,* a moral custom, the introduction of
which would not be amiss in other cities. The impression of the whole theatre is very fine. How I wished
within myself, to be able to transplant it into our own
dear capital! There is something of the time of Louis
XIV. in these wide halls, built by one of his successors, to
whom also descended a part of his pomp-loving and creative mind. The works of that spirit remain, but the
spirit itself has vanished with his times. How beautiful
would it be if this theatre resounded with enthusiastic
applause, with patriotic exclamations, or with the strains
of a national hymn, instead of resounding with one of
these Italian Operas, which I love so little!

Roadstead of Naples, August 11, 1851.

We had not rested more than a few hours, when we had
again to start. It was one of the finest mornings when our
boat carried us to the interior harbour, chiefly reserved for
the men-of-war, where Count Aquila, the brother of the
King, was waiting for us on a war-steamer, 'Fiera-mosca,' to
carry us to the King at Gaëta. Count Aquila was standing
on deck, surrounded by his officers, and I there had the first
opportunity of making his acquaintance. He is not tall,
and a little too stout for his age, but his features have the
noble spirited form of the Bourbons. He is at the head
of the navy, and devotes himself to his profession with
extraordinary zeal and great knowledge. He has already
had the good fortune to make two voyages to the Brazils;
on the last one he attended his sister the Empress there,
and brought home for himself a transatlantic bride, a sister
of the Emperor. During my longer stay in Naples I became more acquainted with him, and learned to value him
as a clever and very agreeable young man. He wins the
hearts of all those with whom he comes in contact, by

* Pit.

E 2

his unaffected and lively manner. Besides being a most ardent sailor, he is a great lover of horses, and has introduced, with much success, English fox-hunting into Naples, without ever having been in England.

The signal was given, and our large and powerful steamer sailed majestically from the harbour near the royal palace into the beautiful gulf. Our way ran along the picturesque shores of Puzzuoli and Baiæ, and we soon saw these two towns shining on the wide secure bay, in which appeared the small rock-island crowned by a monastery. The pillars and single arches of the old Roman bridge, by which the tyrannical Emperor Nero intended to manifest his power over the elements, arose out of the sea. The tuffastone of the hills on the shore glittered like gold, and exhibited every variety of form; the sky was blue and pure, the sea still bluer. We approached the island of Procida to enter the high sea by passing between it and the continent. The island is small, but very picturesque, on account of the undulations of the ground. The costume of its female inhabitants, which retains its old Grecian type, is the most remarkable in the whole kingdom. The voyage from here to Gaëta is of little interest; the four hours required to go there from Naples passed in pleasant conversation with Count Aquila, who in a short time succeeded in completely captivating my heart. The ship, although intended for war, offered all possible conveniences. Being quite new, its cannons were not yet aboard, but some of the most heavy calibre were expected, to ornament the deck. The 'Fiera-mosca' has, notwithstanding her youth, a singular history. She was ordered in England by the Sicilian revolutionists, and when their regiment fell under the royal shells, and the white banner waved again on the walls of Messina, Lord Palmerston would not permit the ship, which had been finished only after the revolution, to quit England. The firmness of the Neapolitan Government succeeded at last in getting it as a lawful prize, and now it is one of the finest ships of the royal fleet. Officers and crew had an excellent sailor-like appearance, and, from the order prevailing everywhere, one might draw favourable conclusions in reference to the value of the Neapolitan navy.

One could now see in faint outlines the mountain behind Gaëta; these outlines became more distinct, and the blue haze of the distance broke up into light tints, and single masses of houses appeared; the projecting rock forming the base of the fortress was seen distinctly, and at the foot of the rock washed by the sea, Gaëta, the princely asylum, the protector of tottering crowns. One can imagine how eager I was to see the place of which the name has been rendered famous by the events of the year 1848; this pool in which anchored the little ship of St. Peter, for protection against the storms of the world. The widely opened gates of hell, it was believed, had already swallowed up the glittering tiara, and the head of Christianity was overthrown, never to rise again; but from among dark clouds it thundered mightily, and the scornful varlets of the prince of this world tremblingly heard a voice calling to them: 'Tu es Petrus, et super hanc Petram ædificabo ecclesiam meam, et portæ Inferi non prævalebunt adversus eam!' The sun was shining on the picturesque although bare rocks, the houses at their foot glittering brightly. We had entered the bay; I looked out in vain for the residence of the King; I expected, at least, to find a tolerably pretty villa; at last Aquila showed me two little houses connected with each other immediately behind the wall of the fortress, over which only a few windows under the roofs were to be seen. That was the place where King Ferdinand dwelt. The ruler of Naples lived in a bare place in two patched-up little houses, behind the stifling bastion dotted with

cannon, scarcely offering room for his numerous family.
Who would believe that the same prince possesses those
beautifully situated palaces, the mighty Capo di Monte, the
crown of Naples; Caserta, Portici, and Quisisana, palaces
which would be envied by many greater monarchs; and
yet he found his *sans souci* in a rocky nest. But, no
doubt, the quiet retirement of Gaëta possesses many qualities to win the hearts of the royal couple. The King feels
grateful to this rock, on which his weary head finds quiet
and rest. He occupies himself with military matters here,
where he has time and leisure for it, and daily strengthens
the already powerful protection afforded to him by the fortress. On the other hand, the Queen loves to live in her
family, which she can do, to her heart's content, at Gaëta.

Several fine men-of-war were lying in the bay, and
saluted on our arrival. Amidst the sounds of music and
the cheering of the sailors the anchor was cast, and the
boat, with some well-bestarred grandees of the army
and navy, attended us from the ship, to land us at a
small gate in the wall of the fortress, where we were
received by some chiefs of the court. We slipped through
the narrow gate, and found ourselves suddenly under
the gates of the residence. A tall strong man, with short
cropped hair and beard, and with a laced three-cornered hat, received us; my good genius whispered to
me that it was the King. Indeed, it must have been
a higher revelation, for I had imagined King Ferdinand
to be a different man. His figure still floated before
me indistinctly, as I saw him fifteen years ago in
Vienna, when he was a young man of twenty-six years of
age. Now, to be sure, he was forty-one, but, from his
appearance, one would have taken him for a man considerably above fifty; so much has the destroying power of the
South and the influence of the years of revolution worked
upon him. Later, when I had an opportunity of examin-

ing him more closely, I recognised the features of his youth, but his fine black hair had turned grey and his face had become wrinkled. He wore the rather plain uniform of one of his regiments of Grenadiers, which he prefers, I was told, to all others since the revolution. The riband of the Austrian Order of St. Stephen was hanging over his shoulder. He received me in the most friendly manner, and conducted me directly to the Queen. It was fifteen years ago since she also had said farewell to her country, when she left home a blooming and graceful figure. Since that period the German princess had become an Italian, and a mother of nine children; one therefore can imagine how she had changed. She is a little slim lady, and, though she has a resemblance to her father, and to her sisters and brothers, the Nassauvian features still prevail. She seems to be very serious and quiet, is wrapped up entirely in her children, and, I was told, loves seclusion. The King formerly found entertainment in festivities, but since his second marriage, and especially since the revolution, the large state-rooms have been only opened for the tedious drawing-rooms on birth- and name-day festivities, and on New Year's Day. On these occasions the King and his family receive the congratulations of the grandees and Government officers, and both gentlemen and ladies must perform the so-called *baccia-mano*. I must mention how highly I was astonished when, on my first appearance as a prince in this kingdom, I saw the highest in the land bend their left knee before me, and hold out their hand towards my right one with a movement like that which is made, perhaps, before the holy water. Not used to such a thing, and utterly unprepared, I felt most disagreeably affected by the ceremony; I made the most comical excuses, and tried to escape. Some of the good people listened to reason, but others insisted on this expression of their respect.

When the usual formalities were dispatched, and I had been invited by the Queen to take a seat on the sofa, the numerous royal children entered from a side door. There are nine living, six sons and three daughters, the crown prince being the only issue of the first marriage of the King. The crown prince is rather a tall young man of fifteen, but still a boy both in manners and dress, very much resembling his cousin the Duke of Modena; his brown eyes are good-natured, his features gentle, and his figure small. In some of the other children the Austrian blood can be seen, especially in the three sons, who immediately follow the crown prince, and who look very bright. The daughters have soft kindly faces, but not one of them is strikingly handsome. A peculiar taste of the King, with which the Queen is not at all pleased, is to have almost all the hair of the children shaved off. I was quite a stranger to the royal family, who knew very little of their more recent relations in Austria, and therefore I had frequently to carry on the conversation alone, which not unfrequently came even to a stop. At last the King himself graciously led me to the rooms prepared for me, where I was left to myself till the dinner hour. The rooms in which the royal couple live are small and plain, nay, I might say, too plain, particularly as regards the furniture; one might be inclined to take the dwelling for one of a not very high officer; plain furniture stands in the rooms, a few antiquated nicknacks fill the table, and on the papered walls hang large English prints, representing tiger and bear hunts, such as are perhaps to be found in the apartments of our bachelors; each window has its balcony enclosed by smooth iron rails. On stepping out on one of them one looks out immediately on the narrow dirty street, whilst from another one sees the bastion of the fortress, which, if I had to live in these rooms, would be a little oppressive to me. From the

windows of the new part of the house in which my rooms
were situated, one has a view of an ugly old house, at the
few windows of which may be seen the disagreeable details
of a provincial household, and now and then the wrinkled
face of an old woman. This house, however, is soon to be
removed, and the bulwark extended; then one will have,
as from the rooms of the Queen, a view of the bay and its
bare hills. From the back part of the house, towards the
great rock, one can, from the upper story, step on a garden
terrace, where, with great pains, a grape-vine arbour and
several trees and plants are made to grow. Though there
are not any rare flowers in the many vases and pots standing about, yet this narrow place offers, in my opinion, the
chief attraction of the house. If one has no view from
the little garden, yet it ascends in lovely terraces up the
rocks, beautifully connecting the vines with the walls and
the yard of the house. I availed myself of the time remaining till dinner to pay a visit to the crown prince.
The poor young man is very timid, which may arise partly
from the manner in which he is educated; he is kept out
of the world, that he may remain child-like. When he
comes of age next winter the prince will have his own
household, and it is said Count Ludolf will be placed at
his side. The Count is one of the few presentable beings
at the court of Naples. He was Neapolitan minister at
the Apostolic See; came to Gaëta in 1849, was liked by
the royal couple, and is now as a kind of 'maître de plaisir
in partibus,' vegetating in the royal court, which is said to
be very simple; so much so, that a man like Ludolf, who
succeeds in spinning out of the merest trifle a whole string
of pleasant phrases, can make a great sensation. At meals
and in the promenade the old gentleman must amuse the
Queen, and dish up innocent remarks and anecdotes of his
political career.

The King is very busy; and, as is frequently the case with

people who work all day, is fond of a commonplace, insignificant company. He is of the same opinion as that great French statesman, who, when asked how he could associate with such utterly insignificant company, answered, 'Je me repose.' Ludolf is therefore the only one who is in some way an exception; this may be the reason why he is assigned to the Crown Prince. The habits he has formed as a diplomatist in various situations will be of service to him in his new career.

At dinner a part of the suite appeared, who were most peculiar figures. The cooking was Italian, and therefore not much to my taste; in my eyes the everlasting Naples macaroni alone gave brightness to the table. One can understand how this dish may be eaten by high and low, all day and every day. I am sorry that I could not ascertain whether in this fine kingdom macaroni is substituted for bread in the prayers. The King, to my greatest astonishment, ordered cigars after dinner, and compelled us, notwithstanding our remonstrances, to smoke in the presence of the Queen.

Since our arrival at Gaëta the weather had become thick; a heavy thunder-storm was raging among the high mountains, and on the opposite shore of the bay, dark clouds were looming, which on breaking, dissolved in a beneficial rain, mitigating the heat of the day; so that the intentions of the King to make a trip with me, were delayed for some time.

After the rain had at last subsided a little, the King invited me to take a drive in the fortress. The Queen, also, who was most kind, and who condescended to address me always in German, which is said to be an extremely rare case, joined us. The King, the Queen, his three eldest sons and myself, stepped into a light char-à-banc, whilst the rest of the company followed in other equipages. We were driving along the enclosure of the town to the landgate

not far off, when we saw a great number of prisoners in
scarlet dress and with heavy chains, who were working at
the repairs of the wall; they were military prisoners,
expiating important crimes.

Immediately outside the landgate there was a detachment
of cavalry, which generally escorts the King in his drives.
To-day, however, I suppose in honour of me, he waved
them off. Outside the enclosure one comes at once upon
a bare narrow isthmus, forming the connection between
land and rock. Towards this ground, from which a land-
attack would have to be made, the fortress has steep
enclosures of natural rock walls, which surround the
fortress towards the high sea to the entrance of the
bay. Two years ago thousands and thousands assembled,
the people of the surrounding country and the Neapolitan troops met here. A poor fugitive from the heights
of this fortress, from a spot marked by an inscription
in marble, gave them the only good thing left to him
to give by the evil nature of the times, to wit, the Apostolic blessing. A second time Pius stood on the rock
of the fortress, and again he pronounced the benediction;
but this time to a multitude that promised him help—to
the Spanish troops sent by the most Catholic queen, and
who had landed at Gaëta to receive the Papal blessing. I
am assured by eye-witnesses, that it was a most imposing
spectacle to see the prince of the church, in his simple
white garments, standing aloft on the ramparts of the
fortress, pronouncing the blessing on vast numbers of
the faithful, who, wrapt in devotion, bent their heads
before him. The place seems made for such a solemn and
august act.

We returned to the fortress, and visited its single bastions. The King is improving them constantly, and indeed
they seem to be very strong. In one of these new avenues
the wife of a condemned criminal, with a little boy on her

arm, rushed towards the carriage of the King and clung to it, crying and shrieking, and would not let go, notwithstanding the danger of her being crushed by the wheels. At last a soldier caught her arm, on which the poor raving woman dropped her naked boy on the ground, and flung herself on him in wild grief. The scene was a sad one, and illustrated the strong, perhaps exaggerated, feelings of the people of the South. Both here and in Naples I frequently saw the people appeal immediately to the King and the Princes, and hand petitions to them whilst in their carriage.

Near the surrounding wall, towards the land, is a monastery, belonging to a peculiar kind of Franciscans, not known with us. The King entered with us. At the entrance was a chapel, before which the Royal Family knelt down to say a short prayer. By a cross walk, adorned with pictures, before which my august guides crossed themselves, we came to another chapel, in which knees were again bent. From this chapel we came to a chasm in the rock, about four feet wide, and reaching from the top of the hill to the surface of the sea; this is said to have opened at the great earthquake which took place at the moment when Christ died. This peculiar narrow deep chasm is perhaps the greatest curiosity in Gaëta; whether its origin is miraculous I cannot decide, and leave the explanation of this phenomenon to the scornful infidel.

A small staircase leads through this awfully narrow place to a little church, built on a vault over the chasm. In the right-hand wall of the rock is to be seen the impression of five fingers, said to have been caused by a Mahometan, who, when told of the miracle, said that he despised this soft stone, and struck with his hand against the rock, which, tradition says, henceforth retained the impression of his fingers. Overpowered by this miracle, he allowed himself to be baptized with the water, which suddenly trickled out of a small opening in the stone wall. The same little spring still runs, and the devotees cross themselves with it as with holy water. In the chapel, in which there is the Host, a short devotion was again performed. From a window to the right of the altar one sees how the sea has entered the chasm. It is said that the French under Napoleon intended to take the fortress by help of this cleft, which was not necessary, as, a short time afterwards, the commander of the place, the Prince of Hesse-Philippsthal, died by a French bullet, after which the garrison surrendered.

Before leaving the monastery, the King, with his wife and children, knelt again at the entrance chapel. These genuflexions, made so repeatedly, might be thought ridiculous with us, but in the Southern country it is the general custom to express one's feelings in a more lively manner ; and as the great are ever bending their knee before the King and his family, so the King prostrates himself before the only Being that is above him.

We returned now to the little town, to inspect one of the batteries before it. I was shown a mean-looking house, which has become renowned by the shelter it gave to the Pope; it is immediately beside an inn, where the holy Father, on his clandestine arrival, late in the evening, could not find a lodging. In the simple attire of an abbate he alighted upon this modest private house, upon which the Bavarian minister, Count Spaur, who attended him, sent at once a letter to the King of Naples with the news of the arrival. The sun had scarcely risen over the mountains of Gaëta, when a steamer cast anchor in view of the fortress, and the King with his wife and his children threw themselves at the feet of the Lieutenant of Christ. He had received the news of the arrival of the Pope in the middle of the night, and at three o'clock in the morning he left his palace at Naples to greet the father of Chris-

tianity as his guest, and to lead him at once to a house
formerly inhabited by the King on his trips to Gaëta.
Soon fresh fugitives arrived; the Grand-Duke of Tuscany
and his family also sought protection behind the walls of
Gaëta. The house in which they alighted is close to the
above-mentioned battery, and is, like the other places of
this town that have become historical, provided with Latin
inscriptions. The Grand-Duke moved later to ' Mola di
Gaëta,' where he lived in the villa of the great Cicero.

Gaëta could scarcely hold the guests pouring in from
all sides. Fugitive court-households, numberless diplo-
mats and cardinals had to find room in the little town.
To get, under such circumstances, a tolerably good room
was one of the happy events of the moment. The above-
mentioned Count Ludolf told me that he in his room, of
which the furniture consisted of a bed and two chairs,
received in one night the unexpected visit of six cardinals.

We drove now to an eminence where there is a military school established by the King. The boys, to the
number of more than eight hundred, were all marshalled
on the road, and looked perfectly healthy and cheerful.
This institution, which is not yet in order, had scarcely
been established when soldiers from all parts sent in their
petitions for the admission of their children. The King
finds it difficult to refuse any request of his much-beloved
army, and thus the pupils increased to the great number
just mentioned, without arrangements having been made
to give them a perfect education.

From this rocky height on which we stood, a staircase,
ornamented with vases, many flowers and vine-garlands,
led through the little garden back to the house of the
King. It was time for us to think of our return. I took
leave of the royal couple, thanked them for their cordial
reception, and returned with Aquila on board the ' Fiera-
mosca,' as the day waned, in four hours to Naples. Supper-

time excepted, I was almost always on deck, in conversation with my amiable cousin, who had to tell me many interesting things.

Roadstead of Naples, August 12, 1851.

Very much fatigued by the exertions of the preceding days, we were glad to pass this morning more quietly, visiting the shops of Naples. Every city has its peculiar productions, for which strangers at once enquire. Who would not ask in Naples for the nicely-cut corals? With this object in view, we made an excursion from the quay of Santa Lucia towards the Villa Reale, and from there into the street Santa Catarina. The first shop we visited was on the quay of Santa Lucia, and contained chiefly clay copies of Etruscan vases, of which I bought several very little specimens; but the best we saw were in the street Santa Catarina, and on the place before the Villa Reale. They consisted in sundry nicknacks of corals, amongst which the celebrated Jettatura-hands, and very nice little views of beautiful Naples and its environs, painted with much skill in oil-colours, recalling the lively picturesque tints for which the gulf is famous. Having done with our purchase, we went into the 'café Europa,' to wait there for the departure of the railway train, as we intended to steam to Pompeii in the afternoon.

Who would imagine that the principal coffee-house in Naples is not in the least to be compared in beauty to the coffee-houses in the suburbs of Vienna? The 'café Europa' is, notwithstanding its proud name, a dirty and small vaulted room with bad furniture, in which the painted ceiling and all the frames of the looking-glasses are covered with gauze, as a protection against the numberless flies. A horrible 'dame de buffet' stands behind a wooden bulwark, watching like a dragon the movements of the comers. We refreshed ourselves with orange-granit, a refreshment suitable to the climate, consisting of half-frozen orange-juice and sugar; I preferred it by far to the celebrated 'gelatì di Napoli,' which, in my opinion, are not equal to those in Vienna. We had scarcely rested a little, when Field-marshal Lieutenant Martini came to tell us, that we could only go at a later time to Pompeii, and proposed to visit meanwhile the Museo Borbonico, where we proceeded at once.

The Museo Borbonico, one of the few imposing build-ings of Naples, is, like Capo di Monte, built of red bricks and grey stones. It is, like most of the buildings of Italy, of the new Roman style; its foundation stone was laid by the Duke of Osuna, viceroy of the Spanish King, and was then intended for a grand riding-school.

Later viceroys continued the building, and, in 1616, under the lieutenancy of Don Pedro de Castro, Count of Lemos, the university was transferred to it. After having been used also as a tribunal and a barrack, it was in 1816 used for its present purpose by King Ferdinand I., and there he brought together all the antiquities of the country, hitherto scattered in different places. The large imposing vestibule, from the sides of which extend the squares, is ornamented with colossal antique statues; to the right and the left of the chief entrance, leading to the wide and beautiful staircase, are the casts of the equestrian statues of Charles III. and Ferdinand I., standing on the piazza before the residence.

Our time was, however, too short to do more than run through the most remarkable rooms of this interesting col-lection, and we occupied ourselves with the antiques only. The mediæval works and the collection of pictures we left unexamined. We commenced with the marble and bronze statues, amongst which I was struck by many great treasures of art. The most celebrated work of Naples, the so-called 'Toro Farnese,' is one of the largest groups that remain to us from antiquity. It is hewn out of a single block of Grecian marble, and represents Dirce before the eyes of another female figure, being tied by two young men to a furious bull. The spirit of Greece breathes through this splendid masterpiece; Grecian vigour is exhibited in these artistic figures. What inimitable life there is in the furious bull roaring between the two athletic figures, whilst despair is expressed in the figure as well as the face of Dirce, who is prostrate before the bull and attached to it by her luxuriant hair. I can scarcely name another work of art in which there is such true life, and where the cold block has been made to yield such a genial group. The vigorous female figure standing at the side also deserves notice, and amongst the smaller animals belonging to the group a greyhound is remarkable for its light excellent work. I looked long at this artistic group, and became still more and more convinced that the Greeks were endowed with that creative power which changes marble into flesh and blood, and animates the dead stone with an ardent spirit and deep life-like truth.

Opposite this group stands the celebrated Farnesian Hercules, a statue much spoken of both in ancient and in modern time. The strength expresses itself symbolically in the exactly drawn, anatomically correct muscles; it is a work which has acquired so much fame that one feels scarcely at liberty to speak of it otherwise than with praise, and yet it has in my eyes two faults: the moulding of the muscles is exaggerated, one might say unnatural, and the head appears too small for the massive figure; but this may perhaps have been done purposely by Glykon, who may have thought by these means to render more prominent the figure of the god of strength. This marble statue, as well as the group before mentioned, were both found in the baths of Caracalla in Rome.

The gallery of Flora is named after the colossal statue

of this goddess. This work proves that Roman art has also produced great things. The large voluptuous figure of Flora exhibits in her pure noble features mildness and dignity; a light tunic enables us to admire through its splendid drapery the symmetry of the limbs, and seems to be of a transparent material. One almost overlooks a Juno and a Minerva which stand in this hall, and hurries to the celebrated mosaic, which so justly attracts the eyes of the stranger. Of its kind it is one of the most extensive works that has been preserved to us, and although it is still surpassed in size by the mosaic in the court-garden of Athens, this one has the preference in the eyes of antiquaries, in possessing the advantage of representing a historical scene, the battle on the Issus between Alexander and Darius. As a mosaic, it is of an extraordinary value in regard to colour and design; but it appears to me rather stiff and cold. It has been excavated at Pompeii in the so-called house of the Faun. In another hall there is the statue often repeated in a smaller size, of a dolphin, which, with its curled upright tail, playfully embraces a Cupid. I must also mention the hall of Jupiter, in which a splendid torso of a Psyche of extraordinary softness and beauty is to be found.

No gallery in the world can boast of such a large collection of splendid bronzes; but there is also no other country besides Naples which can show three old-world towns delivered over to modern times hermetically closed. Striking, indeed, above all is the statue of the intoxicated Faun. It is at once spirited and full of humour, and executed with great truth and ingenuity. Two wrestlers are distinguished by the fine movement in their bodies. Then there is a sleeping and a dancing Faun, and a very sweet, lovely Venus. But one of the greatest masterpieces is a reposing Mercury, deserving, indeed, the praise of connoisseurs, from its excellent *pose*, and the easy rest of its

limbs. An antique head of a horse, and two most lovely
nearly life-sized roes, in which, even in the cold metal
you recognise the soft timid step and the nodding of their
heads, could scarcely be represented more truly and more
like life. You may see a curiosity in this branch of the
bronzes in a very large basin of an antique aqueduct, in
which, on shaking it, you may, notwithstanding the two
thousand years that have elapsed, hear the splashing of
the water which is inside.

· The greatest treasures which art owes to Pompeii are
the numberless encaustic paintings, and these were to me
the most interesting objects of the museum. From them
may be seen how correctly and genially the Romans drew,
not softly and indistinctly, but in a truly artistic manner,
with those firm marked lines which give a distinct character
to a drawing. There are to be seen, amongst these objects
of art, the most lovely *genre* pictures, the most interesting
historical paintings, and even well executed still-life. A
new branch of antique art was opened to me by this collection. I had frequently regretted that the paintings of
the ancients could not resist the influence of time, and yet
found myself now placed in the middle of them, seized
with astonishment and admiration. I am sorry that I had
not time and leisure to examine the details more fully;
but I could see that the Romans, the pupils, indeed, of the
great Greeks, deserved our admiration in the art of painting; for what must have been the best masters of their
time, if even such little towns as those buried by Vesuvius
could show such excellent drawings! One of the most
lovely remains of this branch of art is the celebrated
Female Dancers, a painting of great delicacy, and charmingly executed on a dark ground. How masterly are the
movements of the figures, how light and delicate the
drapery! A little picture, representing a parrot drawing a
car driven by a grasshopper, proves that the serious Roman

also indulged in caricature. The parrot represents Nero, who is driven by the grasshopper Seneca.

The museum also possesses a most excellent collection of mosaic pictures; and its fine Etruscan vases and collections of many Pompeian utensils excite admiration and interest. Amongst the utensils may be seen some of the most curious and the most odd, which the fine ashy ruin of Vesuvius has so excellently preserved for us. Arms, utensils for eating and for sacrifices, chirurgical instruments, objects of the toilet, nay, even rouge, eatables, seeds, colours, and many other curious things are to be seen in the large, wide glass cases of the museum, piled up in boundless quantity. We were also shown a very fine collection of cameos (though not to be compared to that in Vienna), in which there is only one large cameo, an offering cup, in which is worked a splendid Medusa head. The size of the stone and the value of the work almost make it a companion to the celebrated triumph of Augustus, the largest cameo in the world, and which is the pearl of the Vienna collection. Before leaving the museum and going by rail to Pompeii, I should mention three things —the large staircase of the museum, the papyrus collection from Herculaneum, and the large hall of the library. The first is wide, and beautifully planned, but what struck me most in it was a large statue standing in the middle. Looking on it from a distance, I took it for a Minerva; but, on stepping nearer, the features of the goddess became marked and old, and I was told that it was the statue of Ferdinand I. by Canova. This work, to be sure, is one of the most indifferent of this much-praised artist, and it looks most odd to see a by no means handsome male figure attired in the long garment and the large helmet of the goddess. The collection of the papyrus deserves to be noticed particularly for the ingenious manner in which the papyrus rolls, which have been carbonised, have been read and preserved. The carbonised mass is slightly moistened with gum, and by means of fine brushes is delicately pasted on gold-beaters' skin, and in this way it is slowly unrolled. A Neapolitan priest, Antonio Ciaggi, is the inventor of this process, and notwithstanding the exertions of France and England, it is, up to the present time, the only means of making these rolls, so important to history and art, readable. Already more than five hundred of them have been unrolled in this manner, of which a great number have been published. I mention the hall of the library for its extraordinary size and height, and for the correct meridian placed here by Professor Caselli in 1791.

Noon had passed, and we went to the small, mean-looking railway station at the end of the town, from which the railroad goes to Nocera, viâ Portici. We entered the small but elegant carriages of this miniature line, to steam to one of the finest tracts in the world. On our right was the sea with its oft described shores, to the left the rich plain, then the hills of Vesuvius, from which peep between the lava the fresh luxuriant grape vine, and a good many pleasant houses, defying the Damocles sword always hanging over them. After the slow train had meandered through the artificially made ravines of the lava, the eye perceived with delight a new valley of exquisite loveliness, extending from the sea between the hills of Castellamare and Vesuvius; it is the fertile Valle di Nocera, in which Pompeii is situated, at the foot of Vesuvius.

When we were passing near Vesuvius, immediately on the shores of the sea, we saw a very amusing picture. Several boys bathing on the gently sloping shore, as naked as God had created them, came out of the water on seeing the train arrive, and rolled themselves in the *dark* sand, so that face and body became as black as coal. Uncouth as the joke was, we could not help laughing heartily, and threw them money and oranges out of the window.

With a holy awe we approached the town of the ancient Romans. As it was dug out of the ashes, it lies so deep that it is to be seen only when one is immediately before it. Through a narrow street of dead houses, we came to the principal place, the Forum, with the Basilica and several temples. This space is, as it were, the exchange of the ancients. It interested me much to see the nature of the columns, which were made of bricks coated with stucco, showing that the Romans used this paltry manner of building, which was not known to the Greeks. By the side of the Basilica stands a house distinguished by the view from it, and which we examined in its details. Like all the houses in Pompeii, it has such small rooms that one cannot understand how people could move about in them. The rooms are situated round an open court (atrium), ornamented, like the other parts of the house, with mosaics and in the centre of which is a small sunk place for the rain water (impluvium). Notwithstanding the confined space, the inmates were strictly separated from each other; the men had their andronitis, the women their gynæconitis, and there were besides also the cœnacula for the slaves; the provisions, cellars, and the cisterns were underneath the atrium.

All the houses of the city of the dead are arranged for the most part in the same manner, some a little more ornamented than others, some are adorned with fine wells in the shape of shells with small mosaics; on many walls are still to be seen traces of lovely paintings and ornaments; but all the proportions are so small that it may be supposed that the inhabitants of Pompeii lived, like the Neapolitans, very much in the streets. They had, however, their forum, a large fine place, surrounded on the right and the left with temples, upon which Vesuvius looks admonishingly, and from which one enjoys in full measure those wonderful views which are the prin-

cipal charm of Pompeii. In all its temples and public
buildings I see nothing grand or sublime. The Acropolis
of Athens, with its delicate and yet gigantic building, is
still too vividly impressed on my memory. It is true,
one does injustice to Pompeii, if one forgets that it is
only a small town of very little importance, owing its reputation to the fires of Vesuvius. But it has the merit of
having preserved to us a piece of antiquity with all its
details, disclosing, in a manner almost indiscreet, a vivid
picture of Roman life. That which was brought from
Pompeii to the glass cases of the Museo Borbonico certainly shows us only a skeleton of the former life; the
spirit has departed from these things. The shops can
be recognised, and on their walls stand written words and
names; and in the streets one sees the ruts of the wheels,
and the stones leading over the gutters. Pompeii is almost
awful in its ruins; the little rooms still glitter in glaring
colours, like painted corpses; that yesterday still clings to
the walls, which requires a night of almost two thousand
years to become to-day. The total impression is, however, more that of a town destroyed by fire, than of a
careful excavation, and is not in the least grand; and all
of us were more or less disappointed. To see it once may
suffice, whilst one might gaze on the antiquities of Greece
again and again. Pompeii is to the learned an explana-
tory dictionary, but Athens is an enrapturing Epos. Only
a fourth part of the town, however, is excavated. We
attended at an excavation; the fine ashes were peeled off,
and a few vessels, and a marble shell-fountain were discovered; but the people there were so proud, that they
would not let us have even a small piece as a keepsake.
Only two things made an impression on me: the amphitheatre built of solid stones, and the town of the dead, the
Street of the Tombs. Though the amphitheatre is much
smaller than that of Verona and Pola, it is still grand; it

is a gloomy ruin, such as I love, grey and strong, interwoven with fresh green, and made glorious by the splendid
colour of the southern evening. When it began to get
dark the street of the tombs became stern and ghostlike,
without being awful. Evening enfolds the objects in a
mystical dusk, and leaves room for the fancy to divine,
and to add what is wanting. The dusk appertains to the
past, to the dead: whilst the clear light of the sun analyses
too minutely; to a tomb a torch is suitable; and Pompeii
is a tomb.

Roadstead of Naples, August 13, 1851.

This morning we devoted to the arsenal, ships, &c. In
every part of it are work and activity, everywhere ham-
mering, everywhere the newest inventions in the military
branch. The King's pet is Petrarsa, built by him on the
shore of the sea, this side of Portici. For such a small
country, it is an establishment on a grand style; moved
by steam, the roaring of the engine is everywhere heard,
everywhere is to be seen and felt the glow of the busy fire,
vying in activity with the sun of August; and amidst all
this turmoil of our steam-engine century, flower-beds are
to be seen in profusion. The same water that assists in
the making of a war-engine waters roses and oleanders;
and around the wells and the iron columns of the military buildings creepers wind in graceful festoons. It is
an attempt to combine poetry with material productions,
but only with a half success. The establishments which
we saw to-day exhibit two striking features—the great
profusion of galley-slaves, dressed in red, who meet you
on all sides, rattling their heavy chains, and the numberless
portraits and busts of the King. I do not like to see,
during a monarch's lifetime, monuments everywhere erected
to him, out of base flattery.

If the morning was devoted to prose, the evening brought
us some pure poetry. We were driving along a long avenue

Amidst pleasant conversation with the amiable Aquila, and constant admiration of the coasts of the gulf, we soon reached the end of our voyage. A light boat carried us on to the cool sand of the amphitheatrical and picturesque shore, where a crowd of horses and donkeys was waiting to carry us to the ruins of the imperial palace. As the heat was dreadful, I was offered a white parasol, which however I declined with some astonishment, and with the remark, that we Northern inhabitants of the earth could stand the heat much better than the Southerners, who almost succumb to it. We galloped along the steep shores which zig-zag round the hill, now between picturesque formed rocks, now between gardens and houses, always with a beautiful view of the sea. Beyond all other parts of this magic gulf, Capri is impressed with the glowing stamp of the South. Here one feels the power of the sun as in dear Hellas. Capri is not Italy, it is more than Italy. From its stony loins abundantly proceed the plants of a hotter clime; on its shores soft, melting, melodious Italy, with its sweet Petrarch songs, yields to a deeper-felt passion. Italy is a delightful sonnet, sung by soft lips; this island, like the shores of the gulf of Lepanto, is a poem of passionate magic love, from a wild and fiery heart. Were I one of the rich people of Naples, I would live here, live amidst those sunbeams, which effeminate in Naples and invigorate in Capri. The inhabitants are fresh and handsome, and their glowing black eyes tell of passion; they have, besides, the most excellent teeth one can imagine.

Whilst riding along, I saw an old man in a dark cowl, galloping on a donkey, bringing home a filled beggar's-bag; I took him for a monk, and, as I like to get into conversation with these people, I urged my horse on and came up to him. But how pleasantly was my romantic vein tickled, when in the donkey-rider I found a hermit, the first I had

seen in my life. A veritable hermit was sitting before me
on a little donkey, grinning in a friendly manner. His
appearance was calculated to inspire ridicule, from the
great hurry of the solitary man, the quick time he kept
on the unsaddled long-eared donkey, by the sides of which
his sandals and cowl were shaking. In the movement of
the body, a club foot showed itself. He was altogether
a strange contrast to the quiet, serious picture, which is
our ideal of these world-renouncing beings. Our roads
were the same, as the cell of the hermit stood on the
ruins of Tiberius' palace. Of its former splendour, a few
decayed plain walls, mean-looking mosaics, and the commencement of a covered way, which is said to have
served the Emperor as a secret communication between
the heights and the sea, are the whole remains. Luxuriant weeds grow abundantly on the ruins. The situation
chosen for his palace imbued me with an admiration of
Tiberius' intelligence, for it is one of the finest spots
in the world. He was not deterred by the height, and
thus from its terraces he saw the magic picture of the
matchless gulf, the imposing Vesuvius with its mysterious
heavenward undulating column, and the deep mystery of
the unbounded sea. This great pleasure belonged to the
ruler of the world, which is now fallen to the lot of a
hermit, who has been attracted hither more by the numerous visitors, than by pious disgust with the world,
and who is, indeed, still busy with thoughts of it. He
assured us that the pure air of this marvellous height,
where he has enjoyed himself for thirty years, gave him
an immense appetite, which he only half-satisfied with the
kind gifts of the villagers. He was just returning from a
' razzia.' However, he is by no means adverse to money
contributions, and a notice affixed to the wall of his cell,
written in French, warns visitors to place the money only
into his own hands, and not into those of the cicerone.

One of this latter kind, who of course accompanied us, was a queer old typical figure, who, when roguishly asked by one of the company, ‘Whether the hermit was always a solitary?’ answered maliciously, ‘Non si sa!’ The poor slandered one brought bad Capri wine, and a visitors’ list. When we sat down, he commenced playing some merry tunes on a flute, then all dignity vanished, and the black cowl, the club foot, and the covetous cunning features made a diabolical impression upon us.

We were shown the spot, on a steep dizzy precipice, from which Tiberius hurled down into the sea all those who had become troublesome to him. From this spot, the pure transparent sea looked up to us, like a deep beautiful human eye; but the eye had also its dreadful mysteries. The notice of the visitor is also drawn to a white tower from which the gloomy tyrant observed the stars. How frequently these dark minds read evil and danger in those eternal orbs, which yet yield comfort to others!

We went into a little house, where some handsome Capri girls entered and commenced dancing the tarantella to the sound of the tambourine, and snapped their fingers to imitate castanets. The old cicerone, seized by the excitement of the dance, forgot his age and his stiff limbs when he heard the sounds of the tambourine, which were now wild and now gentle.

The inhabitants of Capri were another proof that the character of the people is expressed by its dances. They danced the tarantella, which is so full of wild, beautiful, and intoxicating passion, quite simply and artlessly. Respecting one of these dancers, a magnificently handsome girl, with an ardent fiery look, and a row of pearly teeth which the bold smile could not show sufficiently often, there was whispered a little romance about a prince from the other side of the wonderful gulf. During the dance

cactus figs were handed about, a very rustic refreshment,
which, when carefully disarmed by taking off their small
thorns, were much to my taste. We again mounted on our
horses and donkeys, and, accompanied by the dancing girls,
commenced our return in the best humour. The steamer
brought us, by a few turns of the wheels, near a steep rock
of the island. We stepped into small boats, and rowed
towards it, and it appeared as if one would have, as in a
fairy tale, to glide through the rocky wall, to be opened
by a spell, that we might enter a fairy temple. And so it
was. There appeared suddenly an entrance, not more
than three feet and a half high, and just wide enough for
our dwarf boat. A few strokes of the oars, and we glided
gently, as if moved by the breath of Elves, through the
narrow stone-ring. Behind us closed the world, with its
terrestrial doings and its sunny days, and, borne on the
wings of Zephyr, we were floating under the dome of a
grotto, around the columns, and under the projections, off
which glittered a blue twilight, which, like the reflection
of the moon in a fairy tale, shone mildly on the marble.
We were in the love-bower of the Nymph of Capri; but
the Nymph fortunately for us was not in her home,
for how should we have gone through the hard trials of
Ulysses? Thus it is, that as long as the immortals dwell
in the blue grotto of Capri, no mortal is allowed to find
them; and when the mortals discover them, the immortals
have disappeared.

I felt mysteriously delighted in this cool grotto of the
Naïads, and envied the sailors, who, like silver fishes, were
moving about in the moonshine. Each of their limbs
seemed to be coated with magic metal. A few strokes
of the oar soon brought us again to the ring of rocks;
the sea-hall of the Nymphs disappeared, the fairy tale
dissolved, and day again broke upon us with golden
brightness, as if the splendour of the earth would try its

metal against fancy; and I could not forbear exclaiming, 'By heaven, the sun is beautiful!'

Again the wheels of the steamer were in movement, and we were off to Sorrento. To Sorrento! What melody is in this name! Does not Tasso come before our mind? Do not the most handsome women of the kingdom pass before us? And what a paradise is this splendid Sorrento! It is completely imbedded in orange groves, and is situated on a high rocky bank, on mighty stone-terraces, like a little piece of Switzerland.

Whilst sitting quietly on the terrace, looking down on the wide gulf, and listening to the strains of the Neapolitan marine band, the guests suddenly looked at each other, astonished and perplexed. The table had moved, and the pulsation of an earthquake had been distinctly felt. I was the only one among the whole company who had not remarked anything, and yet the concussion was so strong, that by it, as we heard afterwards, two towns were destroyed, and a great number of men killed or injured. This is the unfavourable side of this splendid country.

We stepped now into a country coach, drawn by two horses, oddly ornamented with shells. Cigars were lit, and, amidst constant jingling, we drove along between the sides of large orange gardens. 'The spirit is willing, but the flesh is weak,' especially after hard riding and a good meal. Fanned by the southern air, and lulled by the music caused by the movement of the horses, I fell asleep. But when we had turned round the hill projecting into the sea, the spirit got strong again, and I woke to take a farewell of the bay of Sorrento. Sorrento disappeared, and left upon my memory the impression of being the throne of the poet's love.

Our carriage stopped in a charming bay, at the arsenal of Castellamare, where my long-cherished wish to see a ship of the line was satisfied. It had as yet no riggings, and the arrangements in the interior were not completed; but still I could see and admire the structure of the ship, and the wide majestic dimensions of this real water-castle, justly named 'Monarca.'

The palace of the King, situated above Castellamare, round which runs a wide terrace, is rich in splendid views, but its rooms are bare and uncomfortable; the small garden towards the hill is furnished with great abundance of trees and flowers from all parts of the world. It is a pity that dahlias also are seen here; rich as they are in colour, they always appear to me like a pretty, but stupid and vulgar woman, quite *parvenue*, and without grace. They do not understand here how to arrange the flowers with coquetry; generally too much is left to mother Nature, or, if a thing is taken in hand, it is made crushingly grand, or appears full of paltry childish taste; the good people are spoilt by the splendid climate and the excellent ground; the flowers grow and bloom, without any help, wherever the seed falls upon the ground! But what wonderful things could be accomplished with such means, if only there was some understanding. The garden of Prince Lieven here is a very lovely sight, and commands a charming view of Vesuvius and a part of the gulf. It shows what the Northern creative mind can do. I would not, however, apply to this country the English mode of cultivation, for nature is here of itself already too park-like. Fragrance and coolness are the requisites of these Southern regions; and grassplots, so difficult here to be maintained, must be avoided as much as possible. Yet Prince Lieven has succeeded with them, at considerable expense. The most successful trial in this Southern Russia has been made on a small terrace, on the hill-side of the house, into which creepers roguishly peep with their flower eyes, and where large trees gently wave their heads over the balconies, so that one sees the splendid Northern oak-wood from the slope of the hill, and dreams of the fresh Alps in the fragrant South.

Roadstead of Naples, August 15, 1851.

As we are living in the age of railways, we cannot do better than swim with the stream; and as everything has its good side, so is it also with the materialising railroad. One gets rapidly over the ground, and this was very convenient in our trip into the country to-day. We were flying through that cultivated plain, which looks so beautiful seen from the heights, but from the plain itself is so monotonous and tedious. I was warned not to fall asleep on account of the malaria prevailing in the low country during this time of the year. Fortunately it was not after dinner, so that we had the less difficulty in escaping the danger, and arrived at Caserta, where the largest palace of the King of the Two Sicilies is situated. The first impression is not favourable; the avenues are neglected, and the dimensions are more barrack- than palace-like. The whole looks a little the worse for wear, and I had continually before my eyes my dear Schönbrunn, with which I heard Caserta compared, and almost to the advantage of the latter. But the impression is more favourable after passing the vestibule of Caserta. When one sees the four colossal squares, and their gigantic halls, which, beautifully arched, support the lofty domes of the massive palace; the large staircase, which seems to be created for the steps of gods; the garden with its giant cascade, one feels that Caserta, although built upon the least pretty, or rather the only place that is not pretty of the country around Naples, is not a royal folly, but a work of which the idea could only be conceived by that courage that speaks in all the works of Charles III., and which could only proceed from the time that had

produced Louis XIV. and his genius. The staircase of
Caserta is so adapted that its possessor seems to make
the world climb up to him, and he then receives the
crowd respectfully, approaching it with a gracious look
and smile.

The garden corresponds with the magnificent staircase,
and its grass-plots, waters, and trees, bear the impress of
the same mind. How majestically do these cascades and
canals flow down the slope! How these fountains and
statues, these close-clipped tree-walls and parallel avenues,
suggest ' pumps' and hoops! Is not all this so trained and
dressed that even nature may not put an impediment in
the way of the ceremonious walk, the measured step of a
court, surrounded by the nimbus of majesty? Do not the
cascades murmur in time? Do not the trees stand in
order with respectful etiquette before their master? What
a spirit of pomp speaks out of all this, so that even nature
has to succumb to its power! Nature in our gardens may,
indeed, be maimed, but it is not subjugated; crooked
country roads and rough bushes are imitated, which may
be found much finer outside, and we attempt to improve
where we only disfigure; whilst our ancestors used power
and genius in their gardens, at least they formed out of
nature a magnificently dressed, though perhaps rigid, lady
of the first rank, imposing, even as a matron, and putting
to shame the free manner of the young soubrette. The
parterre in Schönbrunn is the imperial sister of the royal
garden at Caserta. I should like to have seen both in the
time of their greatest splendour, in that of their powder
and hair-bags. In what stately, rich attire must have
stepped along these walks the courts of Maria Theresa and
the Bourbons of that time!

Before leaving Caserta I must also mention the monster
trouts, living in the cool freshness of the grotto, in the
clear beautiful water in the background of the main cas-

cade. They appear at the call of the keeper, to astonish
the eye of the stranger by their unusual size, like the
monster carps in Lachsenburg. They are, however, only
fit to please the eye and not the palate, and live joyously
on a princely pension.

I took an agreeable dinner at my good aunt's; and it
was already getting late when I drove to the grounds of
the royal palace at Portici.

Roadstead of Naples, August 16, 1851.

This morning was devoted to the antiquities around
Baiæ and Puzzuoli; but I am ashamed to confess that it
was the only tedious morning during our stay in Naples;
and yet few of my acquaintances are so enthusiastic about
antiquities as I am. But it is not only the mind, but the
body also which must be in health, in order that one may
admire and enjoy; and as the latter, in consequence of so
many excursions, was exhausted, and the heat of the glowing sun was so insupportable, I felt quite sick, and not at
all disposed to admire the monuments of Roman greatness
and tyranny, the more so as they are far below my recollection of what the Grecian antiquities were.

We commenced our excursion with the tomb of Virgil,
marked by a long Latin inscription at the entrance of
Posilippo, but the grave itself is on the height, and passing
through a vineyard one comes upon a little stone house
and its insignificant walls, with a few laurel shrubs. Here
rests the poet who created the ' Œneid.' A silly French
inscription commemorates his glory, and confers on Virgil
the great honour of raising him to the rank of prince
amongst the poets, by calling him ' le prince des poètes.'
It is the fashion to take a laurel leaf, or, if possible, a
branch from this spot, which may serve as a poetical
enchanter's wand. The place of the great heathen is used
as a burial-ground for non-Catholics, which is certainly

most improper; German, English, and Jewish tombstones are to be found here ' pêle-mêle.'

After having duly gathered my memento from the grave of the poet, we drove to the ' Grotto of Posilippo,' one of the famous spots around Naples. A long dark tunnel has been cut through the Tufastone mountain: it is by no means so grand as the cuttings on our railroads, and although of the time of the Romans, it scarcely deserves to be called a Roman work. The rockgate in Salzburg, with the fine inscription, ' Te saxa loquuntur,' is indeed a far more picturesque and a grander work, not to speak of the stone galleries in the imperial road of the Wormser Joch. A good effect is produced by the light penetrating through the disagreeable clouds of dust, which, like the silver veil of a fairy, enveloped that dark road.

An old hermit, the second specimen of the kind which I saw, was begging at the entrance of the grotto; a kind of private toll-collector, thus showing the world that even at the entrance of a large capital city one may be a hermit. Through real waves of dust we came to the very unhealthy ' Lago d'Agnano,' on the shores of which is another of Naples' great sights, namely, ' the dog-grotto.' I looked out for it in vain, and to my astonishment I was led to a small door, behind which I supposed was the entrance to the grotto; how much was I astonished when, on the door being opened, I saw before me a small hollow, at best a few feet deep, which ought to have been called rather a dog's-hole than a dog's-grotto! A deadly gas is here exhaled, as at many places in Marienbad; we heard the poor dog whine, as it was held up before our eyes in the hole. It quivered convulsively several times, its tongue became blue, and at last, when almost dead, it was brought out into the fresh air, where it panted and slowly recovered, after which it staggered away as if it were drunk. A truly horrid and barbarous sight—a

suffering which the poor beast has to undergo frequently
for the profit of his master.

We came next to a place where formerly stood the villa
of Cicero, and then on to Puzzuoli, a little town situated
on a hill near a bay branching off from the gulf, and on
the shores of which is also Baiæ, that favourite resort of
the Romans, who passed there a kind of fashionable bathing
season at the ' Stufe di Nerone,' corresponding to our
modern vapour baths. Here there is also a large basin
for sea-fish, the Piscina mirabilis, a colossal water reservoir,
and many ruins of temples and villas. We proceeded first
to the Solfatara, the former crater of a volcano; the tunnel
is now green, and the crater has a white bottom. The
abundance of sulphur in Sicily, however, has proved
ruinous to this business. On stamping the foot upon
the ground, a dull and mysterious booming is heard; a
knocking, as it were, at the door of the lower regions. It
sounds as if there was an empty vault beneath, which is
especially strange and uncomfortable to those driving over
it. I wonder that a trial has not been made to ascertain
something about it by digging. The white ground was
glowingly hot, and I was very glad when we left the crater,
which was as hot as a baking stove. We proceeded towards
Baiæ, and then on to the so-called ' Mare morto,' a natural
dock for the ships of the ancients, which is now slowly
drying up.

Looking over the vineyards we see the height of Miseno
projecting into the sea; this historical point glowed
in the sun, and formed a fine Southern picture, seen over
the blue sea and under the blue sky. In sad contrast
were the prisons of Nero. We were led with torches into
these deep black holes, which branch off under ground in
several ways, forming a horrible labyrinth, where the
smoke of the torches almost stifle. We soon returned, and
I was glad to get out of the dark bowels of the earth into

the daylight. Several women of the neighbouring place here danced the tarantella so clumsily and gracelessly that it scarcely recalled to us the tarantella danced at Capri.

On the coast of the bay of Baiæ the temple of Diana may be seen, a high vault half in ruins, and the temple of Mercury; neither are distinguished by their architecture or by their size. But who looks for great monuments in a country-seat? The small rooms are interesting and are hewn out of a rock, as are also the low dark passage of the Stufe di Nerone, leading to the vapour spring. The steam of this spring is so hot that an egg is boiled by it in a short time. An old man managed this operation; and though on returning his gasping was exaggerated in order to produce pity, I am yet unable to see how he could stand a heat which was insupportable to me even at the entrance of the passage. These numerous vapour and sulphur springs, this smoke breaking through, this heat of the ground, these eruptions of obnoxious gas, are so many unmistakable tokens of a great chemical laboratory which has its centre in Vesuvius, and who can tell how far the smiling crust of Naples is undermined, and how soon perhaps a new volcano may burst forth where at present merry mortals live in villas surrounded by orange-trees, unconscious of the near approach of death!

We closed the inspection of the curiosities with the temple of Serapis in Puzzuoli, which has once been very fine, but has now come down to a kind of swamp. The ground of the temple is several feet high, covered with water, which comes from the chemical spring, and from the sea hard by, and has got so mixed as to afford a favourable ground for fishes; at a certain season, 'horribile dictu,' people flock here to find health by wading in this water where it is low, certainly a very disgusting operation.

How does a 'via tedesca' come to be found in the boot

of Italy, where the Germans are termed barbarians? The via takes its origin from the time when in the twenties of this century the white-coats had to keep order here; in memory of that happy time when they lived in golden Naples, this road has been constructed, which passes along the gulf on the heights of Posilippo, and after passing the most wonderful views, villas, and gardens, enters into the Chiaja.

On one side of the slope hang smiling country-seats, and on the other is the sea. Built in the old feudal style on a rather peculiar site, one sees here the fort-like villa of the Marchesa S——, a very equivocal English lady.

I made one more visit to Capo di Monte to take leave of my aunt and cousin, for now unfortunately they might say to me: 'My prince, the fine days of Aranjuez (reading Naples for Aranjuez) are passed,' and I thanked my dear relations very much for their friendly and genial reception. On board our frigate to-day was nothing but cleaning and cooking and frying, for I intended to invite Aquila to our floating palace for the last evening. The meal was merry, but the farewell was hard; I had found a friend in Aquila, a friend who made the agreeable recollection of Naples still more agreeable; and so it happens that I cannot leave this place where I have had so much happiness without an indescribable longing and a sad heart. Aquila's boat glided away amidst the strains of the Bourbon hymn, and standing on the quarter-deck, I looked long after him.

The youngest' brother of the King, Count Trapani, visited me in the course of the evening. I had seen his amiable wife the previous evening. The features of this daughter of the Grand-Duke of Tuscany are of the same type as those of the Austrian family, and remind me strongly of those portraits of the Empress Maria Louisa painted in her youth.

The last evening I drove through the hubbub of the streets of Naples.   On the quay of Santa Lucia—where I had first landed, and renewed acquaintance with our amiable minister, Field-Marshal Lieutenant Martini—I took my leave of this kind, obliging man, whose name I retain amidst my brighter recollections.   The boat put off the shore, and sleep soon embraced us in its dark leaden arms.

H. M. Frigate 'Novara,' August 17, 1851.

After midnight I rose to be present at the weighing the anchor : we had fine weather and a light breeze through the channel between Ischia and Capri ; Naples, that city of wonders, that terrestrial paradise, was all alight, notwithstanding the late hour, and life seemed still to be busy in it.   I took one last look at the city in which I had spent such a pleasant week, and I hope had learned so many things.   Though I might not select Naples for a lengthened residence, yet few cities offer such charms for a short one.   One could almost fancy that Nature had here set up an exhibition of her powers, and, after looking around her for a spot on which to fix it, had finally selected this charming and unique scene.

At one point rises a mountain, rent asunder at its top, that the astonished human race may get a glimpse at the hidden powers.   Brimstone from its abyss of every colour; crystals of the finest form, glowing streams of lava pouring over the sides of the mountain ; and close to this lava, grapes, the fermented juice of which yields the delicious Lacryma Christi; these are some of the extraordinary sights yielded by Vesuvius.   In the plain below we have the fig tree and the olive, the cactus with its juicy fruit, and the cotton plant with its useful fleece, palm trees and oaks, whilst the lemon and orange trees spread around the most delicious fragrance.   In the mountain masses we have the Tufastone, through which the 'Grotto of Posilippo' has been cut. Picturesque rocks rise from the sea and form natural fortifications. Sweet water lakes in the mountain cauldrons; sulphur fields which save man the trouble of mining; islands rising from the sea, guardians of the gulf, and in one of which is that miracle of beauty, the blue grotto; Naples can show specimens of everything which is most charming, and most fairy-like, alongside with that which enables us to imagine the horrors of the lower regions.

And has not nature succeeded in her plan? man falls down admiringly before her gifts, and thinks himself fortunate that he is allowed to embellish and enhance these gifts by those of art. This is the city to which I said farewell, and left it with the satisfaction of having at last enjoyed everything possible in so short a space of time. With an easy conscience I therefore went again to my bed, and when I awoke in the morning the fine dream had vanished. Fogs had enveloped it, but Capri and Ischia were still at our side. We had to move around the latter island for a long time, so that we still had before us the tormenting view of Vesuvius partly shrouded in fog, the shores opposite Procida and the islands, for I call it tormenting still to see them after having taken leave of them, to see places half obliterated that one has learned to love; too distinct not to remind us of the past happy moments, and too far to enable us to reach them.

August 18, 1851.

All put on their holiday dress and prepared for High Mass, which was to be read in celebration of the birthday of our emperor at ten o'clock. It was a fine moment, full of emotion; on the left of the battery a tent had been made out of Austrian flags, and in it stood a simple but decent altar. Officers and crew were marched, *en parade.* Our ship chaplain, a very worthy young man, read with calm devotion the holy mass, and sung after it the

Te Deum. During the service the music played in different parts. At the Te Deum the ever-beautiful ' Gott er halte' resounded; I felt very sad during service, for it was the first time that I had not been with my brother on this happy day. I was alone, quite alone in strange seas, under another sky; besides I had thought so long and so deeply of one of my beloved at home, about whom my heart was anxious, that I was in one of those forlorn dispositions of mind in which man feels a sort of sweet despair and longs for home. My family had made me too happy at home; but it is well that such a life should have an end, and these heavy hours are a bitter, but wholesome medicine. With the evening came pleasant thoughts which drowned home-sickness. To celebrate the day I had invited the officers of the ship and the chaplain to dinner. The music played, we were all in full dress, and slight as the festival was, it was well received. At noon the island of Ischia was still to be seen.

August 19, 1851.

To-day the sea began its tricks: it commenced a game with the proud Novara, and engaged her for a dance, which did not agree with many of her passengers; the dancing of her slender body had a rather strong effect on most of them. The little island of Ponza and Cape Circello, and later, the island of Palmarola, were in sight. Between four and six in the evening we had a calm, but still the ship did not stop her dancing. When we were sitting together after dinner some storm-birds were shown to us, which had been caught on board. They are very nice grey and black little birds, with black, pointed, long bills, dark lively eyes and little feet provided with web-membranes. The arrival of these guests did not forbode any good, and yesterday the appearance of small dolphins foreboded a rough sea.

[August 21, 1851.

I was suddenly awakened by the tumbling down of my bookcase with everything on it. The movement was extraordinary and all was dark. I groped my way on deck. Here I must accuse myself of a little weakness. I had retained one of the storm-birds, which had been caught the day before yesterday, and in my mania for animals I kept and nursed it; but in the night when it stormed and raged, when wave succeeded wave, I felt uneasy about the ominous character of the storm-bird, and the idea occurred to me that whether it remained on our ship or died on it, it would be equally fatal to us. I felt as if the bird were the spirit of a drowned sailor. I took it out of its prison, wrapped it up in my handkerchief and carried it on deck, where I gave it its liberty, but I placed it behind a gun because of the storm. Who is there that is at all times free from fits of superstition, and especially on the sea?

August 22, 1851.

The weather was fine, and the Papal States were in sight. At noon Monte Argentaro was within view, in the direction of Civita Vecchia, and the Tuscan island Giglio was sighted. It was a sad thought to be so near those Papal States one would have so liked to see; but as it was not in our plan of voyage we had to be satisfied.

August 23, 1851.

On awaking this morning, we saw, besides the island Giglio, Monte Christo, Elba, and Gianuti. Monte Christo, which has got such a reputation since Dumas' novel, 'The Count of Monte Christo,' is a rather high rocky peak rising from the sea, very much like Stromboli, and discovering, notwithstanding its bare and dead appearance, curiously peaked forms. The grotto, with its celebrated treasures, we could not, unfortunately, discover. No diamonds glittered, and we came to the conclusion that Count Monte

Christo must have taken them all with him in his corvette, and have sailed away, never to return.

Elba, that cage in which the eagle was imprisoned, with every facility at hand for escape, and which has acquired its fame through its prisoner, is a rather large, rocky, mountainous island without much vegetation or much life. The side on which Porte Ferrajo is situated may be more attractive, but that which we see is rough and repelling.

August 24, 1851.

In the morning we were between Elba and Pianosa. The latter island corresponds perfectly to its name ; it is a broad rocky plain which, rising very little above the sea, is surrounded with so many shallows that it is dangerous for vessels, especially at night-time. The rocky cliffs encircling the island slope so regularly that the island looks like a cake. To-day at noon I went, for the first time, into the maintop, and found it by no means so fearful a situation as one would think, and if it were not that the movement at this considerable height is much stronger than on deck, one would not be so dizzy. The evening was fine, and the form of the island of Corsica, famous for its celebrated son, was distinctly to be seen. It is mountainous, and of considerable size.

August 25, 1851.

Enjoyed the sunrise in the maintop. In tacking we came rather near to Corsica, and could distinguish the town of Bastia. It does not seem to be an important town, and has the same character as other Italian towns. The day passed without anything worthy of notice, and Leghorn was still far off.

August 26, 1851.

The Tuscan coast could be seen more distinctly towards noon. We passed the island Gorgona, and saw at last the

Monte Nero, at the foot of which Leghorn is situated. In the morning twenty-two ships were in sight, from which one may judge that we were on a track much used. After a tedious calm we came in sight of that commercial city, Leghorn. It is situated in a plain on the shore between an amphitheatre of finely-formed hills, and seems a city of considerable extent. Out of the mass of houses rise two lighthouses and several forts. The white and red banner waves over the forts, showing Tuscany to be a State of the Austrian House. A large dark mountain arises to the right of the city as seen from the sea, on which villas and gardens are erected. This is the Monte Nero just alluded to, and is a celebrated resort of the Leghorn people. On the left, at some distance behind the city, rise the lofty mountains of Lucca, and the even outline of the Apennines. I was not aware that Italy could boast such lofty and romantically-shaped mountains, which gave me quite a feeling of home. The roadstead is too wide; but in the walls of the fortress of the city this is so shallow that even small merchantmen cannot enter it laden.

Whilst looking for ground to anchor, we saw coming towards us two boats ornamented with the white and red flag; uniforms could be seen on board, which we at once recognised to be Austrian. The excitement to know who was coming was great. It was even surmised that the Grand Duke and his sons might be on board. But they soon proved to be General Count Crenneville, commander of the Austrian troops in Leghorn, Baron Hügel, our minister, and several Tuscan notabilities, amongst whom was my old acquaintance, General Sproni. The first who reached the ship was the brave Count Castiglioni, colonel of that excellent regiment Kinsky; what a pleasure it was for me to see friends again, and especially Austrians! I declined the Grand-Ducal dinner, and invited Crenneville and Hügel to a poor dinner with me, for the voyage, being

unexpectedly long, had much exhausted our provisions.
Seven letters which I now received gave me great pleasure;
they were the first I had received since I left Trieste. I
opened them, not without fear at what might have happened since I had been away. Fortunately the news was
good. After dinner we rowed towards the city. It took
some time, for, on account of the bad anchorage, we had
to cast anchor at a considerable distance from the city; but
it was such a splendid day that we could not regret that
our passage was a long one, for it gave us plenty of leisure
to enjoy the fine evening. The mountain-chains stood
out in a purple and blue haze on the clear sky; nearer
objects were gilded by the intense rays of the sun, and the
beautiful sea, slightly stirred, lay dark blue before us; it
was one of those evenings to which the heart opens in
delight, and in which the eye cannot feast enough on the
charms of nature. We passed close to the 'Dragon,'*
whose crew saluted from the rigging; her friendly captain
had visited me before dinner. We soon rowed to a fortified mole stretching its arm into the sea, and offering but
a scanty protection against dangerous winds. On its walls
we saw the friendly sight of an Austrian sentinel. On all
sides resounded the home-like 'Gewehr heraus!' and
through a small opening between two walls of the fortress
we came to the inner harbour, and stepped on shore. The
first thing that we examined was the monument of 'Giovanni Gaston di Medici,' which is close to the shore, near
a wharf. This large statue is of white marble, and Gaston
is in picturesque harness, with the marshal's staff in his
hand. To the corners of the pedestal are chained four
artistically-formed slaves, of bronze. These four bent
figures, with their hands tied behind their backs, and their
heads looking up to their conqueror, are intended to repre-

* An English vessel.

sent the four different races of Africa. Each figure is a
single piece. The stranger is generally led to a point from
which he can see the five noses of the figures, which are
placed in five different directions. We stepped into the
Grand-Ducal carriages, and drove through the celebrated
'Strada Lunga,' which passes through the whole city, and
is full of fine shops. The number and variety of the
foreign merchants living here may be judged by the
English, German, and Grecian sign-boards. Life here is
active, but not so lively and so ensnaring to the senses as
in stirring Naples, but you see here, amongst the women,
far more handsome faces. The Strada Lunga crosses the
principal Piazza, on which are situated the fine but small
Palace of the Grand-Duke, and the not very remarkable
Cathedral.

The principal curiosity of the place is that it is, as it
were, a broad bridge under which the Arno flows like a
canal.

Another Roman work, perhaps still grander than the
last-named, is the 'listernone' at the boundary of the
city; a stone-water reservoir supported by columns, which
can provide the city for forty-six days. There is an inscription on the bottom of the basin, two yards beneath
the surface, a very good test of the purity of the water.

Night spread its friendly veil over city and land, but
the Italian does not enjoy it like the German; for him
the nights are only the cooler half of the oppressive
summer, and he devotes them to noisy festivities. To-day
the band of the regiment played on the square, which,
lighted by gas, was transformed into a city-hall; truly it
is a happy climate which permits such halls with the sky
only for a ceiling, but then the comfortable home-like
feeling has no place here.

Lucca, August 27, 1851.

Very early in the morning, and soon after a magical

sunrise, we left our ship to pay a visit to the Grand-Duke by railroad to Marlia. We steamed through a plain, which is redeemed from a swamp, and is becoming useful land. In the midst of this plain is Pisa, that old stubborn Republic, which had formerly something to say on the affairs of this part of the world, but is now deserted and scantily peopled; a big coffin for consumptive patients. There are some things one has heard of from youth, and the leaning tower of Pisa is one of these.

I went rapidly through the city and saw its beauties as in a dream, intending to examine them next day at leisure. The railroad first ran through well-cultivated land, but suddenly pierced a mountain-gorge, and we found ourselves in a luxuriant garden, which scarce has its match in all the world; this fairy garden is the little country of Lucca, and its happy possessor is the Grand-Duke of Tuscany. The gorge leads to a wide valley bounded by the finest mountains; a little fortified town, with the most splendid trees on its ramparts, sits wreathed with laurel on the luxuriant meadows. This is happy Lucca; over its main gate the arms of the republic are placed—a *libertas* in stone. At the railroad-station outside the wall of the town I had the pleasure of meeting my cousins again. We drove together to the town of Lucca, and afterwards to Marlia, the country residence of the Grand-Ducal family.

This summer-residence of the merry princess Bacciochi, sister of Napoleon, united Italian charm, Southern abundance, with Northern freshness and Northern care. This not very large palace, or rather villa, looks over the green meadows through splendid rich trees on the blessed plain and its surrounding hills; whilst on the other side of the hill a crescent-shaped cascade-fountain, in the noble old Italian style, closes the garden with an ever fresh and animated picture. As in Marlia, so also in the whole valley of Lucca, there is a peaceful rest, which fills the mind with a sense of happiness, as you view the green fertile country under the deep blue sky. I found the Grand-Ducal family well, and was received by them in a truly affectionate manner.

It was arranged that I should stay for dinner, and then pass the night in Lucca. The forenoon was devoted to the surroundings of Marlia, and we went at once to the ' Specula,' an unfinished building intended for an observatory, the lofty position of which offered a fine view, made more charming in the direction of Florence by a lovely lake. From this we drove to the garden of Marlia, and looked at some horses kept there by the Grand-Duke. The stable was once a chapel, where the former Bourbon Regent of Lucca took it into his head to hold Greek and Roman services at great expense; from this we went to the villa Bernardin. This villa and its garden were of the genuine Italian type of times past. I like everything that has a characteristic stamp. How sublime are the wide avenues of melancholy evergreens! How dimly shine the dark leafy walks! How excellently well the parterres combine with the not always large, but always grand buildings! and how adapted to a country residence are the water-works which refresh the eye, and the mysterious grottoes, genuine ' *bagatelles de grand seigneur !*'

After dinner I drove out with the eldest son of the Grand-Duke through the beautiful country to Lucca, the former capital of that little paradise, which combines every charm of nature and art: beautifully-shaped high mountains, a most fertile plain, a lovely lake, beneficial baths, and an interesting miniature capital, which exhibits, however, very little life now, as there is no Court whatever kept here. Looking around upon town and country one can understand the difficulty Duke Charles felt, after the death of Marie Louise, in changing this Court for the

throne of the larger state of Parma. Most of the Italian
cities have a mediæval stamp, and so it is with Lucca;
but as the numerous divisions of this Peninsula have
been done away with, and the smaller states have been
swallowed up in the larger, these towns appear deserted
and dead, an impression which is increased by the scarcity
of shops. But in all these towns you are certain to
see three things: churches, palaces, and at least one
theatre. We looked at three of the Houses of God in
Lucca. One of them, St. Ferdinand, was an extremely
old Byzantine-Lombardic specimen of architecture, with
a mosaic on its façade, and an old Lombardic baptismal
font of white marble. The front of the cathedral is rich
with ornament in the best Lombardic style; over the
entrances runs a graceful gallery. I love columns, and
carved work, as I do painted windows in churches. It
beautifies but does not distract; but the rococo ornaments
look clumsy and cold in churches. The interior of the
church is severely simple, and full of dignity; the ceiling
is painted in fresco, ornamented with stars; the interior
is embellished with paintings of Fra Bartolomeo, a monk
deeply imbued with a love of art, who endowed his angels
with the innocence of his own soul.

In most of the Catholic churches that beautiful custom
prevails of a wonder-working image, which forms the
centre of devotion; and here, therefore, is a small chapel
in the nave of the church, which is the centre of faith for
devoted souls. Il Santo Volto is the one to which the
people of Lucca pay their devotions. It is a very old
crucifix, on which the Redeemer is represented crowned
with very valuable jewels, and wrapped in a dark gold
embroidered coat. This dress had a touching effect upon
me, for never before had I seen the Saviour suspended on
the Cross in the garb of a king. The contrast is powerful
and does not miss its effect.

The Grand-Duke came with his younger son from Marlia, and found us already in the palace, a fine and somewhat sombre building in the cinque-cento style. The staircase, a more modern work, is admired, but I cannot see anything remarkable in it; it leads to a fine gallery, which contains marble copies of the most celebrated statues; but copies are after all corpses of the originals, the soul of which is wanting. In the evening we went to the theatre, where Luisa Miller was given, a tedious opera of Verdi, for the end of which we did not wait, but went to bed.

Florence, August 28, 1851.

Very early in the morning we hurried to the station, and steam carried us only too soon beyond the boundaries of the lovely Lucca, and on to Pisa. It might be thought, perhaps, that our first visit at Pisa would have been made to the Cathedral Square, to see the leaning tower, the Campo Santo, &c.; but I confess that my first wish was to see the camels bred in Pisa. On a wide meadow, at the skirts of a wood, we first saw with eagerness these sand-waders going to their work. What a pleasure it was to see them again! It transported me to my dear, bright Smyrna. The camels, with their half-swimming gait, with their dry desert-skin, recalled pleasant recollections. The most ugly animal that went forth from the creative hand of God is so closely connected with the rich fancies and traditions of the East, that on their appearance the dreams of the East, the sorceries of the Arabian Nights, were immediately kindled. The camels of Pisa are smaller than those of Asia Minor, as is the case with most animals when man in his tyranny transports them from one zone to another. It is princes, chiefly, that have these odd passions, and who like to subjugate nature to their whims; and the camel-stud of Pisa is a princely freak, ascribed to my great-grandfather, Leopold II.

Large woods surround the stables, and the camels are made to carry the wood from them on their quivering humps. Not contented with seeing these animals, I, of course, must also mount one, that I might transplant myself entirely back into the desert. But the lying down and getting up of these long-legged, heavy creatures, is such an awkward operation, and one hangs so between heaven and earth on their high backs and clumsy saddles, that a ride on a camel is decidedly one of the most disagreeable things in the world. If the animal commences trotting, body and soul can hardly be kept together, and even a steeple-chase could scarcely be more dangerous for one's bones than a camel ride; for in the first, one breaks at worst a leg, but here you may get all your bones broken. We also saw a giraffe of rare beauty and size; the present of some Bey on the African coast to the Grand-Duke, a wondrously lovely animal and a mysterious combination; for its head is that of an antelope, its neck a snake's, its skin a tiger's, at once graceful and awkward, an animal having to reach its food from the palms, to wade through the Nile, and too free to be useful to man for anything.

The cathedral Piazza, and the banks of the Arno, with the old palaces, and the lovely Spina, are the most interesting parts of the old town of Pisa. We first examined the baptistry, a large cupola rotunda in the finest Byzantine-Lombardic style, standing apart, opposite the cathedral. In this lovely building, the heads of the columns, the many statues, the rich ornaments, and varieties of stone, and the dome, like a finely chiselled tiara, are most interesting. My attention was particularly excited by a pulpit in the Byzantine form, like those in St. Mark, supported by antique columns of the finest stones; and, again, I admired the mystical ornaments of our ancestors. The richly-coloured chapel gave us the first idea of the Pietra-dura on a large scale, which we saw

later, and on a finer scale, in the Cathedral of Florence.
From this we went to the Campo Santo, a fine conception,
such as could only be created by the believing middle
ages. Round a large grassplot runs, open towards it,
a light and yet stately gothic gallery, supported by five
columns and arches. The interior of the hall is ornamented with frescoes of Giotto, tombstones, and a kind of
museum, which is not in its place there. In the middle
of the grassplot stands a simple stone cross, beautifully
interlaced with roses. The frescoes are the first things
which attract attention : they sprang from the childhood
of Italian art, and one can recognise in the bold lines, in
the animated grouping, the transition from the typical
period to the perfection of nature, and, indeed, I prefer
those periods of art in which the spirit is awakened in the
type, and aspires towards a more beautiful future—the
age of Raphael, to the later schools which exhibit the
genius of the classical times in a state of decay. This
school is the worst contrast to the typical school, as the
latter means the vigorous awakening, and the other the
luxurious falling asleep of art. How should our faithless
material time be able to express the mysteries of simple
Christianity? A painter, making the painting of religious pictures a business, and painting merely for his
purse, can only produce earthly figures, and he gives
them, because it is part of the business, a name from the
Sacred Calendar.

The frescoes of the Campo Santo have an original
freshness. It is an unparalleled Vandalism to have
placed between them clumsy and tasteless monuments;
Grecian tombs in a Gothic hall and under Italian fresco
paintings! To my great amusement, the cicerone became
furious at being compelled to show the Tedeschi around,
the more so as they expressed themselves about these
monstrosities with anger and derision, and were astonished

to find in a Catholic cemetery an antique bronze griffin, idols, and other museum-rubbish, of no consequence whatever. But it is an Italian custom to bring together bigotry and heathendom under the same roof. In the celebrated frescoes of the Campo Santo there is sometimes too great a freedom of fancy, almost bordering on the ludicrous; but this was the strange taste of the childhood of art, and is still the taste of vigorous fresh minds, that reproduce unaltered whatever their childlike innocence conceives. Thus it is with the creation of Eve, the ancestor of our race, who is represented, with biblical fidelity, without any covering at all: and so also you see the empire of the prince of the world in the hideous fancy of that time. A herd of roaring wolves, exhibiting the most peculiar caricatures, is quite diabolical. The poor sons of man are treated in the most barbarous manner, and are fried in hell; I perceived in their company many tonsured heads. The painter would seem to be no friend of the ecclesiastical orders, as several of its members are discovered in very strange positions. The soul of the dying is represented by the artist as a homunculus, which either as an angel or as a devil, according to circumstances, marches out of the mouth of the expiring mortal. It looks very odd to see how painfully wide the mouth has sometimes to be opened to let the soul pass. The souls which require more room are probably the strong ones. But, O horror! who is that dark boy, who is busy carrying away by force the soul of a nun? he seems to be no angel of light! I perceive two little horns: O, Heavens! it is a servant of Satan! Indeed art was then free in Italy, and could be so, for it had fixed the limits of faith. The Pisans recognise with delight the head of Napoleon in hell in one of them, and this is but natural; it is characteristic of mankind to condemn the hated fallen enemy, and to rejoice over his disgrace; one does not risk anything by it, for he has become harmless. As long as the Pisan hell-figure was called Roi d'Italie, there was not gold enough to be found to represent the nimbus in his apotheosis; but the god of the day fell from the heavens, and the holy light was converted into the glow of hell. *Sic transit gloria mundi.*

Before leaving the Campo Santo with its grand past, its old-world poetry, and its new destinies as a pantheon, I must mention that earth which gave it its mysterious charm and its chief attraction in the eyes of our believing ancestors. It is said to have been brought from the Holy Land by the Crusaders, and in addition to its being on that account sacred amongst Christians, a peculiar quality is ascribed to it, which is very curiously shown in one of the frescoes. A corpse is exhibited in three phases: in the first the soul is only just departed, on the second day decay is in full activity, and on the third the skeleton is freed from the flesh, and nothing is left but framework. This is the virtue of the earth from Jerusalem, which destroys the bodies buried in it in three days. The Pisans rejoiced at this extraordinarily rapid destruction, but this hunger of time shocked me.

From the Campo Santo we went to the Cathedral. How magnificent is this rich marble building, with its long nave, at the end of which, over the altar rises, as an everlasting canopy, the lofty cupola! I do like to ascend to the House of God by broad steps to a large portal, and not, as is too often the case in Italy, find it on a level with the coffee-house and the theatre.

We Germans use the word 'erhaben' to express something great. The sublime must stand high; this is a desire of the human mind; it elevates in order to be elevated. The ascending is ennobling, and the descending is only becoming to the great ones, and is then called 'Herablassung.' And how religion awakens this inclina-

tion! At the sacrifice of the mass we look up, and in the
communion, in the mingling of earth and heaven, the Most
High bends down to us in the shape of the bread.   As
with the Church and the altar, so with the throne, and so
with everything that, according to the laws of the world,
is placed high : everywhere must steps or degrees separate
the uncommon from the common.   So in the Cathedral of
Pisa one walks up large broad steps, through artistically
carved doors, into wide sacred spaces.   On high columns
rests a light elegant Gothic gallery, which also runs over
the side naves, and round the large principal nave.   This
is the manner in which many churches are built in Tuscany.   A wide, high arch spans the principal nave, the
ceiling of which, constructed by the pomp-loving Medicis,
is replete with gold.   The most curious thing of this rich
church is a dark bronze lamp, which unconsciously enriched
the world with a great invention, by throwing a spark into
the mind of one of the giants of science, and causing it to
flare up in a bright flame.   It was vesper time; the dark
lamp was burning to the praise of God, and the sacristan
having just drawn back his hand, the lamp swung to
and fro.   A man in a plain coat stood musingly leaning
against one of the high columns; he looked for a long
time at the steady swinging of the lamp, then looked down
thoughtfully, and Galileo had found that which gave life
to mechanism, namely, the principle of the pendulum.
In the leaning tower, which we ascended, this great man
discovered, as a marble inscription states, the principle
of gravitation, by letting a stone fall through the hollow
interior from a height of one hundred and forty-two feet.

   The tower is peculiar, and has character, but I cannot
call it handsome, neither can I get enthusiastic about its
obliquity; it is an interesting object for architects, but
only in the same degree as an abnormal crooked body is
for medical men.   For my own part I should prefer to see

the tower straight; as it is, it looks like a drunken man, whose tumbling down one expects every moment, or resembles the constrained oblique position of a tightly-laced minuet dancer. From the upper platform of the tower one enjoys a view that is reputed splendid; but I thought it only extensive; in a different light it may appear more to advantage. After examining the building more closely, I cannot believe that the architects, William von Insbruck and Bonano, created this architectural monstrosity on purpose; obviously the stone ring of the base has sunk. Such a jejune joke might perhaps have sprung from the last century; but in 1174 they had a too pure love for art to commit such absurdities. A noble axiom is better than the best wit, and so it is also in art. Pisa suffers much from earthquakes, and to this circumstance I imagine the Pisans owe their condescending, polite tower.

Pisa possesses a genius of a rare kind, an artist who in his own time has not been surpassed. He does not work in marble, nor does he paint in colours on the dead canvas; but he creates life from skin and bones, and uses the remains of nature to form new beings; in a word, he is a stuffer of animals, and enriches the museum of natural products, near which he has established a kind of manufactory, with zoological specimens, which seem to be only arrested in their functions of life. In general, I do not like such stuffed things; it reminds me too much of the artificial preservation of corpses, to which, as an enthusiast for the burning of the dead, I am adverse. The body seems to fly after the soul in the flames that devour it; it is not crammed in a dark coffin, nor exposed to the will of those remaining behind; but notwithstanding these philosophical ramblings, in which I like to indulge, I found the animals in the museum of Pisa worth notice.

One word of Lung' Arno and its lovely Spina. Although the Arno is here tame and brook-like, yet the palaces and houses along the quays are picturesque, and give an interesting picture of past times. Amongst the palaces, the stranger is shown that in which Byron lived; it is, in an architectural point of view pretty, and reminds one, as does the Lung' Arno, generally of Venice. The Spina, of which the supports stand in the bed of the river, is a chapel in the Gothic style, with thousands of delicate ornaments, with little towers and points (from which it derives its name), combining all the loveliness and seriousness of the old style of building, a true jewel, a relique which one fancies is built of a finer material than marble. It was a pity that we could not admire the interior of the old building.

In the palace of the Grand-Duke, a mean-looking private house, we met its possessor and his younger son, in order to go with them to Florence after breakfast. Before this short meal, I became acquainted with the Tuscan hymn, and was struck and pleased with its enthusiastic, nay, its almost wild strain. It has no religious, sublime music like the matchless Austrian hymn, but there is enthusiasm in it, and it suits Republican countries very well.

Good-bye, lovely, sedate Pisa! Friendly cemetery! The steam is hissing, and we rush from the dreams of the past in a prosaic and material fashion over classic, historical ground. The little land looks very cultivated and happy. Naples is said to be a piece fallen down from Paradise— fallen down from the clouds, a favourite of fortune; but the Florentine country has been changed to a paradise by the industry of man. It is a child of the earth raised to its high position by ceaseless exertion. And then this lovely plain of Florence, girt with hills, which we now enter. This peaceable blooming country, where hundreds of friendly villas, villages, and luxuriant gardens surround the city of the arts, like a fragrant wreath of flowers. The cupola of the cathedral, with its golden cross, greets us from amongst the masses of houses, which, amidst the green of the plain, gently ascend the hills. It is no grand, overpowering picture, but one of peaceable, pleasant rest. Naples is the city of youth; Florence that of those whose minds seek repose. The city of Vesuvius excites, that of the Arno lulls the soul to a balmy rest. From the large fine railway station we made our way into the architectural streets of Florence. This first entrance into an unknown, remarkable, and much-talked-of city created a peculiar feeling, for there rises before the mind, which glows with expectation, a chaotic picture. One tries to explain everything, one guesses at everything, and the head gets dizzy with the hundred impressions that fly past. After some experience one recognises the wonderful sights, learns to love them, only to be compelled, after a few days, to leave what has become a friend. One has just time enough to discern the beautiful, without being able to enjoy it at leisure. So it was with me with lovely Florence, the mild daughter of the muses. As yet I did not understand all I saw. I knew only that I had crossed the Arno, and was astonished at its bridges, of which one is so light and full of poetry, and is yet built as strong as marble; the other, resting on secure arches, and bearing, like an odd joke, a little town of booth-like houses, as a gay decoration left from the middle ages. Another thing I recognised, when I found myself opposite a large dark rock-castle, standing majestically on a height. I knew that it was the gigantic house of the proud Pitti, piled up by a citizen in 1440, from rough pieces of rock, in spite of the pomp-loving Medicis, to whom, however, he had to leave the finishing, and who gave to the gigantic work the name ' Pitti.' Earnest, terribly earnest, is that sublime rock-castle, and behind the rough uncouth walls one would expect cool stalactite grottoes, and not golden halls. How surprising appears, therefore, the back view of the palace! Three sides of the dark building surround a rather small

yard. On its fourth side, from a terrace at the height of
the first story, over a grotto, with a fresh spring, the
wide Boboli garden opens magically, which, with its fountain, its avenues, its grass plots, marble statues, and its
Belvedere crowning its height, contains within itself all
the advantages offered by nature, enhanced by those of
art. Thus the garden runs along the two side aisles of the
palace, and suddenly arrested in the middle by the high
stone wall sustained by the grotto, leaves space for the
court lying below. The Pitti palace enjoys the wonderful
advantage of a building built on a hill. It commands all
around it, and is in turn commanded by a garden, which,
without being suspected from the city side, is seen from
the windows of the pleasant rooms. It is a pity that the
grand staircase, although large enough in itself, is not
large enough for this rock building. How suitable here
would be the staircase of Caserta! But modern art creates
grand details, and rarely a great whole. The Greeks only
were equal to both. On the Acropolis only is to be
found a Parthenon, with its matchless harmony. We
entered the large apartments; but they are in the style
de l'empire. All the solid magnificence of the Medicis has
been destroyed, to be replaced by Napoleonic insipidities.
But one treasure of a rare kind has been spared by the
passion for renovation. This is the ' pietra dura,' the
solid, delicately-worked monumental room-furniture, which
belongs to a branch of art peculiar to Florence.

But this branch of art can only be recommended for
furniture. The tables, with garlands of fruit and flowers,
with shells and strings of pearls on the mild lapis
lazuli, or on dark deep reflecting ground; the high re-
naissance-cabinets, glittering like little castles or temples
with all the wonderful colours which nature has given to
her stones; all this lovely detail, by years of exertion
brought together, has, indeed, a grand and princely ap-

pearance, and exhibits the riches of the old Florentine sovereign-house. No gold can replace the enamel of the polished stones, and where marble and porphyry, lapis lazuli and jewels are in abundance, there is genuine wealth, solid luxury, the value of which does not change with years.

But now I had to make a hurried visit to a family, a member of which I had already seen and admired in Dresden, and I felt an irresistible longing for her heavenly mild Florentine relations. I was still filled with the impression of the Madonna Sistina, who feels so deeply and understands with such a sad pride the wonderful child she bears on her arms, and that her hands are the throne of the great Son of God. In her look one reads that she venerates herself as the instrument of the Almighty, that she feels the greatness of her duties, the greatness of her sufferings, but also the immensity of her transfiguration; and so she steps out of the clouds with majestic bearing, as the holy queen of the angels, and exhibits to the expectant multitude in that child their Redeemer. She hears the hosannas of ten thousand rejoicing lips, but she has also a foreboding of the crucifix. No glory ornaments the head, neither gold nor jewels are woven in the simple modest garment. In this picture the mother of Christ is not surrounded by pomp, no glitter draws the attention from the chief object, which the artists of our time so much like to apply, to divert the scrutiny of the visitor. The greatest ornament of the Sistine Madonna is the Son, and her most holy glory, that of her large clear eyes— those sublime eyes, filled with devoted faith. In them are comfort, truth, and infinite depth; they mirror, as in a calm lake, the pure heavens. And how glorious beyond all things is the child resting in her arms! In this creation Raphael forecasts the Redeemer; for in the serious features of the child may be read the task to be accom-

plished.   From under the dark hair open two large black
eyes, looking full into the dark sinful world, as if they
would say, 'I shall conquer you.   Tremble, worldly sinner,
before the child who, at some time, will judge and punish
you.'   He is bending backwards, his shoulders drawn up
in calm lingering expectation of the struggle with the
world.

This grand picture was before my eyes, and now I was
to make my first acquaintance with the Madonnas of the
Pitti palace.   I am often angry and sorry that I cannot
be enraptured at once, and lose myself in decisive admiration.   So it happened at this first too short visit to the
Madonna del Seggiola and del Granduca: I could not duly
appreciate them at the moment, and the Sistine Virgin
floated triumphantly before my mind; for in her I saw in
one figure the lofty mother of Christ and the servant of
the Lord, whilst the Madonna Seggiola is only the contented blooming mother, and that of the Granduca the
humble devoted servant.   But a second more leisurely
stay before the pictures will, I think, modify these feelings.
The Pitti gallery, that rare jewel in Florence's rich crown,
is situated in the right wing of the castle, from which, as
from a throne, one has a splendid outlook on the city and
country, on the distant villas, gardens, and mountains.

In the afternoon we went into the cathedral, passing
over the bridge of houses, a floating little town, inside
which is a bazaar containing scarcely anything but gold-
ware.   To the right and the left glitter gold and silver
boxes, earrings and chains, reminding one of the East and
Smyrna's goldsmith streets.   The cathedral is a pure and
noble work of Italian architecture.   It is built in the form
of a cross, with a high, wide, sky-like cupola over the
high altar.   The steeple and outside walls are covered
with the finest rich-coloured marbles, offering a beautiful
picture, which would be perfect if the casing of the façade

were not wanting, which was torn off to make place for a
modern one, which never was completed.

The interior is wide and sublime, at once majestic and
simple. Almost all the altars were cleverly removed, so
that an undivided attention is directed on the high altar,
over which the Last Judgment arches with its hundreds of
figures. It produces an excellent impression, for all is
united round the altar, which, by the light passing through
the fine glass paintings, is enveloped in a mysterious twilight. Round the main altar in a half-circle there are
some chapels with altars; everything else is in simple
harmony. I ascended to the cupola. Round its interior
run two galleries, and over it, like a case, is a second
cupola; between the two one creeps to the lantern. From
gallery to gallery, and from the height of the lantern, I
was constantly looking down into the church. The objects became smaller and smaller, bringing out the imposing grandeur and boldness of the whole. As the
details became less distinct, the whole mass sprang out,
and the view gained repose and clearness. Just the
reverse was it with the fresco pictures of the Last Judgment. What caricatures the figures became! How the
Satans stretched themselves out, and how improperly near
one comes to the sometimes rather free details of the artist's
fancy, which of course when seen from below disappear in
the *ensemble!* We stepped on the outside of the lantern,
and before us lay Florence. A long silver ribbon divided
the city. To the left is the more modern half, with the
dark Pitti Palace, embellished by the green Boboli, at the
top of which looks peaceably enough from amidst fresh
vegetation, the Belvedere; farther on is a sombre avenue
of cypresses, like a green colonnade, to the Poggio Imperiale; that part of the city loses itself in the lovely hills;
single villages and steeples beckon from afar, till at last
the mountains finish the picture. To the right of the old

river is the heart of the city, the seat of the palaces, of
art, and of the churches, and out of its dark roofs the
cathedral rises like a fresh flower.   There, one sees the
Palazzo Vecchio, with its tower and battlements.   There,
appear the long roofs of the Uffizzi, Santa Croce, Maria
Novella, and all the genuine religious buildings of past
centuries.   By the side of them could be seen the little
interiors, little gardens and terraces, and above all, the
wide, green, happy valley, the soft hills, and at the out-
skirt mountains as the closing background.   Lovely villas
crowned the hills and hung on the mountains, the tops of
which, however, are not so fresh as the country.   Happily
and sweetly, Florence reposes in the green Arno valley,
like a tender blossom with refreshing fragrance; and a full
right has the city to a flower in its escutcheon, for one
rarely sees a place so abundantly gifted with the fresh
gifts of Flora.   Everywhere one sees gardens replete with
roses, jasmine, carnations, and other flowers, of such
fragrance that one lives in a balmy atmosphere.   My
climbing-rage had not yet been satisfied by the ascent to
the gallery of the lantern.   I had heard of the globe
under the cross. ' Forward !' was the word, and up the
interior of a column, like a chimney-sweeper, from one iron
bolt to the other, I got into the middle globe, from which
I became acquainted with the temperature of the Venetian
lead-chambers.   Still a few more turns, and I was on the
highest eminence in Florence, with the upper half of my
body outside, immediately below the cross of the cathedral.
My fancy was satisfied, and I felt free and alone.   I had
an idea of the joy of the swallow on the top of a roof.
The penknife of my cousin was sacrificed that I might
engrave my initials upon the Christian symbol.

We next drove to the Cascine, the arena of Florentine
lions; and in the long leafy avenues, stretching along the
Arno, we met the most elegant equipages, so that you

might fancy yourself in Hyde Park, or on the Boulevards, or in the Prater. At the Grand-Ducal farmbuildings Cascine (after which the popular promenade is named), stood a perfect host of carriages around an Austrian military band.

Florence, August 29, 1851.

Our morning-walk was to the Pitti gallery. Such a collection could only have been made in the youthful glow of art two centuries ago. The Medici had a fore-taste of this, and acting upon it were creators of the immortal monuments of their time. They wedded to the learning of Greece the art of a Christian period. In the first room into which I came stood the Madonna della Seggiola ready for copying. Why, in looking at this, does the Sistine Madonna always come into my mind? There may be perhaps a resemblance in the features. Both have the same body, but not the same mind. The Sistine Madonna is a vision of one glorified after combat and suffering, the Seggiola is a wanderer upon earth, whose hour of trouble has not come, who is calmly, nay com-fortably, sitting on a chair which her coming glory has not yet changed into a throne. She bends softly over the Redeemer who is clinging to her, and looks with those contemplative eyes, which only Raphael can paint, mild and touching, like the moon on a pure night.

The colours of this picture have that mysterious haze, that freshness without brightness, that soft, veiling film, peculiar to his art and to some only of his works.

Raphael painted the Sistine Madonna with heavenly insight, the Seggiola with passionate love, the Granduca with the heart of a child. The latter, indeed, has a nearer resemblance to a German than to a Jewish maid. She is a prayer, still and peaceful, whilst the Sistina expresses ecstasy. In speaking of Raphael, the king of artists and embodied angels, I must not forget the Madonna del

Baldacchino and the Santa Familia dell' Imparmata. I
cannot help following my taste and not the judgment of the
world, and confess that both pictures made no impression
on me, and the latter displeased me in spite of my desire
to like it. Two portraits, representing Angiolo Donni and
his wife, interested me, as they enabled me to understand, or rather not to understand, the immense difference
between these works of Raphael and his master-pieces. The
Madonna Sistina and Magdalen Donni show the development of the human soul from the seed to the blossom.

Before the vision of Ezekiel I should like to stand
for hours. A gold frame, a foot and a half high and one
foot wide, contains the heaven in its glory and in its in-
finity. This God-Father is the creator and director of
the world; as a ruler of the universe he is reposing on
the throne of clouds supported by the mysterious symbols
of the Evangelists; a God of the Old Testament, Jehovah,
before whom one tremblingly sinks into the dust, absorbed
in adoration, and yet elevated by the thought that each of
us has been created after his likeness, and that the eternal
soul in the perishable vessel emanated from Him who
was, is now, and ever will be. If I might be permitted
to say so after what I have just said, I should say that the
figure of the Almighty had something of that inhabitant
of the Parthenon, the thunderer Zeus. But the God of
the world, the aim of all faith from the commencement to
eternity, and the unchangeable in Jupiter and Odin, are
blended in this figure. The grey hair and large waving
beard float grandly around the earnest features full of the
dignity of age and of power; his arms lifted up in blessing
are high over the clouds. What a different picture from
this, how full of effect and yet without any charm, is that
picture of his contemporary, the Parcæ of Michael Angelo!
These seem created by the chisel, not with the soft brush—
bronze Parcæ, who can only spin an iron thread, a thread

of Michael Angelo. He has with the strength of a hero dragged them from the lower regions, to give us a solid earnest *memento mori.*

Murillo has paid his tribute to the collection in two Madonnas. One of these Madonnas is a mistake: she is painted to represent the features of a Duchess of Urbino and her child; a handsome, serious woman, but no mother of the Lord. The other is a worthy sister of that in Dresden, a charming picture of religious reality; it is no hierarchic-aristocratic mother of the Lord, but a mother from amongst the people, not severe and divine, but delicate and full of enthusiasm; quite in contrast to a mother and child of Rubens, which belong to the fat, well-to-do class of the people, to the Dutch citizens. Rubens is a painter of men, vigorous and genial; but his female figures are over-healthy and too well fed, stifling the spirit. But what a splendid picture is that in which he has represented himself, his brother, Justus Lipsius and Hugo Grotius. From these features a noble, energetic life speaks plainly; with broad firm strokes, without too much finish, he has given what he intended to give, a company of able, interesting men. Here also is my dear Vandyke again, in connexion with his finest and most charming theme, England's unfortunate royal couple. It is only painted as a bust: one sees the airy figure of the tender queen, not quite as in the gallery of Dresden, but still this picture has a melancholy charm of its own; one sees Charles and Henrietta in mourning, sombre and lovely, unhappy and melancholy. On Charles' serious features the mournful future has settled like a crape; he is a victim of the noblest kind who submitted to fate too passively, too unresistingly; he failed through weakness and yet must have been exceedingly graceful, and in no way repulsive, like Louis XVI. Both had an opportunity, if not to live well, at least to die well. How was it that the

wives of both were so handsome and so lovely? Why
must the sweet and gentle be ever the victims?

With Marie Antoinette I became acquainted in Inns-
bruck and Dresden. I was ever enthusiastic about the
former, and the latter I was taught to admire by Vandyke.
I have never seen any picture that attracted me so mag-
netically as that of Charles I.'s consort. Her lily head
rests proudly and sweetly on her slender, fine neck; her
complexion and features are delicate, and shine like ivory,
and yet they are decided; and under the dazzling forehead,
ornamented with lightly-falling little curls, dwell a pair of
eyes to which only melancholy and a wounded heart could
give that softness and that indescribably attractive force.
Grace is the word for Marie Antoinette, pensiveness for
Maria Henrietta.

Andrea del Sarto, the simple unpretending Florentine
artist, *par excellence*, whom I learnt here first to value and
admire, is endowed with one of those divine sparks which
light, and warm, and kindle. His works are earnest, and
full of Southern glow — altogether the expression of
ardent devotion and deep faith. Could one compare religious painting with church architecture, the style of
Andrea would correspond to the Byzantine-Venetian;
Raphael's, to that of the old Italian, and that of good
honest Durer to the pure Gothic German. Of the latter
a poor Eve naked, and feeling cold, is lost among the
Italian fulness. She is standing awkwardly amongst all
the richly-formed Madonnas; but she is true and full of
character, like the old painter himself—full of life, but
not sensual. But to return to Andrea; I only recol-
lect his Holy Family in the Stanza di Marte. Whoever
has seen this picture of devout faith must love and vene-
rate him. Opposite this masterpiece hangs the imposing
Judith of Allori. This great God-inspired woman, this
proud widow, who, for the sake of her faith and her people,

rose with antique strength, and proceeded after penance
and prayer to the bloody but necessary work, is to me one
of the most interesting figures from the book of life.
There are only a few amongst the better artists who dared
to represent this gigantic woman, and only a few succeeded
in creating a Judith in her dreadful triumph, earnest and
glowing with devotion—they either created a frantic Bacchante, or a weak soul that would have never sacrificed
the commander of the enemy to her country. Allori and
Riedl have accomplished that task. With both it is the
worthy Jewish widow, the woman of the Old Testament,
who undertook the deed because she must do it; without
any quaking of the soul, and also without any vain longing
for the triumph that was awaiting her. It is this sad necessity, this melancholy necessity of sacrificing to be herself
a sacrifice, in which the German master has, perhaps, carried
off the palm. These are the pictures of which I think with
love, and which have become dear friends to me.

Benvenuto Cellini is a poet who uses, in the place of
words, gold and the lively rich colours of enamel. His
gold cups are surrounded by sweet pictures of fancy, groups
from rich and sweet dreams, amply shown in the small but
exquisite collection of his works of art in the Pitti Palace,
which, like a rough large mountain, has in its veins the
finest treasures and the most precious metals.

On the ground floor of the Pitti is a collection of statues
and a chapel. The latter I disliked altogether for its
heathenish style and its bas-reliefs—mere trash, and not
worthy of the royal palace. To give the mind time to
digest the hundreds of fermenting things, we drove to the
Boboli, and rested there. This is a garden as a garden
ought to be—grand, princely, as is befitting to such palaces.
In the Pitti garden breathes the spirit of the Medici, with
their proud pomp.

From these gigantic avenues we went to a manufactory,

but a manufactory producing works of art, and the institution of which does not belong to our material age, but
is still a witness of the richness and pomp of past days
in the manufacture of pietra-dura. These clever stone
combinations furnish table tops, rich coloured ornaments,
altars, cabinets, and similar objects, real monumental works,
massy and yet light, as smooth as mirrors, and charming
the eye by harmony of colour. In future times, when the
pietra-dura shall be dug out of rubbish and decay, it will
excite the just admiration of posterity. The works made
of it are constructed with extraordinary pains. Amongst
hundreds of pieces one must be found which has the shade
of a certain flower, or the colour of its leaves. This is
now cut to a paper pattern with a wire besmeared with
emery, and then fitted to the other stones which make
the picture, or rather so set, that, except it is required by
the drawing, the jointure is not perceived. The stone
out of which that little portion has been cut is now laid
in a box containing the ore resembling it in material and
colour, and there it remains until it is again wanted for a
shade or a colour. The expense and trouble caused by such
a manufactory may, therefore, be imagined; but the re-
sults are splendid. Of the things we saw already finished
I was particularly struck by altar walls for the Chapel St.
Lorenzo, which, on the finest lapis lazuli ground, represented attributes of the Church. These really perfect
works have a very agreeable, peculiar, and brilliant freshness, produced by the polished stone. The crown of all
that has yet been produced is the table of the Muses,
finished after twenty years' work. In the middle of it the
visitor admires victorious Phœbus, worthily represented in
the manner and colour of an antique; and both horses
and driver are drawn in a masterly fashion. It is one of
those masterpieces which, like the cameo of Augustus, or
the salt-cellar of Benvenuto Cellini, will have an everlast-

ing name in the history of art; it is also, probably, the last grand masterpiece on lapis lazuli, as this beautiful precious stone, which hitherto came from Persia, is no longer an article of merchandise, and is not now sent to the manufactory.

The value of the academy which we then visited we could not thoroughly appreciate, as several rooms were covered with grey holland previous to the opening of an exhibition of modern pictures; but I saw that the arrangement in regard to the placing of the pictures was excellent, as it gives to the amateur, and still more to the artist, an excellent insight into the gradual development of art. One sees from picture to picture how the angular and meagre limbs in those of the old artists, become more free and filled out; at a later period one sees how the typical traits must give way to the living model, how with the more active fancy the devout, childlike imagination flies away, and the spirit of Christendom takes a mythological form. I was most particularly interested in a picture by Raphael's master. It is with art as with love; before Raphael it is a childlike love, the nearer it approaches to the grand masters it becomes conscious, though still innocent, of sensual enjoyment. With Raphael comes the first, glowing, all-comprehending, penetrating, enjoying love. Our time is that of love satisfied, love over-excited, finding gratification only in extremes. We were shown with pride the plastic work of their newest artist, whose name unfortunately escaped me, Cain and Abel represented after the murder of Abel, cast in bronze, so beautifully and so highly finished that I have not seen the like of it even in Munich. The figures are executed on a somewhat small scale, and I was not pleased with Cain, who is turning away in horror when for the first time he sees the death of a man. This group and the table of the Muses were intended for the London Exhibition in England's big

glass coffin; but as the English minister in Florence spread
the news that the Grand-Duke intended to present the
table to the Queen, and this prince did not like that a work
of so many years in execution should pass out of his
country, nothing was sent to London.

In the Church of the Annunziata, where we now proceeded, are also some excellent Andrea del Sartos, which
delight one by their fine composition, and soft yet firm
treatment, and increase our admiration of this Florentine
master.   Though the principal parts of this hall are protected against the weather by glass windows, yet the
pictures are already somewhat faded.   I noticed in the
entrance-hall two bronze basins of fine shape.   The
church is ornamented in the rich, but overloaded taste
of the last century.   A true sanctuary for magnificence
and richness is one of these chapels, which is replete
with the finest works in silver and pietra-dura.   I noticed
two slabs, which are so well executed that the shades
represent the sun and the moon, the former half wrapped
in vapours.   In the cloister-hall over the entrance door,
is Andrea del Sarto's celebrated fresco picture of the
Madonna del Sacco, which the artist painted for the pious
friars for a sack of flour, which fact he has perpetuated in
the picture.   At that time the part of a Mæcenas seems
to have been very easy.   Through sundry turnings we
were led until we stood astonished before a Last Supper
of Raphael, a fresco only recently found in the store-room
and saved from destruction, which in spite of the dreadful
risks and damages it has had to undergo, is still excellently preserved; but I fear that it is only half-saved yet,
for I heard the stamping of horses behind the wall; the
humidity of the adjacent stable cannot possibly be very
beneficial to the fresco.   Stable and store-room were once
the refectory of a cloister.   The judges of art have settled
that the Cena is by Raphael.   If this is the case, the

work belongs to his middle period and stands half-way on the childlike ground. The Cena makes a genial impression : one feels inclined to sit down at the hospitable repast and study without fear its excellent details ; there is something of the old German in it, and the key to this picture seems to me to be furnished by the portraits of the Donni couple in the collection of the Pitti, although these belong to a still earlier period. I was especially pleased with the youthful head of an apostle, probably John, in a listening position. That one on looking at this picture should sometimes have doubts whether it is really by Raphael, is I think pardonable ; the judges of art are too quick and easy in their decision ; it made on me, however, an agreeable impression and under this Cena I could enjoy the food of the cloister. We had yet to see two chapels : the chapel of the Medici, in which repose Guillo de' Medici, and Lorenzo, Duke of Urbino, acquired its fame by the sculptures and the architecture of Michael Angelo ; it contains Buonarotti's Day and Night, about which so many rave ; but I confess that I utterly disliked this chapel, nay, that it made on me a most disagreeable, cold, and repulsive impression. Here are deposited the remains of those for whose speculative philosophical vanity this tomb has been erected ; Michael Angelo, deep thinking and clearly perceiving the times, has perfectly succeeded in this repulsive monument. The indecent statues without grace, without soul I might say, lying about, show only too plainly from whence the spirit came that housed here. The half-sitting, half-lying position, clearly represents the aversion of the vain, foolish philosophy to the repose of death ; it struggles against the covering of that veil which has not yet been lifted by any one, but which wraps the faithful in its peaceful folds. These monuments exhibit a morbid struggle of earthly greatness with the nothingness of death, and the marble has a coldness as if death were mocking life from out of it. The word 'peace' can never resound from this hall, which is not imbued with a Christian spirit, but with a cold mythology. These statues of Buonarotti appear to me to be too grotesque, and to have already in them the germ of the rococo time. I liked no better the Lorenzo chapel, the apotheosis of the later Medici, commenced by Ferdinand I., but not entirely finished even now. Everything is replete with a cold, tawdry richness, without the least grace, and one thinks discontentedly of the splendid marble grandeur of Caserta. Coffins with many-coloured escutcheons, of which I will mention only those of Cosmo II. and Ferdinand I., rest proudly against the walls, surrounded by the splendour of colours, which, however well adapted for other purposes, is absurd in a hall of the dead, in which there is not even yet an altar. Death has nothing to do with other colours than those of the flowers which have alone a right to bloom upon the coffin. If one were to remove the sarcophagi and give the whole the name of a festival hall, the ornaments would at once become fresh and pleasant, and the mocking emptiness would be replaced by vigorous life. Constantinople had fallen before the sword of Mohammed, Græco-Byzantine art and philosophy and the rich sciences of the East found a home in Italy, through the luxurious spirit of the Medici, which in its turn conferred splendour on their new dynasty. The tiara was borne by a Medici and the hitherto forgotten treasures of Rome were wedded to Greek recollections, which brought forth a new epoch in art, the Mythologico-Christian. The Lord's Supper was celebrated in the Temple : Venus got the same court-rank as the God-mother. It was in harmony with such a state of things to blend the customs of antiquity with those of modern times, and to call this philosophy. But from this resulted an unsatisfied Ideal. Men discovered that

the gods of antiquity only represented men, and the pride
of the senses which first produced great things in art and
science, took possession of the heart, and laid in it the germ
of atheism. The very princes believed themselves to be
a kind of divinity, needing no longer to be afraid of the
old God. They nursed religion only as a convenient state
or institution for their subjects. In France Francis I. was
the chief supporter of the worship of the Syrens, round
which he attempted to throw a nimbus by the arts of
Italy. Catherine di Medici was too zealous in the service of Aphrodite, and Louis XIV. Jupiterised himself
entirely. A vanity that could be satisfied, vanity and the
apotheosis of sensuality became the philosophy of rulers.
These ideas soon descended to the people, and were fed
by their rulers and celebrated in their songs, and finally
had their chief representative in Voltaire. France saved
Italy partly by concentrating these ideas in herself; but
she had to pay for this glory with her blood. The tombs
of the Medici produce thoughts of a very cold and terrible
kind.

Returned from the Pitti, I went to the wife of our
Minister, Baroness Huegel, to whom I was presented by
her amiable husband. The Baroness is an English lady,
born in India, possessing an amiable and graceful countenance, combining beauty with intelligence; nor could
our country be better represented than by her and her
husband.

A pleasant, agreeable dinner with Leopold brought us
all together again in the Pitti, after which I drove with
his eldest son to the Church of Santa Croce, the pantheon of
Italian greatness. Rows of massive columns support the
basilica-like entablature of the high roof, the light shedding a mild glory, comes through wonderful glass-paintings, veiling softly from the eyes of the faithful the garish
world outside. A broad space, free from stools or seats of

any kind, leads solemnly up to the high altar, and on its right and left are small oratories around the nave. The whole church has the form of a T, and like the cathedral, wants unfortunately a façade. The Lombardo-Gothic would here be seen to perfection, were not the interior meanly disturbed by monuments along the church walls, of which many are modern, and great failures. Italy is not fortunate in her monuments to the dead, as is shown here more than anywhere else. Monuments in imitation of the antique are out of place in a church of the Middle Ages, and the naked body of Dante, half covered with a sheet would be well replaced by the body lying on the cover of the coffin, waiting patiently for the last trump. Could his marble lips open, it would be with an epigram on his own mausoleum. Three statues, representing respectively painting, sculpture, and architecture, mourn over Michael Angelo. There are many insignificant monuments put up by those who were rich enough to buy a place of honour in the Pantheon. Celebrated men join hands with the rabble to disfigure this beautiful work of bygone days by their paltry trophies.

The Church of Santa Maria Novella, with the Dominican monastery attached to it, famed throughout the world for its pharmacy, is likewise built in the Lombardo-Gothic style, and Michael Angelo called it his bride. It has three naves with pointed vaults, and is filled with treasures of art. In the two cross naves chapels are raised, and in one of them is shown a celebrated picture of a Madonna, and in the other the Last Judgment. In this church I had an opportunity of admiring the glass-paintings so much loved by me. The crosswalk, used once as a burial-ground, is ornamented with frescoes of the oldest time, which are said to be painted with the juice of plants instead of with colours. My cousin called them, not without reason, potato frescoes, an expression which for its correctness made me laugh heartily, and which very much scandalised the learned man of art who led us about. Still more curious appeared to us in a chapel of the cross-walk the so-called 'Capitolo degli Spagnuoli,' where amongst other frescoes are represented the fighting and the triumphant Church, with Pope and Emperor at its head, whilst dogs in the colours of the Dominicans (an allusion to the pun *Domini cani*) chase wolves, representing the heretics—from which we may learn that our forefathers indulged in witty, if not in very fine, caricatures. The Dominicans of this day feel highly honoured and pleased by this fancy. In the same picture are pointed out the likenesses of Petrarch, Laura, and Boccacio, whether rightly must be decided by the learned. We followed our guide to the state rooms of the monastery, which are furnished luxuriously; to the Speceria, and to a hall only recently finished, and which is designed for the reception of princely guests, where crystal chandeliers, golden candelabras, and velvet furniture, ex-isting to this day, witness to the wealth of this monastery. The good, cordial Dominicans treated me with Alkermes liqueur of their own manufacturing, with which I did not forget to toast the monastery. After we had bought from their apothecary department, which affords so much help to the poor, some of the celebrated essences and the Poudre d'Iris, we took a cordial leave of the friendly monks, and drove through rich gardens to Pietraja, a château of the Grand-Duke, which takes its name from its site on a stony hill. It was built by the Medici in the fine old Italian villa taste, and is wrapped in the fragrance of a charming garden. To the left of the broad staircase stands, amidst a flower-garden rich with orange-trees, a tasteful fountain, on the top of which is placed Giovanni di Bologna's celebrated Venus, cast in bronze. She is rising from the bath, jets of water issue from her rich

hair, so that thousands of glittering diamonds play
around Aphrodite. To the right the terrace is densely
shaded by extremely broad green oaks, really colossal
in the circumference of their tops, so that a cool green
tent is spread over a wide space. These trees belong,
without doubt, to the phenomena of nature; for without
being very high, they form by their number alone,
and by the length of their branches, quite a little wood.
Behind them stands a cedar of Lebanon, planted by the
Grand-Duke in his youth, which has already reached a
tolerable height. I saw here also camellias in the open
air.

Florence, August 30, 1851.

The parade appointed for this morning could not take
place on account of the rain; I availed myself of the
time to see the rooms in the Pitti gallery which had
been closed on the first three days. But something
yet more splendid was in store for me to-day. One of
the longest passages I ever saw, led me through a part of
the city, over roofs, then over the Arno by the Ponte
Vecchio, from the Pitti to the Uffizi. The interesting,
but by no means handsome, portraits of the old rulers of
Tuscany line, with other daubs representing historical
scenes, this enormous irregular corridor, from which, in
the middle of the Ponte Vecchio, you have an amusing
double view along the Arno, resembling a view from our
Vienna river, and in which the Florentines comfortably
fish by means of large nets from out of their very windows, which looks very odd. The Palazzo degli Uffizi is
a state building in the old Italian style, forming a rectangular building open towards the Piazza of the Palazzo
Vecchio, supported on one side by the Loggia, and ending
opposite the palace; it rests on arcades ornamented with
statues of celebrated Tuscans, among them Cosmo I., the
builder of this stately, regular palace. A fine staircase

ornamented with statues leads to the first story, where another corridor-like gallery runs round, from which one enters the rooms and cabinets lying along it. In these rooms the finest productions of art are united under the name of the 'Galleria degli Uffizi.'

In the first, the busts of the Medici interested me chiefly, those supporters of the finest and last period of art based on the old foundation. The family of the Medici particularly interest me, for they offer, with Venice, the only instance in history that men engaged in commerce can create and preserve great things, and have woven around their heads a lasting halo by their superiority in the department of the arts. They and Venice prove that merchants also may have a mind for something else besides Mammon, and that one may rise by Fortune without becoming a parvenu. The Medici rose as princes from the Exchange, and Etruria's handsome daughters soon wooed the sons of European kings.

In the second room were representations of the animal world: a splendid horse, a boar, and two dogs, pleased me by the *naïveté* and vigour of their representation and the noble spirit which is exhibited even in this branch of art. The first corridor exhibits a great number of busts of Roman Emperors and Empresses, in which the gallery of the Uffizi is particularly rich, and which showed me, to my shame, how much one need be versed in Roman imperial history to know all the names and characters of these high personages; to an archæologist a rich field is here opened out for the study of historical faces. Amongst the statues in the second corridor, I found the celebrated Thorn-drawer, so frequently copied; this ingenious statue, full of movement, and in which the marble almost becomes flesh and blood, and the very joints bend naturally, delights one by its rare and artistic imitation of nature in a difficult position.

At the end of the third corridor we find Baccio Bandinelli's copy of Laocoon, a grandly conceived, fanciful
dream of antiquity; my taste, however, leads me rather to
leave this group to the anatomical examinations of a
surgeon, and to return to the youthful, fresh wantonness of
life, and to Michael Angelo's Bacchus, whose jovial, tipsy,
voluptuous, broad face is thrown backward, and who
languishes for the beloved juice from the raised cup,
whilst a full bunch of grapes in one of his hands shows
that he is ready to renew a pleasant enjoyment. In this
youthful body of the God, and in the merry roguish
little Faun at his feet, there is the fullness of antique
life, and none of those too-much-developed muscles—
which are such a feature in Michael Angelo's works—disturb the delighted eye. One cannot but admire the
creator of that longing face, in which there is a trace of
the animal. An unfinished Apollo by the same artist was
also very interesting, showing as it did the creative power
of Michael Angelo like an uncut diamond; the completion
of which, however, is foreshadowed; and one seems
hereby to see the working of the art, and the manner in
which the sculptor confers immortal life upon the dead.
We find several works of Michael Angelo in which the
master has only chiselled out a firm sketch, and given
birth to the idea without taking time and trouble for the
complete execution of it. To this class belongs a relievo
of the Holy Family preserved in a passage of the gallery.
These half-unveiled ideas of Michael Angelo attracted me
particularly, and I liked them better than many of his
finished works in which there is something grotesque and
too muscular. Near the Laocoon group is a John the
Baptist, by Donatello, very graceful and noble; and
many Roman busts of historical note, of which the most
remarkable perhaps is Nero when a boy. The face of a
monster when a child is a curious study, but this bust

lacks the expression in the eye, which must be added to the other features in order that we may read in the face the prophecy of the future man. As I had so little time to spare, I did not stop in a room of Etruscan antiquities, which branch, moreover, is better represented in the Museo Borbonico, although we are now in the heart of Etruria. However, in the cabinet of the new bronzes were many things worth seeing. The jewel amongst them is Giovanni Bologna's Mercury, which formerly ornamented the Villa Medici in Rome, and from which, as from the Venus of this master, water is spouted from small openings. A little Æolus-head blows with full cheeks a column of air, on which rests a bold statue of Mercury on the point of his left foot, and the upward-striving light movement of the slender vigorous body removes every doubt that this divine youth will successfully cleave the air.

We then entered the hall of Niobe, and stood astonished before the tragical group which the word of a god changed in a moment into marble, and preserved the expression of a soul trembling with pain, by petrefaction. Niobe and her children were too handsome, and too godlike, for their noble forms to crumble to dust and ashes; they were, therefore, rendered immortal by art. Peter Leopold, Austria's Leopold II., possessed this group, which was found near the gate of St. Paul in Rome in 1583, brought from the Villa Medici to the gallery in Florence, where, in a large tasteless hall with light walls, it finds a place, than which no worse could be found; for the great and the beautiful deserve a corresponding habitation. That these statues, which in a passage in Pliny are ascribed to the master of Phidias and Praxiteles, stood in the front of a temple, is obvious from the different scale and the movement of the single figures. A mother with her youngest daughter, a youth running forward, a

daughter holding up with her left arm a cloak of many
folds as a protection against the arrows of Diana, are,
without doubt, worthy to be ranked amongst the most
brilliant conceptions. Despair and agony, the sight of
the blood of her sister, causes the youngest daughter to
throw herself on her knees, and to lean against her mother
as upon a column; her dishevelled hair falls over her
slender youthful figure, the arm is raised in fear whilst
the mother presses her to her, only to suffer in the death
of the youngest the extremity of pain. In all the figures
one cannot but admire the life, the splendid form of the
limbs, the exquisite softness and the masterly drapery. The
noble blood of the brother and sister is spilt by the
arrows; Niobe and her children succumb with dignity to
the vengeance of fate; and a tragedy of a rare kind is here
acted in marble. As even despair has sometimes its ludicrous side, so the awkward tutor of the unhappy children
made me smile by his alarm; for though probably ex-
celling in theory with his lance, he does not know how to
defend with it the pupils confided to him; certainly these
are arrows of gods, arrows of fate, which may serve as
some excuse for the poor 'Philister.' The upper parts of
the walls are ornamented with pictures, amongst which is
Henry IV. at the battle of Ivry, and his entrance into
Paris by Rubens. Here Rubens gives wings to his fancy,
throwing about the masses as no other artist can; but
this genial artist gives us too much flesh, too much of the
healthy *corpus*. This is further illustrated, though in
this case appropriately, by his Bacchanal, which we met
with in the hall of Barocchio, and finds some explanation
in the excellent portraits of his two wives, Elizabeth
Brand and Helena Forman, who, in their fullness and
freshness give us a hint as to the models of Rubens. The
portraits of this painter are, however, my delight; they
are more than portraits, for from them one may study

physiognomy itself. There is not only a fleshly resemblance, but there is life and soul, and the whole power of the eye conjured up by a few touches on the canvas. One may comfortably and leisurely examine his portraits, and look straight in their faces; in their company one feels quite *sans gêne*, whilst one looks up to the creations of Vandyke with veneration as to something higher than ourselves. One may imagine the interest excited by the portrait of Galileo by Sustermann in the hall of Barocchio, in which science is immortalised by art; and the delight one feels in this head with white beard, and sombre features, that of a man who shook the earth from its lethargy, and conquered the pride of mankind, which deemed their world so important, that even the sun should adoringly revolve round it. And though centuries have past since that earnest mouth spoke out the great truth, a large part of mankind still live in the old error.*

In the Egyptian cabinet are exhibited mummies and sundry trifles, proving that the greatness of Egypt consists chiefly in its colossal works, in obelisks and temples, more in the whole than in the detail. We come now to the two saloons in which is a collection of portraits of painters, painted by the artists themselves. This collection, matchless in its kind, was commenced by Cardinal Leopold di Medici, and since then continued, but unfortunately not enriched by the modern artist who is not worthy to untie the shoe-strings of his predecessors. As each artist must paint his own portrait, these pictures show, at the same time, the artist and his work. Here I found my three favourite stars amongst the painters :—Raphael, Rubens, and Vandyke. Enthusiastic, earnest, not vigorously manly, not womanly weak, a melancholy hybrid, living on this earth in a delicate

---

* I met once a young American, from Louisiana, returning home after having finished his education in a Jesuit College at Vienna ; he firmly lieved that the sun turned round the earth, as he had been taught so by s Jesuit teachers.—TRANSLATOR.

over-sensitive body, Raphael, half-cherub, half-genius,
looks with deep melancholy eyes out of the picture which
responds to his creations much better than the portrait in
the gallery of Munich. He it is who has penetrated
deeper than them all, who, in a loving rapture of love, has
executed his divine conceptions, and whose excess of feeling has not deprived him of vigour and strength. Vandyke is handsome and serious, like his splendid pictures;
he is the painter of princes of lofty greatness, an aristocratic artist, and as such he looks with genial dignity from
the frame.

Voluptuous, almost bold, with eyes that have already
enjoyed much, and a nicely twirled moustache, thus
Rubens represents himself to us. Raphael succumbed
to the fever of his art; Rubens thrived in merry enjoyment, and found strength in it for great works.

In the middle of one of these rooms stands a trophy of
antique art, the so-called Medicean vase, of the best
Greek period, and made of the finest marble. Light
grape-vine garlands surround a basso-relievo, representing
in excellent figures the sacrifice of Iphigenia. This vase,
in its detail, as in the whole, tasteful, large, and well-
preserved, is after the old models, and said to have served
at the banquets of the ancients for the mixing of water
and wine, and to have been called ' Krater.' This shows
again, with what a luxury of art, quite unknown to our
time, the ancients, and especially the Greeks, surrounded
themselves ; whilst amongst the Romans a too great
luxury brought about a decay of art. What a joy to the
eye in the merry repast, or at serious work, to be surrounded with such beautiful forms ! Two rooms contain
the productions of the Venetian school. To become acquainted with, and to appreciate the vigorous rich drawing,
the always fresh, well-tinted, deep-glowing colours of this
school, one must examine with leisure the ' *accademia delle*

belle arte' in Venice, one must have seen the palaces of
Venice, the imposing magnificence of the sea-city, in
which the earnestness of Europe is blended with Eastern
richness of colour, in order to understand that its celebrated painters knew how to unite soberness and bril-
liancy. Florence is in possession of a jewel of a rare
kind of the Venetian school, Titian's Flora—a splendid
woman, proud and captivating; the reddish-fair hair,
in seducing rich waves, frames a calm, clear, perfect
face; a light white gown encircles the dazzling bosom,
and in the beautiful left hand are the flowers which give
this masterpiece its name of Flora, though she is rather
an aristocrat brought up in gold and purple, a daughter
of a Doge, than a sweet goddess of spring; the flowers are
only a plaything, not the business or care of the lady.

The cabinet of gems, I might call it the jewel boudoir, is
ornamented with columns of Oriental alabaster and verd
antique, and its show-cases contain the most beautiful
vessels, and fancy-things of lapis lazuli, achat, amethyst,
and rock crystal, some of them cut by Benvenuto Cellini;
a real treasure-house of the most lovely and most precious
objects. The French painters' school, with their affected
trifles and artificial primness, I shall leave unnoticed.
Germany and the Netherlands are better represented in
other places, although this division is ornamented by a
landscape and storm by Ruysdael and a Claude. But to all
this we only give cursory looks, for we approach the
temple of temples—the Most Holy of Art; a pleasant
quiver of excitement runs through us, for we see the entrance to the 'Tribune;' we have still to go through one
room of the Italians, in which our impatience will only
permit us to admire a striking head of Medusa by Cara-
vaggio, and, with an expectation highly raised, we enter
the centre of the world of art.

The dark-red octagon room is vaulted over by a cupola

richly ornamented with plates of mother-of-pearl; three doors, one from the corridor, ornamented with statues, and two from the adjacent picture-rooms, lead to it; the most favourable light comes from above, through a circle of windows, and can, by means of curtains, be concentrated on a single object. The floor is inlaid with marble slabs. In the architecture of the Tribune everything combines to produce a mysterious repose; a glorifying light beams from above, lighting upon the desired picture, and wrapping the rest in a favourable soft twilight.

The Tribune offers a rare philosophical harmony; the most different schools, the most different associations of ideas, the impulses of all times are here intimately allied in one whole by a power penetrating everything, and uniting all periods—the power of art. I stepped over the threshold with a strange feeling. 'What will you find?' and at the same time I was seized with a peculiar embarrassment before what may be termed the indecent in art, before the free naked, which I was afraid would not let me enjoy the spectacle calmly, and only allow me to steal furtive looks. There I stood before the Venus di Medici, and now only arose in me a genuine feeling for art—an art-enthusiasm, in whose eyes indecency has no existence, which only sees the sublime and the glorious—and my embarrassment at once disappeared. Aphrodite rose from the foam of the sea; the golden waves under the sun of the South, and wafted by the zephyr, danced as they leapt upon the shell-covered shore. Like a bud bedewed, a woman rose from the gently murmuring sea, too handsome to be born of flesh and blood—a poetical idea. This wonder of fancy, as shown by a Greek inscription, was a marble dream of Cleomenes, the Athenian. The child of the waves, the goddess of loveliness stands before us in sweet unconscious shame, born perfect; scarcely has the sun kissed the sea-mist from off the softly-swelling limbs, not yet fettered by golden clasps. She is naked, yet the harmony of her beauty does not suggest naked-ness; she is too perfect to be subjected to the dissection of the eye. In this statue the marble ceases to be stone, the free delicate hands are imbued with feeling, in her youthful bosom slumbers the breath of spring, and coyly and sweetly the elastic limbs incline forward, the right foot gently raised, and Aphrodite steps from the wave to tread lightly upon the flowery ground. ' This jewel was found in Hadrian's Villa at Tivoli, but unfortunately in thirteen pieces, which, however, the hand of a master united in such a manner, that the eye is not in the least disturbed by the excellent joinings.

About 1680, during the pontificate of Innocent XI. and under the reign of Cosmo III., the Medicean Venus was purchased, together with the statue of Apollino, and brought to Florence. Under Napoleon the Venus sub-mitted to the sword, and followed a conqueror to Paris, a victim of that forced enthusiasm for art which was then enriching that great city. During that time she was— *horribile dictu*—represented on her ancient throne in the Tribune by the Venus of Canova; a ballet goddess risen from paper sea-foam, took the place of Aphrodite the daughter of the waves. But Napoleon fell, Venice again saw on the Piazza of St. Mark, her famous horses, and the Venus di Medici was restored to her old friends and to her old throne.

The Slave whetting his knife is a vigorous muscular figure in a crouching position, which is very difficult to execute well, supporting himself on a strong, beautifully modelled hand, and leaning only on two fingers of the same. A slave useful to his master, built to do heavy, mean work, but without the least spark of any higher idea ; a most useful model for artists, a ' Famous Body,' much valued as such in the Academy. The group of the wrestlers is full of life and truth, a faithful representation of antique strength and skill, boldly conceived, and executed with a lively fancy; it transplants us into the midst of the times of the Olympian games, when the body was still healthy, and the physical still harmonised with the intellectual, and bodily strength was considered to belong to the requirements of manliness. One can imagine that these wrestlers are waging their battle amidst the applause of the people, who have come from great distances and many countries. The contest is getting exciting, and the issue in doubt, for both are giants in strength. Their eyes sparkle, their muscles swell, and behold now they fall together on the sand of the arena; a light cloud of dust for a moment conceals them from the spectators. Once again he who was thrown succeeds in rising, but the conqueror has seized him by his shoulder, has planted his sinewy knee in his side, rendered an arm powerless, and has secured his prize, the plaudits of the people. All Greece, young and old, are present; in this consists the reward of the victor. This last movement of the more skilful wrestler, the firm conquering embrace of his defeated antagonist, this the crowning moment of the combat, has been chosen to hand down to posterity in marble.

How the fancy of a genuine artist, excited by the sight of a mutilated statue, can be stimulated to attempt its restoration, is exemplified in the Dancing Faun, where limb has been joined to limb, and a head improvised for the headless statue. This work, found without head and arm, but with limbs of exquisite mould, ascribed to Praxiteles, so infused the old Greek spirit into Michael Angelo, that with his chisel he brought this statue to life again.

The dancing Faun is animated, rude, joyous, full of wild humour, in a word, 'a brave fellow,' full of animal enjoyment. Only the deep lines of Michael Angelo could produce a corresponding half-tipsy, brutish, voluptuous head, in which is clearly seen an extravagant pleasure produced by the sound of the cymbals struck together by his sinewy arms, and by the scabellum, which pressed by the foot gives a squeaking sound. To me the Faun was an old acquaintance, for, several years ago, I had drawn it from a cast; I was therefore much interested in seeing the original. In the same manner I had made acquaintance with the lovely, delicate foot of the Medicean Venus.

The round of the statues is finished, and after admiring those most noble forms, after my delighted eyes have re-'cognised with what wonderful life art can endow stone, I shall occupy myself with the splendours of colour. I have already spoken of Raphael, and of his gradual development; how he, first as a great pupil, and afterwards as a glorious master, revealed his artist soul. The Ascension in the Tribune exhibits these gradations in a remarkable manner, and one extremely valuable to the thinker ; picture by picture brings us nearer to that comprehensive masterpiece, the Fornarina. He commences with a Florentine lady with golden rings on her fingers, a little cross on her neck, and long hair falling down over the shoulders, a good-natured picture full of innocence, drawn in firm lines which almost give the picture the character of a hard carving. Had Raphael not gone beyond this step, he would scarcely have reached the entrance to the Tribune. In the Madonna del Cardellino, the figures are animated with a Raphael-like spirit; the limbs are free, body and features acquire softness; the charming Christ-child leans gracefully on his blooming mother, lovingly turning his head towards his first friend the little John. Raphael is here awakening, but it is still an awakening upon earth, after a lovely, pleasing, but not grand dream. And the other group of the Madonna with the children, already shows

in the deeper features, in the more intense colours, that the
foreshadowings of a higher world are beginning to be disclosed to the great master, though even here the movements are too quick, and too lively, and there is not
as yet the celestial, all-compassing, triumphant repose.
The boy John in the desert indicates this latter period;
in it is shown the triumph of colours, the philosophy of
art, and yet, like the portrait of Pope Julius II., it did not
make a deep impression on me; the reason of this may be,
perhaps, an unfortunate restoration, which gives to the
picture a hard, too-much-varnished appearance, which
also impairs the picture to which we next come, but it
shows him on the high road to that goal kept in view by
the great love of the master.

Enraptured by love, Raphael's large melancholy eyes
rest now on the great object of his love, now on the likeness that he made of her. Love guided his heart and his
hand, love gave the colours, love drew the features, a
kiss of the soul gave the immortal spirit to the created,
and the love of Raphael, the sad but glorious Fornarina,
was preserved for posterity. In this picture Raphael
advanced to perfection; he attained it first by means of
woman, and enters, through this womanly perfection, like
Dante led by Beatrice, into Paradise. The Fornarina is
one of those sad, enrapturing faces whose sweet calm
conquers us; brown, enthusiastic, glowing eyes; almost
sharply-cut, horizontal eyebrows; a broad forehead, which
is low, like all the antique heads; a straight-lined, finely-
shaped nose, with broad strong root, a proof of strong
sterling character; a lovely shaped mouth with softly
swelling underlip, animated by a sad smile; a shining,
transparent complexion imbued with the glow of Rome's
animating sun; full chestnut-brown hair, ornamented with
a light golden wreath of leaves; the heaving bosom retained by the blue velvet bodice, delicately covered with

hazy linen; the fine, and yet vigorous hand, the dazzling arm playing with the soft tiger-skin hanging over the shoulder; all this painted in deep powerful colours, overflowing with tropical glow by the creative mind of Raphael, gives us one of the most perfect pictures; and if the Medicean Venus is the diamond in the Tribune crown, the Fornarina is the ruby which shall shine eternally.

Of my friend, Vandyke, we find two pictures: Giovanni di Montfort, dressed in black, one of those noble physiognomies full of life and truth, a piece of history; and Charles V., on a high Spanish horse in full armour, overshadowed by an eagle holding a laurel-crown. He who would understand the great emperor, on whose possessions the sun never set, who thundered over the ocean the '*plus ultra*,' and who had carved on his buildings by the side of the columns of Hercules, Jove's lightnings as his symbol, must step before this picture, and he will be seized with respect and enthusiasm for this king of men. The 'by the grace of God,' shines powerfully from the commanding, earnest face of the emperor, too great to feel flattered that humanity lies in the dust before him; his large hand leans on the marshal's staff, on a high powerful white horse, which seems conscious of its noble burden; the finest pedestal for a warrior-sovereign. The eagle, chosen as the symbol of the House of Hapsburg, floats over Charles to crown his majestic head with laurel. Vandyke, as I said above, has painted history by perpetuating with his brush the immortal spirits of great men. This he showed in the most perfect manner in this picture of a man who, of all others, was the most difficult to understand in his time. Difficult it must be to paint him who feels himself the first in the world, who recognises none above him but his Creator; who dares with unyielding pride to besiege the Pope in his castle of St. Angelo, who counts the King of France

amongst his prisoners, and who, at the same time, understands the secret that it is not good to wait for twilight,
but who leaves his throne in broad sunshine, to die the
death of mortals.

The vigorous Rubens also pays his tribute to the
Tribune, and presents us with his Hercules between Virtue
and Vice; strong, stout figures, healthy and fresh as everything the jolly Fleming creates ; unfortunately the picture
hangs too high; and Rubens has painted many finer
things, that would more worthily represent him in this
select collection. So, also, with Titian, whose two recum-
bent Venuses, though handsome women, lack the sublime pure spirit of the Goddess. One cannot but admire
the voluptuous body; but these two pictures are rather
unsurpassed and unsurpassable models of the female body,
than the embodiment of any sublime idea. One of these
pictures is said to be the portrait of a mistress of Titian ;
this explains the by no means ideal head. It is a pity for
the worthy representation of the greatness of Titian that
his ‘ Tributary Penny ’ from the gallery in Dresden, the
chief of his works, has not a place here. It shows us
Christ, as none have yet succeeded in doing, combining God
and man in one being, with that seriousness, and beyond
all other conceptions of Christ, with that noble expression, with that mild penetrating look, which analyses the
bad and detects the good, speaking the words : ‘ Render
unto God the things which belong to God, and unto
Cæsar the things which belong to Cæsar,’ and so con-
founding the cunning Pharisees. Titian has in this picture, by two figures, painted a contrast which I have never
since seen. To the right stands the representative of the
purest principles living on earth, the high commanding
form of the Redeemer, with bodily weak, but spiritually
strong features; to the left, the brownish-red, rude, cunning Pharisee, the lowest Jewish type. By means of a

gold coin, the artful Pharisees set a trap, the hands of the
two principal figures approach ; the bony, broad, dark fist
of the bad one holds the glittering coin, and the white
finely-veined right hand of the Redeemer, made only to
break the bread and to heal by miraculous power, is point-
ing to it. He who understands, and has enjoyed the
deep philosophy and truth of this picture, will ever regret
that the creator of this masterpiece is represented in the
Tribune by two naked women.

Correggio is not my friend, he is of excessive sweetness,
his Madonnas and angels smirk too much, the messengers
of heaven dangle and fly about with contorted limbs. He
paints too much the idyll, and so loses strength and expression ; behind his porcelain colours one misses the firm
drawing, it is rose-coloured angels' flesh without bones.
These kind of painters, to which class Carlo Dolce belongs,
have a disagreeable, unnatural impression ; but honour to
whom honour is due ; these artists, also, and perhaps more
than any other, have fortunate moments. Thus we see
here with astonishment and admiration Correggio's head
of John, just cut off, lying on a plate. Is that the same
master, almost mannerist, of ' the Night ? ' One can
scarcely recognise him in the cold, dead-look of John; in
that head, which to look at, produces a shudder, with its
pale cheeks, its blue lips, which, because of the truth they
spoke, were silenced for ever ; in those sublime features,
to which death has given eternal rest and silent victory.
Here is no idyll, no holy shepherds' scene, here is a great
tragedy, a martyrdom represented in a single dead face.
As Correggio gives us, in this little picture, so full of
meaning, the close of the tragedy, so Bernardino Luini
paints the chief actor in it ; the daughter of Herodias,
the originator of that deed, which Correggio represents by
the dead head. The shameless, cold, and yet attractive
girl, brutally laughing, a used-up plaything of the pas-

sions, receives the bloody head of the Baptist to show it
to the uncle. The art of Bernardo Luini had not wandered outside the walls of Milan, but Florence acquired
his daughter of Herodias by an exchange, and placed it in
its cosmopolitan temple of art. Andrea del Sarto is also
worthily represented in the Tribune: his Madonna with
St. Francis and John the Evangelist is an altar-piece of
rare beauty, of southern fancy and vigorous faith. I
learned to appreciate still higher this master, formerly
unknown to me, the Florentine, *par excellence.* A wonderfully hearty picture, full of feeling and colour, is Paul
Veronese's Madonna and Child, whose foot is kissed by
the little John; on the works of this master a soft sober
tint rests like a veil; there is no brightness, but yet a
tenderness like a longing eye veiled by long lashes.

Annibale Caracci's Bacchante, which is a picture full of
life, exhibits a beautifully rounded, soft, back, and a sensual joyous profile. Michael Angelo's Holy Family is
grotesque and hard, without grace and without love, as if
carved and not painted. A few naked figures in the
background of this cold, stony picture, indicate the time
before Christ. Worthy of his master, his pupil Daniele
Volterra represents a Murder of the Innocents, a picture
rich in sturdy limbs and brave movement, and full of a
sort of acrobatic effect. In this picture the master is said
to have assisted his pupil to a great extent. As Volterra
is an exaggerated Michael Angelo, so Parmegianino is an
imitator of Correggio; Parmegianino is represented here
by a Holy Family, an elaborate picture, of sickly sweetness
with golden locks, and rich enamel colours, highly var-
nished. It is difficult to understand how such a picture
could find a place in this exquisite collection. Equally
incomprehensible to me is the reputation enjoyed by a
Madonna of Guido: it appears to me a most tedious, ex-
pressionless picture. Our Durer, and the fresh, fair Lucas

Cranach, have not been forgotten, and a worthy place has been assigned to the art of the old German Empire. In looking at the works of these patriarchs, I always feel respect, which, however, does not enable me to repress an involuntary smile, as at the appearance of an old man that has become too old.

When it happens that a man well placed in society has the courage to assemble in the noble rooms of his palace a company from every rank of society, differing in age, in religion, and in worldly circumstances, regarding only the bond of intellect and good-fellowship, his assembly will, notwithstanding the great differences alluded to, and in defiance of etiquette, be an excellent intermixture, most piquant on account of that imperceptible intellectual fermentation that is going on. There will be discussions that will not degenerate into disputes; they will sharpen each other's wits without heating each other's tempers. There will be no cold formalism in such a society, nor will time hang on their hands. This is the sort of assembly which is gathered in the Tribune. Here genius has collected, and tact has harmonised, Madonnas, Adam and Eve, Aphrodites, Apollos, Bacchantes, Christs, and tipsy Fauns. The same genius has discerned the possibility of bringing together the age of Praxiteles and of Raphael. This genius belonged to the Medici, and to them I owe some of the happiest hours of my life. To see the Tribune is alone worth a journey to Florence, and how I regretted that I had but five days to stay in this city! A room adjacent to the Tribune contained the pictures of the Florentine school, and, without wishing to depreciate its contents, I felt a repellent sensation at passing to the ordinary, after coming from the supernatural.

Before the Grand-Ducal dinner I visited the cabinet in connexion with the Pitti. The animal organs, almost too naturally imitated in wax, and intended to teach the pupils anatomy, compelled me to a hasty retreat, as I should have been very sorry to spoil my excellent appetite.   But I was very well pleased with the somewhat theatrical hall, in which the tools, as well as a finger of Galileo, are preserved for posterity.   A rich flooring in marble, and a cupola ornamented with fresco-pictures, form a good *ensemble*; the busts of the late and present Grand Duke exhibit the founders of this mausoleum.   In the afternoon I visited the Church of St. Spirito, which, built in the shape of a Latin cross, forms a basilica with a cupola in the middle; the arches of the supporting walls of the middle nave rest on Corinthian columns.   This church is by no means one of the finest in Florence, and is unfortunately disfigured by the new Roman taste.

After having visited with my cousin one of those celebrated shops for marble and alabaster, objects of art in which Pisa and Florence are so rich, we drove late in the evening, *pour l'acquit de ma conscience*, to Montui, a little villa which the Grand-Duke bought from a Bonaparte a few years ago. To me these Trianons of princes are not without significance, for in them one discovers the character of the proprietor.   As far as twilight and rain permitted me to distinguish, Montui is situated on a hill rising softly towards a mountain, in a nice little flower-garden, enclosed by friendly orange-trees, and from its position it must offer to the eye a fine and peaceful view. The interior of the house is simple, nay common, but comfortable and clean, an unpretending, private house, full of little souvenirs, which artlessly reveal a happy family life ; but all these details we examined by the light of candles that we had to carry in our own hands ; I find also on a page in my note-book that I wrote against the explanations of my merry cousin, ' *Montui coi lumi.*'

We drove home to enjoy with our amiable minister an agreeable evening. My carriage stopped before the little house on the bank of the Arno; a brightly lighted glass corridor led me, amidst the strains of our popular hymn, to the neat staircase, arranged in English fashion, at the upper end of which the amiable lady of the house met me charmingly and gracefully, and conducted me to a tasteful saloon. A select circle of Florentines and our Austrian garrison were assembled there; graceful toilets, without glaring colours or ridiculous finery, testified to the fact that foreigners have had a favourable influence on Italian habits; but Italy faded before the brilliant appearance, blooming beauty, and fairy charm of the Northern lady, who was dressed in rich moiré antique with tastefully distributed jewels. As the daughter of an English general, born in India, the lovely lady of the house unites in herself English dignity and education, with childlike frankness. A dance was commenced, for which one of our military bands played. A pleasant little supper enjoyed by the side of our amiable hostess enhanced the charm of the evening, and this little festive meeting proved to me that Baron Hugel in his new and honourable position had not lost his talent for arranging everything in the most excellent manner.

It was most interesting to me to see in a room of the Galleria degli Uffizi sketches of the greatest masters, where from a few distinct lines we recognise the spirit of a Perugino and a Leonardo, and where we are taken, as it were, into the studios of the masters of art and obtain an insight into the first conception of their works. How easy and precisely everything is sketched there!—what graceful studies are to be seen there which were the foundation of masterpieces!—how perfectly Raphael throws his figures upon the paper; how vivid is the creative power of a Leonardo! One gets to know the greatest masters, and feels happy in finding them great also in little things. No colours flatter the eye and dazzle it, no light

effect brings the work out; here it is the form only which
is given by red pencil or by pen. I hurried once more to
the dear Tribune, which I left with regret, and then through
various corridors and rooms in the Palazzo Vecchio, the
old residence of the Senate of the Florentine Republic,
and later of the first Medici. The palace is a towerlike
castle in the picturesque forms of the middle age, built
of freestone, darkened by time, and ornamented by a
crown of battlements resting on buttresses. Escutcheons
in the freshest colours shine under them: a high grey
tower rises at the side with a stone garland, which com-
pletes a romantic picture of a time-honoured stronghold,
something between a German town-hall and a Zwing-Uri,
and which answers to the old Florentine history, which
united the peaceful arts with war and commerce.

There is a large hall in the palace ornamented with
frescoes and statues, reminding one of the splendid rooms
of the Ducal Palace in Venice. One of the frescoes represents Boniface VIII. solemnly receiving twelve ministers
of very different sovereigns, from the King of Bohemia
to the Khan of Tartary, all of them born Florentines,
which fact proved the intellectual superiority and the
culture of Florence. The statue of Leo X. is majestically
placed in a centre niche on a throne, raising his right
hand in blessing, and at the same time spiritually threatening. In the square of the building stands a strange
fountain with a boy strangling a fish, cleverly cast in
bronze. Stepping out of the gate on the fine Piazza, you
see, as a sort of giant guarding the building, a Hercules
killing Cacus, by Baccio Bandinelli, and the shepherd
boy, David, by Michel-Angelo.

On the left of the palace is a large and beautiful fountain of Neptune by Donatello, and at its side a bronze
equestrian statue of Cosmo I. To the right one enjoys
the view in the fine atmosphere of the Arcades of the

Uffizi, on which lightly and poetically lean the Loggia dei Lanzi, built in the Lombardo-Gothic style, covering with its wonderful and lofty arches the most exquisite works of art. Originally it was a kind of exchange, later a chief guard-house of the Grand-Ducal lancers, hence its name. At first it was simply ornamented with single monuments of art, only to become at last a kind of museum, in which was brought together, hap-hazard, what has since become a glittering jewel in the art-crown of Florence. The building is light, firm, and original, leaning on either side against the walls of the neighbouring buildings, thereby giving the impression of something accidental, and yet quite unpretending. The imitation of this lucky accident of art arising out of the locality, is not always fortunate, as proved without doubt by the 'Feldherrenhalle' in Münich, which is an unfavourable copy of the Loggia dei Lanzi. What is historical in Florence is unnatural in Münich. Tilly and Wrede cut very sad figures whilst in Florence. This beautiful building is fitted with colossal works of art.

But now to the chief works of the Loggia. Giovanni Bologna furnishes two wonderful groups in marble, the Rape of the Sabines, and the Contest of Hercules with the Centaur, two different sorts of combat, each represented in an equally masterly manner. In the first group a vigorous youth encircles victoriously the powerless struggling virgin, and holds her firmly embraced upwards in the air over the figure of the old father; in the other the god of strength overpowers his mighty antagonist as a fighting and yet a successful conqueror. In these works Giovanni Bologna worthily approaches the antique, which is represented by a fine expressive group in the middle of the Loggia, Ajax carrying the body of Patroclus. Early art has stamped its works with a decided character, and one which is at once intelligible, and so it is in the

case here.   Benvenuto Cellini's Perseus with the Head of
the Medusa, the model of which we have seen in the
Uffizi, is on a large scale, with features, however, too
finely chiselled, showing that the master was a goldsmith,
and his eye used to the minute work of that most precious
metal.   The pedestal of Perseus, ornamented with basso-
rilievos and statues, is extremely tasteful, but also in a
somewhat too elaborate style.   We find as a companion
to Perseus, a Judith by Donatello, also cast in bronze, at
the moment when she strikes off the head of Holofernes,
a kind of votive offering erected by the city *ad exemplum*,
as we are told by an inscription, an embodiment of
heroic patriotism.   Let us hope that the pretty women of
Florence will not deal in the same manner with the Austrian commanders.

We now drove to the Baptistery, which, as at Pisa, is before the cathedral, and whose outside walls, as at Pisa also,
are coated with different coloured marble slabs.   Its chief
ornament is the beautiful worked bronze doors, representing, amidst the richest and most tasteful ornaments, scenes
from the Bible.   Michel-Angelo said these gates were
worthy to be the gates of Paradise.   Some assert that this
Baptistery was once a Roman temple; at any rate, it is
of great antiquity.   After paying one more visit to the
cathedral, we ascended a hill commanding the left bank of
the Arno, and through villas and gardens to the Poggio
Imperiale.

Long, fine cypress-avenues lead to the villa, ornamented
with statues and busts, and which is now used by our
troops as a barrack.   In the building itself there is
nothing extraordinary, but splendid, indeed, is the view
before it, gilded too, as it was, by the finest day.   Calm,
mild and dignified lay the city in serious beauty at our
feet, threaded by the silver Arno, embraced and petted
by its green, smiling valley, filled with the fragrance of

hundreds of the most charming gardens, happy to perfection, situated as it is at the feet of the heights of
Petraja, Montui and Fiesole, and infinitely glorified by
the pure Italian sky. Amongst the many interesting spots
lying before my eyes, I was shown at some distance a
cloister situated on a hill—the Certosa. I am no friend
of novels, but all the more do I like romance, and what
romantic ideas are not conjured up by a Carthusian
retreat! As I had not seen one, I induced my cousin to
visit it notwithstanding the distance. We drove to the foot
of the hill, which we ascended, passing through the vineyards of the cloister, in the greatest heat of noon. The
gate protected by loopholed walls opened, a white little
monk appeared, but only to disappear immediately, and
we entered the lifeless halls undisturbed. Everything was
still and dead; no step but ours echoed through the old
halls. We advanced slowly, and entered a church richly
ornamented with marble, extremely clean and fresh, without worshippers, as if built for spirits; many chapels and
altars surrounded the church, so that all the monks might
be able to read the holy mass at the same time, without
seeing each other; but no bell was heard, nowhere was
the Word of God heard; all seemed to have died out, and
in the middle of the day, it seemed as if there floated
over the cloister a sun-lit night. An uneasy feeling came
over me, and I confess I was glad not to be alone, for
every moment I expected the apparition of a long ghostly
procession of white monks, and ghosts in the clear noon
air, by Heaven! still more awful than in the night, which
seems created for them. Keys rattled, but instead of the
grey vision, a little white monk approached with a grey
beard and a friendly face, and we had, to my satisfaction,
a living guide amongst the dead, still halls.

The obliging monk led us up a long crosswalk, and
we stopped before a locked door, the entrance to the cell

of the master of novices. No sound disturbed the stillness; the door-keeper entered the door and returned with
the news that the monk had slept, and that we could
enter. Each Carthusian has his little house built in the
crosswalk, a little garden with a well, an ante-chamber, a
bedroom containing his couch, a poor table and some
holy pictures on the walls. A hall covered with grape
vine, forms his dwelling, his empire, his world; his meals
he gets through a wicket at the entrance. On certain
days the monks assemble in the refectory, and are only
permitted to speak at certain hours; to walk in the common garden is a holiday enjoyment. What a strong soul
must one have, not to be unsouled here, and find words for
a conversation! Every night a lay-brother knocks at the
doors as a signal to assemble for prayers; if a monk be
wanting, then he is either dead or detained in his couch
by illness.

We entered the picturesque hall, from which is a splendid
view of the rich valley of the Arno. A little below us
was the clean little garden with fresh flowers, a few
orange trees and a clear little basin, in which gold fishes
were quietly swimming, the only living companions of the
lonely monks, a picture of mute, sad melancholy. A tall,
serious young man, picturesquely dressed in white, entered
the hall from his room, astonished at the sight of visitors,
and avoiding speech with them in every possible way;
his lips seemed to be closed by the law. It was the
master of novices. What could have induced him to
choose the solitude of death? Will he not at times
lean on a stone support of his altar, and look down
upon the sunny, laughing, joyous valley, where all is full
of hope and happiness, where the children of earth playfully hasten over blooming fields as free as the birds of
the air; or when, on the evening of St. John, the cupola of
the cathedral is glorified with hundreds of lights, and the

bridges of the Arno are reflected in its silver waves, and the merry songs of the moving crowds are heard in the cloister, will he not at these times be seized with unfathomable woe, by an irresistible longing for a moment of pleasure and joy, for one hour of terrestrial delight? Will his deep eye not be filled with a tear for the past? But his woes have raised the world of separation, and a dead compassionate smile at the fooleries of the world, for which in his heart at times he secretly longs, alone remains to him. Pitiable, very pitiable man! you are proud of your life which is pure, because temptation is removed; you have consecrated your heart to death, and death alone will give it its icy rest. We left the cell, and the novice-master remained; how I should have liked to bring him back to nature, to life! but he is dead to the world, the Carthusian monastery is his tomb, and who knows whether it will not, at last, bring to him, as to many others, rest and peace; blessedness on earth, in which this solitude in his homely cell is a still, serene paradise, of which heaven is only as it were a continuation, to which death is the welcome door-keeper? Our arrival and rank were made known by the little monk, and suddenly life arose. From all sides appeared white figures with their flowing garments and pointed hoods; and we found ourselves in a circle of friendly, nay almost childlike men, disposed almost for fun, to whom the appearance of beings from the world was very pleasant.

We were conducted by them to the simple rooms in which Pius VI. and Pius VII. found a short refuge against the storms of the world. There are some pictures here which commemorate these events. To this cloister, Charles V. retired, April 29, 1536. In the dispensary they gave us a liqueur, which is a hospitable custom; it is made by themselves. Our arrival relaxed their laws for a season, and the poor monks seemed very glad to be permitted to accompany us this fine day down the hill to our carriage.

In the afternoon, the friendly Grand-Duke and his sons took us to the romantic height of Fiesole, an old Etrurian town, a mean-looking mother of beautiful Florence, and to whom the daughter granted alone the odd right to give diplomas of nobility for money, for which reason the noblemen of Fiesole were called Nobili della Strada. The view from the height was beautiful beyond description.

We visited the cathedral only, where at the afternoon service the prettiest girls were assembled, with dark veils and the indispensable fan, a lovely foretaste of Andalusia, which we were soon to visit.

September 1, 1851.

This fine day the Austrian troops entered the beautiful Cascine, where I had the pleasure of seeing them, and admiring their splendid bearing and excellent appearance. Here, for the first time since the Revolution, I again saw the first company of hussars — those splendid, matchless, beautiful hussars that Austria only can show, because Austria alone possesses Hungary; those iron horsemen, full of fire and endurance. This view was very pleasant to me, and my Austrian heart swelled at the sight of the familiar ranks, and under the strains of the great hymns of peace and war. I paid my last visit to-day to the Tribune, from which I parted with regret; may it be my fate to see it at some future time, and to appreciate and enjoy it at leisure. Passing by the fine Piazza del Grand-duca and the main street leading from it, we came to the small place of St. Michael's Church ; a dark warehouse-like building in Italian-Gothic style, with a fine bronze statue representing St. Matthew. There was a sort of fair taking place at this spot, and a bustling, lively crowd was moving to and fro and into the little church. To the honour of the Florentines it must be said there was

not that deafening, confused, Punch-like hubbub of the
Via Toledo, but the whole had a more agreeable appearance, I might almost say it was a piece of South German
street-life. Naples is rude and noisy, whilst in Florence
the male sex are more phlegmatic and the women more
polite; could one over-awe the people by good manners it
might be pleasant to live amongst them, which would be
less the case in the city of Parthenope, where, from the
highest to the lowest, all are coarse and noisy, and only
nature, which is there splendid beyond all things, can
compensate for these defects. Even the type of the features may be called handsome in Florence, especially
amongst the fair sex, whilst in Naples the women are ugly
and mean. We entered the church San-Michele in Orto,
which has beautiful windows, and a tabernacle-like little
chapel with fine ornaments in stone, which latter might
be very well called *pietra dura*. The church owes its
square form to its former destination, for it was a corn-
warehouse, which, in honour of an image of the Madonna,
was transformed into a church in 1337. Passing the
Palazzo Ricardo, celebrated for its grand architecture, we
came to the Grand-Ducal stables to change our horses
there for a drive to the far Pratolino. I availed myself of
the time to try in the yard a splendid little Arabian belonging to my cousin, an exercise doubly agreeable and
pleasant after a sea-voyage. Pratolino, which is an estate
of the Grand-Duke, is situated to the right behind Fiesole,
in a somewhat bare, mountainous country; a large and
by no means fine English garden without any freshness,
with an insignificant house.

Tired and low-spirited, I returned to the Pitti to take
the last dinner in Florence, and as the railway brought
me to, so it carried me away from, the company of my dear
relations and this much-endeared city, this mild valley of
peace. I felt quite sad, for, for a long time, I had not passed

so many pleasant hours full of the highest and noblest
enjoyment, devoted to nature and art. Here I was introduced to the home of art: I had opened to me the productions of the most noble minds; I saw their progress,
their beginning, and their culmination.

My parting with Florence filled me with sadness. I
was parting from a high-souled, beautiful, intellectual
woman. Whilst Naples appeared to me only as a sensual
beauty, a voluptuously charming woman offering herself
for momentary enjoyment, and had only to be wooed to
enjoy on her bosom joyous hours; Florence has to be
understood in order to worship her, and it is at her feet
that one comprehends the present by the past. I looked
many times from the window, but the city with its cupolas
disappeared only too soon.

The separation from my dear relatives in Pisa was hard.
They had made my sojourn so agreeable to me, and I
owed them so many thanks for all their friendliness and
brotherly love during my short stay amongst them. How
would I have liked to follow them to Marlia! But to the
frigate, the times and seasons are appointed, and we follow
the law. We arrived in the midst of darkness at Leghorn,
went on board the 'Novara,' which weighed anchor on
Sept. 2, 1851.

'To Spain!' What a beautiful idea, sounding like
golden melody to the delighted heart! And yet how
strangely constituted is the mind of man! I felt rather
sad and homesick, and the pleasure of travel was overcast
for a time; body and mind were out of tune, but Spain
was to be my cure, and heal me with its beautiful balm.

II.

ANDALUSIA AND GRANADA.

1851

ANDALUSIA AND GRANADA.

The voyage from Leghorn to Spain lasted from the 1st to the 12th of September. At its commencement we were detained by contrary winds, but after we left Cape Palos we sailed with fabulous speed, so as once to make twelve knots an hour.

After we had lost sight of Elba we still continued to see for some time the sea-surrounded cradle of Napoleon with its rough hills, its distant capital, Bastia, glittering from afar, and at a still greater distance, the mountainous scenery of that land which formed the stage of that too active man; France appeared only for a moment, however.

The next sight worth attention was the majestic head of Gibraltar rising from the waves; one of the mighty columns of Hercules on which that physically strong but intellectually weaker god engraved the premature *'ne plus ultra.'* A solitary rock ascending towards heaven, the most imposing sentinel in the world between two much frequented seas. It did not seem like a creation of nature, but rather a monument which a god and that, too, the god of strength, had erected: now a colossus rising from the sea, again as a beast of prey basking in the tropical sunshine, then as a pointed pyramid touching the clouds, slender and yet defying the storms of thousands of years; always changing, and yet a picture of rest and power. Round the foot of the grey mysterious rock runs the most frequented road of the whole earth, the silver band on which the Phœnicians with their small light

barks ventured on the unknown roaring ocean, and on
which now, after thousands of years, the sons of Albion cut
the waves, with their steamers swift as arrows, as if it were
mere play, or a promenade, and the Mediterranean a
pleasant lake.

Opposite the Straits I could discern a new continent,
the third in the course of one year, the glowing hot Africa,
with its Ceuta, the by no means imposing twin-brother
of Gibraltar. It is pleasant to note in one's journal
another continent, though only seen from the sea; and I
saw also that we must see for ourselves to rectify our ideas;
for two of my fanciful pictures underwent a change when
I saw them with the bodily eye: the coast of Africa and
the Straits of Gibraltar. My fancy had clad the former in
the yellow monotony of the sandy desert, with mountains
and blue, lively tints; the latter I had imagined so wide
that the coasts of Africa could only be seen in clear weather;
and now, notwithstanding the not very clear day, I saw the
lines of both coasts distinctly.

The favourable wind carried us through the Straits, and
the mighty foaming ocean lay before us. Whether it was
imagination or reality I don't know, but it appeared to me
that the waves were higher and more boisterous, and their
colour clearer. To my delighted eye there was no longer
a lake, but a boundless ocean reaching to the new world;
and I enjoyed the sailor's happiness at having passed the
columns of Hercules. We sailed fast along the Spanish
coast, Tarifa appeared; we passed through Nelson's bloody
field of honour, the waters of Trafalgar, from which
Britannia, refreshed by French and Spanish blood, rose
terribly, the sovereign-queen of the sea. At last, on a
wonderful afternoon, arose a brilliant white city with its
towers and turrets like a *fata morgana* on the green misty
sea, a second Venice, a ghostly dream of the old city of
the Doges. Cadiz unfolded before our looks, whitewashed

and clean, and built with all neatness; standing out from the sea on a neck of land, it first appears imposing to the stranger, then it has a friendly and inviting air without losing in the least its dignity.

Several gunshots at last brought the pilot on deck, over an agitated sea. Next day, thanks to our careful captain, we successfully made the rather difficult entrance, and cast anchor in Spanish ground at about 3 o'clock p.m., on the 12th of September. The port was crowded with merchantmen, behind which we saw men-of-war. Boats were coming to and fro, and there was plenty of life moving in the roadstead.

We landed at the Puerta del Mar, surrounded by black-eyed, brown men with slim figures, and marked, noble features, with a small plate-like velvet hat on their black, curly heads, and embroidered leather gaiters buttoned round their supple legs. Passing some martial looking but not well-dressed guards, we entered within the city walls and found ourselves in Spain's old commercial city, into which once flowed the poisonous gold of America. The gold is gone, and with it the old greatness, and though the city has now the stamp of wealth it does not possess even a single monument of olden times. Long narrow streets, with excellently whitewashed houses, with numberless green latticed balconies on which can be seen flowers, parrots, and pretty women, cross the city in endless, not always regular, lines; many booths covering the lower part of the houses, line in a picturesque manner the badly-paved streets, in which carriages are a rarity, whilst the people move on foot, on horseback, or on mules. Wherever the South spreads its soft arms, traffic goes on beneath God's free heaven. So it is in Spain, but not with the coarse noisiness that it does at the foot of Vesuvius, for quietness and a graceful dignity belong here equally to the peasant and the grandee. But how is it possible to describe the

Spanish women? They are dressed generally in that colour
best suited to bring out the charms of the fair sex, in black.
The veil falls delicately on the shoulders, gracefully uniting
with the mantilla, which is attached to the back part of the
head; the ever-busy fan moves easily and gracefully in
the small hand; old and young are dressed alike and the
dark colour becomes both well.   The old ones are mostly
fat and too much rounded, the young ones delicate and
light, with dark glowing eyes, splendid hair, ivory skin
and fine neat limbs; yet I found the much-praised Spanish
foot too short, broad, and straight.   The Spaniard is *petite*,
yet full of dignity and grace in all her movements; she
does not show the frivolity of the women of other countries, and she understands how to combine seriousness with
playfulness.   The Spaniard does not know the word
'meanness,' but for all that he knows well enough what
pride is.

Southern street-life with its freedom and with its Spanish
peculiarities here reigns everywhere, offering the stranger
hundreds of interesting studies.   As in Italy, rich fruits
are sold in the streets, so here; and the popular vehicles are
drawn by the donkey and the strong mule.   One sees the
handsomest Murillo-like children covered with filth, and
three objects in the motley scene amused me especially:
devout men with immeasurably long hats which might
well serve as a boat for children; negroes as shoeblacks,
showing the frequent intercourse with America; and bob-
tailed cats, perhaps fated to end as a hare-substitute in the
much-praised *olla podrida*.

Churches are the first thing one must visit in a foreign
city: we saw the old and the new cathedral.   The former
is an imposing work, massively built of yellow stones in
the Roman style; it was the first instance we met with of
the arrangement of the Spanish church differing essentially
from ours.   Immediately in front of the chief entrance the

choir forms a square surrounded by stone walls, open only towards the chief altar, and separated at the open side from the rest of the church by a grating. In a side room we were shown a Mary Magdalene of Murillo. No full flesh, no dazzling bosom here delights the senses; it is not a voluptuous Magdalene who, leaning over the Bible in a state of ecstasy, is being pleasantly enlightened; no, this is Mary crushed, penitent, and pining away. Her arms are fleshless; her thin face pale and yellow. When repentance seized the soul the delights of youth fled; the sanctity of the anchorite possessed the tormented heart. The death of the flesh is vividly expressed in the face and body by dark, corpse-like colours, still the past speaks out of those eyes, out of her very position absorbed as she is in prayer; the stormy times of youth are still visible, which must yet be atoned for. This Magdalene is tired of her sins and exhausted by prayers, the body is dying away, and the spirit, purified by severe torturing trials, struggles to return to its Creator. I saw here the first Magdalene who had really sinned, and had ceased to sin knowingly; whilst all the others, that of Correggio especially, were always too sweet and too handsome to sin with energy, and still too pretty, too choice in their positions, to produce the conviction that they would not sin any more.

The old cathedral is too small and too mean-looking for a city once so great and so rich as Cadiz; but there is a rare sight to be seen in this small church—the absorption in prayer of the Spanish women. Neither kneeling nor sitting on the bare marble floor, wrapped up in devotion and in their black garments, the black-veiled head slightly bent forward, and gently fanning themselves, these foreshortened, dark figures, with their earnest, handsome features, offer a charming picture of deep devotion, blended delightfully with unconscious coquetry. My travels taught me that the Spanish women should be seen in the church and at a bull-fight to become acquainted with that wonderfully magnetic power which they exercise over us.

Cadiz has too much the stamp of a commercial city to realise to the eye pictures of Spanish life in their rich glow and colour; but to-morrow we go to Seville, into the heart of hot Andalusia.

September 13, 1851.

As the steamer does not start until 11 o'clock, we promenaded through the lively city, and visited at the hottest time of the day the *salon de Christina*, a favourite walk on a sea-bastion. These promenades, usually called alamedas, are a principal charm of Spanish life, and are always found, as also an arena for the Corridas, even in the smallest towns. But the chief hour for the promenade is in the evening: when the golden sun sinks into the sea and the cooling breeze fans the gently-undulating purple waves, then the charming daughters of Spain come out from the gardens of their clean, cool houses, decorated with orange and oleander, and saunter about the dark avenues, talking playfully, leaning on the arm of their slender, handsome adorers, with a rustling fan in the busy hand. Towards 11 o'clock we went on board the 'Rapido,' a small steamer plying between here and Seville. The sea was somewhat agitated, and it was amusing to observe the rocking of the many boats around our steamer, and the figures that crowded our ship. Now a stout matron had to be lifted on board with the utmost care, floating between air and water with a terrible liability to an accident; now came a lady, pale and sighing, who in the boat itself had already passed through the preliminary evils of the coming voyage; some arrivals were baptised by the foaming salt water. And not only was the human race represented, but the animal also; a splendidly coloured American bird awaited its fate, many domestic animals were miserably kept in close bondage, and some fine

little silky poodles from Havanna were gently lifted on
board in a basket. I began to look out for a snug place
to observe quietly the world of passengers that assembled on our ship to make the voyage with us on
the Guadalquiver. A tall, slender lady with dark eyes,
shining black hair, a lace veil thrown lightly back over
her head, in a rich blue satin dress, ornamented with gold
jewelry, and a Chinese fan in her hand, moved triumphantly up and down, whilst some fine Spanish dandies
with delicate moustachios and whiskers, and little sticks
flourishing in their effeminate hands buzzed around her.
Conscious of the adoration paid to her as the queen of
the day, she took possession, with grace and dignity, of the
principal place on deck, and the little gentlemen surrounded her like a goddess, proud to be drawn within the
circle of her sparkling eyes. At first we took this rather
striking group for a company of actors; and heard only
later, to our great astonishment, that the lady in blue was
a duchess, and the Duchess of Medina Celi, one of the
first ladies of the empire, who with her husband was
taking a trip to Seville. In San Lucar, a little town on
the Guadalquiver, her mother and very handsome sister
joined the travellers. Some stout ladies also joined, who
suffered later from sea-sickness. Several priests in lay
dress and an endless number of children, full of noise and
jokes, combined to overcrowd the small space. The
anchor was weighed, and the vessel began a little dance
along the level coast; the elegant gentlemen became pale
and still, and absorbed in sad meditations over the
rising and falling of the waves; the stout ladies stretched
themselves on the seats of the cabin in the most comical
positions; but the Duchess kept up bravely, and we enjoyed our little breakfast amazingly in spite of the sighing
and groaning of our neighbours. We were much taken
with a fine, pale Spanish lady, who with closed eyes had

arranged herself picturesquely and immovably, half sitting, half lying on a chair, permitting us leisurely to examine her wonderful white face and her beautifully rounded figure; as she always kept this passive position we called her the handsome corpse. At her side, and out of their basket, those silky poodles wagged their tails —protectors of the black-dressed figure.

Suddenly we shipped a sea, and one of the poor dandies got wet, and looked sadly at his soaked pantaloons; but the terrors of the sea were soon passed; Cadiz disappeared from our eyes, and we entered the Guadalquiver, from the shores of which a cluster of the most splendid palms promised peace. At the mouth of the river the shore of the sea had that appearance which I had attributed in my mind to the coast of Africa; it was level, yellow and monotonous, and ornamented only with a single green oasis and dazzling white roofless houses.

One soon comes to San Lucar, a little town immediately on the shore, celebrated for its coolness in the hot months of the Spanish summer, and visited by the rich of the country like Hietzing or Ischl, and considered as a kind of watering-place.

Besides the relatives of our amiable duchess, whose husband, as I heard afterwards, is related to me in some kind of manner, as the Medina Celis owe their existence to an amour of a Spanish Hapsburg, our poor ship was still further crammed at this station by a crowd of passengers; and, tormented with the heat, the noise, and the want of space, we commenced our voyage on the mighty stream, the old artery of hot Andalusia, which advantageously connected with the sea Seville, the capital of the Moors, and admitted large merchant ships to the very gates of the city. Once more was I disappointed in my too ready fancies, according to which the Guadalquiver ought to have been the ideal of southern loveliness; whilst the

reality reminded me of the insipid country of the Magyars.
Bare, endless, level, brown shores without a tree or a shrub,
peopled by bustards and ducks, partly by herds of cattle,
over which one now and then sees men on horseback, with the little round velvet hat and the poncho,
a kind of cloak in the shape of a square piece of cloth
with a hole in the middle for the head, give a picture of
melancholy monotony which unnerves one's spirit. If
this country could be watered by this brown river, it
might be prepared for splendid crops, like most parts of
Hungary. But the Andalusian only works for the neces-
sities of life ; God throws into his lap what he requires for
the day, and more than this his merry light-mindedness does
not require ; he eats figs and grapes, dances his bolero, and
feeds his mind with his passionate interest in the Corrida
de Toros. It was only at the close of this hot ride, when
one began to feel the mildness of evening, bringing with
it its beneficial coolness, that we perceived traces of
culture and vegetation. Magnificent dense orange-groves
with wonderful thick trees crowded to the very water's
edge, refreshing the eye with their dark foliage; green
meadow plots were interspersed between them. A man
on horseback, in the national costume, with the rich
spencer and the beautifully embroidered gaiters, seated no
the high saddle, on a proud horse bridled in the old
Spanish manner, was riding along the shore. The high
mountains of the Sierra Nevada appeared far off; life was
everywhere; the country became richer, and as the river
turned snake-like, expectation was strained to its highest
pitch, for we felt that we were approaching the end of our
voyage. Suddenly out of the fresh green the world-famed,
tradition-rich cathedral of Seville arose, and the excla-
mation, ' Quien no ha visto Sevilla, no ha visto maravilla,'
expressed my heartfelt enthusiasm. Another turn of the
river, and the city was unfolded before our eyes; to the

right, the large Gothic cathedral with its splendidly winding
Giralda, overtowering all houses and palaces; around it,
the historical city of Moorish and Spanish glory, the city
of the sword and the guitar, the city of battle and of
flowers; on the shore, the Delicias, the favourite promenade
of the handsome ardent Andalusians; the palace of St.
Telmo, newly and splendidly restored by the Duke of
Montpensier, richly ornamented with sparkling lilies; and
a strong tower, in which was kept the first gold which
Columbus brought from America.

The nearly finished, finely arched bridge of Queen
Isabella spanned the river; to the left, the Triana, the
city of the gipsies and bandits, renowned for its crimes
and mysteries; and near it, that cold end of all striving
and doing, a great cemetery with large cypresses, and the
silent symbol of the palms.

The steamer stopped between the Torro del Ore and the
Palace St. Telmo. At the end of the Delicias we came
into the city, and at its gate a few coins saved us from
the troublesome examination of the custom-house officers.
The moon stood high, and shed her beams mysteriously
over the narrow streets, flooding with her romantic light
the old gates, the rich cornices and finely-carved ornaments of the splendid old cathedral.

Passing by the mean-looking house of the barber of
Seville, whose existence in former days the cicerone
warranted, we came to the Place of the Constitution, or
the Ajuntamiento, with the fine richly-ornamented building of this name, which corresponds to our honest
German ‘Rath-haus,’ and from there to our hotel, Fonda
d’Europa, a Spanish building in the genuine sense of the
word, with the renowned yard, the light arcades, the wide
staircase with rich ceiling, and small cool rooms, whose
brick floors and windows are covered with finely-made
straw mats, and from which one steps on the small, lovely

balcony, around which play the sounds of the lute and the nightingale, and the fragrance of myrtle and jasmine; and from which one looks on the narrow picturesque street, where from hundreds of balconies handsome women show themselves with a coquettish grace, half concealed by curtains and flowers.

One of my chief amusements in hotels is to look at the pictures on the walls. Thanks to the feeling for art of these advanced modern times, one finds now all over Europe, and even in other continents, the history of the pious Geneviève, the exploits of the bold Tell, and the transmarine love-adventures of Paul and Virginia, pictorially represented. Here I found on the white walls of my little room, *horribile dictu*! the 'Wandering Jew,' not only with French, but also with Spanish explanations. But the poison of France has extended to this golden peninsula, which, like the glittering, ever-moving drops of mercury, changes the precious metal into a grey, dull mass. I for my part have not read the 'Wandering Jew,' and shall not do so, as I do not see the good of such useless and tormenting books; they neither amuse nor instruct, but cause only a momentary excitement, and relax both the heart and soul; but they are the fashion! and the Spanish hotel grandees must needs prove to the travellers that in this branch of modern literature they are not behind the age. Good luck to you! Eugène Sue will store your souls with hatred to the clergy.

The commissioner told us that there would be a bull-fight to-morrow—the greatest and most remarkable national festivity of the Spaniards—an announcement that filled me with delight. In the charming Patio we took a comfortable supper, and in the cool green arcades, softly illuminated by the moon, I learned how to appreciate the Moresco-Spanish architecture. I say Moresco-Spanish, for in this style many houses of Seville are built, and spring like

our Fonda, either from the poetic days of the Moors, or
are at least good imitations of that airy, skilful architecture, at least in form, if not in the richness of ornament. With their charming interior yards they shade
you against the oppressive heat of the day, and offer to
the inmate a seclusion where he may indulge his tastes
and enjoy his rest undisturbed. Do you wish, on the
contrary, to enjoy the animated life of the streets, you
step either on the small balconies of the out-walls, or
you open the door or curtain of the front hall of the
Patio, and leave only the neat iron railing separating the
house from the street closed. Very interesting it is for
promenaders to look stealthily through these iron railings
into the charming mysteries of the house. Here one sees
lofty arches with pure marble flooring, little fountains
throwing their water into finely-carved basins, blooming orange trees and oleander, and amidst them the
most delightful company, the most handsome women:
illumined by elegant lamps in the day-time, from the
mysterious twilight kept up on account of the heat, for
the Patio is the proper sitting-room of the serious
Spaniard, a blossom from the East; it is the centre
equally of the royal palace and the most simple house.
Yet the dwellings of the Spaniards are to be preferred
to those of the Easterns, for these little balconies are
prohibited by the jealousy and seclusion of Arab life. I
stepped on mine, a fragrant cigarette in my mouth, and
was delighted by the pure splendid sky, and looked down
into the life of the narrow street.

It was very early in the morning when we again assembled in the colonnade of our hotel, round a well-
furnished table; the morning was fine, the air pure, and
we enjoyed our breakfast under the light arcades opening
out upon the pretty yard, which industrious hands had
embellished with orange, lemon, and other southern trees.

The walls of the houses protected us against the glowing
arrows of the southern sun; there was an agreeable coolness in the Moorish walks. Under the bushy fruit-trees
sat, as in the times of the Caliphs, falcons of every size,
anxiously examining with their piercing eyes the objects
around.

We had entered the old Moorish city quietly and unknown, yet a dull rumour had already spread that some
Northern grandee had made a pilgrimage to the more
remarkable places of ancient history. Some had the
inkling of a *Hermano del Emperador*, others believed
old England had sent one of her scions to the splendid
Peninsula. Our landlord, also, did not yet know exactly
what to make of us, but he seemed to suppose that we had
brought with us the appetite of the Northern inhabitants
of the globe, for in spite of the earliness of the morning,
abundance of meat and many other things were on the
table, a proof that he did not hesitate to class us amongst
the carnivorous. We all did honour to that classification.
Coffee was served with goats'-milk at the end of the well-
furnished breakfast. From this low estimate of the
golden beverage, we concluded that our landlord, a Pied-
montese, in spite of the smartness of his nation, had not
yet guessed our Viennese origin. After breakfast the
people in the house proposed to visit the Giralda, the
Moorish tower of the cathedral of Seville. The way to the
cathedral is not long; one has to pass over the Plaza de la
Constitucion, and we there took a closer view of the Ajuntamiento palace. It is of the seventeenth century, and
embellished with the finest ornaments; even its columns are
covered with bass-reliefs and arabesques, but like so many
other magnificent works of the architecture of past times,
it remains unfinished, and it seems also that its preservation is not much cared for. The walls and columns are
of sandstone, and have the character of the Cinquecento

style, and are still handsome, but on the eve of the over-
ornamented and degenerate time.   Here I came across
some family recollections, recollections of a time when
Spain, under the wings of the double-eagle, was on the
highest pinnacle of power, and the greatest empire of the
world; days when a mighty Hapsburger spoke the words
plus ultra, and opened for future times a road through the
columns of Hercules.   The eagle and rock-columns, with
this sublime motto, ornamented the walls of the Ajuntamiento.   Excellent-looking soldiers formed the guard.
From this place we had to pass through a short lane over
the most wretched pavement, for which the cities of Spain
are distinguished, to come to the cathedral, which is the
crown of the city, and one of the finest buildings of our
ancestors.   Here one finds the earnest and mystical Gothic
halls, productions of a period deeply imbued with faith.
Hundreds of ornaments cleverly and gracefully interlaced; narrow arches, which like the clasps of a crown,
span from one dental to another; high, painted windows,
in pointed arches, which permit the glaring light of the day
only to enter softened and subdued into the wide sacred
halls; all these combine to complete the impression.
Here you see the peculiar elliptical arch of the Moors
with the richness of ornament which, almost like fine
laced patterns, embellishes the works of these Arab masters
in a light and transparent manner.   The little double-
arches, and the small marble columns of the Giralda show
that they were almost perfected under the dominion of
Mohammed.

The chief entrance is not at the principal façade of the
cathedral, which has two splendid gates, ornamented with
small, finely-shaped projections, similar to those at St.
Stephen's, but it is at the façade on the left side.   Before it is
a wide yard, which is surrounded on three sides by buildings
of the Moorish time, on the fourth by a more modern

church connected with the cathedral from the interior; the entrance-gate of this yard is Moorish, and distinguished by its fine vaulting. To the right and the left of the heathenish ornaments, four Christian statues stand on Gothic projections under small stone canopies; they are two apostles, the God-mother, and the angel of the Annunciation. The yard, planted with fine orange-trees and with a marble basin in the middle, into which the cool water plays, shows that the Moors had changed the cathedral into a mosque, and the *Patio de los Naranjos* reminds us of the places before the mosques, as I saw them last year at Smyrna. It is a fine custom of the Mohammedans to offer to the faithful, before the gates of the houses of God, the refreshment of shade and water. We ought to have mounted the Giralda first, but I could not forbear entering the interior of the church at once. Five naves rise to an incredible height, and simple Gothic columns gracefully support the imposing dome. In the middle of the church rise the chief altar and choir, both connected by a passage enclosed by iron rails. Towards the chief altar the choir is separated from the rest of the church by an iron railing, and walls reaching up to the half of the building, so that, as in the new cathedral of Cadiz, it conceals the high altar from the chief entrance. The outer sides of the choir are ornamented by small halls and many altars standing behind railings, richly embellished with marble in the Cinquecento style ; the inside of the choir is filled with long rows of seats for the clergy, and over them rise on both sides the organs. It was just the time of the Hora. The high altar is raised several steps and separated also from the church on three sides by walls, whilst the fourth towards the choir is closed by a richly-ornamented golden railing. The outer walls which surround the altar are splendidly ornamented with images of saints close together, mounted on Gothic projections

overhung with canopies. The ceiling of the altar and the
space between it and the choir is embellished with the
finest ornaments, quite new to me, and which reminded me
of honeycombs. The vaulting between altar and choir is
higher than the rest, and under it are small painted
windows, which bring out the boldness of the architecture. The wall behind the altar is ornamented with
pictures, and here hung a large red curtain covering
the tomb of my patron, the holy Ferdinand. I had
forgotten, if I ever knew, that this bold king was buried
in Seville, therefore it made a great impression upon me,
when the servant told me, on a sudden, that here rest the
remains of him after whom I was christened, from whom
I have the good luck to descend, and who, by the Church,
has been appointed my chief representative at the throne
of God.

The coffin with the red cloth stands in the middle; to
the right and the left are high niches, in each of which
stands, under a velvet canopy, a coffin ornamented with
golden cover, crown, and sceptre. Here repose two children of Ferdinand the saint—Alphonso the wise, and his
sister. It was strange to see these coffins standing out, as
if they had been exhibited to the eyes of the people only
yesterday, and yet showing traces of great age. It was an
imposing picture of old Christian royalty. The Saint and
his children are united in that house of God which they
wrested from the Moors, and selected for themselves as a
place of rest; the tombs are full of dignity and sanctity,
not like those monuments of a sensual, mythological
kind, without sign of faith or devotion, such as the proud
Medici have erected for themselves, and such as you find
frequently in Italy, where the conceited race believes that
the dignity of religion may be replaced by a little sculpture,
and by bombastic inscriptions. Here one stands by the
graves of a holy family, in which simplicity and grandeur

humble themselves beneath the sign of the cross. On the railing which separates the chapel from the church, is represented the holy king on horseback, and before him the Moorish prince kneeling and presenting the keys of the city to the conqueror. The cathedral is still further ornamented with a number of chapels; in one of which we were shown the finely-worked marble tomb of a Bishop Cervantes, of the same family as the author of 'Don Quixote.' Before the chief entrance is the grave of Fernando Columbus, the son of the discoverer, who is said to have made himself famous in Spain as an admiral. There are still two Murillos in this cathedral: an Ecstacy of St. Francis, and a Guardian-angel. The first is a truly beautiful picture, full of deep feeling; the Saint kneeling in his brown cowl has his eyes raised towards heaven, before him floats the Christ-child blessing him, surrounded by clouds, in which is a circle of angels. The figure of the divine Child appears to me somewhat affected, as is sometimes the case with Murillo. The little angels, also, did not please me; they are flying, falling, and climbing; I do not admire these gymnastics in such pictures, they are like those which Correggio delights in to excess. But the figure of the holy Francis is exquisitely beautiful. In his features and carriage are expressed so much warmth and devotional depth, that it is a saint divinely enlightened whom we see before us. I saw nothing very sublime in the Guardian-angel. Murillo abounds in the greatest contrasts, not only in different pictures, but often in one and the same work. The beautiful, the noble, and the refined, may be found by the side of the rustic-like, low, sweet Madonnas and mean Christ-children.

Especially noticeable are the chapels, which are arranged to the right and left of the side doors, for their great richness in Gothic ornament.

The Giralda is mounted from the back of the tower; the

greatest part of the building is, as I said before, Moorish, and rich in ornaments, marble columns, and burnt glazed tiles. The upper part was built by the Christian kings, if not entirely, yet almost entirely in the same style. Through the dwelling of the warder one comes upon the interior. As at St. Mark's tower in Venice, there are no steps, but slanting brickwalks to the top. The Giralda is the highest building in Spain. From its uppermost gallery one enjoys a wide view all around ; immediately underneath extends the wide, flat, terrace-like roof of the cathedral with its different heights, slantings and turrets, surrounded with a Gothic balustrade. One looks into the green *Patio de los Naranjos* with its Moorish charm, and so enjoys an insight into the life of the Gothic-Spanish times, into the poetical deeds of the Moors, and the proud grandeur of their conquerors.

One can conceive a whole poem in the court on which we looked, and of which the cathedral and its surroundings would furnish in the highest degree the romantic elements. From this gallery you see the broad stream of the Guadalquiver, which divides the masses of houses. The part beyond the river is called Triana, renowned in Spanish popular life by the many gipsies and smugglers living there. An iron bridge leads to it, which is not yet quite finished. The city which extends on this side of the river is of considerable extent, but according to Moorish fashion the streets are so narrow that one can see from above only a few marked lines, whilst all the rest resembles a wide confusion of houses. A large, fine palace in the style of the last century is a notable object; its wide courts, its splendid façade, and its rich ornaments are very striking. One would think that this building, embellished with so much architectural adornment, was the palace of the sovereign. Charles III., who built it as well as the gigantic palaces of Naples, was desirous either to open to the city of the Moors a new source of gain, or he used utility as a mere pretext for satisfying his noble passion for building. It is Seville's celebrated cigar-manufactory which we so much admired.

During my sojourn in Seville I frequently asked whether this building had not originally been intended for a monastery or palace, but I was always assured that it had been built for the purpose of a manufactory. Close by is a large garden, intersected by avenues, in the midst of which is raised a strange many-coloured palace. It belongs in its principal arrangement to the cinque-cento style, as is proved by its rich columns and the variety of its tasteful ornaments, but still this romantic building is haunted by the old poetry of the Moors; it belongs to the exiled son of the French king, who lives here with his Spanish consort. But what is it which glitters there in gold and rich butterfly colours? What is this lofty romantic building whose shining gable attracts the curious eye? It is the Alcazar, it is the fairy residence of the old Moorish kings, with its motley dreams and its magical charm. To the left of the Alcazar a yellow painted, mean-looking gable of a house is seen, which however has become an object of interest to the lovers of art, for in this house Murillo breathed his last. That large round building on the opposite side, not far from the Guadalquiver, is of particular interest to strangers; here we shall in the course of the day look upon the greatest curiosity of Spain; for it is the Arena, in which the world-famed bull-fights take place. With what an ardent desire did I await the hour in which I was to see one of the few festivities which are handed down to this enervated century from the old chivalrous times! We were also shown a wide space on which will take place to-morrow an act which in Spain is only too frequently necessary; it is the place of execution, on which early to-morrow morning a murderer will be executed by a quick justice, who committed his last crime only the day before yesterday. This act is performed in Spain in a peculiar manner: the murderer is strangled by an iron ring with a vice behind, which is placed round the criminal's neck. Our guide told us that an execution takes place every month.

The bells of the churches commenced a peculiar song, which warned us that high mass had commenced. The ringing of the bells in Spain differs from what it is with us. Young people hang on the ropes and swing themselves over the stone ground, and by this means they bring the bell into motion. We entered the cathedral where the priests had just prepared for the holy offering. We took our seats near the railing before the choir; between us and the high altar knelt a graceful group of Spanish ladies with their black veils and mantillas. The fan, the banner of the belles, was here, in the house of God, in incessant motion; its buzzing and rattling was heard just as in the theatre, and yet it has nothing offensive even to ears that are not used to it. The fan, reserved in other countries for coquetry, is managed here with dignity and grace, and is the result of a real necessity in this warm climate. Several priests with wing-like surplices waved through the wide space of the dome. In the procession of the officiators was a master of ceremonies, in old Spanish costume, with a black cloak and a little pigtail. This prolongation of the hair, once common, has become in our times a rarity. High mass commenced behind the gilded grating, now and then the organ above our heads supported the song of the priests; the epistle and gospel were read loudly but unintelligibly from high pulpit-like desks, at the two ends of the golden railings, and the moment approached, so sublime for faithful Christians. The touching strains of the organ were heard throughout the wide space; the heads of the devoted worshippers bent down at the sound of the bell; the large column of incense rose like a fragrant cloud from the high steps of the altar and greeted the great offering, which brought the Lord of the world, the Son of God, in our midst. It was one of those sublime, solemn, deep-felt moments that exist only for the true Catholic, and exalt men to adoration.

When the mass was finished, we visited the Alcazar. It is the work of a believing people, but who had not been enlightened by the true light. That propensity for sensual enjoyment, which forms such a great part in the life of the Mohammedan, shows itself pre-eminently in this work.

One is astonished, one admires, and yet fancy only is excited, for this work of art lacks a higher earnestness. The chief entrance to the palace is through a light picturesque façade covered with a net of ornament in the most brilliant colours, a wreath of finely interwoven arabesque, and other tasteful ornaments. Graceful little columns, and beautifully curved arches support the vaulted roof, which slightly projects, after the Eastern mode.

As the carpet of the oriental is interwoven with gold and silver threads, so are the external walls of his house; light, warm, and full of art is this building, like the poetical and charmful spirit of its founders.

Over the gate of the outer court, in front of the chief building, is a verse of the Koran. We entered a wide space through the garden before us, in which lay a green sea of various plants between dense and closely-clipped walls of luxuriant orange trees. On the one side the garden was closed by a high wall with arcades, statues and grottoes. Shells and stones formed mosaic-like ornaments in the walls, whilst regular terraces, with fine glazed slabs, led to a pond, in the middle of which was a bronze statue of Mercury.

The garden façade of this palace rests on a vault encircling a white shady basin, in which Peter the Cruel,

surrounded by the intoxicating fragrance of his garden,
bathed with his paramour, the notorious Maria Padilla,
whilst his unfortunate wife, from a little prison that is
still shown, was compelled to see the criminal pleasures
of her husband. Yet well-informed persons assert that
this Peter the Cruel, and the iron Philip II., enjoyed in
Spain the greatest popularity. If Peter was terrible and
Philip inexorable, still they left great historical memories,
and therefore are the right kings for the Spaniards.

We stepped through the green gate formed by orange
trees; the arms of Spain, and the initials of the reigning
queen, are cut here in the fresh box. The greatest curiosity in this peculiar garden, and surrounded by extraordinarily large, thick orange trees, is a pavilion in the
Moorish style, built by Charles V., that dear ruler of
my house, in which the great man used to dine. An elegant colonnade runs round the cool place, in the midst
of which is a small basin; but the fountain is now
wanting to it. When we returned to the garden, some
of the old waterworks were made to play at our request.
How agreeable must it be to promenade amongst these
magical contrivances!—how suited are these fountains for
clear, Spanish moonlight nights! Though this garden does
not date from the time of Moorish greatness, yet their
victorious successors have brought it into harmony with
the building which we now entered. Through an ante-
yard, we come to the staircase. It is broad and in a
noble style; especially noticeable are the carvings of its
wood-ceiling, in which one recognises the spirit of
Charles V. The upper rooms have had to undergo a
restoration, as time and barbarian hands have damaged
them. But there are still to be seen in them many
splendid and wonderful things; the spirit of the Caliphs
still lives in these halls, and centuries could not efface
what they created with a dreamy grace. What is the

Alcazar? a magnificent royal tent with delicately carved columns, over which are thrown the beautifully woven gold brocades of Damascus, the tapestry of India, and the delicate lace veil !

The eye almost expects that the gentle air will lift the fine lace veil, and that, stirred by the evening wind, the golden tapestry will move, but it is only the charm of art, of oriental witchcraft, which produces this effect! This tent, created by fancy, which the kings of oriental origin created on the banks of the Guadalquivir, is of stone and solid material; these tapestries which so excite our admiration, and whose ingeniously interwoven mathematical figures show the knowledge of the masters who contrived them, are a rich coloured mosaic of artfully glazed tiles and finely cut stones, and the lace veils are the finest chiselled work ever produced by human hand from clay and mortar. Each room has its peculiar charm, and would repay study; some of the principal rooms break into two stories, and are encircled at the top with light galleries ornamented with marble columns, from which one looks down on the magnificent space below. On the right wing of the house we were shown a half Gothic, half Moorish chapel, dating from the time of Isabella of Castile. With great skill the earnest dignified lines of the Gothic style are combined with the richness and the poetical imagery of the East. The pointed arches created by the Christian spirit are embellished by the apple of the Moorish kings. The ingenious invention of the Mohammedans, the glazed tile, is here made to serve Christian purposes, and to form an altar-piece representing the Annunciation. Not far from the chapel, which might almost be called a house-altar, so small is its circumference, is a room in which a finely-carved, rich wood-ceiling recalls more modern times, and the builder of which, as the old cicerone said, was Charles V., one of the last sovereigns of

Spain who resided in this magic palace. The ambassadors'-
hall in this same palace is the crown of Moorish art; the
richest abundance of ornaments which men could combine
is lavished here to dazzle the eye. A large entrance-door
leads from the court into this hall; to the right and the
left side spring light Moorish arches, which, surrounded
by the most delicate ornaments, and supported by rich
columns, lead to the side rooms. The ceiling of the hall
is extravagantly ornamented with gold; hundreds of years
have passed, and still the metal glitters, still the colours
glow in their oriental splendour, and are interwoven with
a mysterious charm with the most beautiful and gorgeous
enamel. One of the finest ornaments used in the palace
are vine-leaves finely chiselled in stone, a proof that the
Moors did not use the lines of geometry only for their
ornament, but resorted also to the rich forms of nature. According to the Koran the Mohammedans are not permitted
to represent human figures; and it is the later Christian
sovereigns who have placed in the ambassadors'-hall these
sitting likenesses of the Christian kings, and a few handsome female heads, amongst which is the handsome, proud-
featured Maria Padilla. Haughtiness is clearly expressed
in the features of this bad woman. Under each of the
pictures glitter the escutcheons of the represented, and
the inscription shows their names, and, in the case of the
kings, the year of accession to the throne and of their
death. Especially to be remarked for taste are the
Moorish ornaments over the entrance, which through their
extremely fine network permit access to light and air.
In no other country, where art flourishes, have I seen the
like; nowhere admired anything so delicate, so agreeable
to the eye. The figures formed by these light lattices are
as noble as they are lovely, and only a long study and
lively feeling for art can succeed in producing such forms
by the simple crossing of straight lines. Great art, also,

is shown in the arrangement of the tiles; they are many-coloured, but the principal colour is green, that of the prophet. At the first look one believes it to be a confusion of many-coloured bricks, but on closer inspection it is seen that the figures which in those wainscots surround the walls only at the height of four to five feet from the ground, combine to form a principal figure, repeated throughout the palace, and bringing courts, galleries, and walls into harmony. The large chapel of the palace, in a more modern style, has no other interest than that it was once the dwelling of the notorious, charming Padilla, and leads by a secret staircase in the first story of the garden wing, to the rooms of Don Pedro. From an open gallery we had a view of the lovely, charming, interior court. A double row of arcades surrounds it on the ground floor and on the first story; light columns support the match-lessly-ornamented and finely-curved arches; the mathe-matical arabesques of glazed tiles ornament the interior walls of the lower gallery, and, in the middle of the court, is a double marble basin in which a jet of water produces a cooling murmur. In the arcade-gallery of the ground floor, on the right side of the court, the king's splendid throne was raised, in the time of the Moors, sitting on which they received every year the tribute of the country in hundreds of its finest daughters.

In the halls, where once reigned the brilliant life of despotism, is now the stillness of death, and only the steps of visitors now and then sound here, where once the soft carpets of Cashmere protected the foot of the caliph against the cold of the marble, and the sweet odour of amber floated fragrantly through the wide courts, where wreaths of roses surrounded the fine columns, and the sound of the lute and the murmur of the fountain filled the air beneath the still light of the moon.

Charles V. understood how to adorn the wide court

which the sword of the holy Ferdinand had torn from the
family of the prophet, but Spain's soft air relaxed the
German and Frank rulers, and with them died great ideas
and beautiful creations.

Passing along the gallery we went through a door over
which were painted three death's-heads, into a gorgeously
ornamented room out of which led the secret staircase
forming a communication between the dwelling of Pedro
and Maria Padilla. The walls are embellished by splendid
alto-relievos and arabesques, amongst which is the figure of
a slave in chains, and chained in such a manner that he
must look on a death's-head. Over the door leading to the
rooms towards the garden, is to be seen a place on the
ornamented wall covered with white paint; here were
the painted figures of Don Pedro and the Padilla in an
improper position. When Isabella of Castile moved to
this palace she had this picture painted over. The other
rooms are all adorned with Moorish magnificence, but have
already caught the spirit of Christian times, and we found
here, amongst the ornaments, the eagle and columns of
Charles V.

On the ground floor opposite the chief entrance is a
kind of state or reception room, to which, from the arcades,
a large, splendidly carved wooden gate leads, in which is
cut a little door so small that one can only pass through it
stooping. It is a pity that almost everywhere the magnificent and peculiarly vaulted Moorish door arches have
been replaced by modern doors. Seen from below, the
ambassadors'-hall excited afresh my admiration; one sees
well from that point the side rooms to which those airy
arches lead.

From one of the balconies of this hall Peter the Cruel
purposely commenced a dispute with his brother, Don
Federigo, who was entering from below, in consequence
of which he caused him to be stabbed at a given signal.

An inscription still shows the place where the murdered man fell. For another of his misdeeds he punished himself in a most characteristic manner. In one of his nightly walks he had killed a man in the streets of Seville, and believed himself unseen; but an old woman, by the light of a dim lamp, had recognised him by his peculiar limp. The murdered man was found next morning; the Alcalde rushed to the king demanding justice for this deed. As the king believed himself unrecognised, he made no difficulty in granting what was asked, and promised that the perpetrator should be decapitated and his head publicly exposed. The Alcalde knew by means of the old woman who was the murderer, and now told the king that he had been recognised. Pedro would not order himself to be beheaded, but in order not to break his word altogether, he had his head hewn in stone without a trunk, and exposed it in one of the streets of Seville behind a grate, where it may still be seen to this very day. We saw a few rooms, of which some are renovated, in a not very tasteful manner, and after having put something jingling into the hand of the old cicerone, we stepped out of the palace through the large beautiful gates, passing through richly-ornamented guard rooms, envying those who saw this wonderful work at the commencement of this century, whilst all the walls were still sparkling with the brightness of many colours. In 182– occurred that horrible event, when an Englishman, who was inspector of the Alcazar, whitewashed all the splendid painted ornaments, with their fulness of life, and glory of colours, so that now one can only judge from parts of the magnificence of the whole. There is no epithet for such barbarism, and it is only to be regretted that this miscreant has remained unpunished, nay, has even died *unnamed*.

Before leaving this place altogether I must say a few words about the general impression it left on me.

The Alcazar is not a grand work like the Roman, Greek,
or old German ones; it is not one of those buildings which
impress the eye by its massive proportions; it awakens
no great remembrances, like the Acropolis, recalling the
whole history of a people. The Alcazar is the splendid,
charming creation of a sensuous period, a light, graceful
building, not containing within itself the idea of duration.
Mohammedanism only allows to its faithful adherents temporary dwellings, and camps, on their earthly pilgrimage.
The thought which animates the oriental is of a restless
conquering expedition, till the sword of the prophet shall
have succeeded in subjecting the whole globe; therefore
most of the houses in the Mohammedan cities are of wood.
But the Alcazar suggests the idea, that the caliphs had
intended to execute in stone, as a pattern of their tent or
camp for future generations, such a temporary palace.

The weariness of sight-seeing, an evil which frequently
seizes upon the enthusiastic traveller, had enervated me,
and I had still to see and admire a church containing some
Murillos. Moreover, the stomach, a chief potentate in
human life, was opposed to being any longer left uncon-
sidered; it had to be satisfied. In the heat of the Spanish
sun we tottered over a pavement, which, for its badness,
is one of the curiosities of Europe, towards one of the
city gates, when succour suddenly appeared. A mule
approached with the much-longed-for refreshment in
a basket, full of the most splendid Andalusian grapes.
Supplied with fresh strength, we came to the gates of the
church of St. Catherine. Like the common Spanish
churches this one is simple and insignificant, whilst the
altars are over-loaded with rococo gold ornaments. But the
wealth of this church consists in its Murillos, of which one
is an exceedingly dark picture—one fancies one can distinguish two figures; the somewhat lighter head of another
is full of effect, but not particularly fine. This large-sized

picture is over one of the side altars, on the left side of the church. But it is two large and two small pictures which are the chief attraction to the visitor here. The first large picture, to the right of the entrance, is a Lord's Supper; it chilled me, and appeared to me neither noble nor characteristic, as is often the case with Murillo. The picture opposite shows Moses Striking the Rock, and calling forth the saving waters for the Israelitish people. Murillo's Moses is not that vigorous, grand figure which I could imagine leading the chosen people of God at the moment when the omnipotence and the mercy of Jehovah are revealed to the stricken people. I am too little of a connoisseur to dare to judge, but I believe that this subject is one of the most difficult for an artist, and that he must be imbued with another spirit to give to the features of his Moses that combination of enthusiasm, humility and triumph required. The eye of this man of the miracle ought to light up at the successful deed, and yet he ought to be absorbed in admiration and astonishment, in deep-felt humility before the power working through him, before the grace that is conferred on the people by his hand. One figure in this picture interests in a wonderful and striking manner: it is a brown boy sitting on a donkey and looking at the spouting fountain with delight; one of those clearly conceived, vigorous figures which Murillo has taken from Spanish popular life; one rejoices with the child at the refreshment that the miracle is about to bring to him. The two smaller pictures are, Christ and John the Baptist as children. These are figures which Murillo created with the hand of a master. Though children of the Spanish people, they are lively vigorous natures, in pleasant round healthy bodies. As Raphael and Vandyke are aristocratic painters, so Murillo is the genial painter of the people. He has a fine eye for art, though his vigorous figures are not always imbued with the most ideal spirit; and yet there is a striving upwards, nay, even to the divine, which one cannot fail to recognise in his works. Mostly, however, he is chained to the earthly, by the reality of his Spanish models. A few of his Madonnas and Saints, like his holy Francis in the cathedral of Seville, are imbued with a higher spirit; but I found no picture of Murillo which appeared to me to be altogether penetrated by this spirit, whilst one really feels that the highest works of Raphael have caught a celestial spirit. It is only necessary to remember the Sistine Madonna at Dresden, and the Vision of Ezekiel in the Pitti palace.

From this church we went to our hotel, the Fonda de Europa, to strengthen ourselves by a dinner for the longed-for spectacle awaiting us. To-day I was to witness one of those much-talked-of bull-fights, for which the arena of Seville has become celebrated. The hours did not step quick enough for me, for impatience and restlessness had seized me.

In order to become acquainted with the taste and fancies of the Spanish people in all its varieties, we had ordered for dinner an *olla podrida*, which is one of the most excellent and most delicious dishes that ever tickled my palate. A mixture of different meats, excellent sausages and hashes, abundance of cabbage and other vegetables, amongst which, to the horror of civilised readers, were also onions and garlic, in combination with oil, yield an extraordinarily nutritious dish. Since I have tasted it, I can henceforth appreciate the exceeding pleasure of Don Quixote and other Spanish heroes at the hope of finding it in some posada. After dinner we took our cigarettes, and thus passed the day, which lingered long, whilst we were kept cool by the shade in a Spanish rocking chair on a fine reed-mat, puffing fragrant smoke into the air. Impatiently looking at my watch, I saw its hands at last approach the hour appointed for the fight. Gladly we stepped into our equipage, which might serve for a Cardinal's, from its red lining, and we proceeded to the Arena de las Corridas, a large round building standing in an open place; a detachment of lancers was on guard before it. We should have entered by the middle gate, but according to our tickets we were directed to a side door. After having squeezed ourselves up a staircase, we went through a gallery, and stood suddenly under the interior galleries in the wide, imposing space of the arena. We were directed to a stone seat, between two columns, behind an iron balustrade, which by a special grace to us had been provided with a back.

Under ordinary circumstances I should hate to sit in such a crowded space, but what sacrifice would one not make for the spectacle awaiting us! After we had taken our places, we could look out on the wide open space before us, and the galleries beneath and behind us. The arena, which has a great resemblance in form to the antique, is one half of stone, and the other of wood. Roofs supported by light arcades protect the spectators against the glowing sun. In the middle of the stone compartment rises the Royal Tribune ornamented with the crown, and under it is a large gate; opposite this place is the box of the Impresario de la Corrida, also over a wide gate. The interior space of the arena in which the fight takes place is elliptical; a tolerably high wooden partition protects the public to a certain extent against the dangers of the fight. In certain parts of this partition are openings, with wooden screens before them, painted with the attributes of the Corrida; they serve the fighters as a refuge.

Looking at this wide space, and thinking of what was coming, I was seized with an uneasiness, a doubt whether I should be able to look at the bloody game which was to take place before me. I had already made up my mind to leave the arena; an inward feeling urged me from my seat, but the galleries filling more and more retained me, the aspect of stirring life overcoming for a moment the uneasy feeling. Hundreds of tints of Sunday dresses blend together in boxes and galleries. The slender men with their little round felt hats, their embroidered jackets and red sashes, move about with an incessant restlessness, and make a noise, cry, and whistle, practising in this manner the chorus for the coming spectacle. Hundreds of fans rustle and rattle with a continuous movement. The abanicos * of the rich shine in the brightest colours of China, whilst the poor and the stronger sex, who on other occasions do not use this instrument, are fanning themselves with fans only purchased to-day of cane and paper, on which is printed a scene of the Torillos, and some Spanish poetry for the occasion. Dark little heads moving up and down with sparkling eyes, and fresh roses under the lace veil in their raven hair, the mantilla gracefully wrapped around the shoulders, chatted away on the stone seats. Do these red lips part in order to tell of pleasant ball memories?—are the laughing starry eyes examining the merry ranks of the coming dancers? No! Seville's daughters are only pleasantly excited in expectation of the bloody fight. Some officers in rich uniform entered from the door behind us, and with them one of the most charming and beautiful apparitions I ever came across whilst in the Spanish country. She took her place near us, so that I could examine the play of her features and each of her movements; at this stage she seemed only to be joking with one of her admirers, but I intended to observe her during the terrible moments of the fight. The noise of the crowd and the rustling of fans became ever louder and more impatient. Between the general hubbub were to be heard the piercing voices of the vendors of refreshments. One would expect that the pretty lips of the daughters of Spain would seek for something cooling in ice-creams, that

* The name given in Spain to the elegant Chinese fans.

the pearly teeth with which every mouth in Seville is ornamented, would only crack biscuits. Oh, no! Savage as the Spaniards are in their pleasure, they are equally primitive in the objects which they offer to their palate: only water, and Spanish Wind, were handed round.*

The large wide arena was filled; the sun shone on a part of the building, probably not much to the pleasure of those on whom he shed his ardent beams. A deep blue sky arched over a wide space, and formed a most beautiful ceiling. The picturesque, motley crowd became still more noisy; they knocked against the wooden seats; the people commenced to exercise the right which had belonged to them for centuries: the right to direct the game, at least partly, by their cries. The spectators felt that the hour had come, and I partook of their impatience with incomprehensible excitement. Now the trumpets sounded, the door of the large tribune opposite us opened; the noise became still more general, like the roar of a rushing flood; all looks were directed to a man, who appeared in the arena on a stout and vigorous Spanish horse. Our Italian cicerone told us all about this figure, and what was to follow. It was the impresario, who rode in to receive from the authorities who were sitting in the great tribune, the key for the opening of the festivity. Generally it is the Duke of Montpensier who throws the key, but the prince was not present to-day. The impresario stopped his horse amidst the joyful shouts of the crowd. The Spaniards who, like all southerners, yield to any opportunity for excitement, and then give vent to their feelings, have also subjected this ceremony of the throwing of the key to applause or to censure. Thus, if the impresario catches it with his hat, then roaring and clapping of hands follow; if the key falls on the sand, then the people laugh and hiss. The functionary saluted,

* Spanish Wind. A very light kind of pastry, sometimes also called Windbag.

and from the balcony came flying a key richly ornamented
with ribbons, but it fell unfortunately on the sand. There
was hissing and laughter. Fresh flourish of trumpets,
and the strains of military music created an enthusiasm.
We had a splendid view. There entered with a proud
light step the espados with their quadrilles, the picadores
and banderilleros in rich old Spanish costume. They
were followed by the mules ornamented with little flags
and bells, ready to bring away the slaughtered animals.
Old Spain approached with her ancient customs, with her
splendid magnificence of dress, and with her imposing
movements. Confident of their courage and of victory,
the combatants entered the great assembly with a proud
look. They were greeted exultingly from all parts; the
finest eyes sparkling in the galleries shot at them their
fiery arrows; it was one of those state processions in
which not only money—that petty motive power of
modern times—did its best, but where the feeling, the
consciousness of their own strength alone lent dignity to
these men. How rich, and how favourable to the exhibition of their fine forms, was the dress of the espados
and their quadrilles! Tastefully embroidered, beautiful
silk spencers encircled the slender body; over the
shoulders flowed embroideries of gold and silver, like
rich nets of leaves. No tie pressed the free neck; the
rich hair, to the advantage of the noble features, was
combed back and ended in a little silk tail, ornamented
with a rich tuft of black silk netting; on the head was a
jaunty velvet cap; the waist was encircled by a broad
sash; the breeches, also richly ornamented with gold and
silver, were of the same material as the spencer; from
the knee downward, the well-formed, supple leg was
encased in fine pink or white silk stockings; over their
shoulders hung gracefully and in rich folds silk cloaks
with richly-embroidered collars. In this fashion were the

espados, their quadrilles and banderilleros, clad. The picadores, or mounted combatants, had the same rich spencers, sashes, and mode of dressing the hair as the other combatants, but, instead of the little velvet cap, they had that flat, broad-brimmed, grey hat celebrated in pictures, with the many-coloured bands of ribbon which held the tail horizontally on the head of the horseman. High boots, under the yellow leather trousers, which were discovered by the stiff movements of the men, protected them against the sharp horns of their antagonist. In his right hand each picadore held the pica. He sits on the high Andalusian saddle, his foot resting in the broad Moorish stirrup.

After the combatants had made their proud entry, accompanied by the roaring applause of the people, they distributed themselves about the arena, and changed their cloaks for others more suitable for the fight. The mule teams disappeared through a side gate; the military music ceased; opposite the principal tribune a shrill flourish of trumpets proclaimed the culminating moment. The gates open; the movement becomes more anxious, the excitement indescribable; the bull, a black son of the herd, which, wounded in the neck by a javelin, and ornamented with a white and blue ribbon, rushes forward with powerful leaps amidst endless cheering and loud enthusiasm. Suddenly he stands as if spell-bound, and looks long and wildly on the thousands and thousands of spectators. He proudly surveys the place on which he is to fight and to die. There he is surrounded by the noble forms of the combatants, who flutter their cloaks before his eyes. Irritated, he bows his head, and rushes upon those who wave the cloaks, and who, with a light graceful movement, manage to evade him. Again the cloaks are waved before him, and again, threatening with his horns, he rushes after his audacious enemies; one thinks he must reach them in his wild course; that he must run his horns into their sides, when they with incredible swiftness and indescribable grace jump over the wall of the arena, or save themselves behind the small wooden screens. It is now the object of their art to irritate the furious bull in such a manner as to make him run towards the picadores, who are waiting for him on horseback. He pauses a moment before the horsemen, then he rushes with all his might against them: one expects the most dreadful things to happen; but a well-directed thrust with the lance in his back makes him rebound at once from all three picadores. The bull is wounded; blood, warm blood has flowed, the approaching fight changes my anxiety into a singular pleasure. The frantic acclamations of the people accompany the combatant, and at each movement of the bull, I looked at Spain's handsome daughters who were near me: their features were perfectly calm, nor did they shudder on seeing the gaping wounds. Again those combatants, so beautiful in their movements, wave their cloaks as they hover round the bull, which is now beginning to be furious and to pursue them as if it were mad. If the game becomes too dangerous, they throw their cloaks at its feet, which it attacks furiously, thus affording them time for escape; or another combatant with his cloak allures the pursuer in another direction. Once more the picadores await the charge of the bull. They thrust their lance towards it, but this time, instead of flying, the bull rushes with his sharp horns against the flanks of the horse. The horse receives a mortal wound and the picador falls to the ground.

The interest becomes keener and keener as the fight gets more exciting. Whilst the picador remounts his bleeding horse, the bull in a magnificent rage plunges his horns into the horse of another combatant. As long as the horses can keep on their feet the picadores mount them; their very entrails protrude, and they drag themselves along half dead. The bull makes a fresh attack, throwing the horse, which succumbs to its antagonist, amidst the furious acclamations of the crowd. The bull, having given several mortal thrusts, in none of which, thank God, any picador has been wounded, a fresh flourish of trumpets announces the arrival of the banderilleros. These are most skilful men, who plant between the shoulders of the bull two long javelins ornamented with coloured paper. On their appearance the picadores retire. With matchless ease and dexterity the banderilleros run their weapons into the flesh of the bull, which makes straight for them.

A light and graceful movement saves the man from the sharp horns of the bull; yet the animal is enraged at the javelins which, striking into it on both sides, flutter about its head the more it turns and defends itself. After having been wounded by six or eight of these javelins, the trumpets sound anew, and Luca Blanca, the richly-dressed handsome matador, steps forward amidst the acclamations of the spectators before the chief tribune, greets the authorities, and asks in a few words whether he may give the bull the *coup de grâce*. The celebrated red cloth flutters on his arm, a pointed blade is in his hand. Looking round the assembly, he waves his hat horizontally three times as a death signal; after which, with a grand and firm step, he walks up to his enemy. The quadrilles irritate the bull with the waving of their cloaks; Luca Blanca flutters before him his scarlet cloth; the bull rushes against it with rage; Luca Blanca evades him with agility. Several times this play is repeated, and the excitement heightened by it. Suddenly the bull takes a direction favourable to the matador, stops a few paces before him, throwing up clouds of dust with his

foot, lowers his head and rushes with full force against
the red cloth. The great moment is come, and moved as by
magic the people rise at once without a shudder, without
fear of danger, to observe with the eye of connoisseurs
the mortal stab. This general electrical movement is one
of the grandest sights to the eye of a stranger, and proves
how completely this spectacle has entered into the heart
and soul of the people. Luca stands proud and fearless
as if spell-bound. Suddenly raising his blade, he thrusts
it unerringly sure and up to the hilt, into the back
of the animal. The bull totters and falls down upon the
sand; the exultation of the crowd is boundless, the air
vibrates with their acclamations. A wild intoxication
seizes upon me; I feel myself borne along; and become
eager for the bloody scene. As a conqueror he steps
before the tribune, and bowing, responds to the thousands
upon thousands of looks that are fixed on him with ab-
sorbing interest. He is the king of the moment, and has
electrified the multitude. As a sign of approval, hats
are thrown to him from several parts, which he flings
back with grace to the galleries.

With different eyes I look upon him during the following
scenes. How the feelings of a man can be changed in so
short a space as a quarter of an hour! On entering I felt
uneasy and very uncomfortable, and now a mania for the
bloody spectacle possessed me. The bull and the dead
horses were dragged away by the mules amidst the music.
The people were still in their exulting mood when the
second bull appeared, and the noble fight commenced
anew. This animal was less strong than the first, and
the fight less bloody. A second espado, named José
Carmona, a fine, well-built man, was far inferior to Luca
Blanca in his manner of giving the *coup de grâce*. The
first stab did not hit the spine, so that the animal did not
fall. He had to get the sword out of the wound for a

new thrust; he succeeded, and the bull fell and was stabbed with iron instruments in the back until he expired. I was beginning to experience the genuine Spanish feeling, and I suffered the matador, who was a tyro, to pass before me without applauding him.

And now appeared a third bull, the most vigorous and the most handsome of the animals. He carried his wide horns with pride on his strong forehead, and his sinewy limbs were short and solid. He earned loud applause immediately by his wild, dashing entrance. I could not turn my eye from the animal and its aggressors; each moment of the fight enchained me with irresistible force. How the attention of all were strained to the utmost when the enraged bull placed himself before the picador, measuring him defyingly, and then, with full force, rushed against horse and rider! This is a most exciting moment, but when the bull has plunged his horns deep into the flanks of the horse, he generally leaves off, and does not wound his victim any more, so that the picador brought to the ground is safe against his rage. The bull generally directs his thrusts into the belly of the horse, so that the bleeding entrails protrude. The poor animal's right eye, which is next to its antagonist, is covered with a cloth. Once during the games of to-day the bull caught the horse behind, and lifted it several times. But the spectator's nature is soon changed; his original nature is awakened; wild passion gains the mastery, and he is annoyed when the bull does not succeed in his deadly thrust, when the phases of the fight are not steeped deep enough in blood. This time also Luca Blanca gave the *coup de grâce*, and fresh acclamations filled the air. One horse had died on the spot; another, already mortally wounded, but still standing on its legs, was dragged away by the mules, amidst the laughter of the crowd. The Spaniards are peculiarly wild and relentless. In such moments as these one

o 2

becomes aware of the sort of fire smouldering in Spain. If
a bull is not courageous enough in his attack, the crowd
hisses and roars, and endeavours to irritate him by waving
handkerchiefs.

In the box next to ours, sat an old man with an Andalusian hat, and singularly lively features. He took an actual
part in the fight from his box, bent forward, called to the
espados, and enabled us plainly to recognise the fanaticism still prevailing in Spain for these fights, and how
popular this festivity is. But there is a peculiar charm
in the Torillo; the excitement produced by the sight of
danger carries every mind irresistibly away along the
stream of enthusiasm. I was told of a stranger, who
expressed himself strongly as to the barbarism of this
festival (his tender feeling made him abhor what he had
not seen), that a friend who knew from experience the
charm of this national pleasure, induced him, though filled
with abhorrence, to visit the Corrida. At the sight of
the noble combat he was also seized by the sweet, wild
intoxication, and eagerly asked his friend when the next
bull-fight would take place. I only regretted that my
sojourn in Spain was not long enough for me to enjoy
this splendid sight again.

A fifth bull now rushed upon the arena; a splendid
fellow. This was indeed a bull worthy of the 'fiesta;' his
thrusts were dreadful. Conscious of his strong horns, he
justified the acclamations of the people. All looks are
directed on him; the people rise; they appreciate the
moment of danger, and exultingly roar for blood, for
deadly wounds; horse and rider reel; a second picador
falls with his horse, the spectacle is horribly beautiful,
dreadfully sublime. Horse and rider fall in a heap; a
horse receives a few deadly thrusts and expires. The
people get mad; this is a bull the Spaniards love and
applaud. Trumpets sound, flames and noise fill the air,

the javelins had been provided with rockets to increase the rage of the bull in every possible way. A fresh blast of trumpets; but what surprises me is that Luca Blanca steps gracefully before our box; whilst all looks of the arena are turned towards us. The brave espado addresses me with dignity in a congratulatory manner, and announces that the *coup de grâce* will be given in my honour. A strange feeling comes over me, for the looks of the whole arena are directed upon me; and a murmur runs through the multitude. I cannot deny that I felt flattered by this national homage. I even fancied myself back in the fine old times, when the Hapsburgs were the rulers of this noble people. It was whispered to me that, after the Spanish fashion, a purse with silver was the accustomed reward. We got our Spanish rixdollars ready. Luca waves his red cloth, the bull rushes furiously about, the espado plunges his sword deeply into the back of his antagonist, and withdraws it, to the delight of the people, from the gaping wound. The animal falls. With a triumphant smile, Blanca steps to the front of our box, and amidst the joyous strains of the Tango Americano, and the acclamations of the spectators, a heavy purse falls at the feet of the victor.

I felt a happiness in giving this reward to the brave fellow. Luca Blanca is picturesque in all his movements; proud and calm, he treats the fight as a play. During the Corrida he was pursued by one of the bulls; he retired behind one of the wooden screens, but the animal stopped suddenly as if spell-bound. The espado stopped also; and resting on one foot, he leaned with his left arm calmly on the board wall. The cloak fell down at his side in rich folds, and with a mocking smile he looked at his antagonist, as if it were a lamb. The fight has no *entre-actes*, but after the deed is accomplished, the matador steps behind one of the screens.

The sixth bull, and to our regret the last, now entered
the arena: a fine strong animal of a golden yellow
colour. This fight was full of interest and movement.
At one time it was especially attractive, for the bull
caught the horse of a picador on its legs, and threw it to
the ground; the rider was half under it, on the sand.
The furious animal made another rush against the horse
and ran right over it; the picador was supposed to be lost;
it was a moment of intense excitement; but in his blind
rage the bull rushed over the lancer, and he was saved.
José the matador-tyro killed this animal also, but his
thrusts wanted the firmness of Luca.

The corrida is finished; the people stream into the
arena, and towards the entrances, and I left, with a
sense of the highest pleasure, a place that had become
memorable to me, and in which I had passed the most
interesting hours of my travels. When they read these
lines at home in the warm saloon before the hissing tea-
urn, sandwiches and sweet tarts, I guess the lot which
awaits me. A beautiful circle, preferring little excursions
at home to adventurous voyages, breaking out in idyllic
ecstasies about the note of the nightingale in the grove
close by, or the chirping of a cricket, will sing out in
horror: 'Has the poor youth left us to become a barbarian in far countries?' Yes, they will say so! and
I shall console myself as I answer, with an ironical
smile: 'You poor people do not know what a corrida
is! what strong sense, what a splendid development
of strength and skill is represented in this national
feast!'

I love such festivals, in which the original nature of man
comes out in its truth, and much prefer them to the
enervating, immoral entertainments of other luxurious
and degenerate countries. Here bulls perish, there heart
and soul sink in a weak, sentimental frivolity. I do not

animal remained standing before him spell-bound. The same gentleman, who is at the head of a company in a small city we visited, has established a wide building for the corrida. On noticing with pleasure my enthusiasm for the fight, he told me that there would be an opportunity in December to see a splendid festival of this kind, as the higher nobility of Spain would celebrate the Queen's delivery by a bull-fight, and that the sons of the grandees would themselves appear in the arena. Thus the proud people celebrate the coming of an heir to the throne, and thus the queen is here greeted as a mother. The people love the sport so much that they starve themselves during the week, that, after having attended prayers in the morning, they may pass the hours of the Sunday afternoon in this excitement, and collect material for gossip for the week. With us, the lower labouring classes drink and eat away their wages, and pass black Monday idling and intoxicated. Which is best, I leave to the judgment of my readers.

Almost every town in Spain has its corrida, and July and August are the best months for the fight, as at that time the bull is wildest. May my good luck bring me again to Spain at that season to study this fight still further, and the spirit of the people exhibited in it, and once more to enjoy that intoxicating enthusiasm arising from the fight, at the expense of being called by sentimental lips a bloody barbarian, *un jeune homme dénaturé!* I shall be repaid by exulting Spanish lips, by the applauding glow of Andalusian eyes, and cannot forbear calling out amidst the waving of mantillas and the rustling of fans: 'Spaniards, I envy you this old festival!'

From the arena we drove to the adjacent Delicias on the shores of the Guadalquiver. Though it was beginning to get dark, there were still many carriages of an odd shape and colour moving to and fro in the avenues. It

was a novelty to see the fine strong mule before a carriage,
and to hear the merry sound of the little bells with which
the richer teams are ornamented.   We were astonished at
the *élite* of Seville with their mantillas, lace-veils, and
flowers in the hair, who use the fan in the open carriages,
as if the Delicias were a saloon, as indeed they are.
The air is soft and agreeable, the sun has ceased to glow
in the firmament, the moon softens with her mild light the
fine complexion of the ladies; what more is required for
the noble Spanish lady to appear to the best advantage?
Happy the country where romance has not yet utterly
been stifled by French fashions, where the women have
yet sense enough to understand that the same pattern and
the same head-dress are not suitable for every nation and
every face, and many things may suit a grisette well which
will not agree with the features of the black Manola.

But let us return to the Delicias and look with our
readers at one of the more striking equipages, a rather
large coupé drawn by two stately, richly-ornamented
mules : coachman and footman are in livery, the carriage
is lined with red, and on its cushions reposes an old man,
enjoying the pure evening air.   He is the cardinal-arch-
bishop of Seville; so great is the love of the Spaniards for
the Alameda, that even the aged Cardinal still drives in
the evening on this lively promenade to enjoy the merry
life of the people.   To wind up the day we went to the
fine, great theatre, where unfortunately an Italian opera
was represented, and badly too.   Some strikingly handsome ladies graced the boxes; in one of them I perceived
one of the dandies of the vessel from which we disembarked
yesterday, striving to make the oppressive heat more bear-
able by the use of a fan.   Sleep soon drove me from the
theatre, and after a day of much excitement, I sought and
found sleep behind my mosquito-curtains.

Seville, September 15, 1851.

To-day our pilgrimage was directed to the house of
Pilate where Jesus was scourged, and where Pilate presented the ill-treated Saviour to the deluded people with
the words ' Ecce homo;' and, frightened by the cries of
the roaring people, ordered a basin to be brought, and
washed his hands of that terrible crime, a ceremony frequently repeated in later times with memorable luck.
But how does the house of Pilate come to be at Seville?
It is said that an ancestor of the Duke of Medina Celi, on
his return from a pilgrimage to Jerusalem, had an exact
copy of this house constructed in his native city.   But
either the house of Pilate in Jerusalem has been entirely
rebuilt between the time when our Redeemer was on
earth and that pilgrimage, or the house in Seville is
a fancy building.   The style of the house of Pilate in
Seville, in which the family still lives, is the rich Moorish.
The courts are enclosed by light arcades, the staircase, over
which our Saviour is said to have passed, is covered with
azulejos in relievo, full of the most splendid ornaments in
clay-slabs, like the stoves we see in all knightly castles.   It
was only the various fragments of statues placed in the
arcades and said to come from the house of Pilate, that
reminded us, in a manner by no means agreeable, of the
time of the Roman Emperors.   A lovely garden, full of
roses and oranges, and a cool arbour, in the midst of
which was a small Moorish fountain, which played, no
doubt, in better times, ornament this house so renowned in
Spain.

On another occasion we entered the interior of the
palace-like cigar-manufactory, in which one can trace the
whole fabrication of the raw leaves as they come from
America, to the cigar boxes packed for European use,
the small packets of cigarettes for Spain, and the sealed
tin cases of a most excellent Seville tobacco.   In these

endless vaulted galleries four thousand women and girls
are occupied daily. Their ever-busy industry, the confused merry buzzing and chatting of the girls, and yet the
exemplary order of this female army, constitute, withou
doubt, the most interesting part of this giant manufactory
The female labourers sit at numerous tables, a heap o
large brown leaves before them, which, after they have
moistened their fingers with gum-water, they roll up
quickly, wrap round a small leaf as a cover, and clip the
little roll on one side with a strong pair of scissors; thus
in one moment a fragrant cigar has been made out of a
prepared leaf.

The work-people are paid according to the number of
cigars they make. For the cigarettes, little paper tubes
are filled by means of a funnel, with finely-chopped
tobacco, after which they are weighed with the greatest
quickness by a kind of forewoman. All this is the work
of a moment and done gracefully and amidst merry chatting. In contrast with our own factories here all is life
and freshness, and everybody seems to work with pleasure. Amongst the four thousand females, who, according to the custom of the country, had flowers in their
black hair, I saw few really handsome faces. Many
moved gracefully, many had coquettish ways, but all were
in a military order, which is kept by stout odd-looking
duennas, who, like generals used to victory, walked through
the ranks, proudly mustering them. A few dark daughters
of the Triana, from the celebrated tribe of the Gipsies, sat
between the Moorish-Gothic sisters, and might have told
us many stories of love and murder. Eugène Sue would
find amongst these many figures, and in their history of
happiness and sorrow, material for a novel in a hundred
volumes, and the 'Mysteries of the Cigar-manufactory of
Seville' might take a worthy place by the side of those
of Paris.

The preparation of snuff is left to the men and the mules; the tobacco is cut, pressed and seasoned, and produces an atmosphere which tickles the nerves of the nose; In the ground-floor rooms of this manufactory is prepared the titbit of the nose gourmands, the strong delicious Seville rappee, which, in gold boxes ornamented with diamonds, gives to our diplomatists their unmatched 'countenance,' to our doctors and *savants* their wisdom, and is accepted by all as the first symbol of agreement in important transactions.

From this giant-building, worthy to be a king's palace, we proceeded to the interior of the city to the Exchange, situated in the neighbourhood of the cathedral; a noteworthy building of Herrara, the architect of the Escurial, the eighth wonder of the world. Ascending a fine staircase, one comes to the marble-floored halls in which the celebrated documents of the old India Company are preserved; amongst these are kept in a particular room, letters from Cortez to the king, which are remarkable from the man who wrote them. We were also shown the stamp of Pizarro, which, not understanding how to write, he used as a signature; as it is interesting I give it here. Besides these, the last will of the pilot who made the great voyage of discovery with Columbus was shown; all monuments of better times of poor Spain. How famous a piece of paper made from rags can become, and a matter of pride for a whole people, so as to belong to its richest trophies, if a man, whose name is written down in history, or who has been a witness of some great event, has laid his hand upon it! With such opportunities one regrets that theft is a crime. The walls of this room are ornamented by the portraits of the last sovereigns, amongst them those of Ferdinand VII. and his daughter Isabella.

The innocent Isabella is certainly one of those with whom fate has dealt most singularly. A plaything of the most terrible passions, she was suffered to grow up without principles, to form principles for herself; she was endowed with various talents, and has had the good luck to win the love of her subjects by her great kindness of heart and captivating manners.

In the beautiful Lonja, which, by its solid rich construction, shows us what Spain was when the gold of the colonies flowed into her lap, is a boldly winding staircase of stone without support, a masterpiece of the same Herrara. The terrible Alva, the blood-reeking spectre of modern time, and his all-ensnaring fiery Inquisition, are gone ; but the high, large, splendid orange trees with their fragrant shade, under which Philip walked about brooding destruction, are still standing, and have stood there these three hundred years, enjoying in the garden of the duke their green existence. These trees are not those roundly-cut plants of the Italian gardens, or of our orangeries; they are splendid trees, full of leaves, with long slender branches, affording shade, fragrance and fruit. I have already said, and am also assured by the Duke of Montpensier, that Alva's king, the pale, serious, bloody Philip, though descending from the Bourbons, is respected amongst the people, for he was a man and a Spaniard. However much we may hate Alva, we must admire his orange trees, and acknowledge that the duke had surrounded his Moorish house in an excellent manner.

We admired another building of that kind, which belongs to a rich banker, in which is one of those high lofty halls, painted for us by Arabian fancy, with an entrance from a fresh fragrant garden ; to the right and left are cosy side-halls, to which we are introduced as in a fairy-tale through fine light arches ; the whole is wrapped in that lace-veil of delicate stucco-slabs, and takes one by surprise, the more so as it is found in the unpretending house of a private person. Can one avoid feeling enthusiasm for this Spanish-oriental romance?—is it to be wondered at that the fanciful tales of the South spring forth from this flowery reality? In the works of the Egyptians, earnestness is the principal feature; in that of the Greeks, one admires humanity immortalised in pure marble; the Romans show us that unflinching manliness which afterwards degenerated into imperial insolence; in the Gothic monuments we find deep devotion, but in the poetical architecture of the Moors, as in the silvery moonlight, we enjoy the rich sensuous fancy of the south.

In a large building, which I believe was formerly a monastery, is the Academy of Seville, and in it is a treasure of exquisite Murillos, not sufficiently appreciated. They originally ornamented the large walls of a hall, perhaps the former refectory, but many have not even frames. Murillo is a child of impulse, whose brush is guided by enthusiasm, but whose impulses are succeeded by lassitude and weakness. A man may raise himself by his immortal spirit to the clouds; but it is not every one who succeeds in keeping himself there; he falls back on the earth, to rise again after collecting fresh strength. So it is with Murillo: his pictures sometimes glow with a celestial fire, and as frequently they are only illuminated by the light terrestrial; but his happy moments are enchanting, and at such times he stamps upon his works, which show the very life of the people, a soul that marks him as a great artist, and secures him a place by the side of the most exalted.

Murillo has painted pictures which touch one by their ingenuous grace, and I found here another, amongst so many of his, by which I have been enraptured. It is a Virgin, who places her child in the arms of the saintly Felix as a reward for his holy labours. Words cannot tell how this virgin, half floating, half inclined forward, comes down from the clouds, like a fragrant flower; how sweet and lovely is her bearing, how gentle her peaceable, friendly look, and yet after all she is only a wonderfully hearty girl, a pure angel of light, but not the mother of God, not immortal, as the Sistine Madonna of Raphael: this sweet daughter of the clouds of Murillo could not have given birth to the Saviour of the world.

Whoever admires Murillo, and has in general a feeling for art, must read Hahn-Hahn's 'Travelling Sketches in Spain;' though I do not love Murillo so much as the Countess Ida, I nevertheless confess that few describe as she does; that to few only are given that warm, rich poetical conception, and richness of language. Whoever knows Spain will enjoy this work of the countess, who strews her fine ideas with a graceful *nonchalance*, like pearls on a velvet carpet.

I intended to remain in Seville incognito, but the Duke of Montpensier found me out, and sent his chamberlain to me; so, though I had purposely left my uniform on board ship, I had, *nolens volens*, to pay a visit to the Palace of St. Telmo, which afterwards I did not regret; for it made me acquainted with new wonders in Seville. A rich equipage with a scarlet box and laced servants, drove up before our hotel, to fetch me; it was the prince's magnificent city carriage; we stepped in, and it brought us to the splendid Palace of St. Telmo. The guard was called out; between iron railings, tipped with golden lilies, we entered through a richly carved door into the interior. A chamberlain led me to the fine, wide, double staircase, at the foot of which stood a soldier with his halberd, who announced our arrival by striking it on the marble ground. The walls were ornamented with a select collection of pictures. At the upper end I was met by a tall, fair young man in a black dress-coat with the order of the

Golden Fleece round his neck, and the blue riband of a Spanish grand-cross; it was the Duke of Montpensier who thus received me in his fairy palace, newly arranged; and who led me through two saloons luxuriously furnished, into a third room all gold and colours, in which was a lady of princely appearance, with those Spanish eyes which promise so much; dark and deep as eternity, with antique, regular features, and that Andalusian transparent complexion, shining like ivory. She had a pale rose mounted in her brilliant black hair. This was the beautiful duchess, only nineteen years old, Christina's second daughter, and a picture of Spanish loveliness.

A little daughter, the miniature picture of her French grandmother, stood at her mother's side. When after a short conversation I took leave, the duke took me back into his first saloon, which is ornamented with large family pictures, and also contains some curiosities collected by him; amongst them, some splendid oriental presents, which the prince had received on his voyage in the East, and a lute of the royal Isabella of Castile, the devout consort of Ferdinand the Catholic.

I was invited by the duke to dinner: he received me in his fine library on the ground floor, where amongst other portraits I noticed that of Philip III., the founder of St. Telmo, formerly a naval academy; and also that of the ex-king of the French. Montpensier then led me into his chapel replete with gold ornaments, and thence into his park, laid out by himself. This is indeed a fairy spot, created within two years by industry and taste. By the side of old luxuriant orange trees, forming a dark, shady grove, stretched out—thanks to the rich soil—arbours of vineyard, rich in fruit. Amidst this deep green is a newly-designed pond, with a lovely island containing the plants of all the continents in the world, and a fine Moorish kiosk: on the water are a small boat and a couple of

swans.   There are also aviaries with parrots, and fine
American fancy birds, with which the mild climate of
Seville agrees.   There is also a little farm with a breed of
Swiss cows new to me, and which have the pleasant defect
of being without horns.   On that historical spot where
the Inquisition once erected its pyres stands an artificial
hill with a hermitage.   Even now there are on a mound
of earth, bricks bearing the mark of the dreadful tribunal,
where, scarcely fifty years ago, a so-called ' beata ' was
burned because she had been visited by visions.

Thus times change; on the same place where half a
century ago the unfortunate victims of a bloody fanaticism
met death amidst flames, surrounded by thousands of
scared spectators, rises now a green hill, which the visitor,
ascending to have a wider view, is shown as a curious
garden ornament.   This hill contains the remains of the
dreaded pyre, and now the daughter of a Spanish king
uses the site of the *auto-da-fé* for her charming park.
The greatest attractions of this place are the luxuriant
tropical plants, which here grow splendidly.   Here we
see the much-used bamboo, by the side of the poetical
palm, and wonderful tropical blossoms of all countries.

We found the duchess, who had lately given birth to a
second daughter, with her children in the garden.   The
climate of Seville is so mild that the women may enjoy a
walk as early as the ninth day; just as the handsome
duchess did (who on this occasion wore a yellow dress and
glowing red flowers which became her exceedingly well),
with uncovered head.   As the mild evening came, the sun
departed, and the sky acquired that clearness only to be
found in southern regions. The tops of the palms appeared
in more marked outlines in the silvery twilight; the
frgrance of the flowers became stronger, a gentle breeze
arose from the Guadalquiver, and nature did her part in
seasoning the approaching meal with poetry.

Passing a richly-ornamented terrace, we came into a saloon containing marble columns and jets of water, and filled with pictures; and thence into the brightly lighted dining-room, in which was a magnificently dressed table loaded with silver and flowers. On one of the walls was an excellently painted portrait, by a Parisian artist, of the duchess in an Andalusian dress, and from the open terraces the pleasant Spanish melodies of a military band mingled with the freshness of the evening and charmed our delighted ear, whilst our palate was flattered by a well-prepared French dinner. All these things combined, made me remember the evening in the fairy palace of St. Telmo.

As in travelling, things are incessantly changing and in this way always producing new pictures, so at our hotel a new and interesting spectacle awaited us, to which my dear friend, the amiable commander of our frigate, just came in time. We had ordered dancers to present to us the celebrated national dances. Slim girls with sparkling eyes and well-built men entered with Spanish grace the not very brilliantly illuminated comedor, the hall used for the *table d'hôte*, on the white walls of which numerous copies of Murillos were hanging, to be offered to the unfortunate English as originals. Like a voluptuous sultan I took my seat on a sofa, to smoke cigarettes whilst enjoying the seducing spectacle, a pleasure which at the commencement was also enjoyed, by my permission, by the Russian consul and his two stiff virginal sisters, but who escaped later, frightened by the somewhat uncertain movements of a pretty dancer of seventeen. The guitar sounded, the castanets were set in motion by the pretty hands, and in an old rich Spanish costume they commenced the dance.

He who has not seen the bull-fight and these dances does not know Spain. If the man show courage, strength, and agility in the bull-fight, so does the woman unfold in these enrapturing dances the natural grace and

P 2

dignity of the glowing daughters of Andalusia. The
feet are the weakest part of these dancers, but the upper part
of the body is the more supple, and the bending, yielding
and throwing back of the body is at the same time in-
sinuatingly graceful and perfectly dignified, and lovingly
commanding; especially pretty is the sudden approach
of the dancing couple, the piercing look of love followed by
the quickly bent head, and that again by a playful receding.
The head moves gracefully on the slender neck, the black
eyes sparkle with love, the regular features are serious and
yet charming. The arms also move with grace, and the
well-shaped hand beats time to the rattling castanets. To
hear this little instrument vehemently set in motion by a
whole company, seizes one electrically with the national
feeling. A chorus song was given by two of the dancers
To call this melody would be an exaggerated enthusiasm,
for though the sounds come from the lips of Andalusian
girls, they are nevertheless a barbarous snuffling, which,
as I had later an opportunity of noticing, comes from the
Arabian blood.

As the bull-fighter has, on his light-coloured silk jackets,
gold and silver ornaments, so also these male and female
dancers have on their bodices, which are ornamented
with rich braids. Usually the bodice has a colour differing from that of the petticoat, over which picturesque lace
sometimes falls. On their heads the girls have, besides
ribbons, flowers and pins in their hair, which is further
ornamented by a comb obliquely passed through the hair.
The whole dress is picturesque, rich and romantic.

Amongst the dancers, one dark girl, seventeen years old,
knew how to attract our attention by her prettiness, her
suppleness, and by her droll manner; and she was only
rivalled by a tall, by no means pretty, but really clever and
skilful dancer, Doña Inez, the daughter of the sexton of
the Giralda. If the little one, although conscious of her

prettiness, was nature itself, so Doña Inez was the actress, the coquette produced by art, confident of victory. Our doctor commenced courting her in the most amusing manner, as he, without being able to speak one word of Spanish, commenced a Spanish conversation with her, at which Inez gave herself the airs of a *grande dame*. The daughters of Thalia were urged to smoke cigarettes, which they did after a little struggle. Inez had scarcely given a few puffs when she gave the cigar to a gentleman, who after the Spanish custom had to finish it, as it is considered to be a great compliment to receive from a lady the cigar which she has tasted. So also it is with a glass of sherry.

The order of the dances, which are executed by one, two, or more couples, is: first, Sevillaise; secondly, Fallera de Xeres; thirdly, Bolero and Cachucha; fourthly, Baile de Banderete; fifthly, Bolero; sixthly, Mijares, a dance with many springs, accompanied with a horrible song; seventhly, Seville, also a very lively dance with a very stirring song; eighthly, Ole; ninthly, Bolero; tenthly, Jota. When the music for the eleventh dance commenced, I was quite surprised by hearing homely words, and still more so by seeing Inez dance an affected ' Ländler;' we felt quite flattered that the eleventh dance and song were German.

Seville, September 16, 1851.

To-day we had to pass the Guadalquiver over an old ship bridge (for the fine iron bridge which is supported on stone pillars is not yet finished), to visit the Triana, which is the most remarkable part of the city of Seville. The very name of Triana conjures up visions of night, death, or sin. At one moment these spectres appear as horrible murderers destroying for vengeance or for money; now as dark gipsy girls, who with glowing eyes, and busy castanets, bring about a slow death by some seductive poisons. It is said that in the Triana that charming being was born who

excited her victims to madness, who afterwards left the
stage to rule an empire, and who shows as a trophy of
short rule a royal symbol in her coat-of-arms.

We drove along a filthy and ruinous street. Before
miserable houses with low doors brown gipsies were sitting,
and little children were crawling about like vermin. But it
was morning, therefore the Triana did not show itself
in its black characteristics; and I believe that all is not
so bad there as romantic minds picture to themselves;
and that modern ideas have worked a change even here.
Under a glowing heat we drove thence to a secularised
Cartuja on the same side of the shore as the Triana, which
is used as a china manufactory by an Englishman. In
the middle of a wild and disorderly garden, stands, near a
puddle of a pond, a little temple, in which the delicate
poetical bas-reliefs of the Moors are miserably imitated
by awkward house-painters' bungling. A copy cheaply
produced, is a clumsy imitation, and is always like a
trivial parody, changing poetical ideas into would-be witty
puerilities.

In the Cartuja we were entertained by nothing so much
as by the absurd rage of a dignified turkey-cock, who
took the jokes in which we saucy intruders indulged at
his expense very ill, and strutted about like an indignant
courtier in his bedizened court livery. Perhaps the poor
bird was some enchanted prince, or a grandee of the proud
court of Madrid, who, as a penance for former arrogance,
had to go through this course of purgatory.

The arsenal, the foundry, and the manufactory of gun-
caps outside the city are institutions which, by their arrangement and order, certainly exhibit the satisfactory
progress of Spain. Here, as in Naples, the means of death
are manufactured in the midst of gardens and flowers.
The dangerous fulminating powder, required for the caps,
is prepared in various stages in storehouses, surrounded

ness of evening came on, a dense fog enveloped the ship, the water became of the colour of the clouds, and our frigate appeared to be floating like an isolated body high in the air. Now and then there was an uneasy movement, glowing phosphorescent sparks shot along the sleeping flood, no breath stirred, all was seen through an uncertain light; it was a dismal sort of haunted feeling which possessed us, and the flying Dutchman would not now have been out of his place. Perhaps the sea-god was celebrating his nuptial night. I had never experienced anything like it. The phosphorescence, more particularly, seems peculiar to the Straits of Gibraltar, where we now are, sometimes producing a magical effect, more especially when the oars are moved.

September 20, 1851.

In the morning we came in view of the great monster rock which arises majestically from the ocean and the Mediterranean, offering from either point a different picture. Gibraltar has the somewhat awfully pleasant power which attracts from its dominating greatness. So everything, which rises above the ordinary standard of nature ' and of daily life, captivates weak humanity, and attracts like the awful whirlpool with a magnetic power. In the manner in which it hangs over consist the beauty and the charm of this naked, bare, sun-baked, giant rock. By picturing to yourself a rocky mountain ridge cut in the middle one may get an idea of Gibraltar. The side cut perpendicular to the top, and forming an immense, inaccessible stone wall, stands as a gigantic support or defensive wall towards the great port of the world, the Mediterranean, having at its base scarcely room for a couple of small houses inhabited by Genoese. The steeply sloping outside wall of the ridge, half grown over with dwarf palms and forming up to the crest-line an oblique plain, faces towards the land's end of Spain, separating the great ocean from the wide open bay of Gibraltar. Cutting off the ridge at both ends, one gets on one side the vertical rock wall towards the 'neutral ground,' and therefore towards Spain; this is the only part of the rock not washed by the sea, but which instead is bounded by a plain of sand similar to the surface of the sea. Thus the rock rises with a marvellous freedom like an island.

There are several heights on the crest of the rock, and on one of the most elevated of them stands the telegraph tower. Between the above-mentioned sand plain, across which the Englishmen hold their inevitable course, and the city of Gibraltar, is a narrow road of communication defended by walls and water-ditches, which at the same time leads to the small but crowded mercantile harbour, to which flock ships from all parts of the world after their distant expeditions. Gibraltar is one of those great world-trade stations, which, like the Cape of Good Hope, has been appropriated by Great Britain, to hold the trade of the world by the monopoly of arms. How glorious for England's proud sons, to find in all their voyages, at every turning-point of their wide sea-roads, a bomb-proof hotel! They can everywhere find their countrymen, and everywhere can sing under the blessed shade of their banner, 'Rule Britannia.'

From the Punta de Europa towards the town the new city for the soldiers extends, surrounded by blooming gardens; certainly the most cultivated part of the rock, where officers and *employés* live in English comfort amidst masses of geranium, mixed with rich-coloured southern flowers, dense trees with picturesque rocks, aloes and various bushes, the whole intersected by the most excellent roads. Between this part and the old is the drill ground, by the venerable Moorish tower-crowned town, and between murderous batteries.

But let us return to our ship. We were sitting be-
calmed opposite the big giant, and were annoyed at the
splendid but phlegmatic weather, the greatest enemy of
the sailor. The boats were lowered, and we moved slowly
towards the anchorage, which we reached about noon. One
of the staff of the governor, clad in the fantastic little
uniform of the English general staff, took us by surprise
with a letter containing the most polite invitation from his
commander. We declined, however, for to-day, in order to
be able to roam leisurely through the city. Through gates
and over ditches we entered the most unassailable fortress
of the world, which could only have been acquired by the
English by treason. Through a large square, outside the
barrack, one enters the only great principal street of
Gibraltar, which in an irregular course runs through the
whole city. There are shops, elegant and inelegant, the
exchange, the Catholic and the English church, the latter
with Moorish horse-shoe arches without any ornaments,
bare and clumsy, more fit for a stable than for the exterior
of a church, and the government mansion, a former Fran-
ciscan convent.

In this street may be seen two distinct phases of cultivation : the so-called barbarism, and that which we choose to
call civilisation ; we see the dress of all stations in life, of all
countries and religions, especially of the English. Looking
around we see the gigantic red-haired red coat, or the
blue constable, usually in a spencer or a little white coat,
with a little stick in his hand, without arms, and that
little saucepan-like cap, which, being without a visor, does
but little to protect his blue eyes against Spain's African
sun. They solemnly walk about as if on stilts, and in
doing so preserve the same pace, the same stiffness as on
the drill gound, but Spain's swarthy children are also to be
found in Gibraltar, and form even a chief item in this
human *pot-pourri*. Here again are the Andalusians with

their little, round, velvet hats and embroidered jackets,
and the female Andalusians with their mantillas and brilliant eyes. But the latter are not the genuine inhabitants
of Gibraltar: these wear long, heavy cloaks of red cloth
with black velvet seams, and a cape drawn over their
heads, and look unpicturesque and witchlike. So also the
long, thin young ladies, and the stout soldiers' women cannot justly be called picturesque. Much more picturesque
are the so-called barbarians, the men of Tangier and Fez,
in their wide golden garments of rich colours, with the
large turban, and the overshadowing bernous, which give
to their majestic, earnest figures a poetical charm, increased
by the pure white cape which surrounds, vapour-like, head
and turban.

In contrast to the serious, proud Moor, whose bearing is
that of a victorious caliph, is the African Jew with his dark-
blue caftan, and his small, black hood; supple and smart here
as everywhere, with the same repellent features, the watchful questioning eyes, inviting the bashful Christian with
an uncomfortably sweet smile to trade; with the same bent,
supple spine, which bends to the heavy sack until it is
filled, which he then pantingly, but hoarse with laughter,
carries home.

Two shops strike the eye of the stranger: Mr. Speed's
warehouse of English goods, intended for the outfit
of sailors, and a shop kept by a fine, lively, honest
negro, in which the most splendid objects from the neighbouring continent may be had at a fair price.

One would be extremely mistaken in imagining that Gibraltar had the characteristics of a great city; the houses are
clean, but small and mean-looking, everything is on a neat,
comfortable, small-town scale. It is a garrison town, from
which the practical, sober English spirit has driven out
Spanish-Moorish romance. It is the life of the red-coats
on the hot southern soil. As to trade, Gibraltar, though a

secure harbour, is only a place through which one passes without remaining.

The roomy drill-ground between the park and the town is ornamented by some splendid trees, which justly bear their Spanish name, *sombra.* The park offers some fine views, but is at the present time of the year very much dried up. Two monuments are erected in it. The one a statue of Wellington, standing, and a most humorously executed statue of brave Elliot, the stubborn defender of Gibraltar. With an immense old-fashioned hat on his large head, the hair of which ended in a pigtail, with legs like a broomstick, the gilt keys of the fortress in his right hand, the old hero seems to promenade in the shrubbery of the park like a ghost of his former self. In all matters of art the English are far behindhand: with them, comfort and the practical are the principal things aimed at; art is not understood by them; it is just the opposite with the Italians, who are so enthusiastic 'per le belle arti,' that they, for art's sake, freeze like tailors in their giant palaces under fresco-painted ceilings; Germans and French alone succeed in uniting the two.

The day was warm, and we rested in a tent, looking out for Gibraltar's greatest curiosity, for which every one inquires. Everybody looks out for what so few visitors have seen, and what in Europe, Gibraltar alone possesses: I mean the four-handed monkeys in a wild state, Gibraltar's pride and greatest wonder. It is the only place in Europe where these animals can live, and that too in very considerable numbers; they feed on the fruit of the dwarf palm. If the wind be blowing from the Mediterranean, it drives them towards the lowest sea-batteries, otherwise they are rarely seen, and a dead monkey has never yet been found. Where do these animals come from, if we cannot believe the tradition that St. Michael's cave leads to a submarine connection with Africa and the monkeys'

hill of Ceuta, and that the four-handed regiment marched
in through these caves ? The killing of one of these
animals is prohibited by a heavy fine, and so also is the
slaughter of rabbits, which may some day be useful as
food in case of a prolonged siege.   We did not succeed in
seeing a monkey, and returned disappointed to our ship.

Sunset in Gibraltar is generally a splendid spectacle ;
the southern glow deepens most beautifully the various
colours of the finely shaped rocks, while the picturesque
mountains of Spain, projecting over the ocean and clad in
deep blue, are distinctly marked on the golden, sunny
background. The southern evening then quickly comes
on, then one light after another appears from the foot of
the hill up to the top of the rock, and the brilliant starry
firmament overspreads the black giant, which, seen from
the sea, leaves a vivid impression.

Gibraltar, September 21, 1851.

After mass on board we paid a visit to the convent.
Passing up a neat wooden staircase decorated with arms,
and by a window painted with escutcheons, we came to the
cloister-walk, containing, not the portraits of pious abbots,
but of those brave red-coats with hair powder and pigtails
who took part in the celebrated siege of the invincible
rock.   This cross walk encloses a friendly yard surrounded
by fine, many-branched pepper trees, like weeping willows ;
in the middle a large fountain, in the stone basin of which
turtle doves live.   Here we were met by a thin man in a
black dress coat and white gouty slippers, who shook hands
with me ; it was Sir Robert Gardiner, the governor of
Gibraltar, whom later I learned so much to appreciate and
love.   He led me into a large, clean, simple room, which,
like all other rooms of the convent, was painted with a *café
au lait* colour, and made a comfortable impression, which
was further heightened by exterior passages provided with

Venetian blinds. From the saloon one looks upon a rich garden facing south, commanding a view of the beautiful bay. One loses the consciousness of being in a fortress, and rather fancies oneself with a rich planter, than with a governor in old Europe. Sir Robert commenced the conversation in English, like all Englishmen, proud in self-consciousness, but I insisted upon commencing in French as the language of communication. After having declined all invitations to-day on account of a bull-fight in Algesiras, we returned on board the frigate. In the afternoon a boat carried us in an hour to the little town Algesiras, on the opposite shore of the bay.

It may be imagined with what interest I went to this national festivity. I passed the intermediate time on the Alameda of Algesiras, for, however small a Spanish city may be, an alameda is to be found there. Wide gravel-walks lead through shrubberies of southern plants, and from the shady seats one enjoys a fine wide view of proud Gibraltar, haughtily overlooking Spain, and of the opposite coast of Africa with its blue mountains, its monkey's hill, and its neglected Ceuta, the impotent antagonist of the mighty European column.

The town of Algesiras is small, and has rather irregular and dirty streets, but the houses are neat and clean, as is the case throughout Spain; and from behind the reed-mats, which exclude the heat, and which are substitutes for our wooden blinds, and the far-projecting, almost cage-like, green-painted window-lattices, frequently but very little raised from the ground, glow, in the half-darkness, the black eyes of the roguish female inmates, giving the stranger an idea how pleasant a *tête-à-tête* would be, about the time of twilight, through these narrow, coquetry-favouring chinks, where the girl who is courted is secure in her sort of fortress, and protected against any too passionate outbreak of her admirer. In a mean-looking house, with

two sentinels before it, in a principal street leading to the
Alameda, lives the 'Comandante-general del Campo de
Gibraltar,' one of the best-paid and highest positions of
the Empire. He is a kind of observer of what is going on
opposite, and commander of a camp existing only in fancy,
but once formed against those former enemies who took
Gibraltar. This camp is intended to perpetuate the regret
for the loss of the splendid fortress, which the Spaniards
still flatter themselves that they will get back. Now they
have only to prevent smuggling, which they do unsuccess-
fully; but the general collects enormous custom-dues from
the communication between Gibraltar and Spain, as one
has to pay one colonat, every time one comes or goes,
with loaded or unloaded mule, which is not quite agreeable
to the English.

The commander enjoys the most splendid hunting of wild
boars and deer in the Sierra Nevada. This general-in-
chief, of the name of Calogni, an educated, agreeable man
of about forty, who had served with distinction in the late
wars, had been informed of our arrival incognito, and
hunted us up on the Alameda, in full dress, covered with
decorations, and surrounded by his general staff. To us,
sitting comfortably on a seat in *dolce far niente,* this surprise was not the most pleasant, but Calogni understood
how to make amends by his amiability. He led us into a
building which was formerly a church, but changed by the
circumstances of the time into a barrack, where the men,
like all the soldiers in Spain, looked well and martial, but the
rooms, on the contrary, were beyond everything unpleasant.
We were also led to a sea-battery, a sad contrast to the
great Gibraltar, showing clearly how inexorably history
raises and destroys, according to its fancies, and how
nothing can impede its arbitrary and powerful progress.

The general is a decided enthusiast for corridas, and both
to his influence and to his money it is partly owing that

Algesiras has an arena. He not only invited me to come with him into his box, but went even so far in his politeness as to urge me to direct the fight in person, by means of a white handkerchief which he put into my hand. Though this embarrassed me much at first, I must confess that I was proud to take a leading part in such a national sport. Unfortunately the fight did not respond to the enthusiasm of the leader, the performers were all novices, without strength and courage. The fighters were cowardly *dilettanti*, not even dressed in the old costumes, and not more than two horses fell whilst we were there. The arena built of wood was not filled, and when at last a man appeared upon stilts to destroy the poor calf, I felt too much, as a genuine admirer of this truly noble fight, to be desirous of any longer looking on at this butchery. I forsook my office of director, and turned my back on this shameful exhibition with a deep-felt regret that my remembrance of Seville had been tarnished by it.

Gibraltar, Sept. 22, 1851.

This day was devoted to examining the inmost terrors of Gibraltar, and its astonishing cave buildings. At the water-gate, through which officers only are allowed to enter, the son of the governor waited for us, as well as a few other officers. We mounted horses, and proceeded through the town between neat gardens cultivated by non-commissioned officers, passing the old venerable Moorish tower, over a considerable height, to the first rock-gallery looking upon the neutral ground. My astonishment was great when I found we need not dismount, and that the rough rock of Calpe could receive horse and men. A bold breach in the rock made by iron and gunpowder forms a broad, high cave-passage, without rise or fall.

On one side are loopholes, through which the light of

the day shines in mysterious, yellow tints on the rough walls, leaving the road—which had the firmness of rock, and the stillness of death—in half darkness, from which one, as if standing on a superior world, looks down on the little earth, on the sands of the neutral ground, and on the lazily-moving sea. One has a feeling of pride in looking through the rock eyes of this petrified Titan, as from a secure, immense height, on the ant-like, diminutive doings of the earth. In these rough, unadorned caves stand, like solemn monks in a cloister of rock, apart and silent, the awful guns of Gibraltar : now they are silent as in deep meditation, but when they commence their wide-reaching chorus, the world trembles before the impressive psalms of chastisement of these rough monks ; then the rock smokes and roars like a volcano, and pours its deathly lava from the dizzy height on to the head of the daring enemy. What a spectacle must it be when the white smoke issues in slow circles from the cavities of the lofty rock, surrounding in cloud the forked lightning, and thunder shakes the air, roaring in hundredfold echo the trembling waves of the two seas, proclaiming to ooth continents the revengeful wrath of England !—when the heavy missiles coming from the bowels of the rock, hiss shrilly with a cry as of ghostly owls, without any antagonist of flesh and blood being seen, still less any hostile movement !

But whether, at such a time, life in the interior of the rock be pleasant and free from danger, I cannot say. Firstly, notwithstanding all air-holes, the smoke must take away the view, which is only to be had through small loopholes, and even the air which is requisite for breathing must be impeded. Secondly, it is doubtful whether, after continuous cannonading, the rock could resist the terrible concussion produced by the expansion of the air. Let us ask how that giant wall is to be defended from the flank? But nature and art have provided for that also. Between the two walls, lying respectively towards the neutral ground and the Mediterranean sea, projects, like a balcony, a rock which, to the height of two battery-tiers, is excavated like a hall, and which rakes with its terrible guns in all directions, as in the most regular fortress. These galleries on the giant balcony are named St. George and William's Hall, and in the former the garrison gave a ball some years ago. It must be extremely beautiful to see a thunderstorm from these rocky halls, through the loopholes of which one has the most comprehensive view of sea and land; when the white waves of the ocean and the Mediterranean dash against the immutable rock, when the heavy clouds sink down towards the sea, and thunder resounds against the rocky walls, the lightnings flashing, and the wind shrilly whistling through the crevices. To be alone in these dark stony halls in such an uproar, must be awful and refreshing to the soul.

It is strange to observe the great number of falcons that fly around the walls of the giant, which as quick as lightning issue from the crevices to float motionless in the air over the dizzy heights; one envies them, for they alone can play around the rock from all sides, know every cave, freely rule in the gigantic space, and discover its most remote mysteries. This right, although in a less degree, is exerted also by the monkeys and rabbits. We ascended to the upper battery, and I made the remark that what has been done here by the hand of man has been surpassed by the celebrated rock galleries on the road of the Stilfserjoch on the Italian side; it is chiefly its natural site which makes Gibraltar so extraordinarily remarkable.

We next visited the telegraph-house, standing on a narrow edge on the highest point of the rock, and from

which one, as from the clouds, enjoys with wonder and
admiration the imposing view all round.   In addition to
a few Englishmen who keep guard here over the world,
an exceedingly malicious, gigantic monkey, a child of the
rock, a noble Gibraltese, is also a guard.   To my regret I
did not get a view of his brethren who were at large,
during my sojourn.

Our road, now on the narrow dizzy edge, now on the
side towards the ocean, led us between numberless fan-
like dwarf palms which cover some parts of Africa and
Andalusia like grass, and serve the monkeys for food,
to the St. Michael's cave, whose wide hall exhibits fantastic stalactite formations, which however are not com-
parable to those of Adelsberg, and from which a connection
with the opposite continent is said to exist.   An English
general, O'Brien, went a great way into this mysterious
cave, and when he either could or would not proceed
farther, he threw down his sword as a present for him who
would fetch it, but O'Brien's sword is still where he left
it.   Riding on good roads along the steep walls of the
rock, we came to one of the most exposed batteries on the
steep side towards the Mediterranean, from which one
sees as from a box the houses of the Genoese village,
built on the sand of the coast, standing forlorn between
the rock-wall and the sea.   We passed the governor's
villa, which is built in the style of an American planter,
and situated on the rock towards the Punta de Europa,
and came to the newly-built military house of correction,
situated between batteries.   I saw here the first peniten-
tiary upon the silent system, where the criminal, through
complete want of occupation, and by a cruel and absolute
solitude, is rendered either better or mad.

In small, clean little rooms, with a little window high
up, a wooden bed, a washstand and a Bible, live these
involuntary Carthusians all along a passage, from which

one can observe them and visit them. If one enters the bare cell, the inmate undergoing his wholesale penance has to turn his back to the comer, and to remain standing immovable. The convicts have a rough but useful dress, and close-shorn hair, and as they wear no irons, one is more reminded of lunatics. A house of God is not wanting here, in which the convicts sit in obliquely amphi-theatrically arranged wooden boxes, so that all can see the preacher and hear his words without being able to exchange with each other either looks or words. Service is held here on Sunday, which is attended by the director, a field officer, with his family. In the week the house of God is used as a school and the clergyman is the teacher. To give the body exercise they have invented a game which blunts the feelings. The prisoners gathered in a narrow space must lift for several hours each day iron balls, carry them a few paces, put them down again, lift them up again, and so, on and on. The feeling that the toil is useless, the perpetual monotony, the perfectly aimless work, is intended to im-prove the mind. I believe this apparent improvement is a dulness produced by despair; the individual is made a machine; a machine does not resist; but whether this brutal thing may be called a better man I do not know; for it is an awful thing to cut off from active life a self-dependent being.

This moving of the balls, by which is to be calculated how many thousand and thousand times a man must use-lessly stoop in a month for a dead piece of iron, has left a painful impression upon me, an idea of the hopeless emptiness of the never-to-be filled vessel of the Danaïdes. The poor men look very pale, and do not seem much pene-trated by the philanthropy of this new system. If one would carry out the much-praised Pennsylvanian system, in which the convict is protected against corrupting in-fluences, and is brought to repentance by absolute seclusion and eternal monotony, one should invent soul-barometers, which to the minute and second should indicate when the unfortunate is bettered, to restore him to liberty and to the world before the soul has sunk into lunacy or misanthropy.

A large, fine carriage-road between picturesque rocks and charming villas, led us past the park and over the drilling-ground, through a gate where a forlorn Imperial eagle still bears witness to the former rule over the world of the Hapsburgs, to the town and to the convent, where a luncheon was waiting for us at the friendly governor's. Unacquainted with the English custom, which requires a guest to ask for everything and help himself, we had to suffer the pangs of Tantalus, to enjoy from afar the fumes of the joints, and to be satisfied with small insignificant bits. When we were asked what we should like, we answered evasively, and the practical English must have taken us for members of the Temperance Society.

In the evening, in honour of us foreigners, a brilliant gala dinner was given in the great hall, the former church of the convent. All the best society of Gibraltar filled the saloons of the governor. The strains of our national hymn greeted us with the most friendly welcome and impressed us with a feeling of festivities at home. The aged governor, in the full uniform of a general of artillery, covered with the finest military decorations, received us as a friend. After the usual presentations, in which Old England always behaves a little awkwardly, every one gave his arm to his lady, and to the strains of music we entered the brilliantly-lit, large hall, which was appropriately adorned with the colours, covered with victories, of the regiments stationed at Gibraltar.

The immense table was filled. I found my place was between the amiable governor and his friendly lady; and now we again noticed an English custom, for at Sir Robert's they still dine after the old fashion. The aides-de-camp at the end of the table carve, and handle the big joints, nay, often whole animals, with dignity and seriousness; every one has also his bottle of sherry and his decanter of water before him. In all these things I was a novice, and felt exceedingly happy to be able to witness the official habits of Old England. We had scarcely sat down when the company rose again. I, in the first surprise, remained sitting, for I thought the English rage for toasts had commenced before the stomach had been strengthened; but the governor murmured a few words towards a person sitting far off, on which the archdeacon said grace. I rose quickly, delighted at this fine old custom, which opens and consecrates the meal with a thought of God, and which has been unfortunately abolished altogether in our Catholic lands, as fashion, the only religion of the educated classes, prevents one showing to one's neighbour that one thinks sometimes of the great God. Strange also to us foreigners, but very friendly, is the custom of the English of drinking to each other; you seek anxiously between the crowd of flowers and table ornaments him whom you wish to distinguish, which indeed is your desire in respect to almost all of them. If you are too far for a glance you call attention by a servant, pour a little sherry into your glass, which is imitated by the person honoured, stare stiffly at him, bow the head forward without moving the mouth, and sip or drink, and then this ceremony, which reminds one by its phlegm of the Chinese pagoda, is finished.

When the principal meal with its large joints is discussed, all the plate and even the glasses are taken away, the covering napkins are rolled off, and fresh glasses are placed on the great table-cloth with little bowls containing fresh water, to cleanse the mouth and hands, whilst those persons sitting in the middle of the table are provided with large bottles of the principal wines. Some trifles were discussed, and the bottles commenced making their rounds: the master of the house calls out, 'Gentlemen, will you charge your glasses?' each supplies himself with port, sherry, or claret of different qualities, according to his taste, and the era of the toasts commences.

The worthy old gentleman rose and gave a toast to our much-beloved monarch, and, to our pleasant astonishment, in the German language. If the grammar was not always correct it went to our hearts, for it was our mother-tongue. Except the master of the house, according to the English custom, nobody else rose, and the applause at the close of the toast was only given by knocking the hands on the table, the effect of which, *en masse*, is not so very bad; after this the 'Gott erhalte' resounded in the hall.

After the toasts, the ladies left the table to await the arrival of the gentlemen in the saloon, who still comfortably gave themselves up to wine and conversation. It seems strange when the ladies, at the desire of the gentlemen, humbly march away from the table. Many blame this habit as barbarous; I like it. The ladies ought to learn that they have to obey the men; and to what an exaggerated and senseless gallantry shown towards the ladies leads, is shown to us by the immorality of France. After coffee we rejoined the ladies, and after a conventional conversation, the company separated, and Austria returned on a fine night and over a sparkling sea, to the frigate.

Gibraltar, September 23, 1851.

To-day we went out into the green country, leaving the rock-fortress, and riding on horseback towards the cork-wood behind St. Roque. This party, arranged for us by the friendly governor, was quite a success. His son and his aides-de-camp accompanied us. During this party we had the pleasure of learning how perfectly hospitable and amiable the English are when they wish to be so. The sons of Albion are endowed with the gift of making their guests comfortable if they really like them, of being cordial when it comes from their heart, but they are stiff and cold, nay, even wanting in politeness, when they cannot see sufficient ground for a pleasant manner, and this unconscious frankness becomes them very well.

By the low neck of land of the neutral ground, we went over the sand of the shore, which reminded me in a lively manner of one of the happy evenings of my life in the glorious gulf of Lepanto. Between dreary hills, the hunting-ground of the fox hunters of the garrison of Gibraltar, our road led us to the cork-wood. It is a large splendid wood, reminding one, by its gigantic, wildly scattered trees, and its festoon-like creepers, of the romantic descriptions of the American virgin-woods. The trees are the celebrated and useful cork-oaks, whose soft, light bark is a large revenue to the possessor, and gives stoppers to our bottles. There is something curious on learning for the first time the origin of a thing frequently seen, and to which one is accustomed by use. How many corks had I seen in my life, and had in my hand, and burned them to make moustachios with, and yet I only knew that the cork was taken from a tree, but how the tree looked, or what kind it was, and where it grew, was all unknown to me! I had not the least idea that it was an oak, and that whole woods of it existed in Europe. But one travels to learn, and probably one learns something new at each step, and that is the unsurpassable pleasure of wandering, which compensates for so many privations, and in which the mind is enlarged, whilst the heart also has its enjoyment. One learns only by seeing, and finds often a pleasure, not sufficiently appreciated, in the smallest details.

The cork, so much in demand, grows on a curious and

fine species of oak, whose elastic, light, but knotty and rough bark is detached from the poor tree, and carried to the sea for exportation by mules, of which we met long caravans. The tree, however, does not die through this rough treatment; nay, it even reproduces I believe from the wounded trunk the much-used material, the obtaining of which is perhaps one of the most easy labours. Looking at our German oak, it is difficult to believe that it is its brother which furnishes in the south the material for corking up the delicious product of the vine. The most favourable time for seeing these cork-woods, which extend for miles, is said to be the spring, as it is for every child of nature; then they bloom and sprout most luxuriantly, and at the foot of the centenarian oaks the finest flowers of the south grow around in great abundance, whilst the creepers extend their soft, green fetters from branch to branch. But in the Spanish autumn-time also, which corresponds to our warm summer, this curious wood is very beautiful.

Where the forest became somewhat lighter we found between green hills a small, broken-down convent with a large orange tree in the otherwise neglected yard ; and after having visited the small church, which according to Spanish taste is rich in gilded wooden ornaments, we entered one of the bare rooms of the convent, now only inhabited by a single priest. Involuntarily I imagined myself in the days of Don Quixote, in one of those dwellings, surrounded by woods void of man but full of adventures, yet my adventures amounted to nothing more than the partaking of some of a cold English monster roast joint, and instead of blood, my greedy thirst was satiated with the most excellent sparkling Moselle, a wonderful kind of wine, the acquaintance of which I had formed only in Gibraltar, at dear Sir Robert's, and in which 'the bouquet' of the Moselle imparts a flavour to the too sweet Champagne.

This delicious beverage is obtained by growing grapes of the Champagne on the banks of the Moselle.

After having refreshed ourselves, we commenced our return home, but we forsook the regular road, took another direction, and came through some romantic valleys and over picturesque hills, past a herd, when W——, in the midst of loud disapprobation from the herdswomen, insisted on playing the picador with a young bull, but had to leave off without accomplishing his purpose. Then we rambled through a wonderfully graceful pine-wood, passed through Ronda, a little town lying on an eminence, with its inevitable alameda, in which a part of the English pass the hot season. We next passed between dense hedges of aloes to the shore, and over the neutral ground to Gibraltar.

In the evening I gave Old England a dinner on the frigate, but besides Sir Robert I had invited the Spanish Captain-General Calogni. Remembering yesterday's toast I drank the health of the 'little Queen,' in the English language, after which other toasts were exchanged. The band played, 'God Save the Queen,' the 'Hymna Borbonica,' and the beautiful 'Gott erhalte.' Scarcely was this cosmopolitan banquet at an end when all rushed into the convent to a brilliant ball which the governor gave to his Austrian guests.

Notwithstanding the excursion of the morning, and other exertions during the day, dancing was going on bravely, in which, however, the daughters of Albion are far inferior to our maids. In waltzing, a Lerchenfelder girl is a queen in comparison with these ladies, who move clumsily and without grace. The prize of beauty was well-contested here, for the apple might be divided between two figures, of whom one was an English lady, a calm, clear, perfect beauty, with round, almost large figure, regular features, and dazzling complexion; the other, a light, graceful, glowing Andalusian, with raven hair, and mildly glowing eyes, beautiful as a dream of love, graceful as a gazelle. The choice was difficult, it was a choice between the calm, fresh North on a summer day, and the Spanish moonlight night amidst orange-trees interwoven with jasmine.

Gibraltar, September 24, 1851.

Sir Robert, in the rich uniform of a general of artillery, mounted a fine, large, black horse to show us some more military curiosities. First, we were conducted to the barracks of a Scotch regiment, and whilst we admired the neatness of the vaulted rooms and the excellency as well as the abundance of the rations for the privates, the Scotch pipers played before the building, in their rich national costume, their monotonous bag-pipes.

It is not merely the body of these splendid soldiers which is nourished in super-abundance with the finest beef and the most excellent potatoes, but an endeavour is also made to improve their mind. A rather rich library has been collected at the common expense, open to every one be- longing to the association, in which are also many papers, and amongst them the 'Illustrated London News,' a luxury not found on the continent, even in many officers' quarters, for whom it would be still more useful than for the common men, with whom it might produce an injudicious half- knowledge. Whatever the private has here, his officer has in a greater degree, and the garrison library which we visited is really very interesting. Founded so far back as 1793, it is kept in a spacious place expressly allotted for this purpose, and already contains more than 8,000 works. Two of the newest struck me by their finished beauty: the one contained drawings, with explanations, of the Alhambra, the other, splendid lithographs of Egypt and its monumental wonders. How they made my mouth water, and what ardent desires were called forth by the view of these remarkable pictures!—how oil was poured by them on the flames of my desire for travelling!

Yes, let everyone travel who can. By travelling one gets the true view of life; in this way only one becomes acquainted with the world, and really it is pitiable to see so many waste their money and their time stupidly sitting by their own fire-sides; but still more to be despised are those who thoughtlessly let themselves be dragged like trunks through foreign countries, without recognising the beautiful and sublime, and who at best only make impertinent jokes over the immortal monuments of art and history. Unfortunately, the number of these travellers is very great in our time. The hopeful youths of the nineteenth century, educated in modern materialism, believe themselves in duty bound to travel; they think it bad style in the highest degree to find interest in anything interesting, or to get attracted, still less excited, by anything beautiful.

They travel because it is *bon ton*, to test the different manners of cooking, to pass through the different theatrical seasons, and to show the people of various countries how they yawn at all that was formerly great, and how insipid and dull a modern *élégant* can be. Such a one annoys himself and others, and becomes a nuisance to all those he comes across.

We now proceeded to the mess-house of the artillery officers, who had invited us to a luncheon. A detachment of artillery in glittering full-dress, with music, stood waiting before the house, to confer on us the most brilliant honours, whilst in the great hall a splendidly dressed table greeted us. The noblest wines, the best dishes, and the finest silver showed the wealth of the English army. Each regiment has its so-called mess, in which all the officers take part, in a suitable locality, where they have their meals together, and pay for them each day, whether they eat them or not, but for which they are excellently supplied. This may be of great advantage to the *esprit de corps*, and, at the same time, prevents the younger officers from exposing themselves to disagreeable scenes, in inferior inns. After the obligatory toasts had been dispatched, we went to the great barrack, where a red-coated and truly splendid regiment defiled to lively music in measured parade-step, like a walking rock.

In the fine, scrupulously clean barrack, I was especially struck by the mess-room of the non-commissioned officers. Comfort, which extends even to this inferior rank, shows the richness of this nation and its thorough knowledge of how to live,—a knowledge exhibited by few nations, and which appears to me highly important. The English sergeant has his dining-hall, his cleanly laid-out table, his elegant and tasteful plate of English metal, as the officer does with us. It is true that the English sergeant can never become an officer, he therefore makes himself comfortable in his inferior position, whilst ours nourishes the hope of becoming an officer, should chance favour him.

Very interesting to me was the examination of the convicts' ship. For this purpose the English use old ships of the line, once rulers of the sea: these, now bare of ornament and painted grey, were distributed about the small bays of the rock. Formerly used for war, and carrying death over the seas, their fine oak decks serve now as large soul-coffins for criminals. The port-holes have become windows, all the spaces are emptied and changed into wide airy cages, above all description clean, and brightly scoured; everything which recalls war and the sea, each tool and arm, has disappeared, and the poor empty vessel offers this advantage only, that buildings are thereby saved, and escape is rendered almost impossible by the surrounding sea. In the batteries where the guns formerly thundered the rabble now sleep in hammocks like sailors—an arrangement deserving imitation, on account of its cleanliness and saving of room. Wooden gratings and partitions separate the different rooms, between which runs an airy passage. By the removal of all objects necessary for shipping, the space appears so large and light, that you no longer think that you are on the sea. Of the convicts the sick only were present in their hammocks, the rest were away at hard labour in chains. They wear a white and very good dress.

The only reproach to be made against this excellent institution is that these men live much too well, and one can understand how hungry people may commit crimes merely to get into such an establishment. One wishes for the poor and honest Irish the abundant and good food here given to great criminals. That where the head can pass the body can also, was here shown by a bold fellow who pressed himself between two cage-rails in a very incredible manner.

Sir Robert Gardiner accompanied us with his suite to the shore, on which was ranged a company with a band, and where he took a most cordial leave of me, to my great regret. We went on board ship, but a calm prevented us from leaving dear Gibraltar.

September 25, 1851.

The calm continued with its leaden pressure, destroying all energy, and not until 5 P.M. could we move, and, amidst the thunder of the English batteries, say good-bye to the proud rock of Calpe and take our course towards Malaga.

September 26, 1851.

Towards evening we came in view of Malaga. Far off glowed the beautiful forms of the proud mountains of the Sierra Nevada. Beneath, on the blue and always beautiful sea, lay the world-famed town of Malaga, with its lofty cathedral towering gigantically over all houses; with its old castle on the broken-down hill; with its unpoetical

factory chimneys lighting up the night, which, like obelisks,
but without ornament or hieroglyph, shoot up into the
glowing blue sky; with its sea-defying pier and its far-
seen lighthouse. Malaga is now one of the richest cities
of beautiful Spain, and in a short time perhaps will be
the first commercial place, for by its rapid rise it promises to outshine Cadiz, once so rich. The principal trade
of this growing city consists in dried fruit, and in a delicious fiery wine, which the sun produces on its numberless bare heights. The pilot was called by a gun-shot,
but night had arrived before us and we had to delay our
entry until next morning.

Malaga, September 27, 1851.

A little after seven we cast anchor in the roadstead.
We soon went on shore and landed under the large iron
roof, which covers a place teeming with people, quite
mercantile in character, and crowded with goods. My first
walk was to the gigantic cathedral. It is one of those rare
buildings found only in Spain, which exhibits to the
lovers of architecture the unsuccessful transition from the
sublimely pure Gothic to the clumsily overloaded Roman
style. Still there are some fine ideas in this building;
still are we surrounded by the delicate ornaments of the
older time in a few favoured earlier-built parts, but the
heaviness of an unmeaning pomp begins to appear in
it. The principal façade is a perfect failure, but it is
shown with pride to the visitor on account of its heavy
richness. Very handsome, on the contrary, is a side-door,
of which the arches are delicately and artistically encircled by the Gothic ornament of a number of little saints
in their neatly carved niches. It is arranged, as regards the
interior, after the Spanish fashion, the choir being separated
by walls and railings from the rest of the church. The
high altar, free and raised, overlooks the other altars,

which are in niches at the back of the round wall of the nave. This arrangement has something dignified and high-priestly about it, directing all looks to the high altar, and separating the officiating clergy from the praying people.

Though our consul spoke of Raphaels, I only found in this church the painted saints carved in wood for which Spain is celebrated, in which the truth to life is often quite awful, and of which I found, as I mentioned before, a superlative specimen in St. Jerome in the Museum of Seville. In the church we were complimented by the worthy old bishop, who was recently appointed archbishop in Granada. I noticed that the bishops of Spain wear grass-green shepherd's hats, with many tassels, which look very well with their purple gown. The palace of the bishop on the Place of the Cathedral has, like the church, a too rich and tasteless façade ; besides these there is not much worth seeing in the city. The streets are narrow and rather dirty, but very lively; everywhere one sees the finest fruit for sale in masses; mules and donkeys are in motion everywhere, pressing and hurrying on; but one misses the calm grace and dignity of Seville.

Malaga, like every town in Spain, has its Plaza de la Constitucion and its Alameda, which is here indeed very fine and grand, in the middle of the city, with a wide triple avenue, and pleasantly surrounded by the largest buildings of the city, amongst which are a few fine, city-like hotels. At the end of the fine airy promenade and towards the sea, stands a fountain of a very curious kind, in which the water is spouted into a basin by stone figures in a very natural way. Fortunately the police, watching over morality, seem to have cut off the water from this joke of the days of wigs. There are some very elegant shops under the cool shade of a very pretty little bazaar. Here the celebrated clay statuettes are sold which, artistically done and well coloured, represent scenes and costumes of the rich romantic life of Spain. The groups of a bull-fight are especially good, of which I, being a warm admirer of this national sport, bought several.

The evenings in Malaga are truly magical in their intense and almost melancholy clear tints; gold, blue, and pink fuse in the pure cloudless twilight, shining on the forms of the mountains and irresistibly calling forth sweet thoughts of the past and of eternity.

Malaga, September 28, 1851.

It was Sunday; I heard the holy mass on board our frigate, and, as I did not feel particularly attracted by the city, remained there all day, and was in my cabin fighting with an extraordinary mass of flies, caused by the warm climate and by the many fruit-ships richly laden with grapes. It was quite an Egyptian plague, which almost prevented me from writing. At last I lit a great number of candles, and crowds of my enemies fell a victim to the sudden *éclaircissement*. The others were on shore, and worked very hard at preparations for an excursion to Granada, which I absolutely, *coûte que coûte*, resolved to make to the flower of Moorish Spain. On all sides impediments arose to our journey: all the places in the diligence had been taken, the governor was obstinate, the road was not secure; horses were not to be had, carriages were wanting. But this was no reason why I should give up a journey on which I had set my heart. If people are obstinate and difficult to bring to reason, then I am still more obstinate and am the more resolved on not being prevented from carrying out what I want. That's the way to conquer. And so a vehicle was found at last, and a man to take us to Granada, the last place of note on our voyage this year.

September 29, 1851.

We started at two o'clock A.M. In the darkness and freshness, beneficial both for body and mind, we rowed to land, accompanied by our amiable commander, who would see us delivered over to the superintendent of our journey. On the Alameda stood two old carriages, scantily illuminated by some lights, each with six horses. Armed men on horseback surrounded the carriages, wrapped in dark cloaks; a few words of farewell interrupted the stillness of the moment, and away we went at a quick pace, as if it were an elopement in the beautiful romantic time of Don Quixote. Night covered us with its shade, and sleep, into which we soon fell, was only interrupted by the cries of the leaders and the rattling of the carriages, reminding us that we were on the high road to Granada.

When morning came with its silvery grey light and the cold awoke us, we were at a great height, and a sublime panorama spread before and beneath us. Hundreds of cones of the curiously formed Middle Mountain rose before us, rose-coloured, whilst between the numberless hills, ascending gradually to the chief mountain, appeared single valleys, beds of rivers, and crater-like cavities, overgrown by fresh vegetation, and from which shone out in the calm peaceable morning, single farm-houses and chapels. Behind, the high and beautifully formed giant-mountain shelters this land from the rough winds of the north, and endows it by the absorption and reflection of the sun's rays with that celebrated climate in which even in winter the temperature is never below 12 deg. of Réaumur, a temperature which enables every American plant to grow on this European soil.

At the foot of the Middle Mountain, on a river bed now dry, and in a rather wide plain, lies the prosperous city, shining in the morning light. Before us expands the endless mirror of the azure sea, on which, as a speck in the wide horizon, our frigate was lying immovable. On the side of a mountain, between vineyards, our road took us to the Rocky Mountain. We frequently met peasants wrapped up in their romantically picturesque ponchos; caravans of mules with goods, or loads of grapes, for it was just the time of the harvest, were hurrying towards the city. The peasants of the country of Malaga, as in the plain of Granada, wear, like all Andalusians, embroidered leather gaiters, velvet or leather knee-breeches, the scarlet sash wound many times round the waist, the jacket neatly embroidered in colours, the knowing black velvet cap or peaked hat, and the above-named poncho, a broad, long, and sometimes embroidered strong cloth, in which the upper part of the body is enveloped as in a Scotch plaid, serving now as a protection, and now as an ornament.

At a little house on the first ridge we halted and took a cold breakfast, as an obliging alcalde on horse back, armed with his gun and bringing home part of his grape-harvest, offered us, politely and gracefully, according to Spanish custom, some beautiful grapes, without the least embarrassment, as if he were dealing with his *confrères*. We rewarded him with the remains of a bottle of Johannisberg, which honest German return he seemed to like very much. Whilst we were stopping here we remarked that our servants were much better off in their carriage, in reference to temperature and space, than we were—if something not at all good may be called better. They moreover numbered three only and we four : this caused us to change carriages, and we now got one of the time of Maria Theresa, with a large closed outside state box painted a cardinal-red colour. The inside was lined with silver-grey and yellow embroidered satin ; in a word we got a gala carriage, excellent a hundred years ago, then indeed perhaps the pride of a grandee, a cardinal, or even a royal prince, but now fallen from its high estate, but which, as I read with a certain pleasant emotion in the travelling sketches of the countess Hahn-Hahn, also served her a few years ago—as probably all travellers to Granada—and was spoken of by her with praise.

The most curious thing about these Spanish vehicles, for the foreigner, is the manner of putting the horses to the carriage. Six horses are connected to the carriage by means of traces, but only the shaft horses have bridles, which the so-called mayoral manages by means of dreadful cries; the other four animals, amongst which is frequently a mule, are led by their own common sense and the zagal, a very nimble boy. The latter is always in motion; gifted with famous lungs, he runs by the side of the front horses and mules, urging them with his stick, throws stones at them, and frightens them with his cries, sitting, if his animals happen to be going in the proper direction, then again running in advance; and thus he is the chief motive power of the whole equipage and at the same time an instance of Spanish endurance. It can be readily understood that this manner of driving does not at first agree very well with nervous foreigners; for to look out upon a bridleless team can never be satisfactory, especially on rocky roads with precipices on either side. But the zagal is equal to all possible emergencies: an indefatigable help in trouble, and the real moving-spring of our very national vehicle. The mayoral, on the other hand, is decidedly the moral power, who in a crisis works by the power of speech, or rather by shouting to his animals; he calls everyone by its name, as Coronel, Castagno or Capitano, to encourage them in their hard duty; but if they excite his ire he calls them the most offensive names, and so attempts to work upon their already somewhat blunted sense of honour, then one frequently hears the 'Anda, perro!' (Go ahead, dog!)

We had, as I said before, reached the first hill, and

now found ourselves on a wide table-land, looking towards a rocky, bare, gigantic mountain; in the plain was
the village of our friendly alcalde and some fields, but
otherwise it was rather bare, especially as we came nearer
to the mountain over which we had to pass, and at the
foot of which everything acquired the character of our
high Alps. The grass was short and greenish yellow, the
plants, amongst which there were no trees, corresponded
with those of our high mountains; single cows and goats
were browsing on the sunny meadows running up to the
rocks. In a word, all wore the stamp of our beloved
Salzkammergut, and homely and pleasant, if somewhat
sad feelings, shot through my heart like a sunbeam from
the sunny past. Ascending the mountain on foot, we met
the diligence, drawn by mules, plying between Malaga
and Granada; it quickly passed us, for the mules go at a
very good pace. We looked astonished at the passengers,
and they looked inquiringly at us, as is always the case
where men meet but for a moment on the wide earth in
places where few living beings are ever seen. In the eyes
of these passengers one feels a sense of importance, travelling as we were. We know that we are a riddle to
them. We stand before those we shall perhaps never
meet again with a sort of coquetry. So it is on a high
mountain, where two people meet at sunrise, so on the sea
when two ships meet, so also on the dreary heights of the
Sierra de Ronda, where people measure each other enquiringly and for a short moment form an intellectual
connection by both being travellers and engaged on the
same errand.

Before we crossed the mountain, which closed before
us like an enchanted wall, through which there was no
visible passage, we stopped at a posada, a regular Spanish
inn, in order to refresh ourselves and our horses. A stable
and a yard with a good well sufficed for the horses; a large

irregular, smoky, and dirty room served as kitchen and larder and sitting-room for the numerous family of the host and as the reception room for the visitors; in a word, it was a room used for all purposes. But the posada contained a treasure in the family of our friendly hostess, who were the handsomest children I think I had ever seen: a truly Murillo-like family. They had the brown fresh face with the large splendid eye, upon which it was a pleasure to gaze ; and withal, the children were so natural and so graceful, that it was a pleasure to converse with them. A painter could not have found prettier models for his Christ-child, his John the Baptist, or his little angels.

A wild, romantic defile, a fine place for a band of robbers, brought us over the crest and down a slope planted with ancient bushy cork-oaks. Over a wide plain we came upon the splendid new road leading to Loja.

The soil here seemed to be fertile, but was now barren ; in one valley only, which we could see from the road, was an extremely pretty oasis refreshing the eye, amongst the trees of which several large buildings were seen, probably a colony of manufacturers. During the day it rained a little, but the evening was beautiful and clear, and the Spanish sun went down splendidly, colouring the mountains with purple. The air, purified by the rain, was refreshing. The country became greener, and towards dark we came upon a little river with overgrown banks, on which, on an elevation, and surrounded with trees, was the little town of Loja, the cradle of the once powerful and energetic Narvaez, duke of Valentia. A few advantages in lighting and some of the walks in this small and insignificant place show that the great man who ruled Spain and its queen did not forget in the height of his splendour his humble birth-place. In a fonda where lamp-oil was used for the salad—from which we may conclude that the one was too good or the other too bad—we passed the night.

Granada, September 30, 1851.

As early as four o'clock in the morning, an unmerciful hour, we had to get into our red state-carriage, that we might enter the Moorish royal city as early as possible. Daylight found us on an undulating barren plain. At the side of the ferry a fine stone bridge is being built over the river. Perhaps in the spring the river will be more swollen ; at present the bridge is a luxury. We had passed the Rubicon and now came upon the famous Vega de Granada —the centre of civilisation in the old Moorish times and the heart of beautiful Spain. To our left were to be seen the woods which a grateful country gave to the victorious Wellington, as a magnificent addition to his English estate; before us in the distance lay Granada with its fresh green chain of hills. Unfortunately it rained, and rain is very unfavourable to romance, and damps enthusiasm. At the station next to Granada a detachment of lancers waited for us. Here we had an opportunity of seeing greyhounds peculiar to the country, and red partridges, which in Andalusia are kept in very small cages, just large enough to hold the body of the animal, probably for the purpose of fattening them. We passed through Santa Fé, a small place with a large church, standing on the spot where Isabella the Catholic heard mass with her husband on the day of the taking of Granada. We were now at the entrance of the city and saw distinctly the charming chain of hills, a lovely terrace at the foot of the mighty principal mountain. Red walls and towers in the manner of our castles, high up amid the fresh green, made me think of the Alhambra.

A few palms and the arena for the bull-fights were the first things that struck us in the city : we passed them under a steady rain, and rattled on to an hotel in a large street on the banks of a river ; but nothing was to be had there, so we wandered on to the Leon de Oro in the neighbourhood of the theatre, where we settled down and had occasion to be satisfied with our choice. We had scarcely disposed of our luggage, when, armed with umbrellas, we made a hurried tour through the city. In the neighbourhood of our fonda we came first upon a place in the centre of which stands a marble pedestal with bronze inscriptions and ornaments—a monument dedicated to the revolution and its heroes. The clumsy statue of a woman of the name of Perez, who would not betray the names of those who had taken part in a meeting for liberty held in her house, and who was beheaded under Ferdinand VII., was intended for a number of years to occupy this pedestal; we were shown the model of this statue, which, to the horror of all friends of art, is preserved in the museum. More interesting and much finer is a pedestal in the centre of the Plaza de la Constitucion, on which stands the old winter palace of the Moorish kings, now the town hall. How the old sovereigns would wonder at finding the word Constitution in the place of their despotism! On this place the splendid bull-fights were first held in Spain, which originally were only games and not fights; there, under the royal balcony, the Moors let bulls loose, exerting against them their utmost courage and strength without killing their mighty antagonists. It remained for the chivalrous Christian time, used to combats, to change the game into a serious one. I could not easily imagine the Moors, in their oriental dress, seriously contending with a bull; the fierceness and strength of the Goths seemed to me much better suited for it. This Moorish custom is utterly extinct in Africa, whilst in the Peninsula it was grafted on mediæval chivalry, and thus imbued with a new life, out-lived all revolutions, and continues even in this humanitarian age to excite this fiery people, and even the foreign visitor, who is caught in the whirlpool of their enthusiasm. The importance of the place bulls occupy amongst the Spanish people is proved by the

following occurrence. When the Duchess of Montpensier came for the first time to Tarifa, where for ages no
royal scion had been seen, the loyal population thought
that they could not express their joy in a better manner
than by letting ten bulls loose in the middle of the town.
One can imagine the surprise of the loiterers; all ran
into their houses and all doors were carefully closed.
Late in the evening one of the court-ladies, who was not
quartered in the house of the duchess, was going to her
lodgings and had to cross the street, when one of the
festival bulls rushed towards her. She turned round in a
great fright, but, oh heavens! from the other side of the
street came also another similar monster, trotting on
towards her; her position was more than disagreeable, it was
critical and dangerous. For a matador there might have
been a chance of a double victory; but our poor doña
seemed lost, when fortunately a door opened quickly and
she found an asylum, getting off only with a fright.
This story, which I heard from the amiable duke himself,
is a good illustration of this Spanish custom.

In the place mentioned above, as well as in the various
genuine Spanish streets running into it, are many well
supplied shops; but in them are sold, be it said to the praise
of the frugal Spaniard, objects more of necessity than of
luxury: unlike our cities, where the latter are oftener
found—to the ruin of the lower classes, who think they
must imitate the rich. The Spaniard does not know this
malady of wanting things above his position. He dresses as
his father dressed, cleanly and simply, nor does his house
exhibit any ornament except in his beloved patio, which
no house in Granada is without, and which is always
arranged in the most pleasant and most agreeable manner. But it is not the luxury which is noticeable, but
the graceful and light style of building, the ever fresh ornament of lovely women and beautiful plants, the strange

subdued light and the lively refreshing play of its little fountains. The ladies also know no other luxury than their mantilla, trimmed with fine lace, the velo, and the Chinese fan. Black which so well becomes them prevents a too great extravagance, and they ornament their rich black hair, which nature always gives them in rich abundance, with roses and jasmine. An additional charm to their attractive exterior, and for which they are much envied by foreigners, are the small fine shoes into which they put their lovely little feet. Everyone knows how frugal the Spaniards are, and frequently their whole meal, to them a very rich one, consists in their beloved and really savoury *olla podrida*.

An elegant ornament of Granada is the silk bazaar, which has come down from the time of the Moors: a perfect garden of little marble columns with beautiful arches, many interwoven arabesques and inscriptions, form a range of small shops, where, in the proud day of the Caliphs, the silk interwoven with gold was sold for their luxuriant oriental garments. Now, everything is sold here, and this spoils the delicate harmony of the fine building.

The large, majestic cathedral stands on the place occupied once by the old mosque, of which the traces are still to be seen on one side, and recalls, without equalling in its exterior, the Gothic splendour of the cathedral of Seville. The exterior of the cathedral of Granada is difficult to understand, as it does not stand free enough, and draws a number of buildings into its net of ornaments. The wide gigantic interior is a mixture of Gothic, New Roman, and Moorish. The Capilla Real, the jewel of the church, is pure Gothic, and a true treasure of historical relics, to which we will return in the afternoon. The lofty cupola, which rests on columns, is New Roman, and arches over the high altar, around which everything is full of gold and tawdry

ornament. The Arco Maravilloso—an arch with an extremely wide span—connects the cupola with the nave,
and forms the gate between the space round the altar
and the high wide church, representing a very curious
transition from the Gothic to the Roman, but where the
remains of Gothic were more numerous than in the
cathedral of Malaga.

In our fonda a dinner awaited us, only too good, and too
well served, commencing with the *olla podrida* and
ending, as if we were in Canaan, with monster grapes, the
juice of which ran over. I do not believe that anywhere
in the world are grapes that can vie with those of beautiful Granada in size and excellency; even in the much-
praised East I have found nothing like them, especially
the blue ones.

Scarcely had we refreshed ourselves when we again
hurried to the great cathedral, to examine its interior, and
to hear the playing of the great organs, whose screaming
and snarling sounds disturb in an unpleasant manner
the serious stillness of the church. It was fortunate that
this by no means edifying concert did not last long. In
general I am no friend of the organ, as its notes are rarely
pure and clear, scarcely ever soft, and too mechanical.
There is too much rattling and groaning. There are a few
sublime moments when one hears the harmony of the
spheres and which correspond with the magnificence and
power of the Catholic Church.

We left the centre of the church, and began to examine
its history in the curious Capilla Real, a masterwork of
perfect harmony. It was in the light of evening, the true
light to look wonderingly in an earnest frame of mind at
monuments of a beautiful past. A rich iron railing separates the chapel from the church; behind it shines the
splendidly carved Gothic altar, in colours and gold, raised
on steps: a sublime production of art of a childlike, pious,

and poetic time, reminding one by its expressive little figures and tastefully interwoven ornaments of a noble christmas *crib-plaything*, as we have it in Germany.

Especially curious is the altar, constructed from two wood basso-rilievos, one of which represents the unfortunate Moorish king Boabdil marching out of the Alhambra, the walls of which are seen, he is bringing the keys of the castle to the victorious Ferdinand ; the other exhibits Moorish women bending over a baptismal basin to receive the con-secration of the Christian religion. These two carvings are curious by reason of the costumes, which are somewhat different from those of the Moors of the present day. Still more curious are four portraits, also carved in wood and painted in colours, of Ferdinand and Isabella, of Philip and his great son Charles V. Philip, called by his con-temporaries the Handsome, has the sharp, large Haps-burgian features which characterise his father Maximilian, and which have something typical and peculiar to that time. Each century, as also every country, has its peculiar physiognomies which are not to be mistaken, and such a one is that of the noble Maximilian which has come down to his descendants. Strictly moral—which is sufficiently indicated by the dress, fully covering the form—proud, cold, and devout, and firm in character, must have been the serious Isabella. The Catholic Ferdinand appears to me more in-significant. There are two other pictures of her husband in the sacristy.

At the foot of the altar are two fine double sarco-phagi of dazzling white marble, on which are curiously-carved likenesses of Ferdinand and Isabella, of Philip and the maid Joan, who look serious and solemn as petrified corpses. Their son Charles caused this fine monument to be erected in honour of the latter. The first monument bears the stamp of the strict Catholic time, but the second is embellished, with truly astonishing art, by the luxurious, heathenish, mystical ornaments of the refining but also lowering Cinque-cento epoch, in imitation of the antique.

I looked right into the dead still face of the stone likenesses of my ancestors; they were great men, who enacted a portion of history, who have done something on this earth, have begotten a mighty, far-ruling race, and now rest alone in a solitary chapel. *Vanitas vanitatum!* Instead of the glittering court surrounding them as formerly, a poorly clad sacristan now takes a torch, opens a small iron door, and leads me down narrow steps into a low, musty vault, without any embellishment, any ornament—where the naked truth grins. On this the eye of the forgetful heir never looks, and what the world does not see, it does not adorn. Here rest these proudly royal couples in these narrow, small, dreadful, bare coffins. One feels the heart oppressed, and the *memento mori* to princes shudder through the soul.

In Spain I was the nearest legitimate relative to the poor dead, nearer than the ruler and the princes of the country. Here I felt that the family feeling lives even after centuries, and a melancholy regret moved my soul to see the great dead thus forsaken and not thought of by the new dynasty. I, in simple dress, stand by the coffin of those on whose sunny throne our family would still rule if there had not been a Charles II.

Beside the two royal couples there lies in the musty vault Don Michael, an elder brother of Charles V., who in his 13th year died from a fall from his horse. The very existence and the fatal end of this prince, who, according to the decrees of fate, had to make room for a man who was great for all time, had remained unknown to me till I saw his coffin. For such a young life history has no pages; it is only when a man either does deeds or resists a progressive development that his name is noted down in the books of Clio; moving-springs or drag-chains alone become known.

Darkness began to creep over those dismal vaults—a veil over the empire of death. The Quasimodo unlocked a small room, stirred about in the darkness, and returned with the regalia of the Catholic Ferdinand and the prayer-book of the devout Isabella. That which a proud nobility and pages formerly vied in carrying, the sexton of the cathedral now brought to the simple stranger. Proudly and yet sadly I took in my hand the golden ring and the once power-ful sword. Would it not be a brilliant dream to draw the latter in order to win the former? All that was once so great is now a toy for foreigners and for the curious, and I asked the sacristan, whether I might be allowed Ferdinand's crown for a few shining thalers; but against that he protested. He had recently been forbidden to exhibit the church ornaments embroidered by Isabella's own hands, because an Englishman had cut off some gold fringe.

Before leaving the cathedral we read over the episcopal ordinance, calling to remembrance that people who conspire or have to do with mujeres will be excommunicated or fined. Availing ourselves of the night, we stole to a dark narrow street in which a woman sells wall ornaments of the Alhambra, stolen by galley slaves; the old woman feigned to be very nervous, and told us that the robbers of Alhambra arabesques were punished by having their left hand cut off. On returning to our fonda we heard through the night air, singing and the jingling of bells; they were people who either in honour of the Mother of God and of the saints, or to obtain alms, went about singing litanies—a singular, rest-disturbing custom.

Granada, October, 1851.

Soon after six o'clock a.m. we left the fonda to do homage to the crown of Moorish Spain, and, in an elevated frame of mind we directed our way towards the Alhambra. We were to enjoy the sight of the crowning point of our fine journey; one of those moments but rarely enjoyed in life. The weather had cleared up, promising a fine day. Passing the grand palace of justice, in the Cinque-cento style, ornamented with a big bell on the roof, and the house of the perfidious Gomer, whose history we shall hear later, we came to that gate, also in the Cinque-cento style, built by Charles V. in the precincts of the stronghold of the Alhambra. At home one imagines the Alhambra to be a fairy residence, but it is a great mistake; it is a strong citadel on a rocky height with mighty walls, numerous towers and heavy gates, including in its interior two kingly residences, the summer palace of the Moorish kings, and the unfinished palace of Charles V., besides several hundreds of houses and numberless gardens, nay even fields. The whole rock-hill with its under world, sheltering during the siege 40,000 Moors, is called the Alhambra, and is still considered a fortress. But what a fortress! A really goodly castle, uniting in its Moorish halls the charms of nymphs and fairies, to the strength of Jupiter in the fine palace of the emperor. Seen from below, the Alhambra appears like an old German feudal castle with balconies, tower and ring walls, and one imagines oneself in Germany, though a more glorious Germany. Entering the fresh, cool park which runs around the hill, and ascending to the castle, the luxuriant trees, always watered by fresh springs, form a magnificent arch; a fine walk with rose-hedges runs under a dome of oaks, beech trees, plantains and chestnut trees; everything shines with an eternal spring. My heart leapt within me at the sight of this beautiful grove, and I imagined myself at home in Heimbach or Dornbach, only there it must not be October 1, but May 1, and be always May 1, to be like what it is here. This is the charm of Granada, that it unites the freshness and the fulness of the north with the mysterious charm of the south.

A second gate, and this time a Moorish one, brought

me into the interior encircling wall on a wide place
opening before the building of Charles V., and the summer
residence, with the Moorish cisterns, which form arches
underneath it, and contain delicious, icy-cold water; to the
left, opposite the kingly residences, rises the Torre de la
Vela, a mighty red tower, from the battlements of which
the Christian banner first proclaimed to the new Spain,
which was then proudly rising, the victory of the royal
Catholic couple of January 2, 1492; towards the park stands
the Torre del Vino with elegant, rich-coloured, Moorish,
horse-shoe arches; here, under Moorish rule, Christian
wives were sold. All this is connected together by irregular walls, and interspersed now and then with patches
of green, forming an interesting picture of a knightly residence which has become a ruin. Stepping between tower
and castle on to the breastworks, a picture of rare charm
unfolds itself; the ancient, venerable, city with its high
churches and many towers lies, a perfect world of houses
and gardens, in the valley of the Darro. On the height
opposite the Alhambra is the old poetical Moorish town
Albaicin, and over it, glittering in southern warmth, the
rich vega, surrounded by mountains, the blessing of the
country, and behind us the bluish-black rocks, with snow-
covered tops, of the Sierra Nevada.

Looking on the buildings before me, I ask enquiringly for
this much praised summer palace, but I only see naked irregular walls; this is, however, quite Oriental, that the buildings from the outside should be mean-looking, and the interior only, which is disclosed to the guest, should discover
the hidden charm, as the shell which is black outside conceals within it the pure pearl. Very imposing in exterior is the summer palace of the great Charles, a splendid
reflex of the noble builder. Charles was an emperor, but
he was also a poet; in travelling through his beautiful
Spain he came upon Granada, and at once fell in love

with it. Here the fresh verdure of his northern dominions
was offered to him united to the rich luxuriance of the
south, satisfying his love of romance. Here must he live.
It was not the emperor, but the poet, who loved the Alhambra. The little rose-gardens, the myrtle-courts, the
marble basins, with the silver purling fountains and the
merry dabbling fishes, the woods of slender marble columns,
the architectural wreaths of leaves and the fairy arabesques,
the dreamy life fed with the fragrance of roses and the
song of nightingales—all this, which was the charm of
the interior of this Moorish palace, captivated him. For
the master of the world, who was not permitted to dream
on a throne eternally lit by the sun, all this loveliness
was useless. Grand must be the dwelling of the great
Charles; he tore down the Moorish winter-palace to build
his imperial residence on the ruins of a destroyed fairy-
tale world. He did a horrible violence to art, but his
palace of large freestone is the idea of a ruler, whilst
what remains of the summer palace of the Moorish kings
leaves only a lovely and romantic impression; as of a
dwelling of elves woven from moonbeams, in which one
may dream but not govern. Charles's palace resembles
a crowned and helmeted prince in serious majesty, whilst
the seat of the Caliphs resembles a siren with pearls in
her wavy silken hair.

Were I a sovereign and had to choose between these
two royal residences I should decide at once for the palace of
Charles. We entered through a horse-shoe arch in the
bare outside wall. Transplanted as by enchantment, we
found ourselves secluded at once from the rest of the
world and in the dream-land of the Alhambra, in a
long charming patio, ornamented at both ends with light
galleries and perforated arches. In the middle, surrounded
by myrtles, violets, and roses, is a rectangular piece of
water with merry gold-fishes; this water is fed by fountains

and little channels in the marble floor of the court. Unfortunately the play of the fountains, a principal charm of the Alhambra, was stopped to-day. Over one of the two galleries, whose marble columns have blue ornamented capitals and arabesques, a passage runs towards the palace of Charles V. In the first storey were wooden lattice-windows, like those of Oriental houses ; and above is a lofty colonnade with a richly-carved wood ceiling. This is the highest part of the whole Moorish palace, which in other parts has only a ground floor or single storey, and seems to have formed the passage to the winter palace, as there is still one gate here which leads to the emperor's building. How delicious must be this patio in the mild moonlight of spring, when myrtle and violet send forth their fragrance, when the sweet love-song of the nightingale is wafted through the air, when the fountains melodiously murmur, and the moon sheds her silvery beams on the untarnished mirror of water !

The wonder of the Alhambra is the Court of Lions, which is the largest patio in the palace. The Moor does not care for system, or regularity, which is the greatest enemy of poetry in everything, and therefore also to architecture. Through beautiful gates which obliquely cross each other one comes upon a rectangular enclosed court, surrounded by a colonnade which is rather a dream than a building. On the two shorter sides it runs out into kiosk-like projections, half open balconies, half little temples, which rest on slender little columns. Everywhere the intersections produce charming perspectives and are perforated like lace veils, everything seems waving or hanging loosely as if negligently attached with diamond pins ; the arabesques part and reunite in everlasting puzzles ; narrow channels carry the silvery flood from fountain to fountain, and the very breath of poetry raises for the looker-on a dream of enjoyment: 124 columns bear the light burden, and form the slender support of this stone tent; for the Alhambra is, after all, like the Alcazar of Seville, an enchanted tent, and even still more so than that; or are these very veils and very lace, which delicately swing from support to support? are these not golden interwoven cloths of Cashmere and Thibet, which fall down in dazzling folds from the lofty walls? does not one expect every moment that all this light delicate web will swell to the air? Yes, here we stand in the Oriental tent which a caliph from the far East has erected, on the green heights of Granada, to the bride of his heart for his honeymoon.

But this work of the moment was too beautiful to be allowed to perish, and art for ever fixed the tent of linen and silk, of purple and golden embroidery. The fine bride's veil of the sultana, interwoven with blossoms, has come down through hundreds and hundreds of years, from generation to generation, a lasting splendour, and still affords a glimpse in the charm of its remains, of what it must have been in its full glory. Still it is but a tent, poetical but not grand, and, notwithstanding its duration of 400 years, an ephemeral picture of fancy without the assurance of stability. I candidly confess that notwithstanding the charming picture stamped on my memory, the Alhambra did not altogether come up to my expectation, it was too small, too neat, too confined; it was not royal enough, and I missed bold lines and imposing masses. Two things may have spoiled the impression: the sun, that gilder of all earthly things, was wanting, and I had first seen the Alcazar of Seville, so that I was not surprised, though this is built in the same manner and in many details is more royal. The ceilings of the gallery of the Court of Lions, as also those azulejos running round the wall, are still perfectly preserved in their rich, fresh colours and their wonderful wood carvings, and form the most splendid instance of drawings arithmetically running into each other so as to produce a beautiful *tout-ensemble*. The colours and lines are calculated in such a manner that they, though forming also in their details thousands of figures, if looked on as a whole mingle in such a manner as artfully to create fresh forms. Each part vanishes in the whole, whilst the whole is divided into numberless details which in themselves form splendid parts. Thus the mind has an opportunity for its ingenuity in uniting and dissolving these beautiful forms. The lines in the azulejos are always straight and in square forms; but the arches of clay and mortar ending in hundreds of points, the basso-rilievos covering the walls of the hall, the graceful arabesques like the finest Persian or Indian embroidery, from the border of the azulejos to the rich ceilings, are more intricate and are woven into each other in circular forms. Throughout the ornaments of the arches, as in those of the hall walls, which are in shape and colour like the finest lace and often, also, transparent as lace, runs everywhere the sentence: 'God alone is the victor.' How graceful a puzzle this sentence makes, may be concluded from the circumstance that the Arab writing is itself arabesque.

As the Court of Lions was repairing when I saw the Alhambra, we missed the many waterworks belonging to each room, and the green plants, which, as in the myrtle court, generally surround the large alabaster basin. The Moors understood the charming power of water and knew how to subject it in their finest buildings and gardens to the most lovely uses. There is no hall without a fountain, no court without a marble basin freshly filled, no garden without the spray of water and numberless small cascades; thus that murmuring is obtained, that delicate play of rising and falling pearls, that eternal freshness which is given to the air on hot summer days, and that soothing murmur in the calm moonlight. Water in the rooms is a poetical

luxury very little known with us, but which I will intro-
duce as much as possible into my little world. Nothing is
perfect, not even nature, where the eye is not refreshed
and strengthened by water. The union of the splendour
of flowers with gold and marble is also one of those
ideas of the Moors showing the skill they had to make
the beautiful also agreeable, and the sublime in art,
homelike. With us, all fresh plant-life is exterminated, in
order that art should stand quite naked ; as if a handsome
woman wreathed with roses did not look doubly pretty !
Everything with us becomes directly museum-like, classi-
fied and tedious; one begins to think that one cannot
admire art without a catalogue in hand and spectacles on
the nose; one does not enjoy it as an ornament of existence; it becomes isolated from nature and thereby loses
its meaning which is to be interwoven in our life like a
golden thread. The most striking proof of my assertion
is Münich, where art is so completely separated from life,
standing formally on the cothurnus, and therefore cold
and shivering. The old Greeks understood something
of art; their temples which were in cypress-groves were
half concealed and half shining out; and round their
gods wound fragrant rose garlands, blooming chains uniting art to nature.

On the right and the longer wall of the Court of Lions
is the Hall of the Abencerrages, into which leads a broad
open door with two low little doors at its two sides and
two elegant niches for the slippers of the Moors. Through
the right entrance-door came, so says tradition, the unfortunate Abencerrages, allured by king Abu Abdillah,
to be beheaded at the fountain in this hall. Traces
of blood are still shown, large red spots in the white
marble floor, a counterpart to the blood of Wallen-
stein shown on the boards of Eger. There are two ver-
sions of this story of the unfortunate Abencerrages, who

were a kind of knightly order at the Moorish court. The one tells that Zoraya, a former Christian lady of wonderful beauty, had been the consort of king Abu Abdillah, whose name is usually contracted to Boabdil, and to whom has been given the surname of 'el Chico,' the Little. At the Moorish royal court, to the misfortune and the weakening of the government, lived two parties of knights hating each other to the full, the Abencerrages and Zegris; the former were descended from Ibn Cerraj, the grand vizier of a king of Cordova, and formed a powerful and widely spread family; the latter were the knights of Saragossa and other cities of Aragon, having after the loss of their province retired to Granada; some called them Thegrim, that is the people of Thegr, the Arabian name of the kingdom of Aragon. One of the most powerful at the court of the little Boabdil was el Perfido Gomer, whose house we saw at the entrance of the Alhambra, who was of the Zegris, and who brooded over an hereditary hatred against the Abencerrages and against the influence of Zoraya the handsomest of the sultanas, she whose face bloomed like the rose of Damascus, whose eye outshone the gazelles of Darfur, and whose hair waved like the palm-leaves of Tyre.

In order to ruin both with one blow, he informed the suspicious king that the handsome sultana had been seen one evening in the Generalife, a castle on the height behind the Alhambra, under a cypress, and in conversation with an Abencerrage. This was enough for Oriental jealousy and sufficient to produce in the king that terrible resolution, in consequence of which the tribe of the Abencerrages perished, and the sultana became a prisoner. The visitor is still shown the iron-grated balcony-passage, in a small mean-looking yard of the Alhambra in which Zoraya obtained a little air, and where at a later period the lunatic mother of Charles V. was kept. It reminded

me vividly of the short walking dens of the bears in the
Schoenbrunn menagerie. In a treacherous manner the
Abencerrages were decoyed into the charming hall, named
after them, to be there decapitated; only some few who
were warned by a page hurrying from the scene of murder
succeeded in saving themselves. Zoraya was more fortunate than the knights sacrificed for her. The news of her
unjust imprisonment penetrated the Christian country
where several young and noble men of the Christian army
resolved to save her. They presented themselves to
Isabella the Catholic with an urgent request that they
might be permitted to fight for the innocence of the
Moorish queen. After having received, though . with
difficulty, permission for the adventure, they entered,
disguised as Moorish knights, and as men understanding
the Arabian language, into the Alhambra, inviting the
calumniator Gomer to a combat before the king. Gomer
afraid of these brave fellows confessed his crime and the
noble queen was liberated.

The other version says: a sultan of the name of Mouley
Abu-l-hasan Ali, called by the Spanish authors briefly
Alboacen, a son of Mahomed X., had two wives, one a
cousin, 'Ayeshah, and the above-named Zoraya, who both
presented him with male offspring. The king was attached
with all his heart to the sultana Zoraya, which roused
the jealousy of the other in the highest degree, and she
became afraid that her husband might prefer the children
of the hated rival to her own. She gained over the Zegris
to her cause, whilst the Abencerrages held by the queen
Zoraya. Abu Abdillah Mahomed (Boabdil), according to
this version, a son of 'Ayesha, fled in June 1482 from
Granada to Cadiz, was there proclaimed king, and returning victoriously to Granada, dethroned his father.
Urged on by the Zegris he wished to be revenged upon
the Abencerrages and invited them under the pretext of

reconciliation with the Zegris to his house, and there had them ignominiously executed. Whatever may be the truth, the history, according to either version, is a bloody one, and this hall derived its name from the unfortunate victims of the crime.

In the time of the Moors these beautiful rilievos glowed in all their freshness of colour; they are now much faded and in many places have been barbarously whitewashed. By order of the government they are just now busy in restoring as far as possible in this hall, those that have received damage. These clay ornaments being slightly relieved produce a picturesque shade. The light projecting lines, and the ornaments, whose graceful drawings are taken from the world of fancy or from nature, are always lined with verses from the Koran of great sublimity, the Arabic letters forming graceful arabesques supported by fine marble columns. Here we see mineralogy with all the wonders of the underground world exhibited in a poetical form, and through its most precious metal.

The gradations of this building, its sharp contrasts of colour, metal, and shape, combined together as they are by a rich Oriental fancy, give an exquisite charm to these rooms, and make it difficult to believe that they are the work of man's hand. They appear rather a dream, a beautiful fancy, a poem, a heart-stirring piece of music. Indeed the whole of the Alhambra is a fairy tale. How delicious it must have been in the old Moorish nights, when the mild moonlight shone through the cupola, the fountains murmured, and the air was fragrant with roses, and resounding with the melody of the lute! The glowing words of Arab and Spanish minstrels bear testimony to the beauty of these moments in these magical halls.

Now these halls are empty and forsaken, and the melancholy murmuring of water is unaccompanied by the charm of song. All this magnificence and beauty glitter now for the eyes of strangers only, or for the galley-slave. It is as still as death, and the moon illumines the poetry of a past time only.

At the other end of the Court of Lions, opposite the entrance in the myrtle court, is the hall of justice, where the princes of the East sat in court amongst the faithful. Here is a perfect labyrinth of larger and smaller rooms and of niches with those golden pyramidical ceilings, like stalactites. These are united to a gallery, divided into seven compartments by wide, airy arches, chiselled with exquisite delicacy. In some of these niches are alle-gorical paintings, painted on parchment by the Christian slaves during the time of the Moors. Amongst these, on a golden ground, are the portraits of ten Moorish judges, full of a patriarchal dignity. These serious-looking men, sitting in a circle on cushions, give us an idea of the costumes of the Moors of that time. A bernous covers all the head, except the face, and is joined to a light-coloured turban; they have also a kind of cravat, a wide caftan, divided in two as in some old Venetian pictures, an under garment of some different colour, and a great sword sus-pended on an embroidered belt. The other pictures repre-sent hunting and fighting between Moors and Christians.

From this hall a charming view is obtained of the Court of Lions, the arches of which seen from this point cross each other in the most curious manner, their numberless little marble columns forming quite a grove. Opposite to the Hall of the Abencerrages is the Hall of the Two Sisters, so called from two large marble plates in the flooring, of equal size. It is one third larger than the Hall of Justice, perhaps a little richer in ornament, especially in its fine lattice-windows from which the hauras of the harem could look at the festival celebrated in the hall. In the alcoves of this hall on the right and left are stone divans adorned with azulejos, the drawings of which are exquisite.

Here also is a fountain. Opposite the entrance is a wide arch, opening upon a magnificent gallery with a balcony supported on columns and low arches, and from which an interior garden can be seen, blooming with the orange, the myrtle, and the rose. This balcony is called El Tocador de la Lindaraja, and was the toilet-room of Lindaraja, a lady of the court, and also the lady-love of one of the kings. This is the jewel of the Alhambra, the gem of this fairy residence, combining in itself all that is beautiful in Moorish art, both in colour and form. The ceiling is a transparent net-work, amidst which are inter-woven the most beautiful verses. Looking out from all this brilliant gold-work, the eye is feasted with the freshly watered orange trees, and with roses bedewed with the moisture falling from a lofty fountain. This little Eden is completely cut off from the world, and the enraptured eye glances upwards from the flowers to the deep blue firma-ment, a fit place for lovers, so protected is it and so still.

The rooms of Charles V. in the summer palace have been arranged for him, according to his taste. Here he lived, for his magnificent palace was never finished. By the side of the Oriental splendour around, his palace is cold and prosaic, and contains nothing but heavy, dark wooden ceilings, like those in the feudal castles of Germany. From the dining-room of the emperor you look into the court of Lindaraja, and on the other side, the windows look towards the little court with the latticed passage of Queen Zoraya, where his poor lunatic mother was im-prisoned. For the honour of the great emperor, I hope that he never knew for what purpose this cage was used. From the rooms of the emperor on the first storey, we stepped into an open gallery supported on columns, which is situated on the outside wall of the fortress, and leads to the neat, bower-like balcony projecting into the Darro valley, the airy, open Tocador de la Reina. Probably, no other queen in the world ever had such a view from her dressing-room. It is a pretty idea to make one's toilet in the free mountain air, so utterly secluded and unreached by the eye of the world, and yet to have at one's feet the whole magnificent valley, the large city, the green and golden vega, nay, even the tops of the plantains which encircle the Alhambra hill and its lofty walls. The business of dressing without this is a dreamy affair to a woman; in a soft leisure the body is prepared for the coming festival, whilst the mind, half mesmerised by the supple management of the waving hair, the ambrosian fragrance of the perfumes, which, by the way, in this Moorish boudoir ascended from below by means of small holes in the marble floor, floats in a sea of half-unconscious thought.

How delightful must it have been to pass the time in this Tocador, under the dominion of thoughts rendered pleasant by this luxuriant nursing of the body! As this open airy room projects on three sides from the crown of the fortress over the Darro towards the city, one may imagine how free, beautiful, and sublime the view is. Imagine the loveliness and natural grandeur of the site of Ambras combined with the southern richness and fragrance of the Moorish country with the kingly view from the Hradisch of Prague, and you will get an idea of the picture presented by the Alhambra. The interior of the Tocador was painted under Ferdinand and Isabella, and discovers amidst its ornaments the F and Y of the royal couple.

In the court of Lindaraja I plucked one of the celebrated roses of the Alhambra. Underneath the Tocador of the beautiful court lady is the Sala del secreto, a musty room, the artful vaulting of which enables you to hear in one corner every word whispered in the opposite one. The devout and severe Philip II. had it arranged for the amusement of his children, intimating that they ought no longer to require to go outside the palace. The banishment of the princes during their hours of amusement to such a gloomy room, the dismal tricks of which were not fitted to replace hours spent in the wood and in the field, was the commencement of that Spanish etiquette, which under the falling Bourbons worked so sadly, so ridiculously, and with such an awfully petrifying effect. This etiquette no longer permitted the king to leave the barren Madrid and its palaces. Etiquette prohibited them from walking in the daytime, by which the night promenades were brought about; it did not allow of balls, banquets, or soirées, and the princes could not even visit the theatre except in the company of the king. Etiquette is the soul of a court and is inevitably attached to every throne ; but the court must have the heart to live, and should have all the freshness of life and its kindnesses. One need not amuse oneself at the court, there are other opportunities for that, but one should feel elevated by the impressions received in the palace, overawed now and then by the splendour of majesty, but tediousness should never be felt, for in tediousness everything perishes as in a Dead Sea. Life dies, and with it progress, as we are unfortunately taught by the history of poor, beautiful Spain.

In an architectural point of view the baths are very interesting. They will be shortly restored. In a large ante-room divided into compartments separated from one another by arches, it was the custom to prepare for the bath as in the East, and one went through a process of kneading and mesmerising at the hands of a slave, and then entered a farther room which contained basins on either hand from the pores of which the steam issued. There were also the bathing places set aside for the children, adjacent to those of the king and his sultana. The room in which they rested after the bath, is in the highest style of Moorish luxury. A gallery runs round the room, from which music issued to lull the royal personage to repose. This room of wonderful loveliness has just been most perfectly restored. In form it greatly resembles a very small court in the Alcazar of Seville, likewise lately restored.

In a vault not far from the bath are the two somewhat immodest statues described by Washington Irving. Their watchful look is directed on that spot where the Moors are said to have buried immense treasures before their flight. Unfortunately these treasures have not yet been discovered. Projecting over the valley of the Darro is a tower of the Alhambra, called, after a son of Boabdil, the Comares Tower, because that king, who according to all accounts was a regular tyrant, had his son incarcerated there on account of a dream. With the assistance of Zoraya, his mother, he escaped through a window. The other son Omer, Boabdil banished from the Alhambra and built for him a palace, the Generalife, on the hill Silia del Moro—on which, by the way, are still traces of a Roman town. He banished him because Omer was too fond of playing on the fiddle, which made the little king nervous. How many princely younger sons would be seized with a passion for fiddling, if by these means they could get such a charming palace as the Generalife! The Moors prayed in the Sala de la Misericordia before they entered the mosque, which under Charles V. was transformed into a chapel.

In a gallery of the myrtle court opposite that visited before, we found a visitors' book, in which amongst the first names is that of Washington Irving, and the respected name of the Countess Ida Hahn-Hahn. From this, one enters into the hall of the ambassadors, Sala de los Embajadores, which is in the Comares Tower. Here one finds the utmost luxury and richness, the space largest, the vault the most lofty, the view from the many balconies the most charming; and the whole hall replete with gold hangs over the valley in architectural contrast with it. On the outside the tower is rough, without adornment, and capable of defying centuries; inside is the room, lighted by numerous windows from the cupola windows, which is the real throne room in all its Oriental fanciful splendour. Azulejos and clay slabs, richer in ornament than ever, cover the wide walls, whilst the floor is ornamented with arabesques, and from the ceiling, finely carved in cedar-wood, shine great pieces of mother-of-pearl, like a starry sky in daytime. In this really princely room, perhaps the only one which responded to the King's idea, it was a delight to step out on the balconies with their double arches and to admire the fairy-like splendour on one side and the beautiful world of Granada before me. From the height of this tower one enjoys the most perfect view all round, and here towards the East we were shown by the cicerone the hill del ultimo sospiro del Moro; the last point from which Abu Abdillah defeated and retreating could see his fairy-like Alhambra; here he paused for a time and the tears trickled down his face. One can enter into his feelings and sympathise with his agony of grief.

To-day before leaving these enchanted courts we were shown, in a room of the myrtle court, a very fine Moorish vase, similar to a Roman amphora, without a pedestal, which, with an old chest, provided with curious locks, and in which were once kept the great treasures, are the only things still remaining from the time of the Moors. In this room are kept, not very carefully, the Moorish archives, which, if made use of before they are destroyed, would certainly yield much interesting information. We now passed through the myrtle court to the palace of Charles V.

The imperial palace encloses a large elliptical yard, surrounded on the ground-floor and on the first storey by colonnades. At festivals, it seems to be used for bull-fights, as it bears the grand stamp of an arena. Its numerous columns are formed out of a composition called pasta almendrada, which looks like decayed marble. There are rooms and staircases all round this colonnade. One can hardly speak of anything in connection with this palace but windows and doors, for there is scarcely anything else. Fresh weeds grew close to a badly-smelling cistern. The steps are effeminately easy of ascent, probably constructed in that fashion intentionally, and because of the gout from which the Emperor suffered.

Except at the plantations of Canosa in Dalmatia, I have never yet seen any vines at once so large and so fresh as there are here. Who may not have tasted of them? Perhaps I may have eaten from the same vine as Philip the Second.

We mounted the Torre de la Vela, in which there is an inscription to the effect that the Christian flag was mounted here on January 2, 1492. The bell in this tower is rung with the greatest assiduity by the girls of the neighbourhood every 2nd of January, tradition promising them a husband within the year in which they perform that ceremony. Every evening after sunset the bell is also rung as a signal to water the vega, an institution dating from the Moors, and to which the country owes its rich harvests.

The Gate of Justice in the outside walls is very interesting. On one of its horse-shoe arches is a hand, and on the portal a key, hewn in stone, respecting which the following tradition is current : Granada was not to be conquered by the Christians till that key was taken by that hand. Nevertheless, the victorious Ferdinand passed through that gate with his royal consort. A similar tradition prevails in regard to Stamboul and Sion. When will the Christians there make a triumphal entry, and destroy the Mohammedan superstition? In Stamboul, this may soon come about, for personal advantage prompts a solution, but it is far different with Sion ; for that work true Christians are required, such as are not produced in this century, in whom poetry and faith have been destroyed by steam and its consequences. The Land of Promise of this age is San Francisco, to which thousands of pilgrims wander.

But to return to the Hill of the Alhambra, to reach which we passed through orchards and kitchen gardens, (for even the inmates of this fairy residence eat cabbages and carrots, and cannot live on poetry and the smell of roses,) to the Tower of the Infantas.

This tower contains a principal room, richly ornamented, which, as is often the case amongst the Moors, breaks through two stories, out of the upper one of which are more rooms. It was used as a residence by three sisters, Saida, Zoraida, and Sulima, with their governess Soraya. They were the daughters of a king who loved them so much that he tried to prevent their marriage by incarcerating them in this tower, and secluding them from the world. But love knows no obstacles, and man yearns for the forbidden. Two young knights, who were imprisoned in the Red Tower, effected their escape, and by means of a rope-ladder liberated their two imprisoned sweethearts. The youngest, Sulima, who was yet too young to know much about love, in the first instance opposed the elopement. She wished to remain obedient to her father's will, for liberty had not the same attractions for her. Her sisters, however, managed to persuade her to escape with them, and with the governess to descend the rope-ladder. Away they went on horseback, at full speed, across the vega. The governess, unused to such expeditions, fell and broke her leg. There was one encumbrance the less. Evening set in ; the sun went down behind the blue hazy hills, shedding a parting ray on the proud Castle of the Caliphs. Then all was consternation and mourning, for the king missed his jewels, the pride of his heart, The bell of the Torre de la Vela rang out, and when its sound was heard by the faithful, fires were lighted on the tops of all the hills. But the lovers rode on swift horses, and love itself has swifter wings, and when the fires had died out, the three Moorish Infantas were beyond the reach of their pursuers. The moral of this story is, that a father's love may be too tender.

Driving through the city we were shown two interesting buildings; the church in which the Moors were baptized, and the house of Sidia Yerriaga, the inventor of cannons. From out of the windows of the top storey some culverins still protrude, and every possessor of this house has with it the right to fire them off at any time, a privilege not particularly agreeable to his immediate neighbours.

Our road led us to the garden of Yarto Real, the garden of Zumera, the mother of the last Moorish king. It is a place of marvellous loveliness and quiet, now the property of a Marquis, whose powdered ancestors look strangely out of harmony in the Moorish Trianon which looks upon the garden through a wide saloon and hall.

What I most coveted here were the laurels, upwards of a hundred years old, trained to meet over one's head, and under whose green vault fountains played and dispensed freshness through the house. The Moorish religion permitted enjoyment in its fullest extent. Wherever their dominion extended, nature opened up to them its richest treasures, which their Oriental fancy knew how to improve. There may be some who think that these fountains, cascades, water-courses, canals and basins, all these ascending and descending streams of water, this diamond shower, these silver mirrors reflecting myriads of flowers, unworthy of attention and childish, but to me they appear excellently suited to the climate, refreshing the eye, and exercising a peculiar charm.

How contrary to all this nature is the absurdly puffed-up spirit of the days of wigs. This spirit one notes in the overloaded church of Santa Maria de las Angustias. Wonderful, here, is the serious face of the Madonna bending her pale marble forehead over the body of the Redeemer. A black and gold mantle envelopes her figure, the attitude of which is mourning whilst her head is encircled by a clumsy crown. Though the ornament is heavy yet the dark mantle heightens the effect of the image of the Queen of Heaven. I stepped up behind the altar that I might see and admire the sad face more closely, and I expected almost to see a warm tear roll down the pale face. The veneration felt for this picture, with its touching name, is general; it has been everywhere copied, and a copy of it is even placed in the church of Malaga; it is said that great miracles have been worked by it and one of these only two years ago. It was very dry and the harvest threatened to fail, the vega thirsted for rain, and all the waters were dried up. At this critical time the people applied to the Mother of God for her intercession, and the image of Santa Maria de las Angustias was carried through the city in solemn procession, and amidst fervent prayers. Scarcely had this taken place when Heaven took pity and sent refreshing rain upon the golden plain. Another instance of the devout mind of the Spaniards is to be found in a large and splendid hospital and church of St. Juan de Dios, which this saint, born in 1495 at Montemôr-o-Novo, a small Portuguese town, was enabled to found by begging, and which afterwards served as a model to all other hospitals. It has spacious premises which are still used for the same pious purposes for which they were instituted by the holy founder of the Merciful Brothers, and it remains a remarkable evidence of what an inspired man may do.

The body of the saint reposes in a sanctuary behind the

church.   Formerly it was preserved in a silver sarcophagus,
but Marshal Soult, unfortunately, took notice of it and removed it as he did so many other things.   Now poor Juan
de Dios lies in a wooden coffin, in the midst of gold and
marble splendour.   But why does he require any ornament? his best ornament is the immense useful building,
the directors of which, however, were secularised like all
other male convents by most atrocious injustice of the re-
volutionary rulers in the year 1835.   A letter and a simple
bread-basket of the saint are still exhibited.   In this
sanctuary is an interesting collection of portraits of all
the sainted crowned heads, of whom there is a wonderfully
great number.   I saw with much pleasure that our mon-
archy was well represented in this company.

The wide, shady alameda, with its splendid avenues, is a
beautiful ornament of Granada, of that Granada which, in
the south of golden Spain, is the spot where the powerful black eye has a deeper meaning than anywhere else.
Granada, watered by the rich springs of the Sierra Nevada,
is the only place on the southern Peninsula which never
loses its spring freshness in the summer.   At the entrance
of the fine wide promenade stands a chapel, historically
remarkable though mean-looking, which is covered with
inscriptions in stone and built on the spot where the Catholic conqueror embraced the conquered Abu Abdillah.   The
Moorish king fled to the sea and bewailed in the deserts
of Africa the glorious days of Granada, and Ferdinand
entered the golden rooms of the Alhambra as master
of the Peninsula.   How dearly the Moors loved the Alhambra, their most charming work, may be judged of from
the circumstance that poor Abu Abdillah could not make
up his mind to leave his palace by the principal gate, but,
bowed down by grief, went out to meet his conqueror
through a side-door.

We concluded the day with an excursion with a few visitors. On the right bank of the Darro, opposite the Alhambra, is a rough slope covered with fancifully pronged cactus plants called Las Cuevas del Sacro Monte. Seen from the height of Tocador de la Reina everything seems dead, and the visitor expects at most to look out upon the caves of reptiles underneath this wide rough cactus wood; and yet it is a Troglodyte town with several hundred inhabitants and with life hiding under the steep sides of the hill. In the daytime all is still and quiet, and when the sun shines it is night in the Cuevas del Sacro Monte, and there is nothing to betray any life in the cactus hill; but when the first bats soar through the twilight, and when the last ray of the sun disappears over the mountains of the Sierra Nevada, then day commences in the cactus wood; a great number of figures glide from the sides of the hill through the narrow paths between the plants, the sound of the tambourine and of singing proclaims to the drowsy city that the Troglodytes are awake.

Numerous dark entrances to the caves of the Gitanos are visible in the dense prickly hedges. These dark chambers in the earth, devoid of light and air, smoky rooms in which bandits and beasts live in patriarchal simplicity, are formed by digging out the soft clay. Egress and ingress is alone to be obtained through an opening surrounded with the cactus. On entering one of these caves a warm stifling air sickens you; and the eye requires time to discern anything in the night of these caves. Groaning and grunting inform you that you are in proximity with a pig and the dirty sick bed of a Gitano. Broken cooking utensils stand on the glowing coals, and the smoke only finds egress by the same openings as ourselves. Rags hang against the black sooty walls; whilst onions and garlic form the treasures of the larder. When, after sunset, we entered the cave-town, the male population were already gone to Granada to profit during the coming

night by theft and robbery; brown female figures and
wild lively children crouched, crying and screaming, before
their dens. Many stared in astonishment at decently
dressed foreigners approaching this thief-district; others
indolently allowed us to walk about, heedless of the
unusual evening visit.

I was much interested by this sight: close to a rich
populous city I was transplanted as by a charm into a
novel of the middle ages, when witches lived on the earth,
when gnomes housed in the clefts of the mountains; or
to the savages of primitive countries, who scratch up
the earth like badgers to find warmth and a dwelling
in it. These Gitanos, wherever they appear on the wide
earth, carry a mysterious romance along with them! In
England they choose their unknown king, and travel to
the fairs to cheat the people; in Hungary they live, notwithstanding the government, as unsettled nomades; in
the golden Peninsula the tambourine sounds in their
hands; the glowing eyes of their daughters ensnare the
heart, and when the cheated world has enjoyed their wild
dance, then the children of the Ganges with bloody
daggers and shining gold glide back into the caves of Sacro
Monte to hide from the eye. And there, withdrawn for
ever from the eyes of the world, may lie in these dark
earthy holes many stolen goods, and much treasure.

Remembering the dark arts in which these people are
said to deal I asked the women through one of our
ciceroni whether any of them could disclose the future
from the lines of our hands. None would acknowledge
this art, until at last, and after much seeking, a woman
took W. . .'s fine white hand and repeated to him a little
verse in which he was given to understand that he would
eat white bread, and that health and long life were allotted
to him. It was already night when we returned to
Granada through the narrow, prickly, uneasy walks of the

Troglodyte town, which ought to be visited by Eugène Sue.

Granada : Oct. 2, 1851.

Our first ramble to-day was again to the wonderful fairy palace where I enjoyed at leisure what I had looked upon yesterday with astonishment. Our request to the governor of the Alhambra had succeeded so far, that he suffered the fountains in some of the courts and rooms to play. Though in consequence of repairs of the pipes, the water was not quite clear and pure, one could hear it murmuring through the golden halls and saw it merrily rippling through the marble floor. Here I must say 'peccavi' to the reader for an offence half poetical, half childish. There was in the inn where we lived a kind of clever Crétin who very cleverly imitated the voices of animals. I had read that above us where the myrtle bloomed and roses poured out their fragrance, the nightingales sang splendidly in spring; this I desired to hear though it was autumn. The Crétin had been taken to the Alhambra, and we hid him in the green bushes of the myrtle court, and the song of the nightingale soon sounded loudly and powerfully. Delighted I stood by the side of a murmuring fountain, but suddenly the rascal made fools of us and we heard the voice of a turkey-cock from the myrtle grove. This was a punishment for attempting to force the enjoyment of nature; and since I would hear the nightingale in October I must have into the bargain the gobbling of a turkey-cock. Too soon, alas, we had to say good-bye to the beautiful Alhambra, and drove up to the Generalife, the château of Omer the fiddler. This palace, built on a smaller scale, lies higher than the Alhambra. The fresh green of the mountain serves it as a background; and from the outside its tower-like shape gives it more the aspect of a cloister than a villa. A very fine portico leads from the principal room into the long narrow garden parterre, in which an abundance of flowers is intersected with fresh-water channels. Along the parterre is a bower from which one has a view of the world. Here everything is Oriental, solitary and secluded, but a paradise of flowers and poetry for the possessor.

Amidst these still and romantic gardens in which one might dream away life, rises an old cypress, under which the sultana Zuraja was said to have seen the Abencerrages. Up the hill and under laurel hedges and rich leafy trees is a staircase, the banisters of which are made to form narrow and regular cascades, a poetical idea which ought to be imitated in our gardens. On the highest point of the garden is a modern kiosk, from which one has an extensive view. This is the true point from which to understand the site and position of the Alhambra: standing higher than the Alhambra one has a bird's-eye view into the Moorish fortress and can see how large a space it occupies on the hill, how many towers run round it, and how many different buildings that curious citadel contains. The finest and most picturesque point is, without doubt, that which is occupied by the summer residence; it stands out proudly with its Comares Tower. From this point it affords to the city of Granada and to the wide vega, a perfectly intelligible picture of the mediæval loop-holed feudal castles, with their irregular towers. One is transplanted to Germany, so strong is the appearance of the old reddish-tinted castle. It stretches itself along on the opposite side, protected against the looks of the outside world by walls all round, and is seated on the high plateau in the midst of which stands the rocky fortress-palace of Charles V.

Behind these buildings, in a western direction from the Generalife, are gardens and fields; the convent of San Francisco with its huerta; the present parish-church Santa Maria; the ruins of the Mufti palace, and separate villas and smaller buildings. Eastward, fronting the palace of

Charles V. at the sharp corner of the hill towards the city, is the Alcazaba with the Torre de Homenaje, the Armeria, the Torre de la Vela, and de la Polvareda, forming a complete whole. Immediately before the palace of the Emperor is the Plaza de los Algibes, where the celebrated cisterns stand close to a steep slope. On the other side of the Darro, far above the Cuevas del Sacro Monte, is a wide mountainous country, amidst which the cicerone pointed out to us, las Cuevas del Diabolo, the devil's caves; robbers and murderers inhabit these caves, and the country around is so watched by them and so dangerous, that not even the Spanish police dare to go amongst them. How much I regretted that the shortness of my sojourn in Granada did not afford me an opportunity of becoming more nearly acquainted with the prince of darkness and his bloodthirsty children. I am convinced that they are not so dark as they are painted.

In the inner rooms of the Generalife are some pictures of great historical interest. There one sees the portraits of Philip I., Philip II., Philip III., and Philip IV., and their wives, those of Ferdinand and Isabella, and of several Moorish princes, amongst whom is a white-bearded aged man, Muza, an uncle of Boabdil. But as a sailor I was more interested in the pictures of the ships in which the great Columbus made his discovery. Navigators of the present time would be altogether startled at the shape of these vessels; and would scarcely have ventured with them along a secure coast from harbour to harbour. This enables us to appreciate the difficulties with which the iron Columbus had to contend.

We now quitted the Generalife, which the Duke of Montpensier intended to buy from a Marquis residing in Genoa, but family laws did not permit the Marquis to sell it. The palace is now empty and forsaken, and has a melancholy romance about it; what might it not have been if the duke had tried his taste on a place so splendidly situated! We drove to the celebrated Cartuja, and on our road to the city to two interesting places: the house of the Inquisition and the place of the Triunfo, a wide open place planted with trees and bushes; on which encamped 70,000 men, the mighty army of the royal Catholic couple. In the middle of it was erected a column of victory. Here was also a large palace for the royal conquerors which, *tempora mutantur*! has become subsequently a lunatic asylum.

The Cartuja is built on a hill commanding a fine view. The large church is rococo; the courts are empty, for the monks had to go out into the world at the time of the revolution, a class of unfortunate, unemployed, therefore despised ecclesiastics. Some horribly painted pictures are the only things which now intimate the past life of the order and the former destination of the building. Of the refectory there remain only four bare, high, long walls; ghostly stillness reigns in the wide courts, and a large brown cross painted on the wall is the only remaining emblem in the forsaken hall. I wonder whether at the midnight bell, when the moon throws her pale light through these windows, the ghosts of the deceased monks so barbarously driven away, assemble here in their white rustling gowns, their grinning skulls topped with their small pointed cowls; and whether according to their old habit they eat their meat here in a dreadful seriousness, with rattling jaws and clattering bones? If there is such a thing as haunting in the world, as seems to be admitted by some, it takes place certainly in forsaken cloisters, where the wind howls through the long bare passages, where the bells only ring in a storm, the mouldy doors of the cells creak on their hinges, and the organ in the choir sighs and groans.

The only things worth seeing in this wide building are

the splendid marble ornaments in the church and its chapels, the elaborate wood-work and the mother-of-pearl and tortoiseshell on the principal door. The tortoiseshell and wood surfaces seem to be only painted, so excellently are the different materials joined. A poor family, with their little ragged children, are the only guardians of the cloister. The father was dying, and the little circle was mourning and in trouble. How sad everything seems in this world, why is everything so perishable, and created with the germ of death in it? By this time the guardian of the proud Cartuja is probably mouldering away.

Returned to our fonda, we once again enjoyed the splendid fruits of the richest plain of golden Spain, and then with a heavy heart we entered our carriage, and said good-by to Granada and rattled towards Loja. Thankful, and yet low-spirited, I frequently looked out of the window back upon the Alhambra.

Malaga: Oct. 3, 1851.

From Loja we ascended the mountains, whilst asleep. We did not forget to put up again with the handsome Murillo family, and arrived after a ride of several hours at the last mountain ridge, from which we had a splendid view of the Mediterranean, nay, even of the coast of Africa. In Malaga, though we were in October, we experienced a South African heat, and a surprising reception from our consul and the governor of the island, the latter inviting me in artless innocence to receive in the palace on the birthday of the king next day, in place of His Majesty, the con- gratulation of the grandees of the city and province. One may imagine that, not a little afraid, I declined this odd proposition, and having rid myself of these Spanish honours, I glided gladly over the waves and back to our beloved frigate, beneath the cool evening breeze and charming moonshine, and such a play of colours at twilight as can only be admired in Malaga.

The thunder of cannons from the shore early this morning proclaimed the commencement of the celebration for Pacho, a word which in Spain is used for Francisco, and by which name the consort of the queen is called by the people. Flags were everywhere hoisted in city and port, and all the bells sounded. Over the sea, too, thundered the guns; the mighty frigate sent forth its lightnings and the white smoke majestically rolled across the smooth endless mirror of the sea. Though a response to the festive signals of the country, our salutes, mass, and Te Deum were also meant for our own high festival at home, which we celebrated on our little piece of floating Austria with all our heart, and with the love of faithful subjects.

To-day I went on shore for a few hours under a glowing heat, over dusty roads, with edges filled with red geranium, to the cemetery of the city which I had seen from the hills, and which I imagined to be interesting. Already depressed by the heat I was utterly disappointed on my arrival. The cemetery is without ornament and without poetry; instead of in graves, the dead are here placed inside a broad surrounding wall, into which the coffins are shoved one over the other. But the covering layer of briars which separates one from another not being there, a disgusting smell spread around the neighbourhood of the more recent graves, which cannot but be unhealthy, amidst such a heat.

We passed this beautiful day in a very pleasant manner. We had hired horses to visit the heights which surround Malaga, and on which Buen Retiro is situated. Away we went, in spite of the heat, in a sailor-like gallop. The wild horde were constantly joking at their queer situations, dashing through a high field of reeds, across which the road led as through the grasses of the American savannahs. We had to cross a river, which was not very favourable to our toilet, already considerably damaged, and ascend a height where a small village is situated, a kind of Hietzing of the people of Malaga.

At an inn with a broad terrace and beautiful view we ordered breakfast. The distance from Malaga to this place we had made in a fabulously short time, to which our continuous and rapid ride contributed. I cannot ride slowly, to trot is wretched, a full gallop delightful, one breathes easier, is careless about the heat; no longer belongs to this weak earth; laughs at obstacles; throws all one's life into the enjoyment of the moment; conceives something of the delight of flying, and is inclined to fancy oneself almost master of the world. We visited the garden of the Prussian consul, distinguished by an abundance of flowers and by a splendid palm; even now in October, everything is brilliant in fresh lively colours, delightful in its balmy fragrance, as it is with us in the month of June. Happy, beautiful country, with an eternally mild climate! how the heart of those who have to drag their life through the cold winter longs for thee. How readily one forgets the heat, compared with the deadly cold of benumbing winter. Yes, you in the north have no idea of the delight of the south, you cannot imagine the joy of the soul beneath the dark-blue wide sky, shining over the limitless azure sea; and perhaps it is better for you not to know it, so that the melancholy remembrance of a paradise once enjoyed does not sadden your heart. The south with its charms has captivated me altogether, and little by little a good climate has become a necessity to me. Those days passed in warm countries in the midst of a vegetation rich in flowers and blossoms, are coveted by me amongst the most beautiful of my life. In the south one lives twice; the spirit easily stirred becomes richer and fuller; the body which in the north is rendered inflexible by ice and iron becomes in the sun only flesh and blood.

Once more on horseback we dashed over rocks, between tall prickly aloe plants, to the Buen Retiro. Indeed, no place in the world better deserves this fine sounding name. It is a summer residence reposing amidst the green of the cypress, amidst rose-hedges and orange-trees, and containing everything which the world can offer in loveliness. Situated on a height, a wide regular terrace is stretched out before the windows of the ground floor; from which is obtained a splendid view of the old rich city with its high-towering cathedral, the nobly-formed mountains of the Sierra Nevada, and the calm peaceable sea. On the terrace itself bloom numberless trees, amongst which glitter statues and fountains in the old pompous style.

As night approached we returned, the moon shone in the blue firmament, and amidst the sound of the guitar and the song, the Majo returned in pleasant company with his black-eyed Manola from the country to the city. You already know what the Majo is; and the Manola is the fair girl to whom the Majo plays his guitar, and under whose windows he sighs. There are also Majas, who are the lionesses of the lower classes, who exhibit themselves on Sunday in rich national costume, and who dance the charming bolero with their cavaliers to the rattling of the castanets. Since the bull-fights have again become fashionable in Madrid, five ladies of the highest rank have appeared as Majas with richly-laced bodices and black lace veils!

Port of Cartagena : Oct. 14, 1851.

With a heavy heart we raised our anchor in Malaga on October 7, and took leave of beautiful Spain, of this country of golden dreams and sweet longings; and as if fate were disposed to make our separation still more difficult, a calm of several days' extent fell on us, after we had made but a few miles with great difficulty; Malaga and the mountains of Granada were before our eyes, and yet we could not lower a boat, for every moment a breeze might spring up to chase away our enchanted ship. At last, a light evening breeze sprang up, and Malaga disappeared before our eyes. During the calm, an epidemic did much havoc on board our vessel, carrying off several victims every day; but thank God, the disease was not amongst the men, but amongst the chickens; the ranks of our noble ones were thinned by grim death, and the big hen-coop was soon an empty temple. In consideration of this misfortune, and our long voyage without a pause to the coast of our own country, it was very wise of our commander to run in to Cartagena, to provide our ship with fresh supplies. At seven o'clock, P. M., just before dusk, we entered this important port, which, on account of two rocks underneath the surface of the water, is not without danger to those entering and leaving the port. On the second cliff in the interior of the basin, a low iron bar has been fixed as in the botanical garden, where the plants are more than usually interesting. Cartagena, little Carthage, according to tradition built by Hannibal, exhibits a red tower on the sandhill, belonging to the period of its foundation, and was once the pride of the Spanish navy. From this port in the days of Spanish glory, the armadas issued which were built in this splendid arsenal. In this harbour, the red and yellow flag of Castile, if threatened by the enemy, might take refuge, protected by cliffs and rocks. Now it has outlived its proud days, is empty and deserted, and is decaying with an ever-increasing rapidity. Spain's once gigantic navy was destroyed by the English; the eighty-six ships of the line she possessed before 1806 have been burned, sunk, or have rotted, and the navy which is now springing up is happy in numbering even four or five of them; but the ships now built are constructed with great trouble in Ferrol or Carraca, so that from the great arsenal of Cartagena, where once a thousand workmen were employed, at this moment only a single brig is being fitted out.

Cartagena: October 15, 1851.

Poor Cartagena is everywhere yellow; the rocks are yellow, the houses, and the people, and nowhere is green to be seen to comfort the tired eye. As Prince Puckler, with his philosophical wit, asserts in his letters of a deceased, that for each day of the week a colour was involuntarily present to his mind, so I felt the same in reference to the recollection of certain cities: at Venice I think of the dark red of the marble; at Granada, of the smiling green; at Cadiz, of the swan-like white; at Constantinople, of glittering gold; at Rome, of violet and blue; at Munich, of forget-me-not blue; and at Cartagena, of the bare, jejune yellow. The steep rocks reach to the entrance of the city, there they slope off, and behind them is nothing. There I hoped at least to find a fresh green Huerta, but in that also I was miserably disappointed, for a wide dusty plain extends from the opposite walls of the city, to the far mountains, behind which is the kingdom of Murcia. The arsenal, situated on the left side of the city, is noticeable from a fine and spacious basin surrounded by brickwork, in which a whole fleet, cutting through the Channel, might anchor safely. The churches of Cartagena are ugly, the streets dirty, and of the buildings the palace of the Admiralty is the only one worthy of notice. The old castle exhibits only decayed walls and is a dismal sight. On the bastions we were amazed by the mechanical drill of the poor recruits who at the sounds of *uno dos*, which the whole row had to repeat after the drill master, were taught how to march very artificially; the mode of saluting in rank and file was also drilled into them with singular inclinations of the body. The Spanish troops, who seem to be excellent soldiers, are very proud of their marching, in which they show a very great perseverance. A double gate leads from Cartagena to the sea, through the left division of which, however, one is not permitted to pass, the sentinels compelling the promenaders to walk through the right one. This custom not only prevails here but in Cadiz also.

Cartagena : October 16, 1851.

As Cartagena offers nothing attractive or interesting, I availed myself of my last day's stay there to make an excursion amongst the cliffs of the sea-shore, to collect shells I enjoyed the small bays and grottoes and the foaming waves, but my feet suffered, and my boots were torn by the sharp edges of the rocks. In one of the small caves I found, to my great astonishment, bedded on soft sand, a man sleeping, probably it was a smuggler, a tribe, to the despair of the government, very numerous here, but if there be a country more than another suited for this business it must be the coasts of Cartagena.

Cartagena, October 17, 1851.

Tired of Cartagena, I remained on board to-day and was ·glad when at six o'clock P.M. the sails were set and our homeward voyage commenced.

END OF THE FIRST VOLUME.

LONDON: PRINTED BY
SPOTTISWOODE AND CO., NEW-STREET SQUARE
AND PARLIAMENT STREET